Dragon Kingdom
of Wrenly

Night Hunt

By Jordan Quinn

Illustrated by Ornella Greco at Glass House Graphics

LITTLE SIMON

New York   London   Toronto   Sydney   New Delhi

LITTLE SIMON
An imprint of Simon & Schuster Children's Publishing Division
1230 Avenue of the Americas, New York, New York 10020
First Little Simon edition May 2021
Copyright © 2021 by Simon & Schuster, Inc.
LITTLE SIMON is a registered trademark of Simon & Schuster, Inc., and associated colophon is a trademark of Simon & Schuster, Inc. For information about special discounts for bulk purchases, please contact Simon & Schuster Special Sales at 1-866-506-1949 or business@simonandschuster.com.
The Simon & Schuster Speakers Bureau can bring authors to your live event. For more information or to book an event, contact the Simon & Schuster Speakers Bureau at 1-866-248-3049 or visit our website at www.simonspeakers.com.
Designed by Kayla Wasil
Text by Matthew J. Gilbert
GLASS HOUSE GRAPHICS Creative Services
Art and cover by ORNELLA GRECO
Colors by ORNELLA GRECO and GABRIELE CRACOLICI
Lettering by GIOVANNI SPATARO/Grafimated Cartoon
Supervision by SALVATORE DI MARCO/Grafimated Cartoon
Manufactured in China 0221 SCP
2 4 6 8 10 9 7 5 3 1
Library of Congress Cataloging-in-Publication Data
Names: Quinn, Jordan, author. | Glass House Graphics, illustrator.
Title: Night hunt / by Jordan Quinn ; illustrated by Glass House Graphics.
Description: First Little Simon edition. | New York : Little Simon, 2021. | Series: Dragon kingdom of Wrenly ; 3
Audience: Ages 5–9 | Audience: Grades K–1 | Summary: "Ruskin is back on Crestwood to witness the Night Hunt, a legendary event wherein the bravest young dragons on Crestwood are chosen to participate in a high-stakes scavenger hunt"–Provided by publisher. Identifiers: LCCN 2020027677 (print) | LCCN 2020027678 (ebook)
ISBN 9781534478633 (paperback) | ISBN 9781534478640 (hardcover) | ISBN 9781534478657 (ebook)
Subjects: LCSH: Graphic novels. | CYAC: Graphic novels. | Dragons–Fiction. | Scavenger Hunts–Fiction. | Fantasy.
Classification: LCC PZ7.7.Q55 Ni 2021 (print) | LCC PZ7.7.Q55 (ebook) | DDC 741.5/973–dc23
LC record available at https://lccn.loc.gov/2020027677
LC ebook record available at https://lccn.loc.gov/2020027678

Contents

Chapter 1

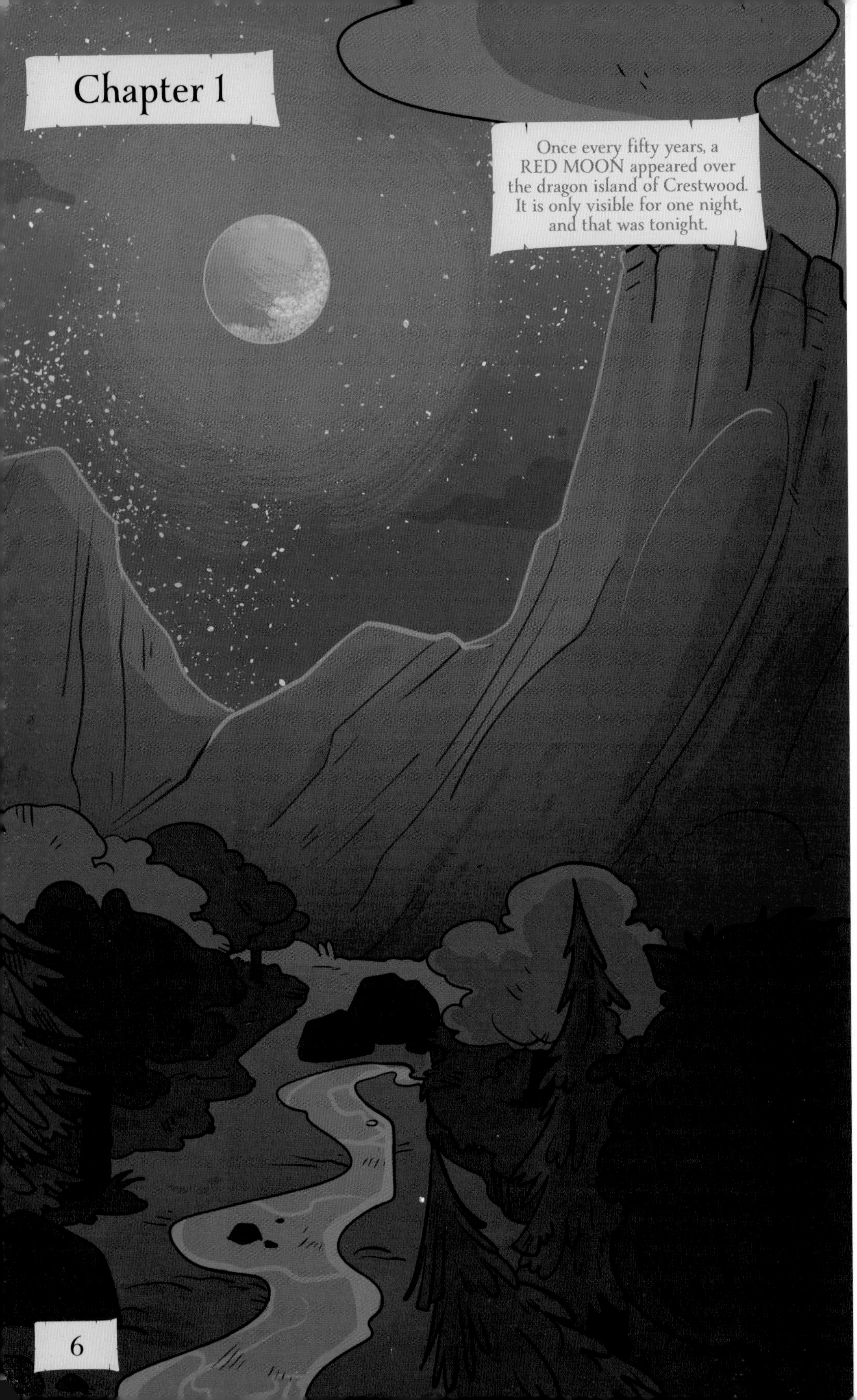
Once every fifty years, a RED MOON appeared over the dragon island of Crestwood. It is only visible for one night, and that was tonight.

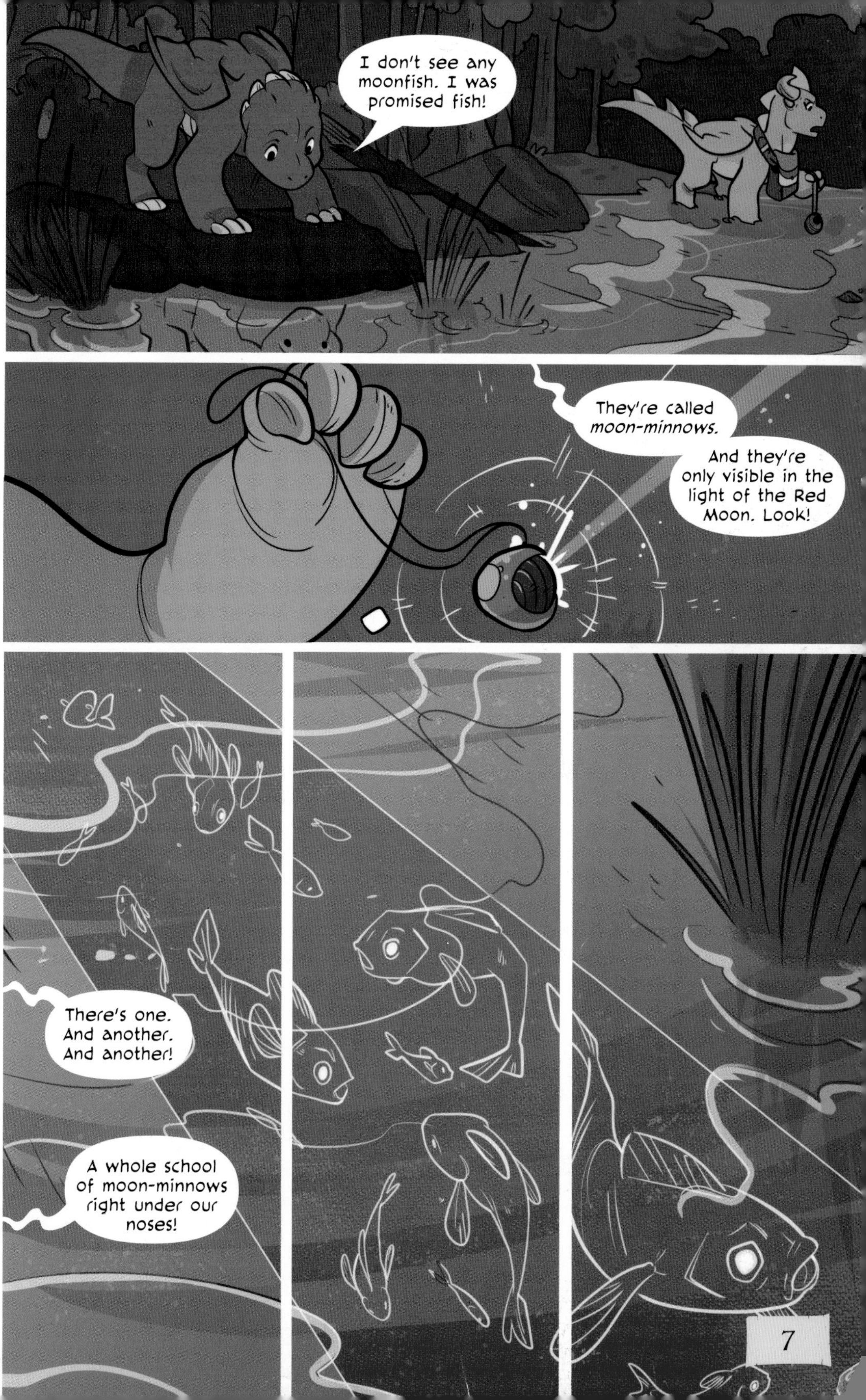
I don't see any moonfish. I was promised fish!
They're called *moon-minnows.*
And they're only visible in the light of the Red Moon. Look!
There's one. And another. And another!
A whole school of moon-minnows right under our noses!

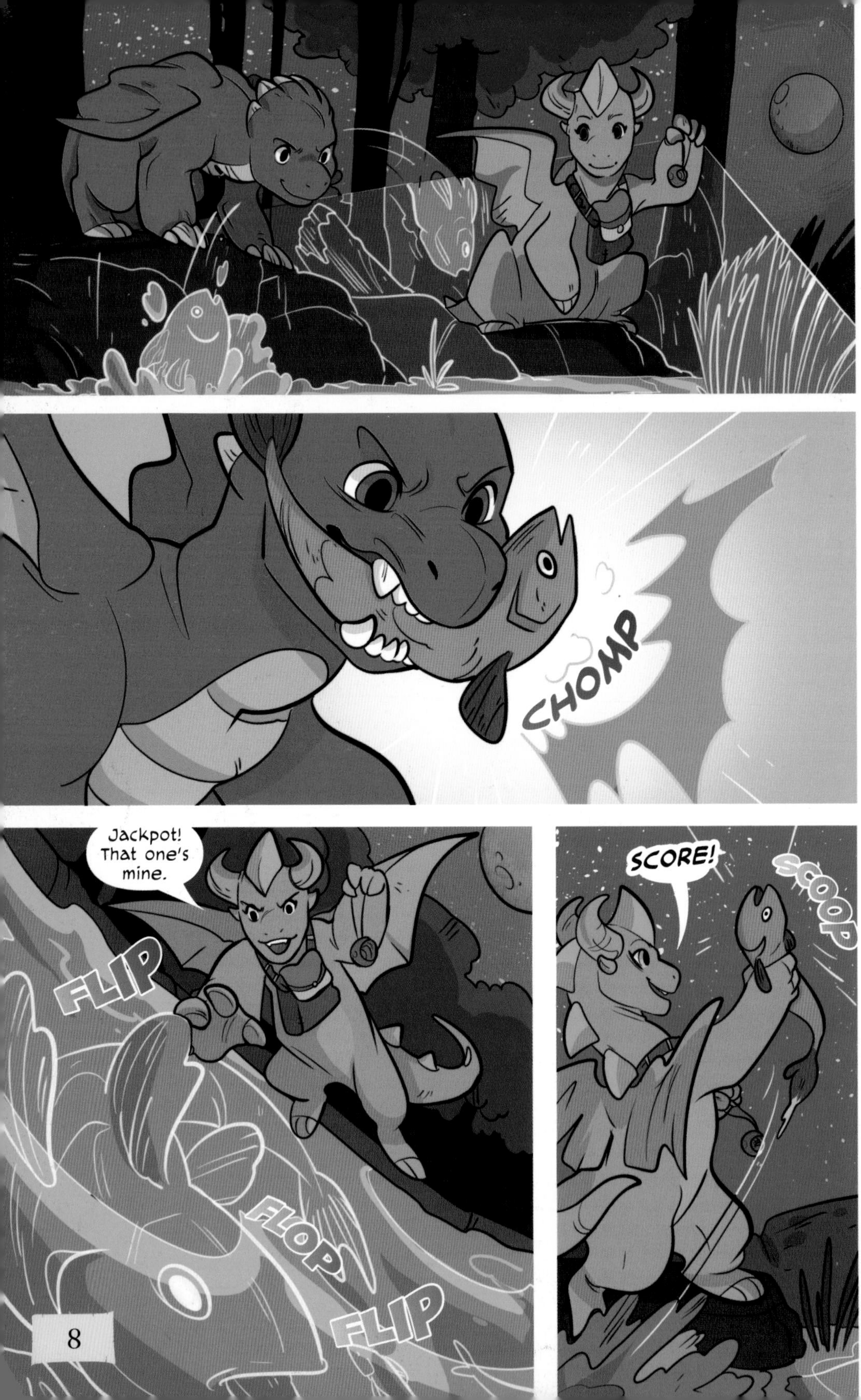
CHOMP
Jackpot! That one's mine.
FLIP
FLOP
FLIP
SCORE!
SCOOP

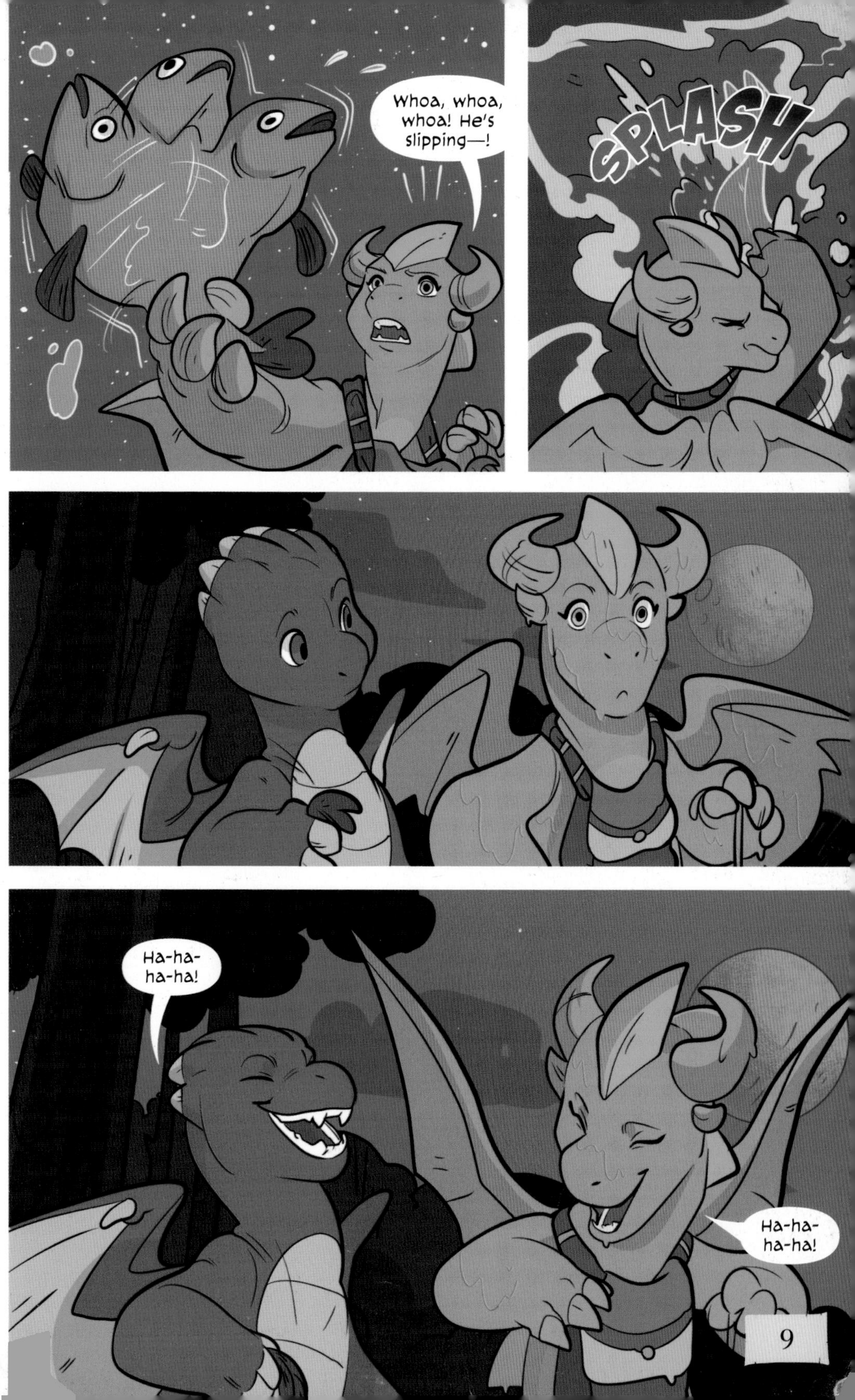
Whoa, whoa, whoa! He's slipping—!
SPLASH
Ha-ha-ha-ha!
Ha-ha-ha-ha!

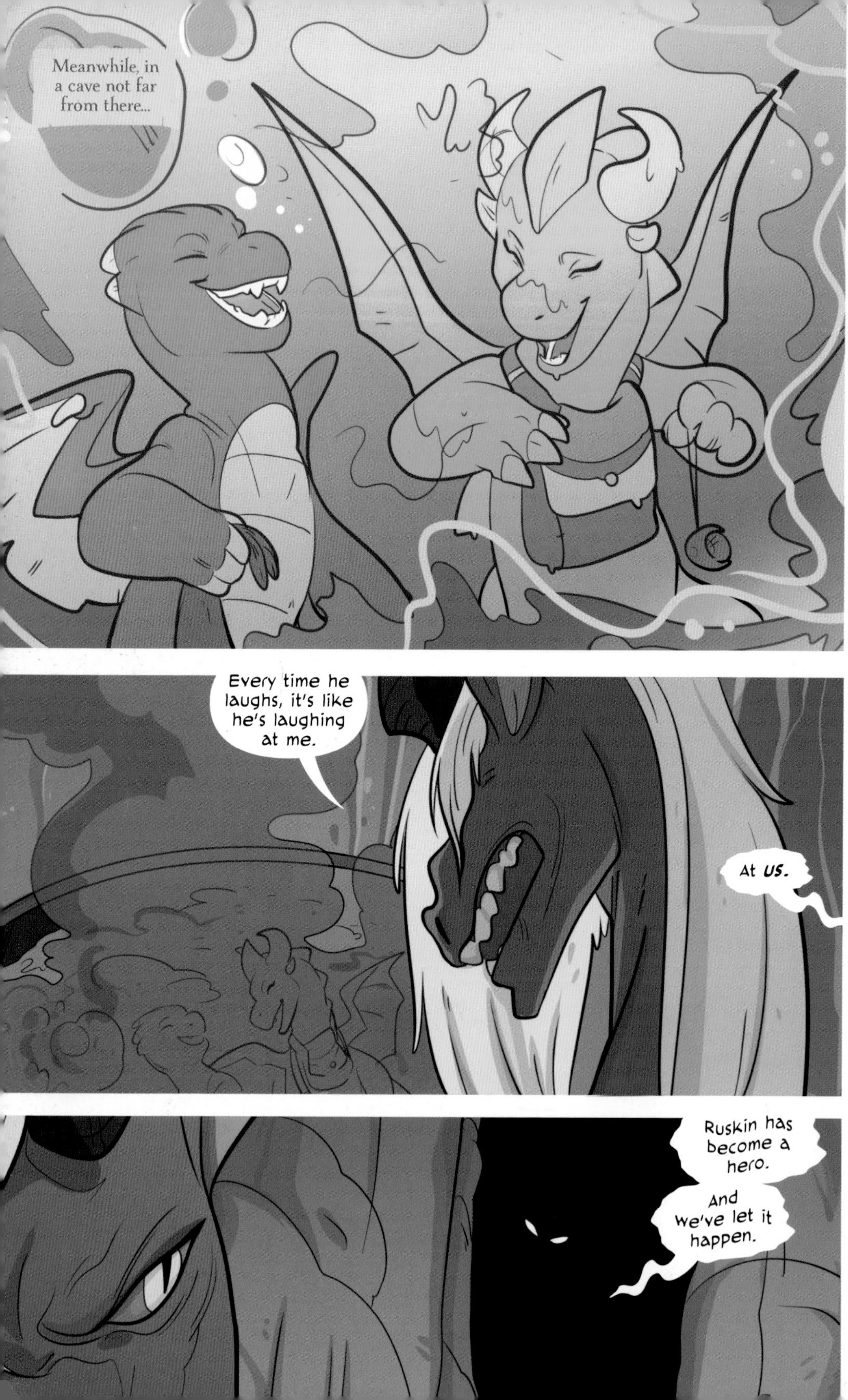
Meanwhile, in a cave not far from there...
Every time he laughs, it's like he's laughing at me.
At US.
Ruskin has become a hero.
And we've let it happen.

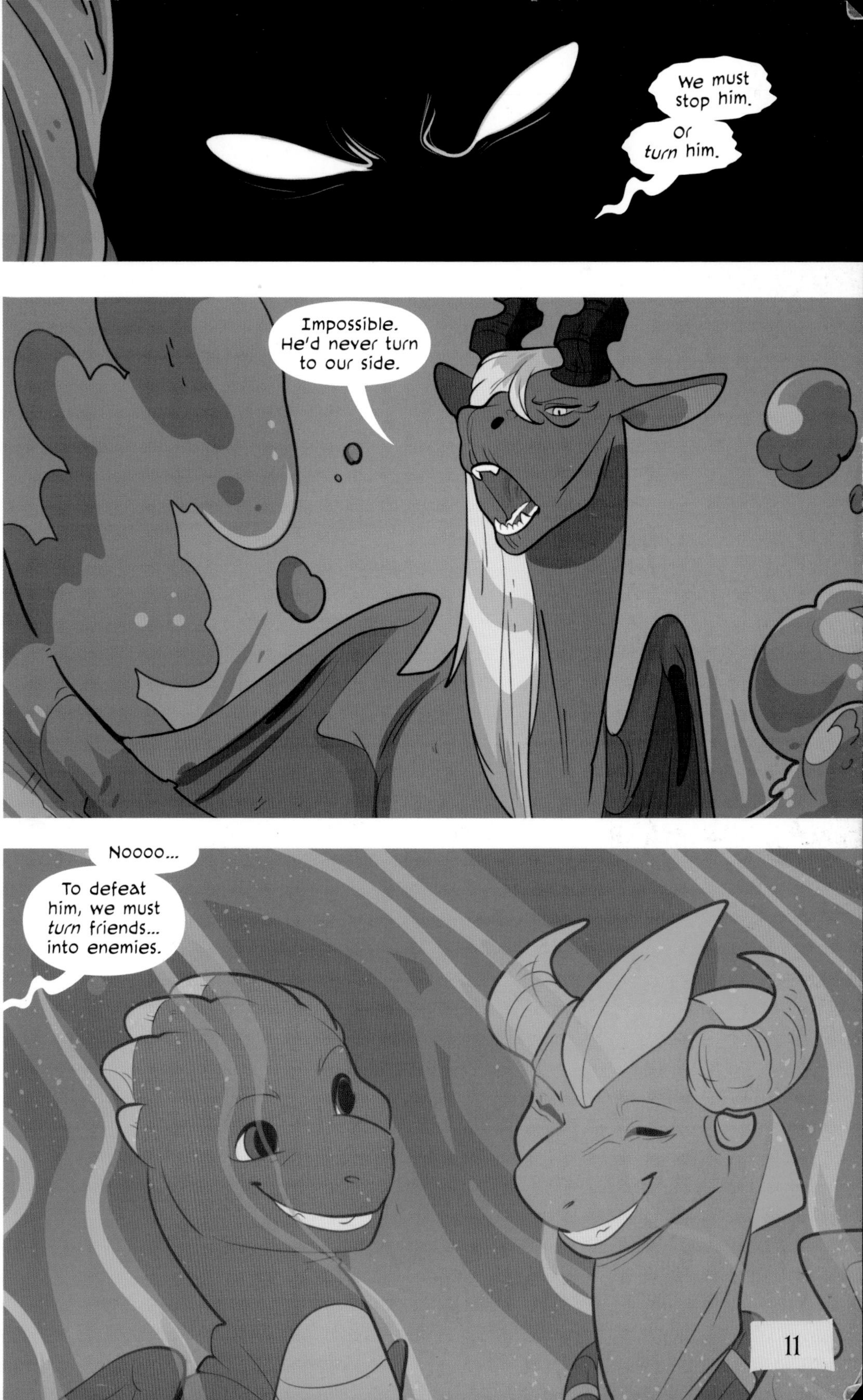
We must stop him.
Or *turn* him.
Impossible. He'd never turn to our side.
Noooo...
To defeat him, we must *turn* friends... into enemies.

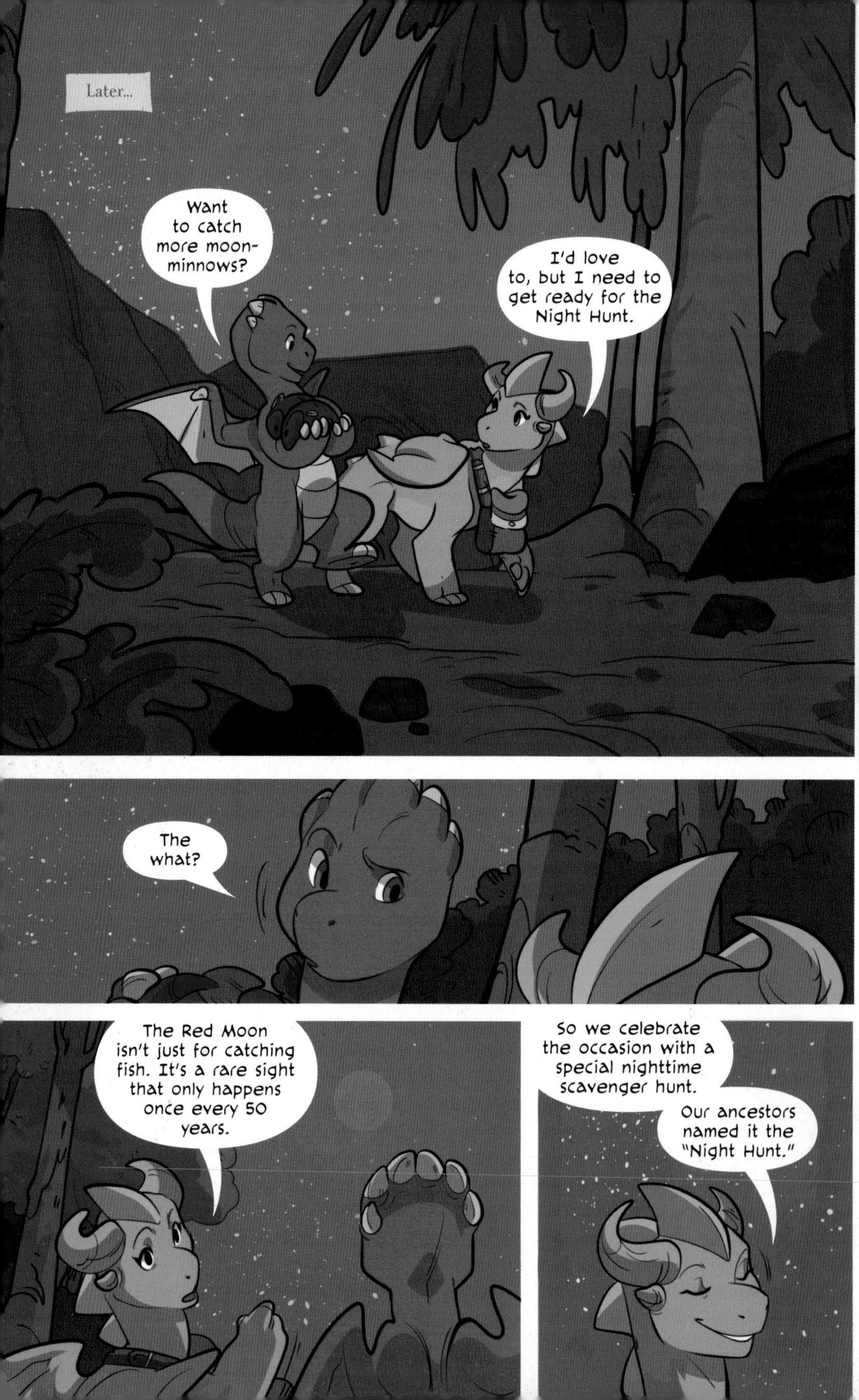
Later...
Want to catch more moon-minnows?
I'd love to, but I need to get ready for the Night Hunt.
The what?
The Red Moon isn't just for catching fish. It's a rare sight that only happens once every 50 years.
So we celebrate the occasion with a special nighttime scavenger hunt.
Our ancestors named it the "Night Hunt."

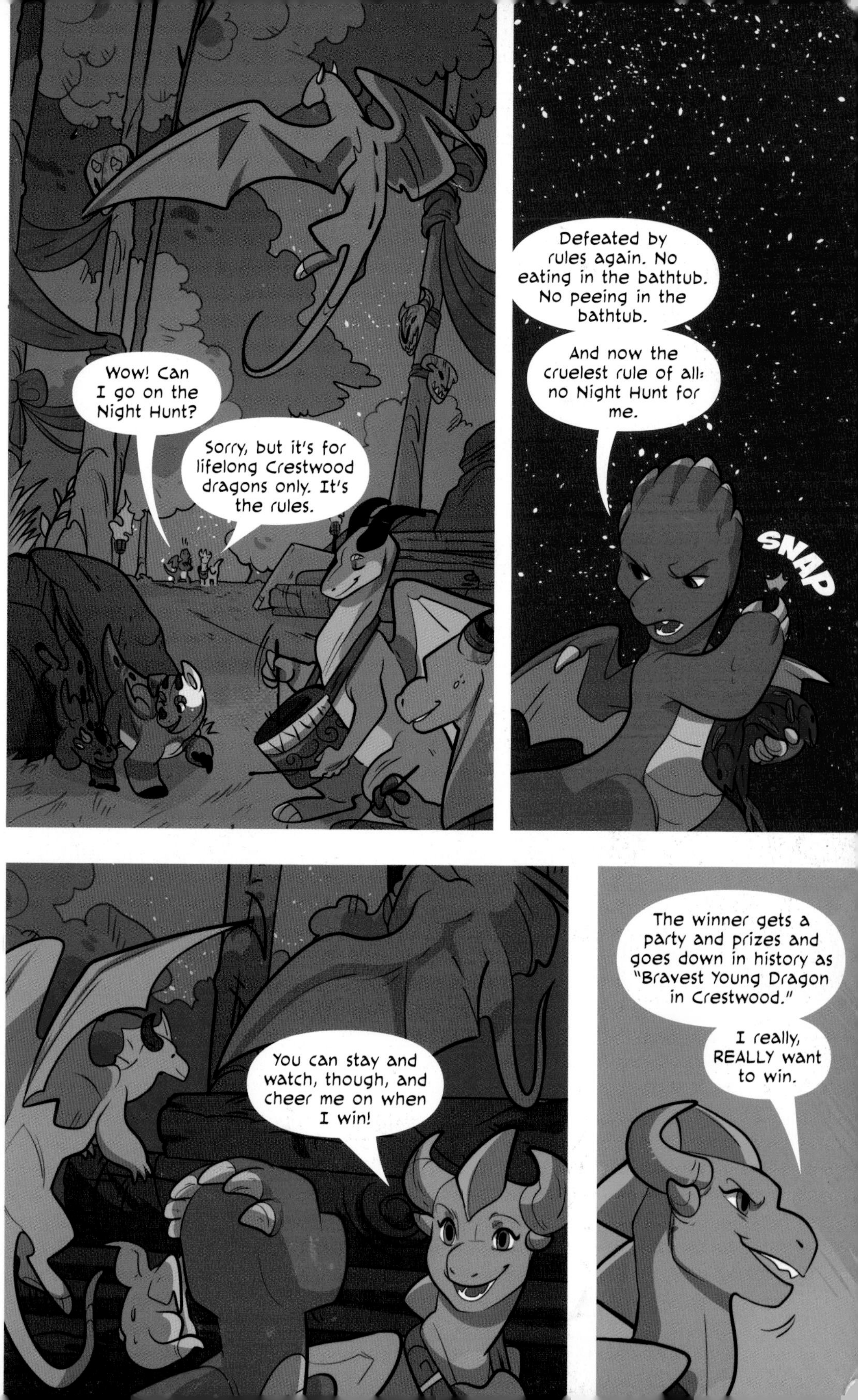
Wow! Can I go on the Night Hunt?
Sorry, but it's for lifelong Crestwood dragons only. It's the rules.
Defeated by rules again. No eating in the bathtub. No peeing in the bathtub.
And now the cruelest rule of all: no Night Hunt for me.
SNAP
You can stay and watch, though, and cheer me on when I win!
The winner gets a party and prizes and goes down in history as "Bravest Young Dragon in Crestwood."
I really, REALLY want to win.

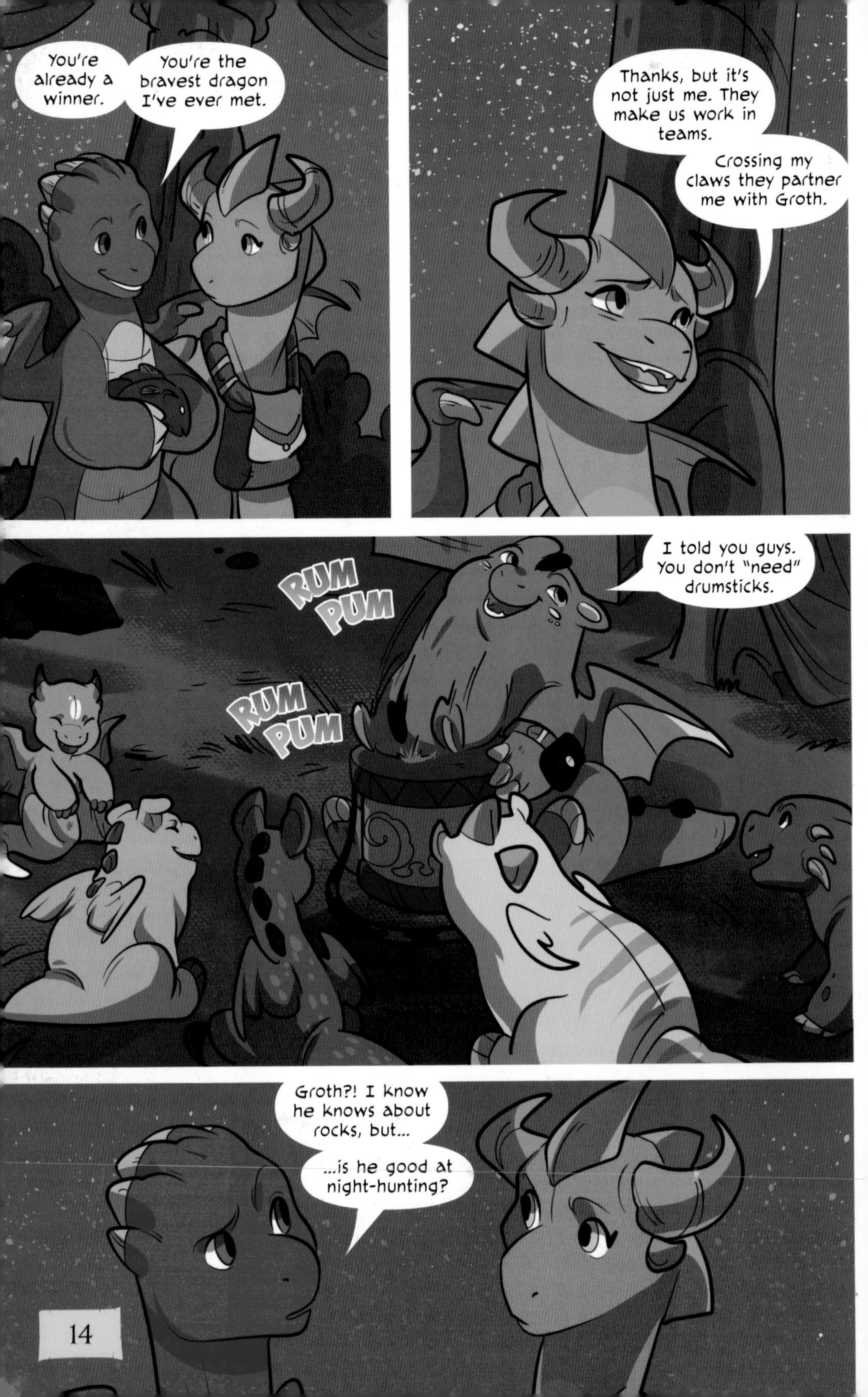
You're already a winner.
You're the bravest dragon I've ever met.
Thanks, but it's not just me. They make us work in teams.
Crossing my claws they partner me with Groth.
RUM PUM
RUM PUM
I told you guys. You don't "need" drumsticks.
Groth?! I know he knows about rocks, but...
...is he good at night-hunting?

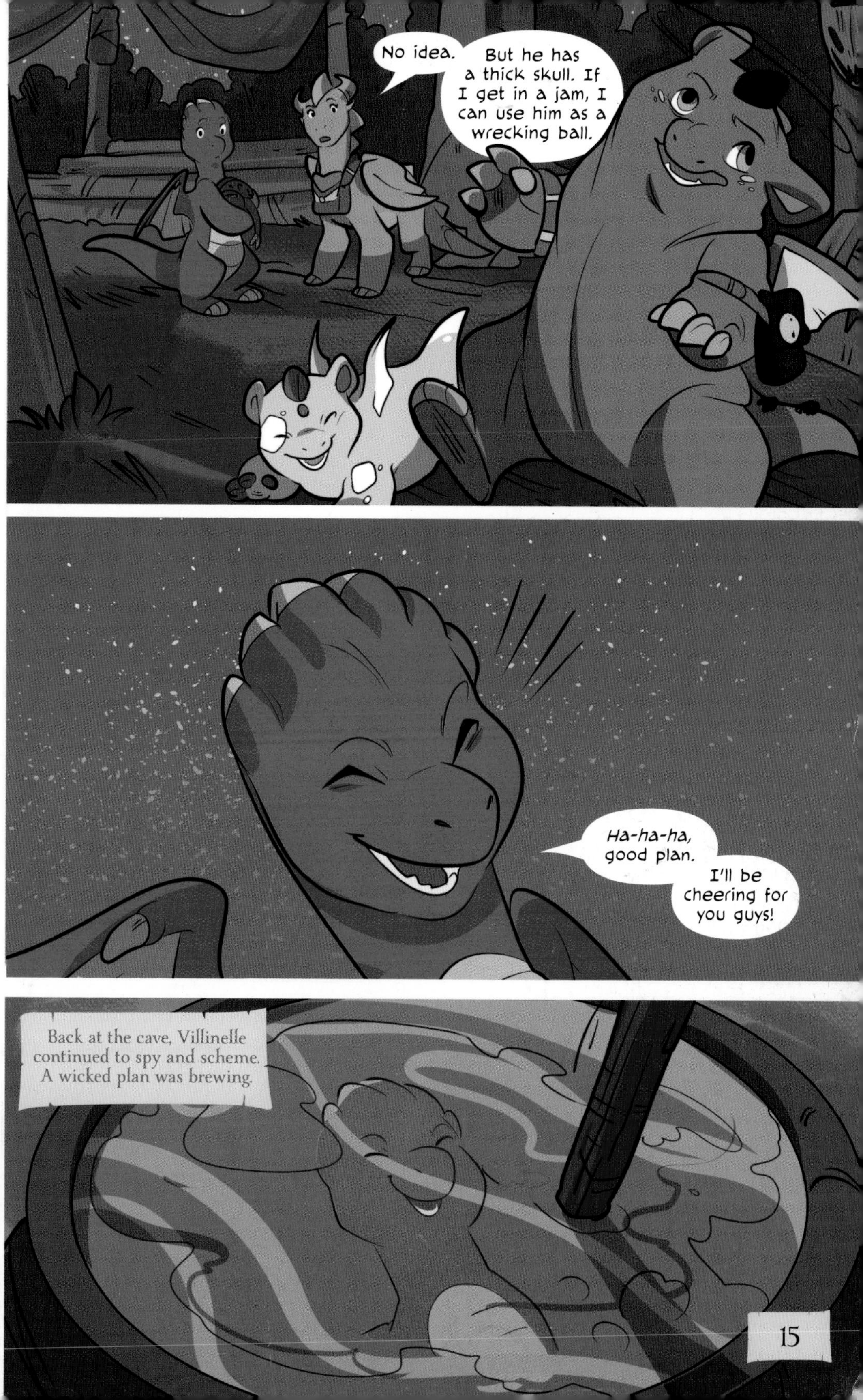
No idea.
But he has a thick skull. If I get in a jam, I can use him as a wrecking ball.
Ha-ha-ha, good plan.
I'll be cheering for you guys!
Back at the cave, Villinelle continued to spy and scheme. A wicked plan was brewing.

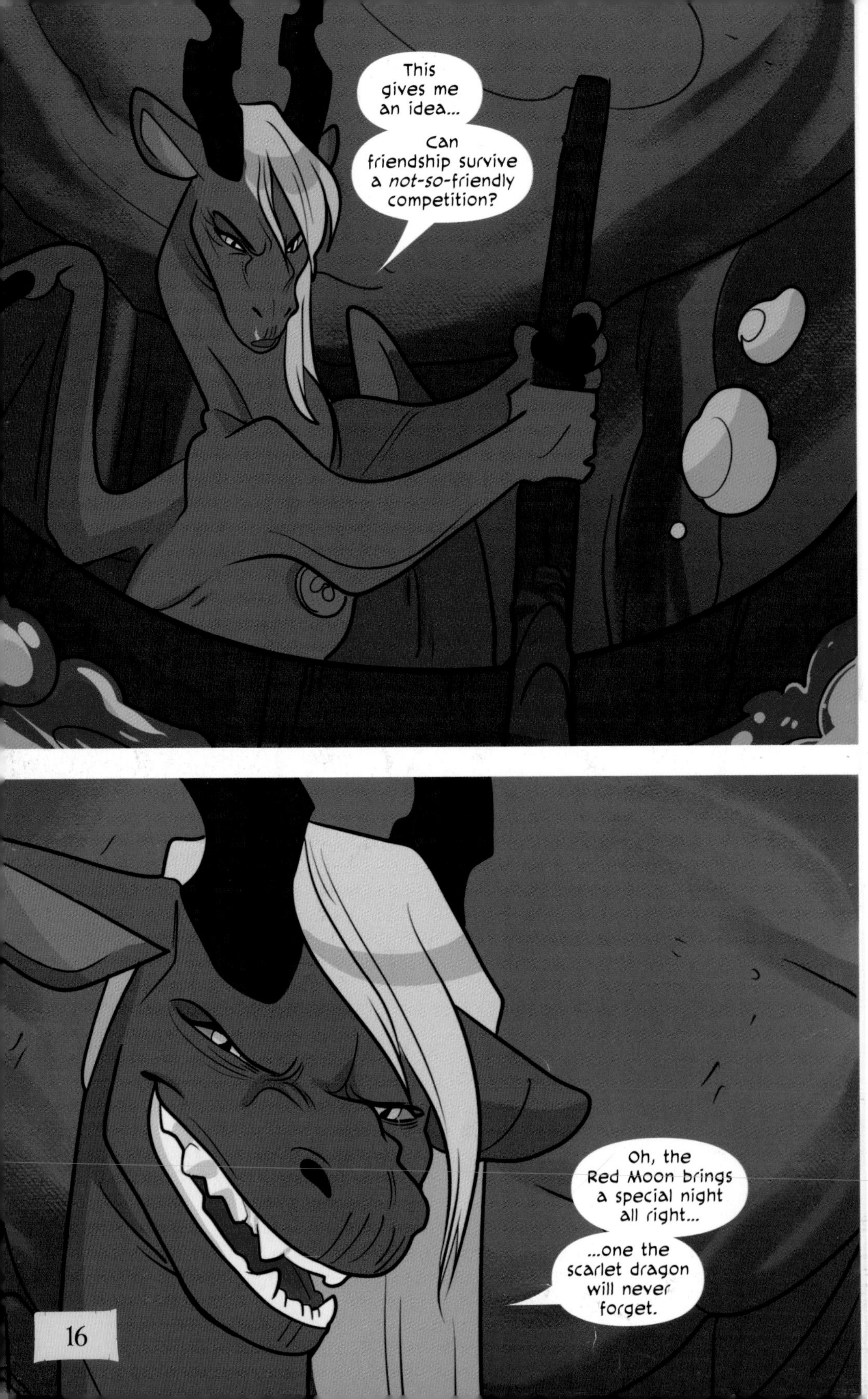
This gives me an idea...
Can friendship survive a *not-so*-friendly competition?
Oh, the Red Moon brings a special night all right...
...one the scarlet dragon will never forget.

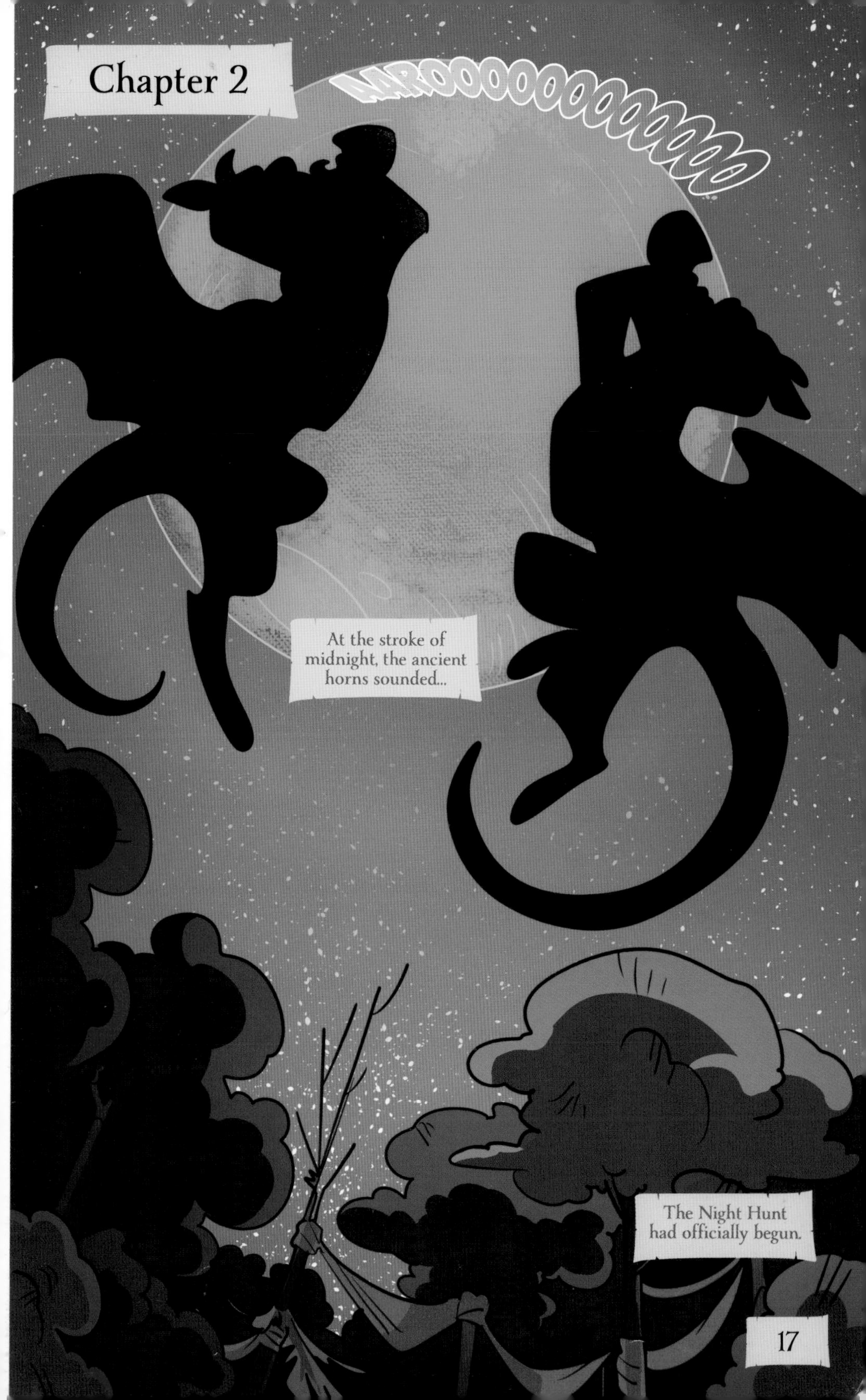
Chapter 2
AAROOOOOOOOOOOO
At the stroke of midnight, the ancient horns sounded...
The Night Hunt had officially begun.

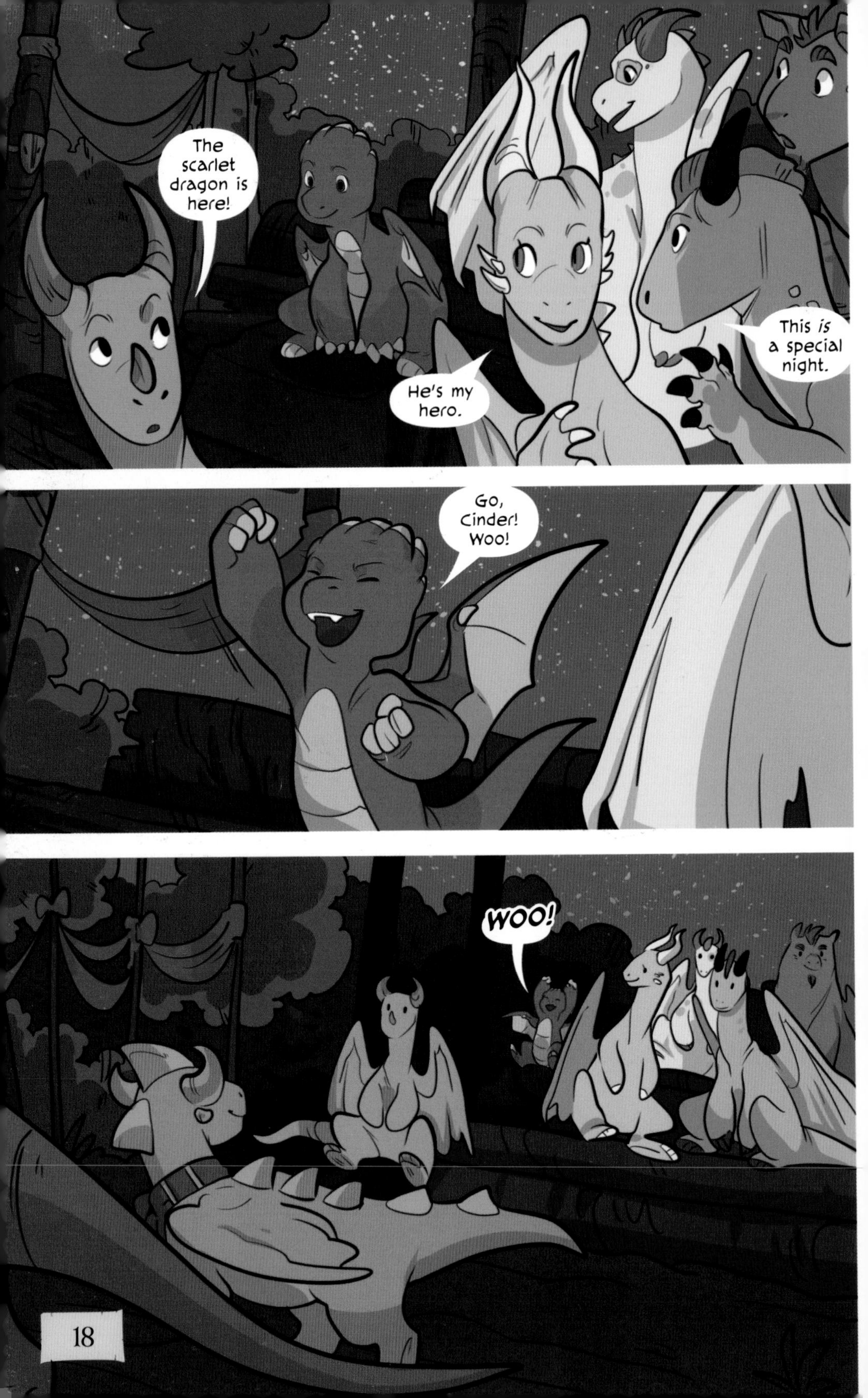
The scarlet dragon is here!
He's my hero.
This *is* a special night.
Go, Cinder! Woo!
WOO!

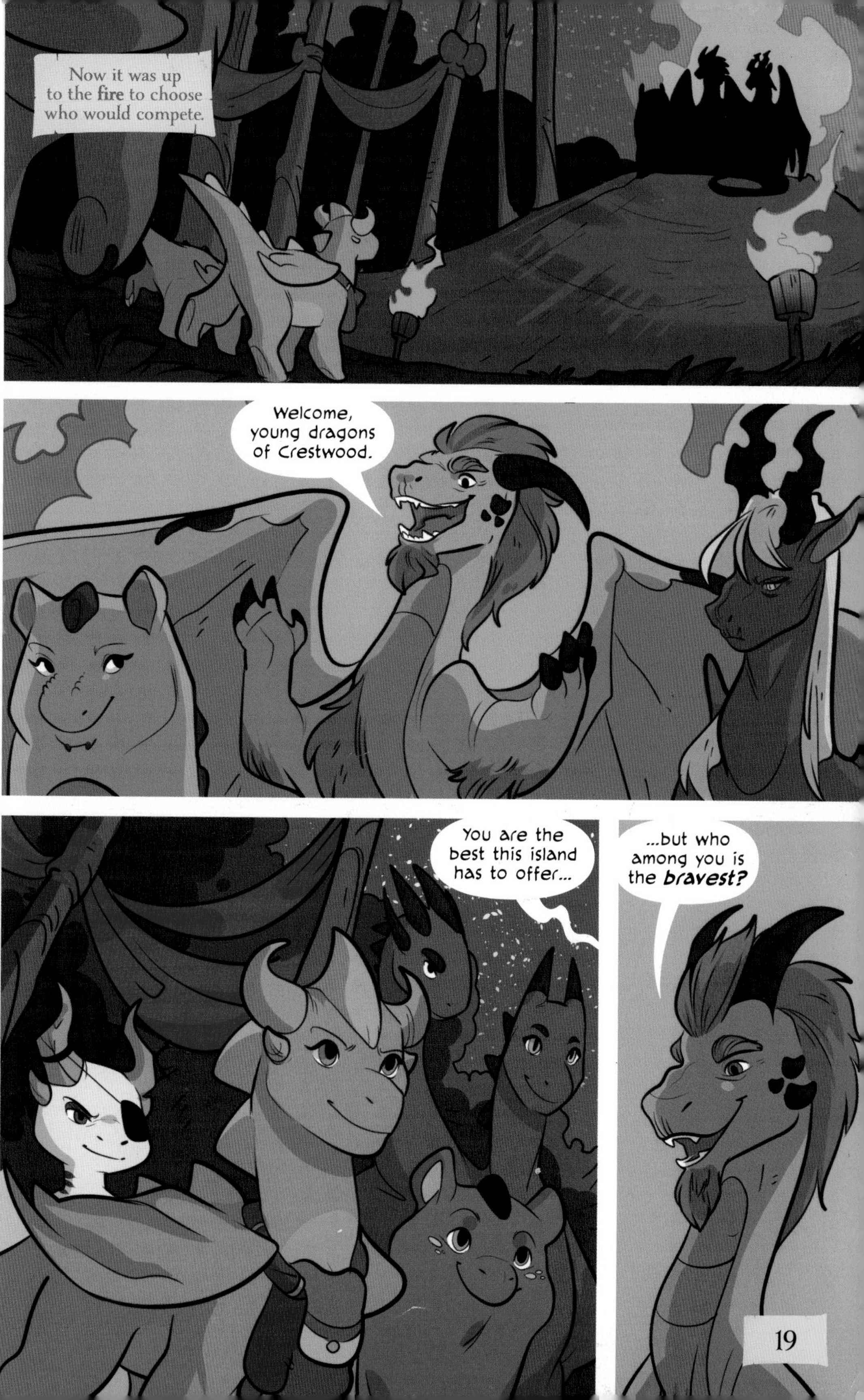
Now it was up to the **fire** to choose who would compete.
Welcome, young dragons of Crestwood.
You are the best this island has to offer...
...but who among you is the ***bravest?***
19

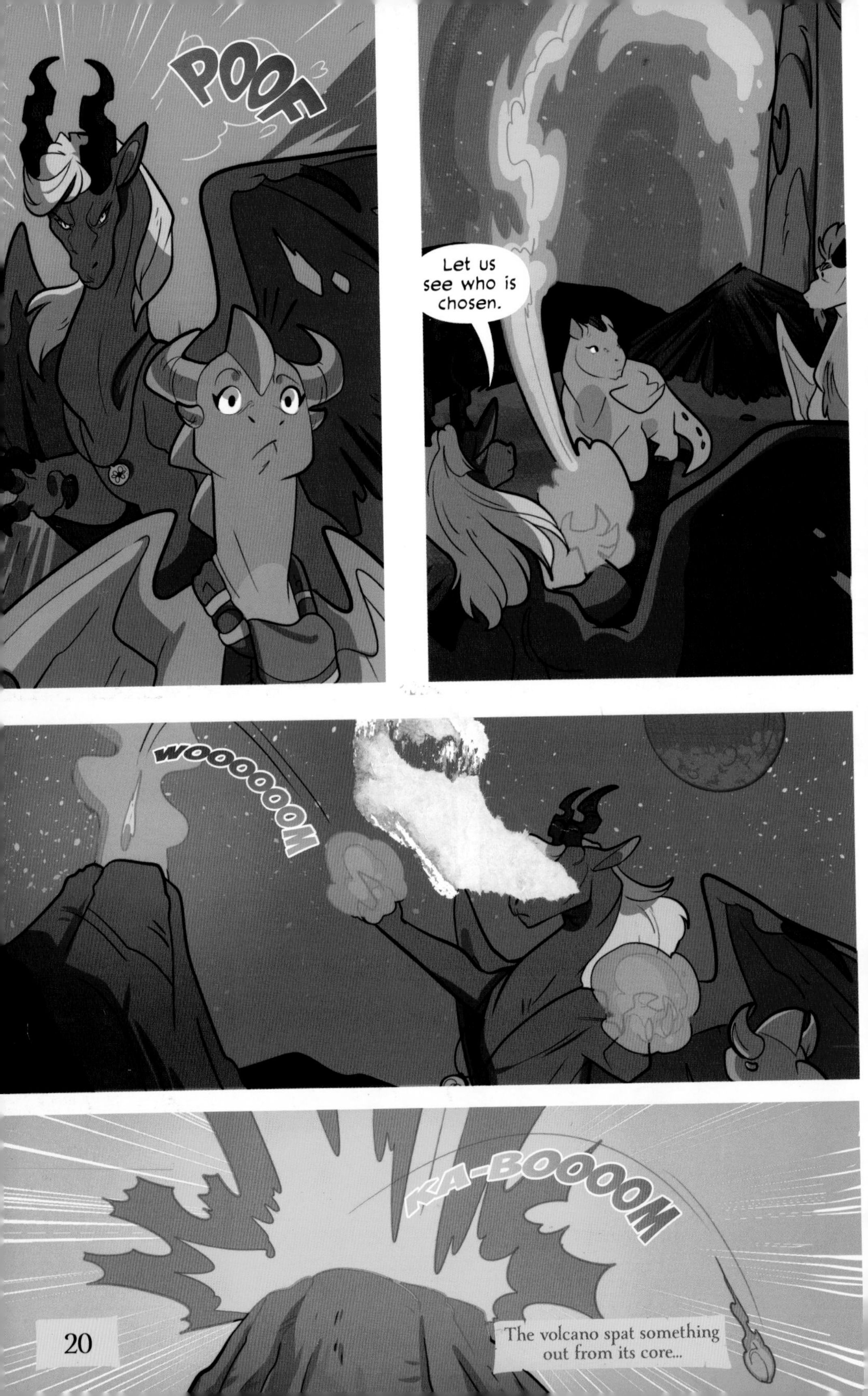
POOF
Let us see who is chosen.
WOOOOOOM
KA-BOOOOM
The volcano spat something out from its core...

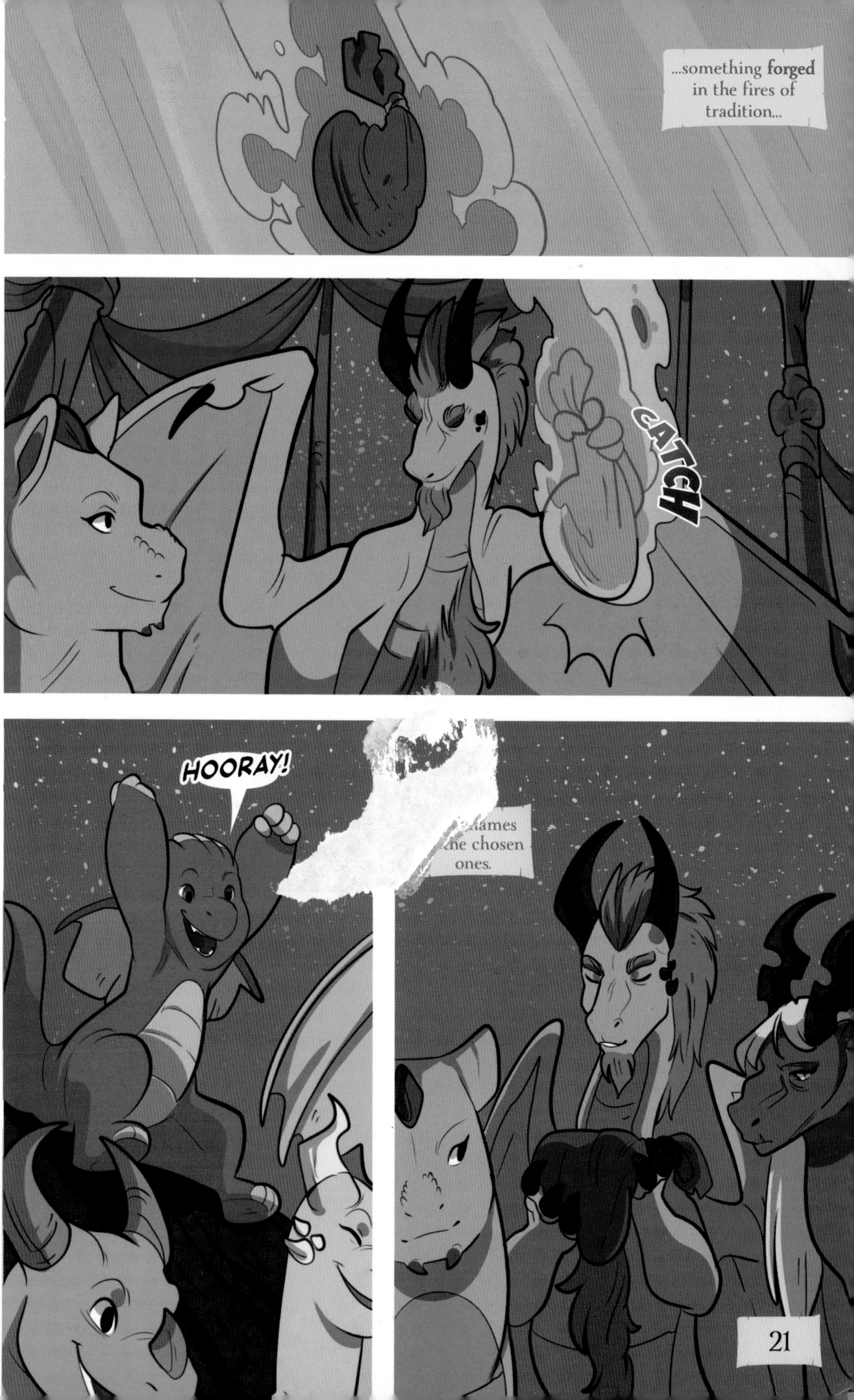
...something **forged** in the fires of tradition...
CATCH
HOORAY!
ames
he chosen
ones.

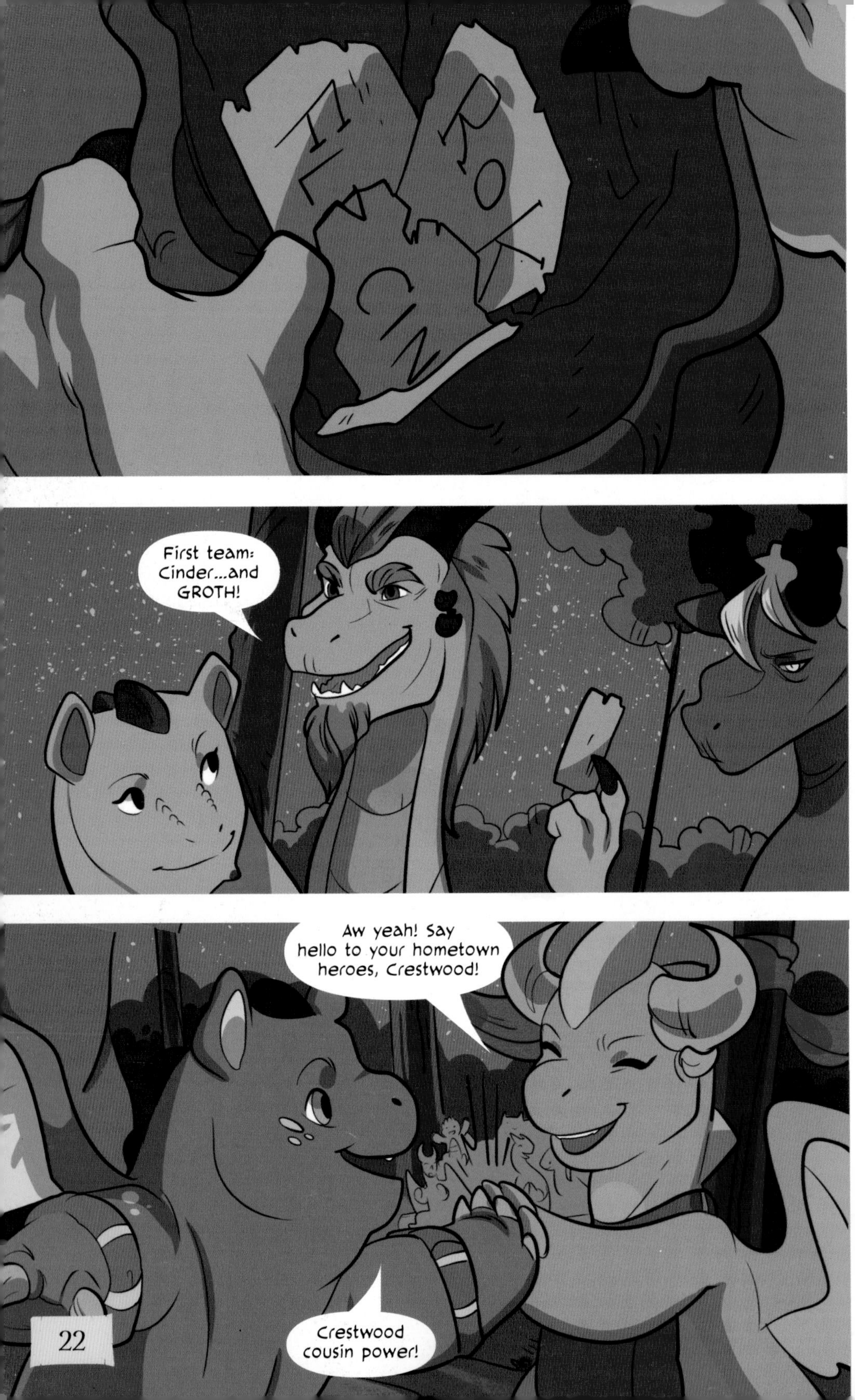
First team: Cinder...and GROTH!
Aw yeah! Say hello to your hometown heroes, Crestwood!
Crestwood cousin power!

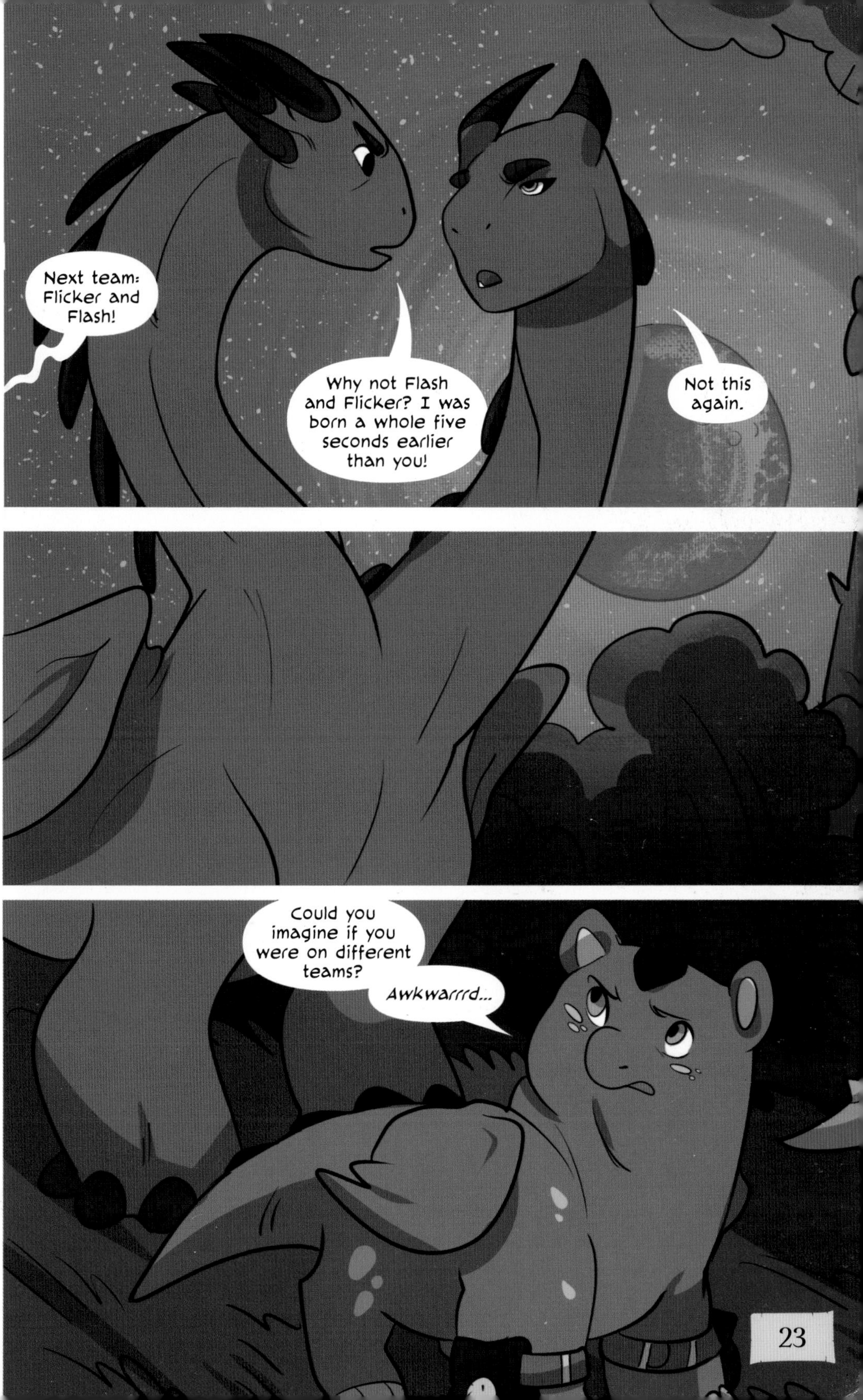
Next team: Flicker and Flash!
Why not Flash and Flicker? I was born a whole five seconds earlier than you!
Not this again.
Could you imagine if you were on different teams?
Awkwarrrd...

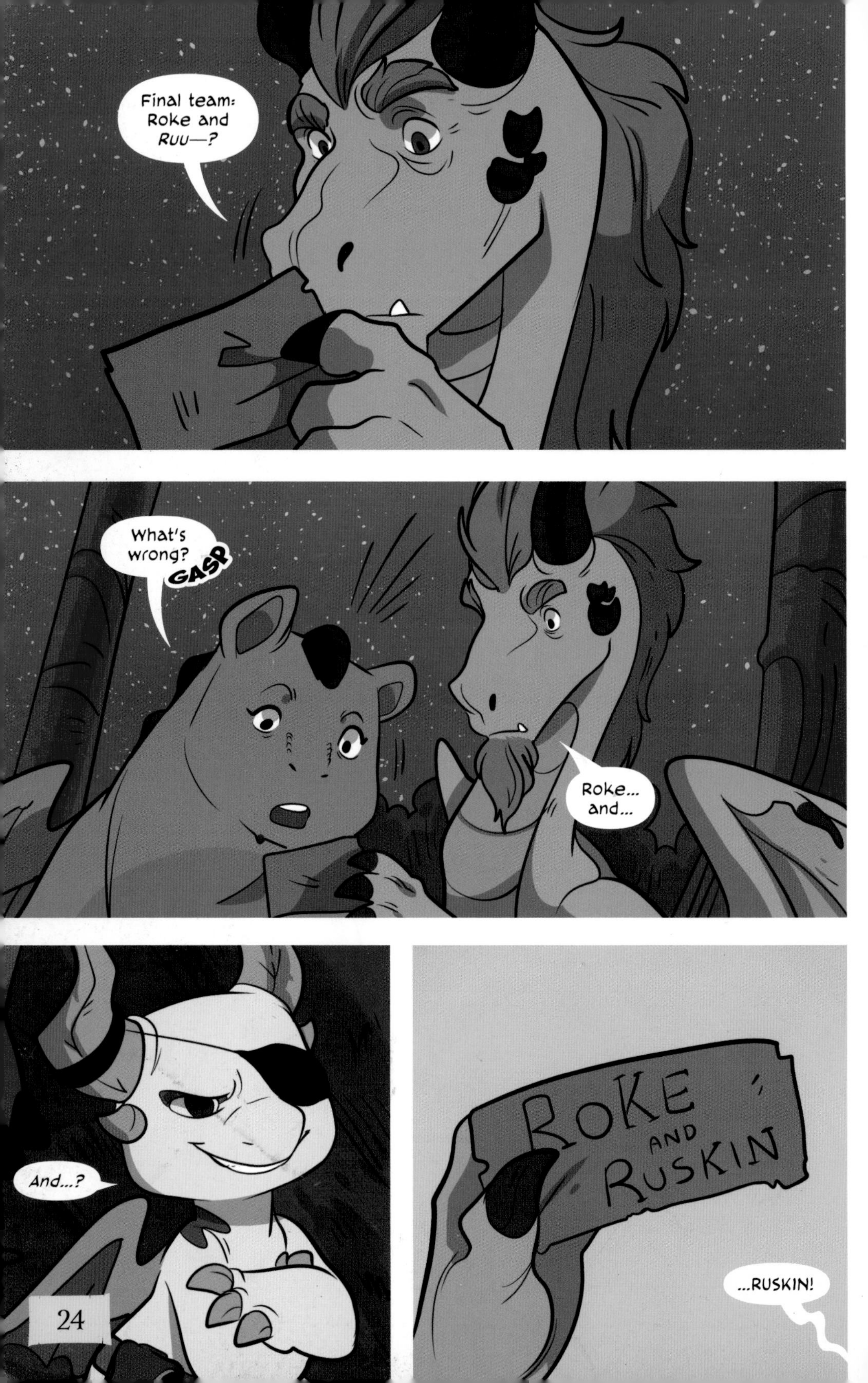
Final team: Roke and Ruu—?
What's wrong?
GASP
Roke... and...
And...?
ROKE AND RUSKIN
...RUSKIN!

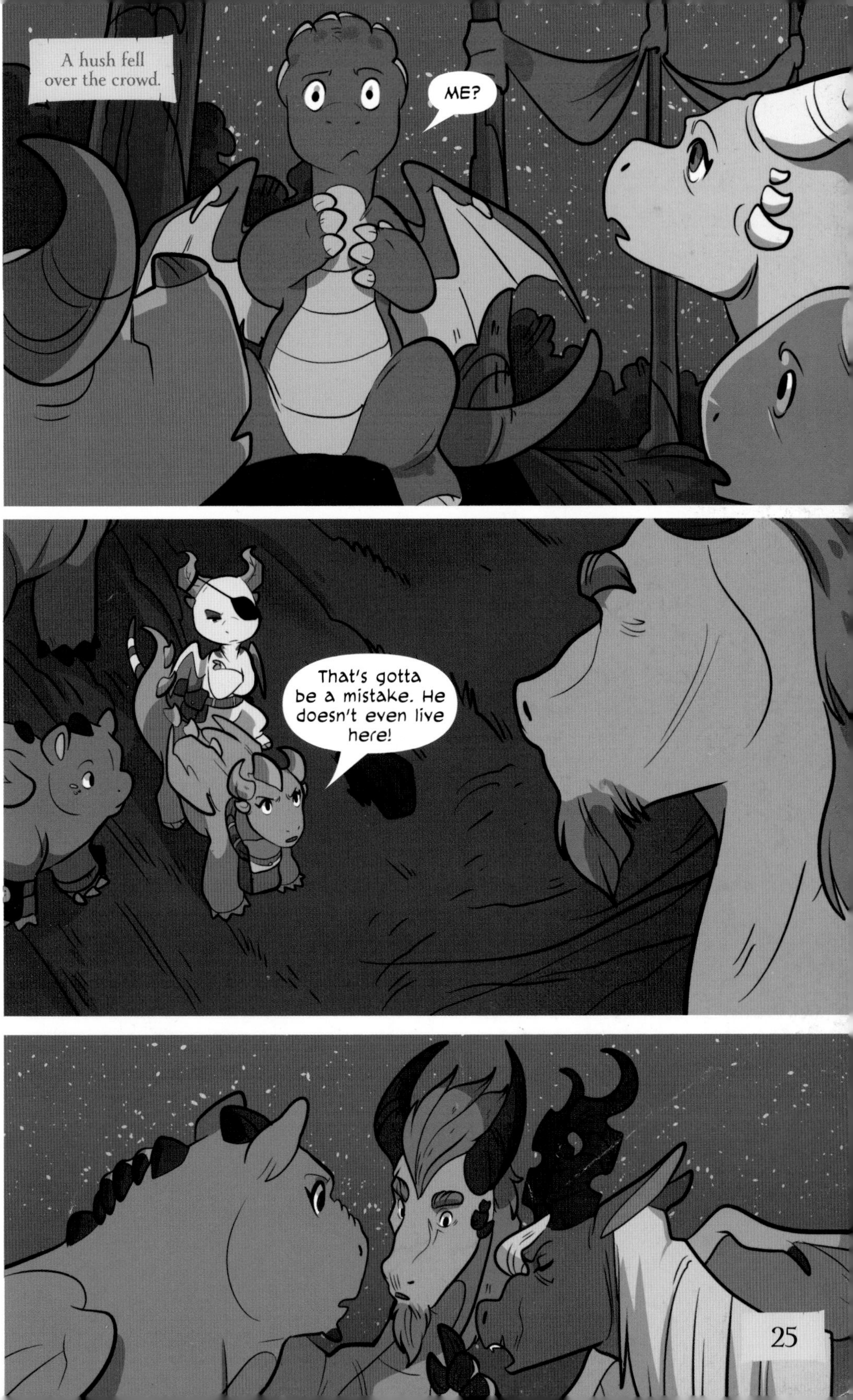
A hush fell over the crowd.
ME?
That's gotta be a mistake. He doesn't even live here!

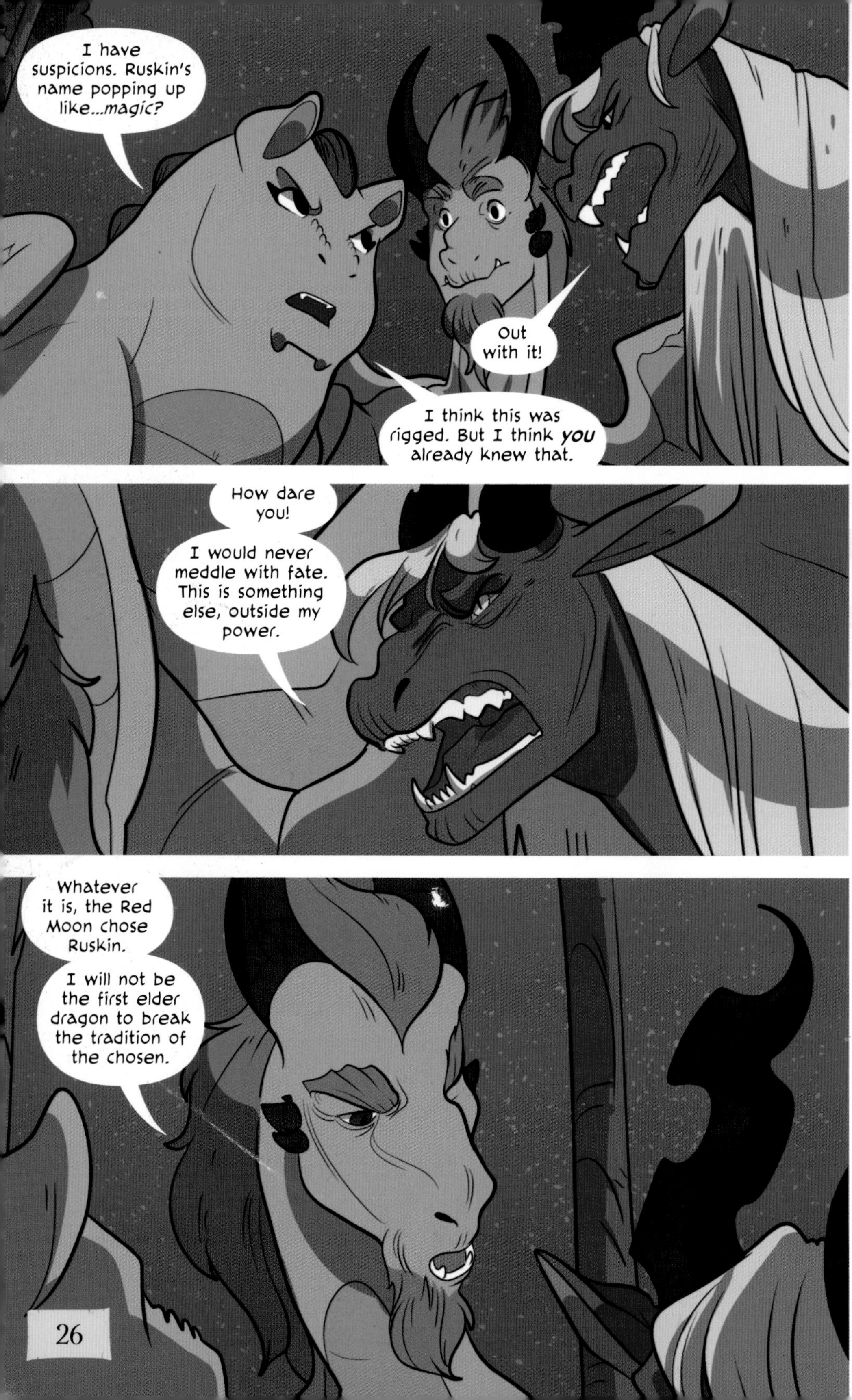
I have suspicions. Ruskin's name popping up like...*magic?*
Out with it!
I think this was rigged. But I think ***you*** already knew that.
How dare you!
I would never meddle with fate. This is something else, outside my power.
Whatever it is, the Red Moon chose Ruskin.
I will not be the first elder dragon to break the tradition of the chosen.

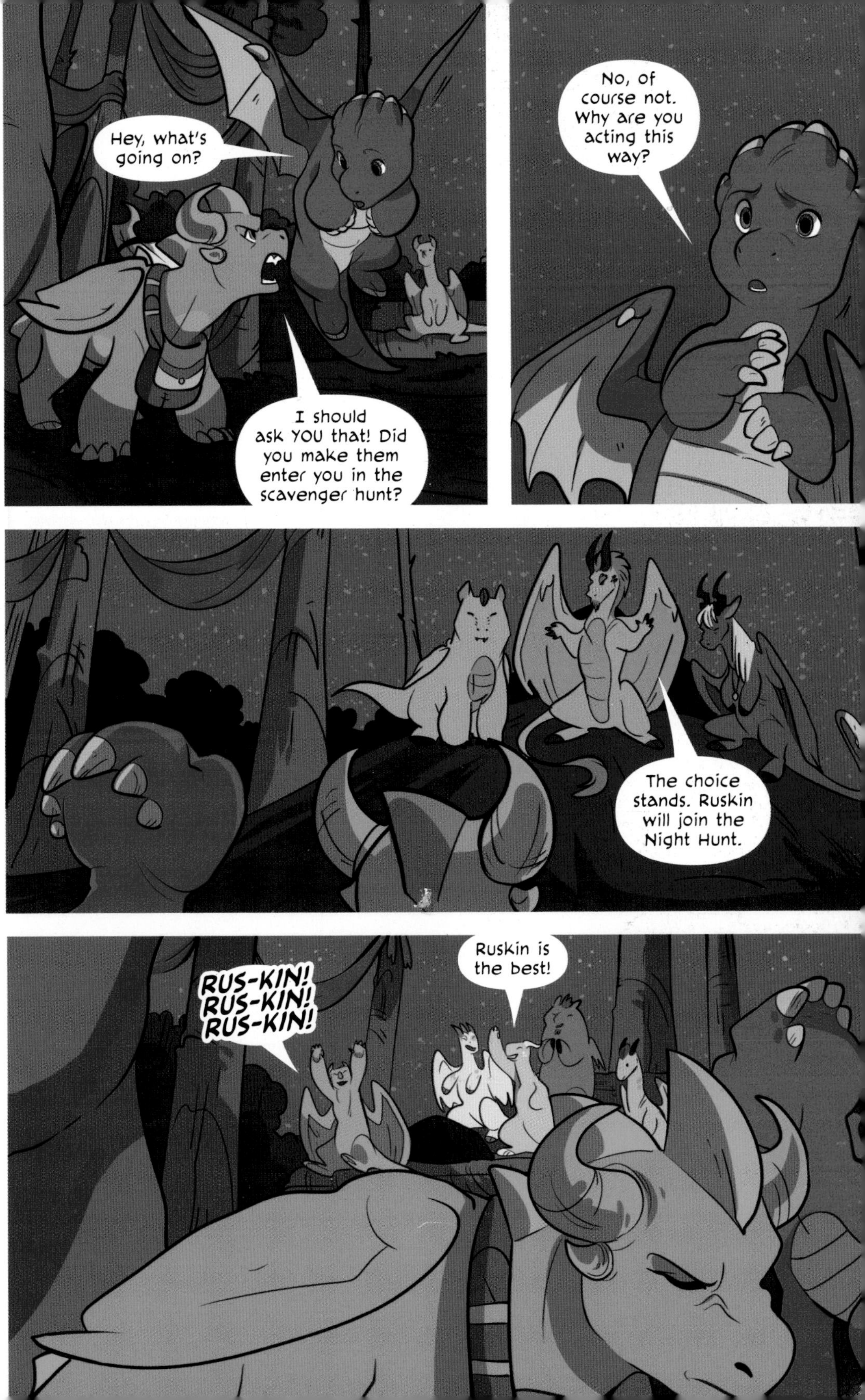
Hey, what's going on?
I should ask YOU that! Did you make them enter you in the scavenger hunt?
No, of course not. Why are you acting this way?
The choice stands. Ruskin will join the Night Hunt.
RUS-KIN! RUS-KIN! RUS-KIN!
Ruskin is the best!

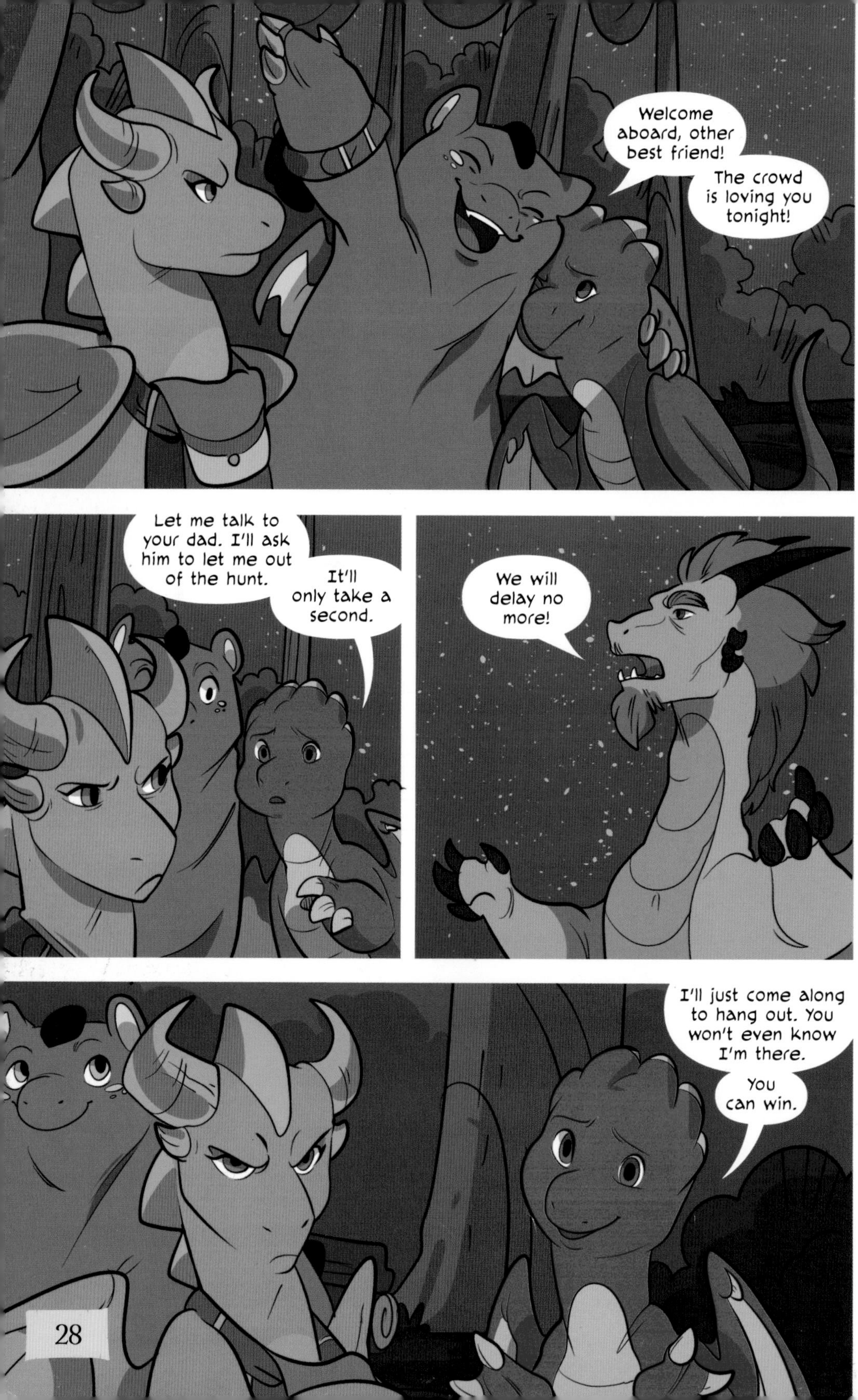
Welcome aboard, other best friend!
The crowd is loving you tonight!
Let me talk to your dad. I'll ask him to let me out of the hunt.
It'll only take a second.
We will delay no more!
I'll just come along to hang out. You won't even know I'm there.
You can win.

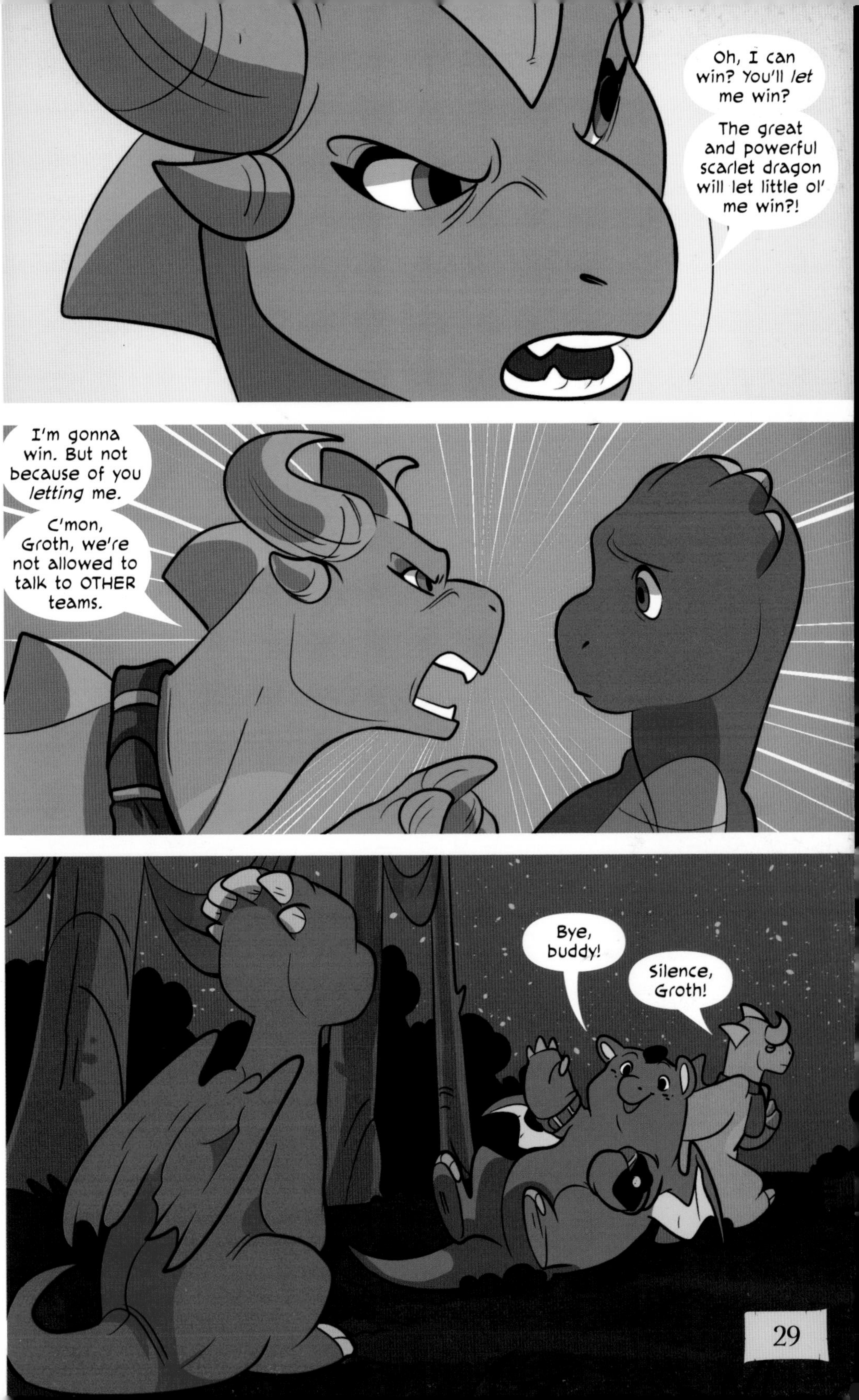
Oh, I can win? You'll *let* me win?
The great and powerful scarlet dragon will let little ol' me win?!
I'm gonna win. But not because of you *letting* me.
C'mon, Groth, we're not allowed to talk to OTHER teams.
Bye, buddy!
Silence, Groth!

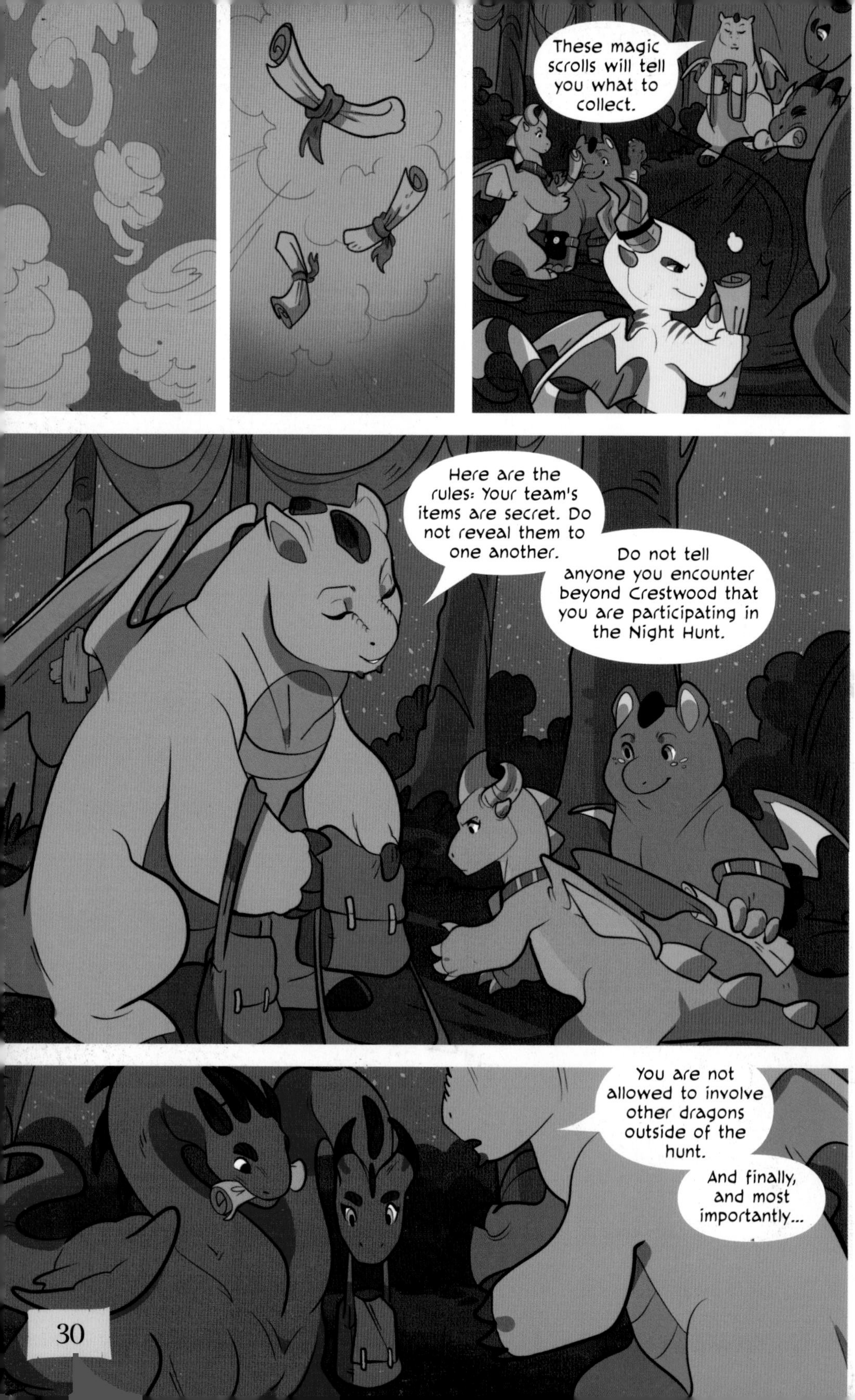
These magic scrolls will tell you what to collect.
Here are the rules: Your team's items are secret. Do not reveal them to one another.
Do not tell anyone you encounter beyond Crestwood that you are participating in the Night Hunt.
You are not allowed to involve other dragons outside of the hunt.
And finally, and most importantly...

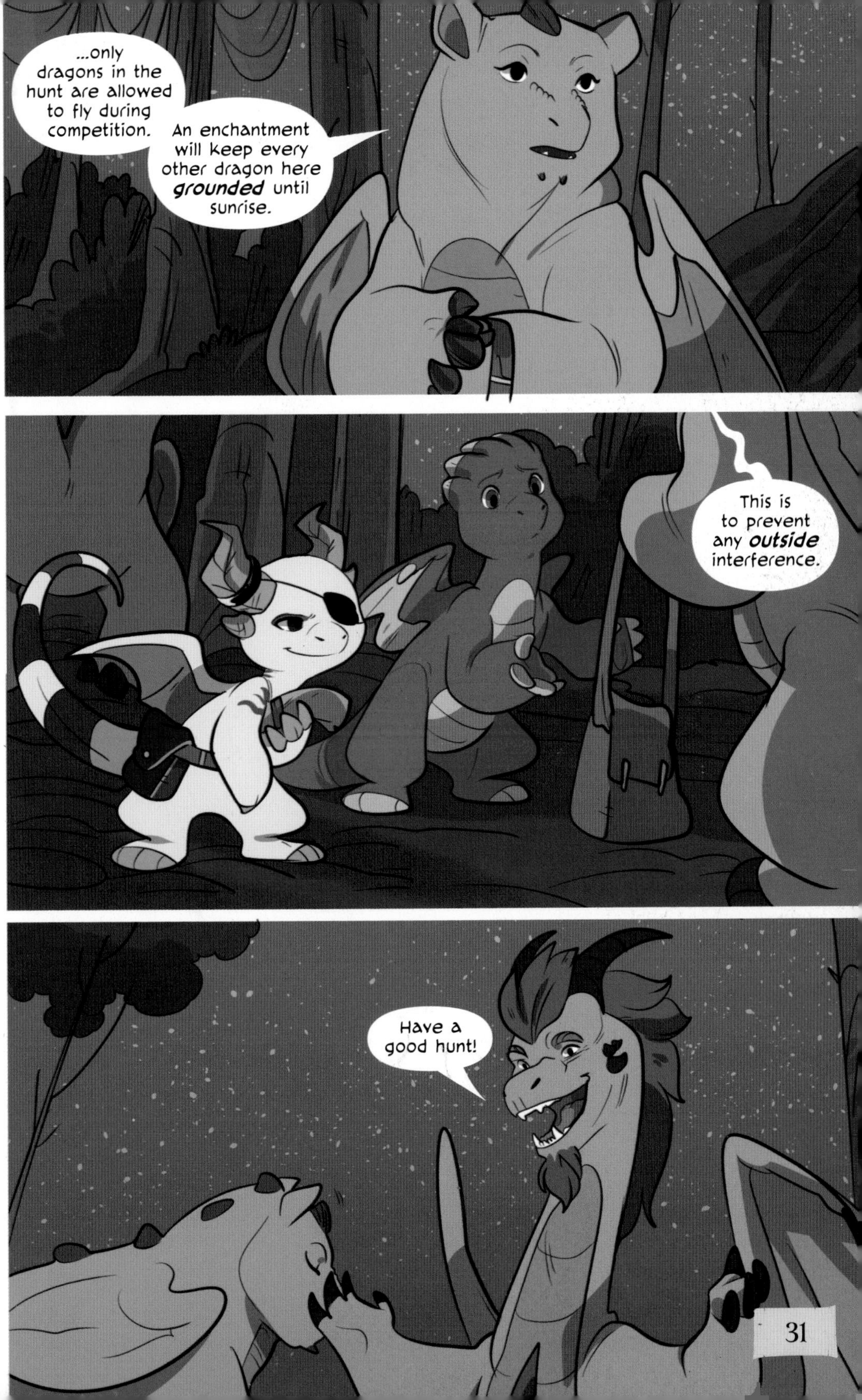
...only dragons in the hunt are allowed to fly during competition.
An enchantment will keep every other dragon here ***grounded*** until sunrise.
This is to prevent any ***outside*** interference.
Have a good hunt!

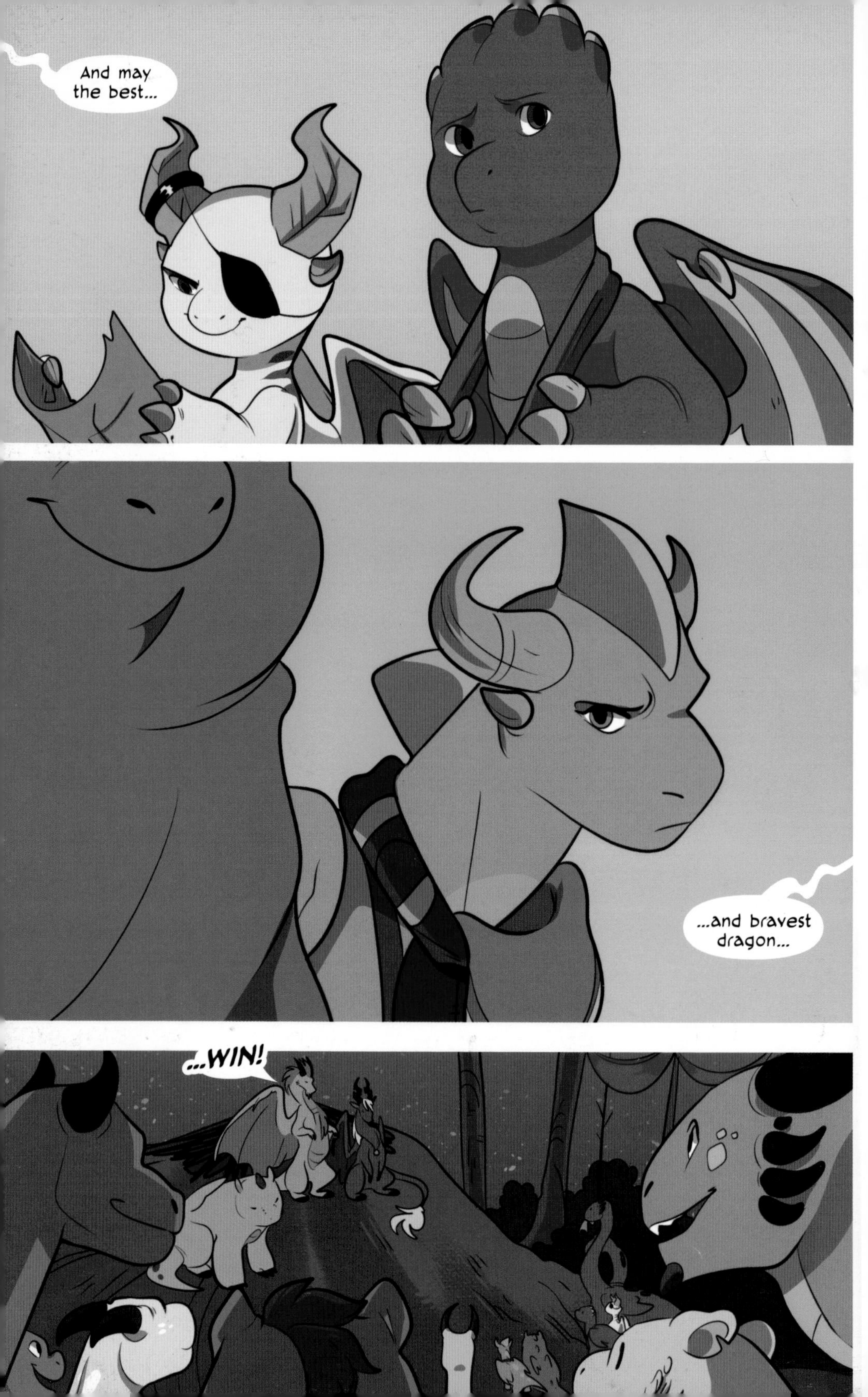
And may the best...
...and bravest dragon...
...WIN!

Chapter 3

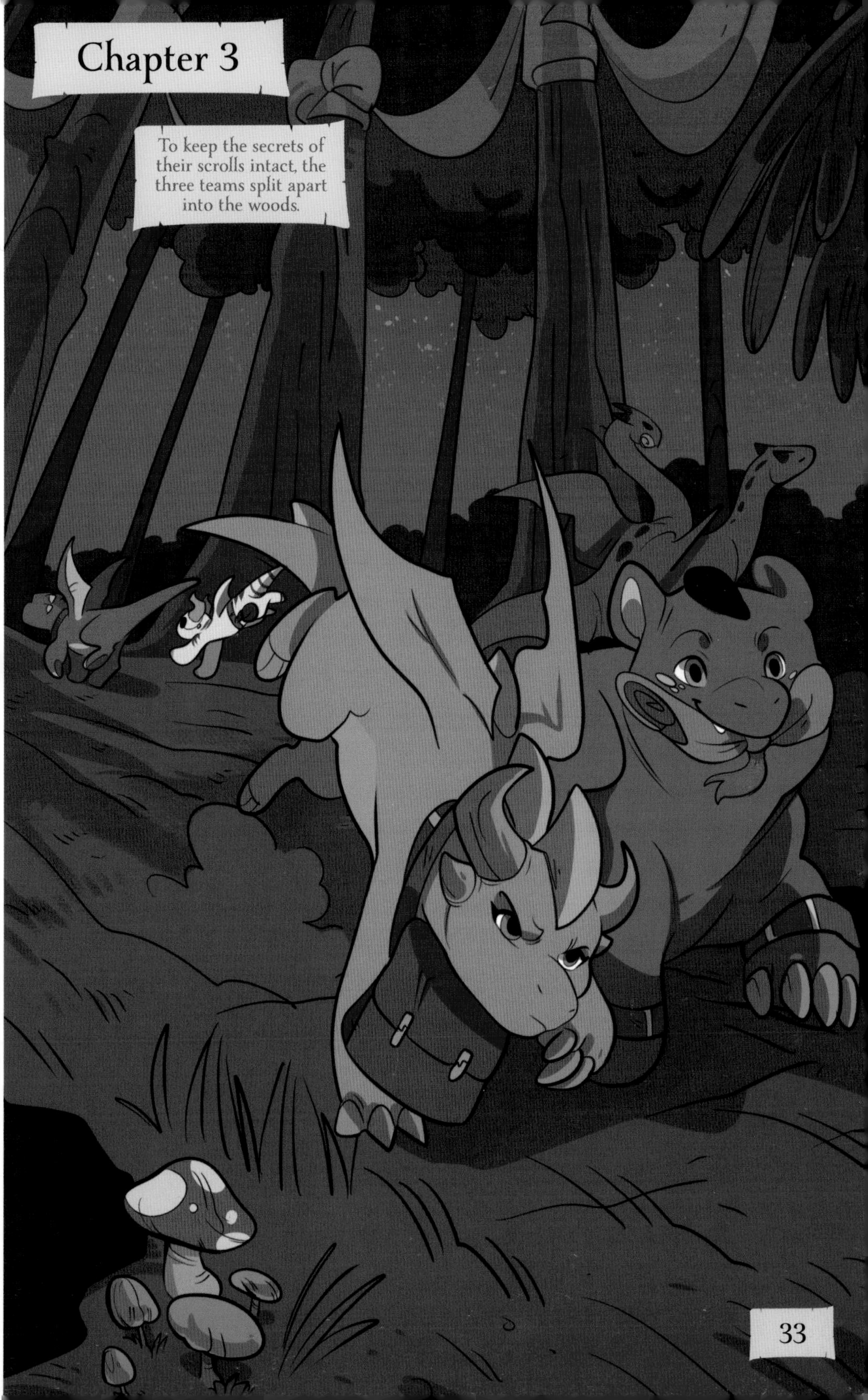
To keep the secrets of their scrolls intact, the three teams split apart into the woods.

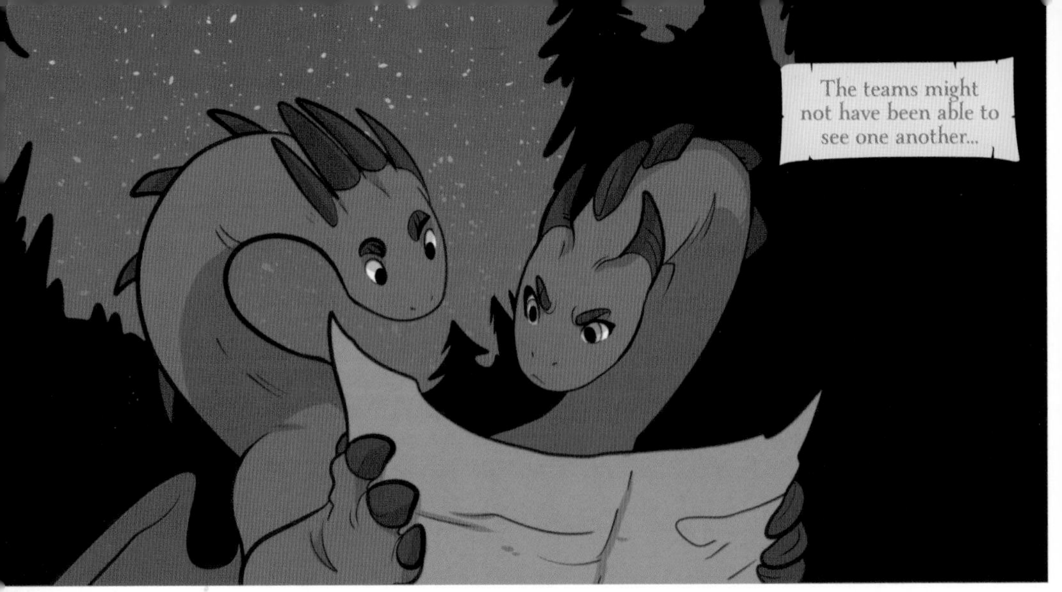
The teams might not have been able to see one another...

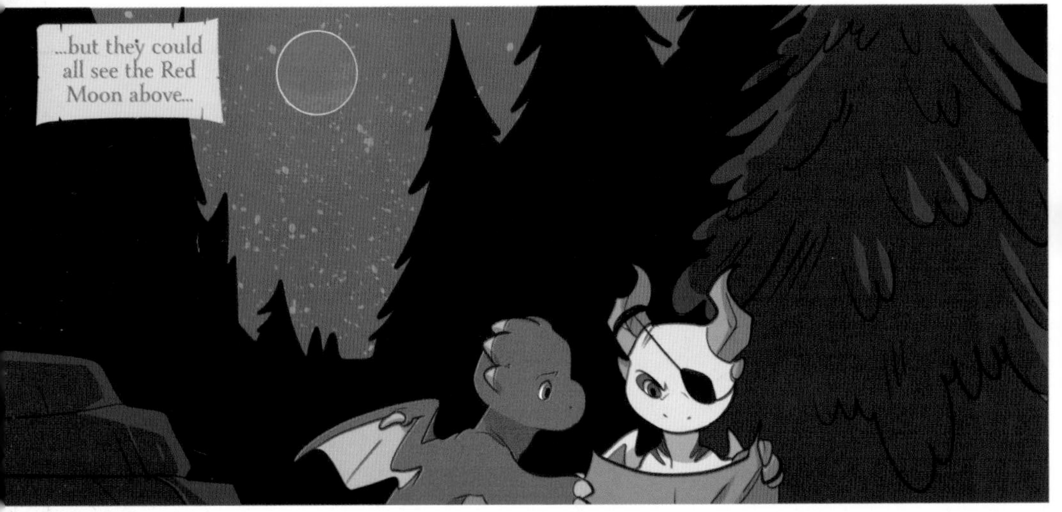
...but they could all see the Red Moon above...

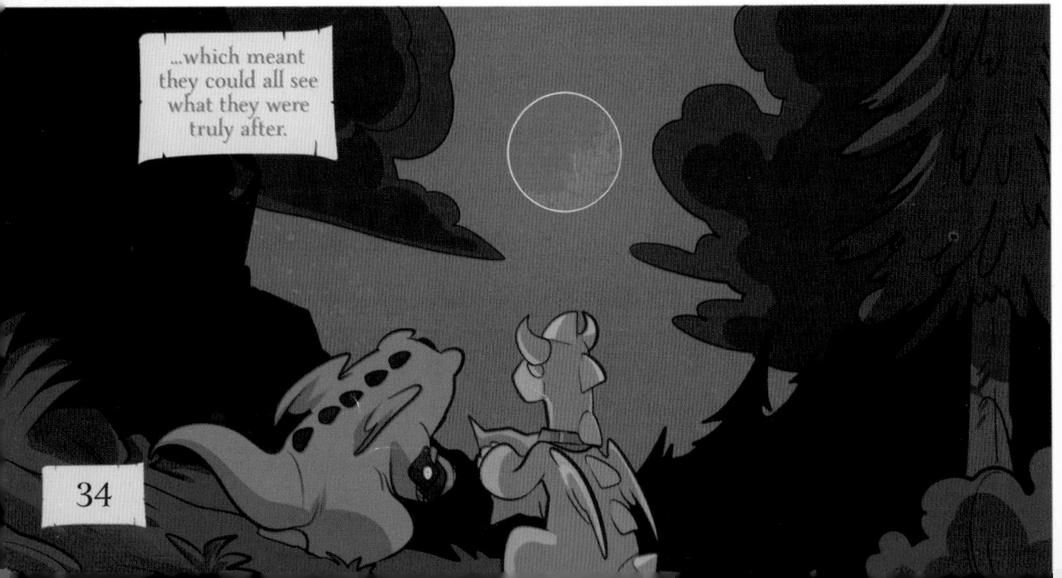
...which meant they could all see what they were truly after.

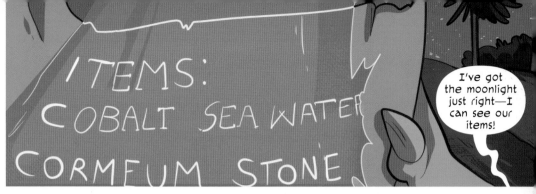

ITEMS:
COBALT SEA WATER
CORMEUM STONE

I've got the moonlight just right—I can see our items!

We have to win this, Groth. Failure is not an option.

Right, so we should read these items—

We've gotta prove ourselves!

All of Crestwood is watching, and they need to know that Ruskin isn't the only hero around here.

We're brave too!

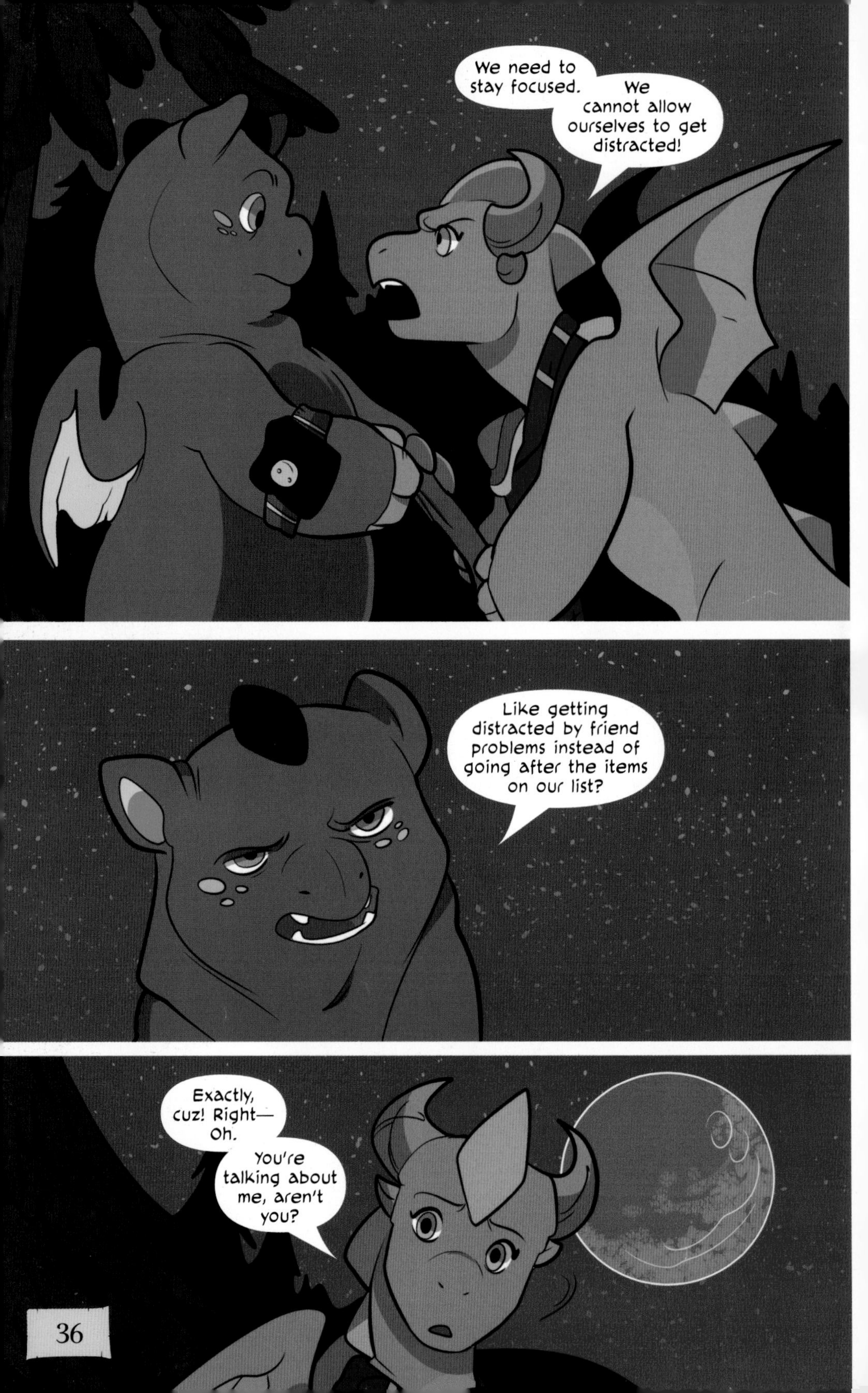
We need to stay focused.
We cannot allow ourselves to get distracted!
Like getting distracted by friend problems instead of going after the items on our list?
Exactly, cuz! Right— Oh.
You're talking about me, aren't you?

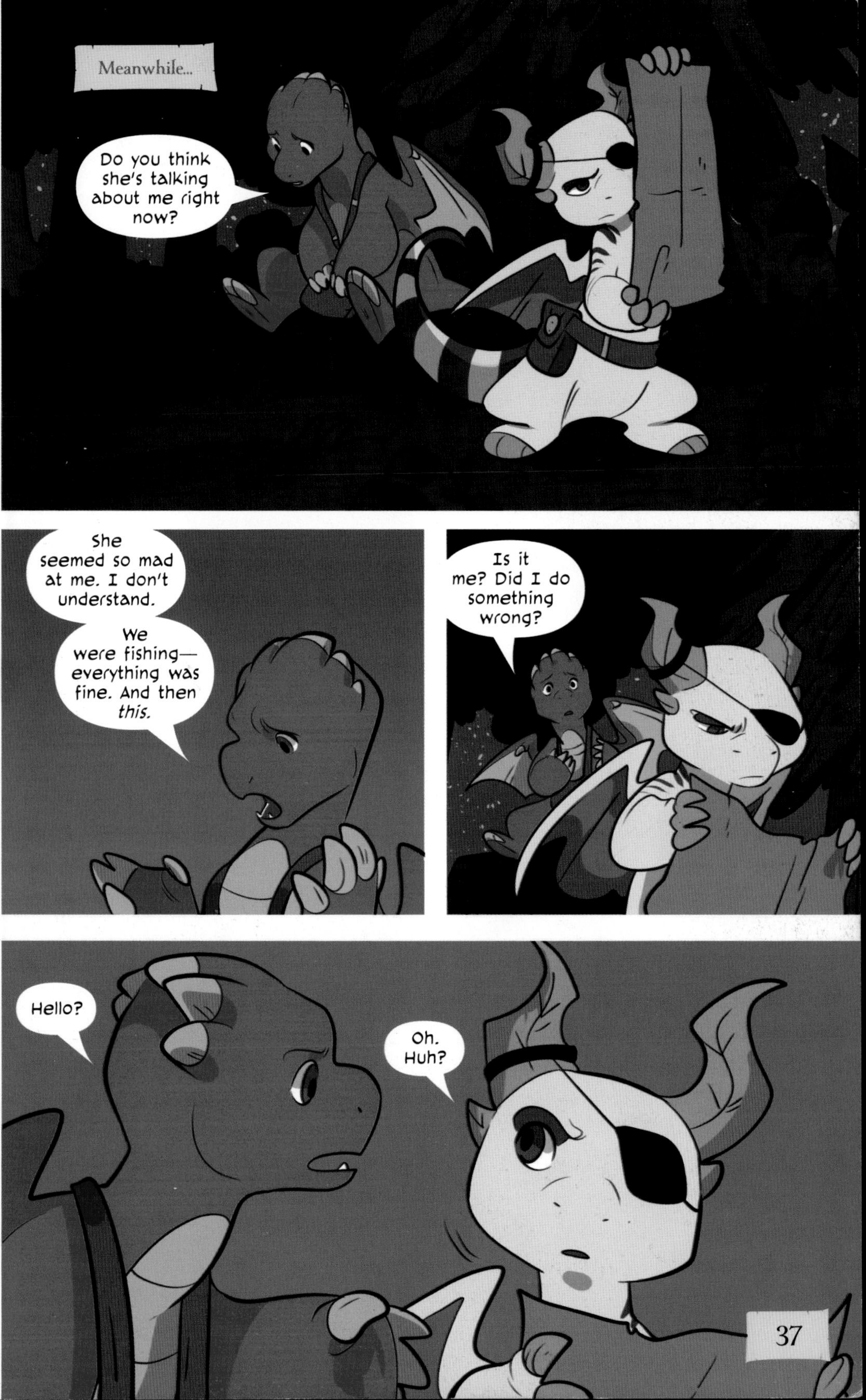
Meanwhile...
Do you think she's talking about me right now?
She seemed so mad at me. I don't understand.
We were fishing—everything was fine. And then *this.*
Is it me? Did I do something wrong?
Hello?
Oh. Huh?

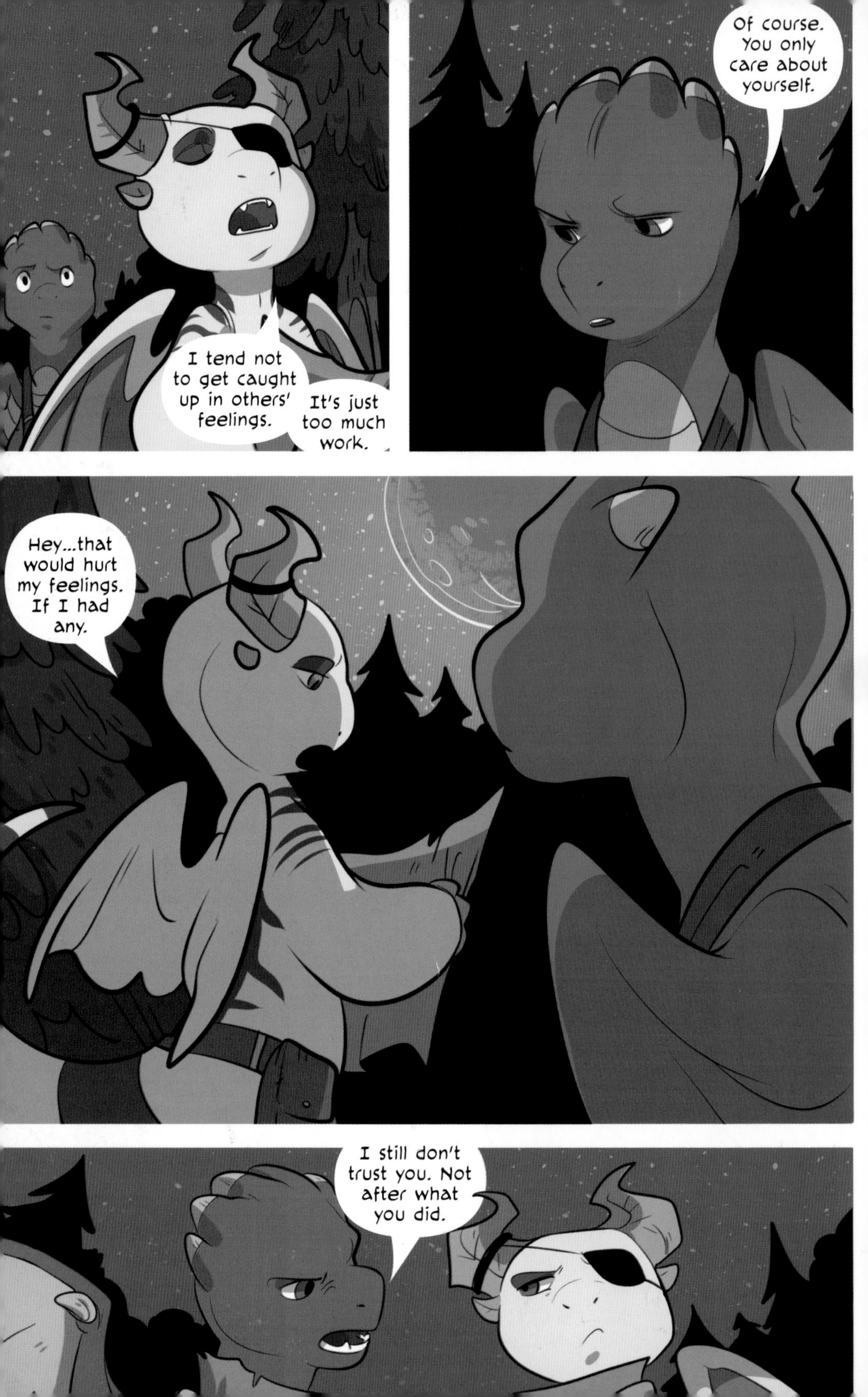
I tend not to get caught up in others' feelings.
It's just too much work.
Of course. You only care about yourself.
Hey...that would hurt my feelings. If I had any.
I still don't trust you. Not after what you did.

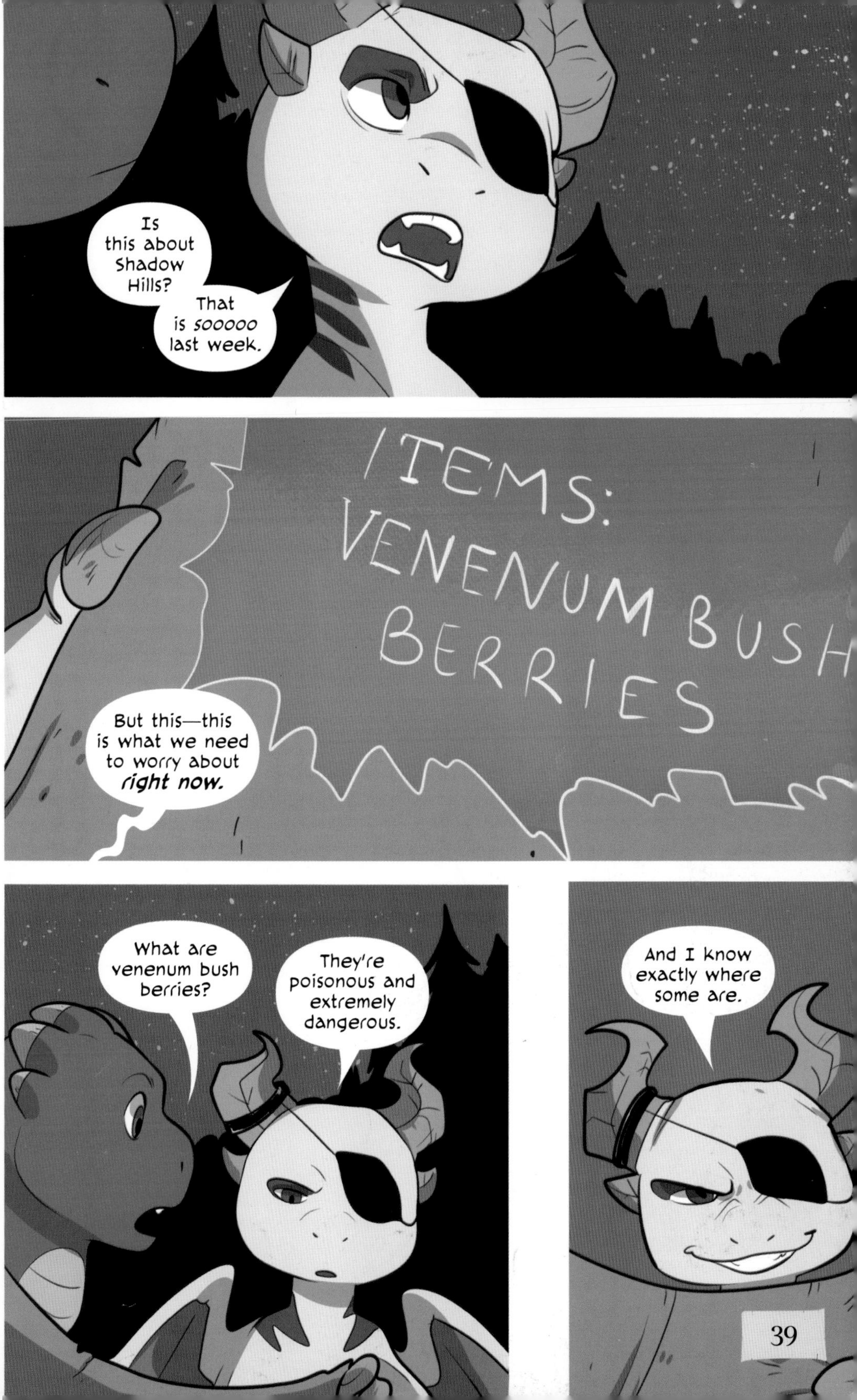
Is this about Shadow Hills?
That is *sooooo* last week.
ITEMS: VENENUM BUSH BERRIES
But this—this is what we need to worry about ***right now.***
What are venenum bush berries?
They're poisonous and extremely dangerous.
And I know exactly where some are.

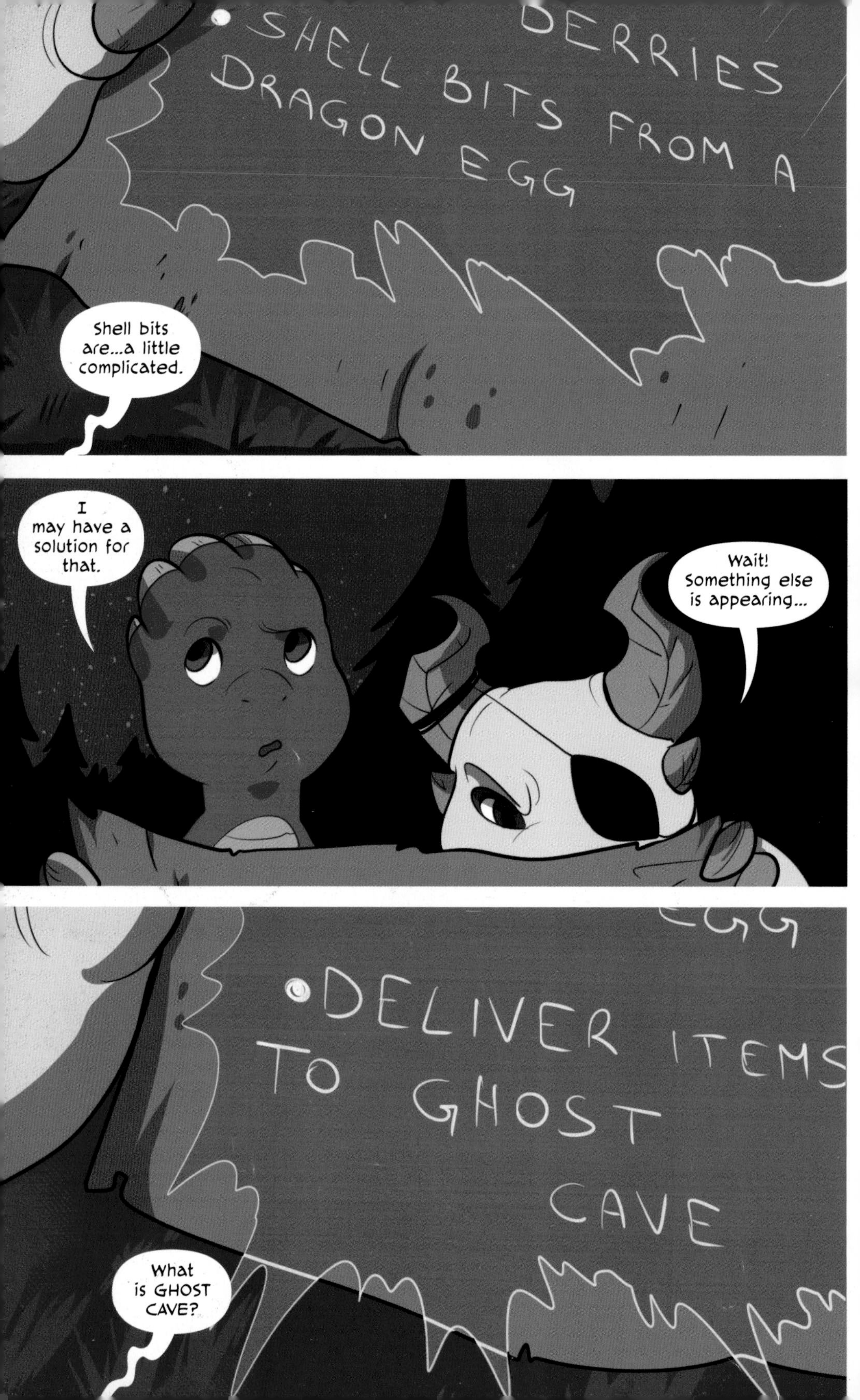
BERRIES
SHELL BITS FROM A
DRAGON EGG
Shell bits are...a little complicated.
I may have a solution for that.
Wait! Something else is appearing...
EGG
DELIVER ITEMS TO GHOST CAVE
What is GHOST CAVE?

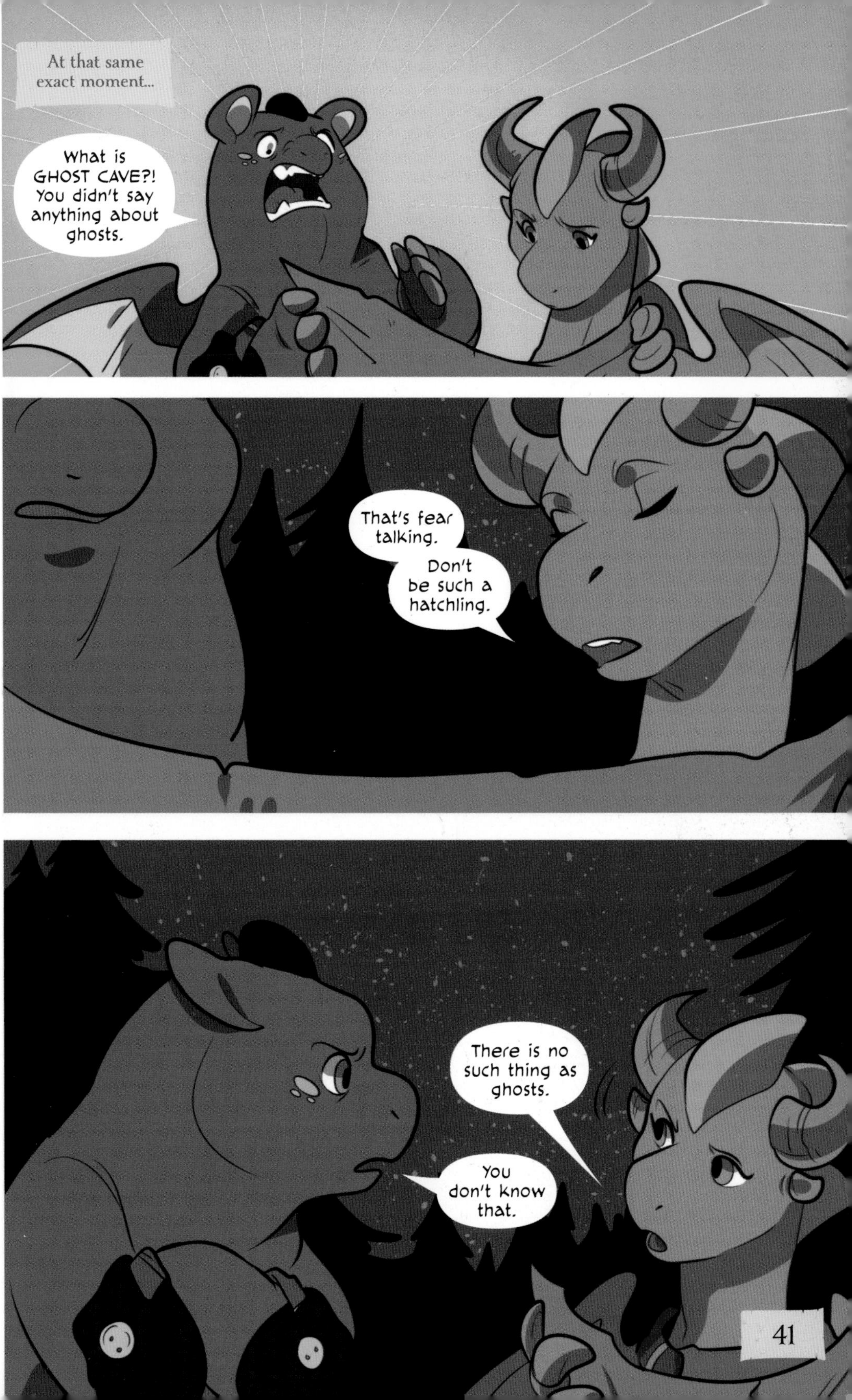
At that same exact moment...
What is GHOST CAVE?! You didn't say anything about ghosts.
That's fear talking.
Don't be such a hatchling.
There is no such thing as ghosts.
You don't know that.

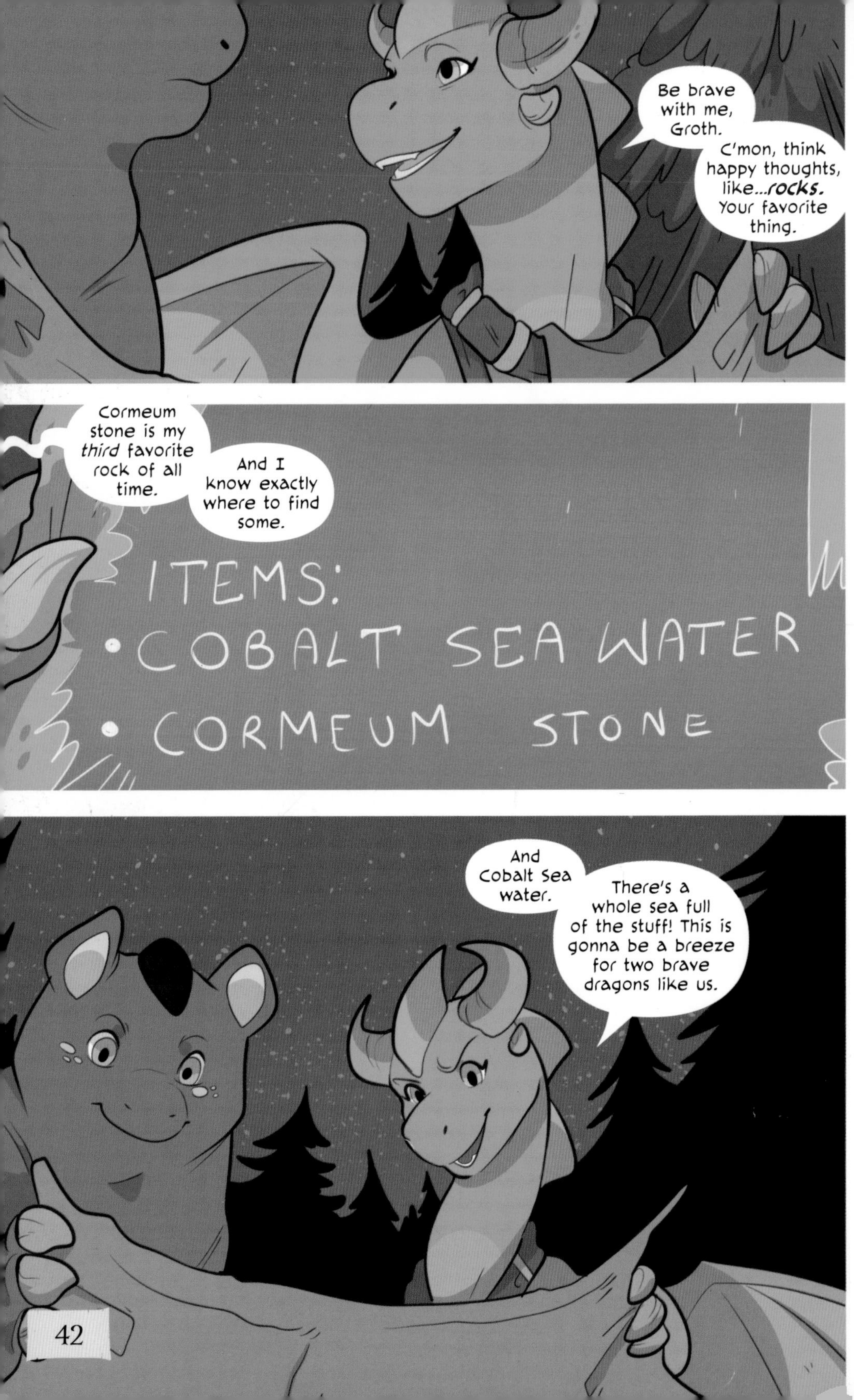
Be brave with me, Groth.
C'mon, think happy thoughts, like...**rocks.** Your favorite thing.
Cormeum stone is my *third* favorite rock of all time.
And I know exactly where to find some.
ITEMS:
•COBALT SEA WATER
•CORMEUM STONE
And Cobalt Sea water.
There's a whole sea full of the stuff! This is gonna be a breeze for two brave dragons like us.

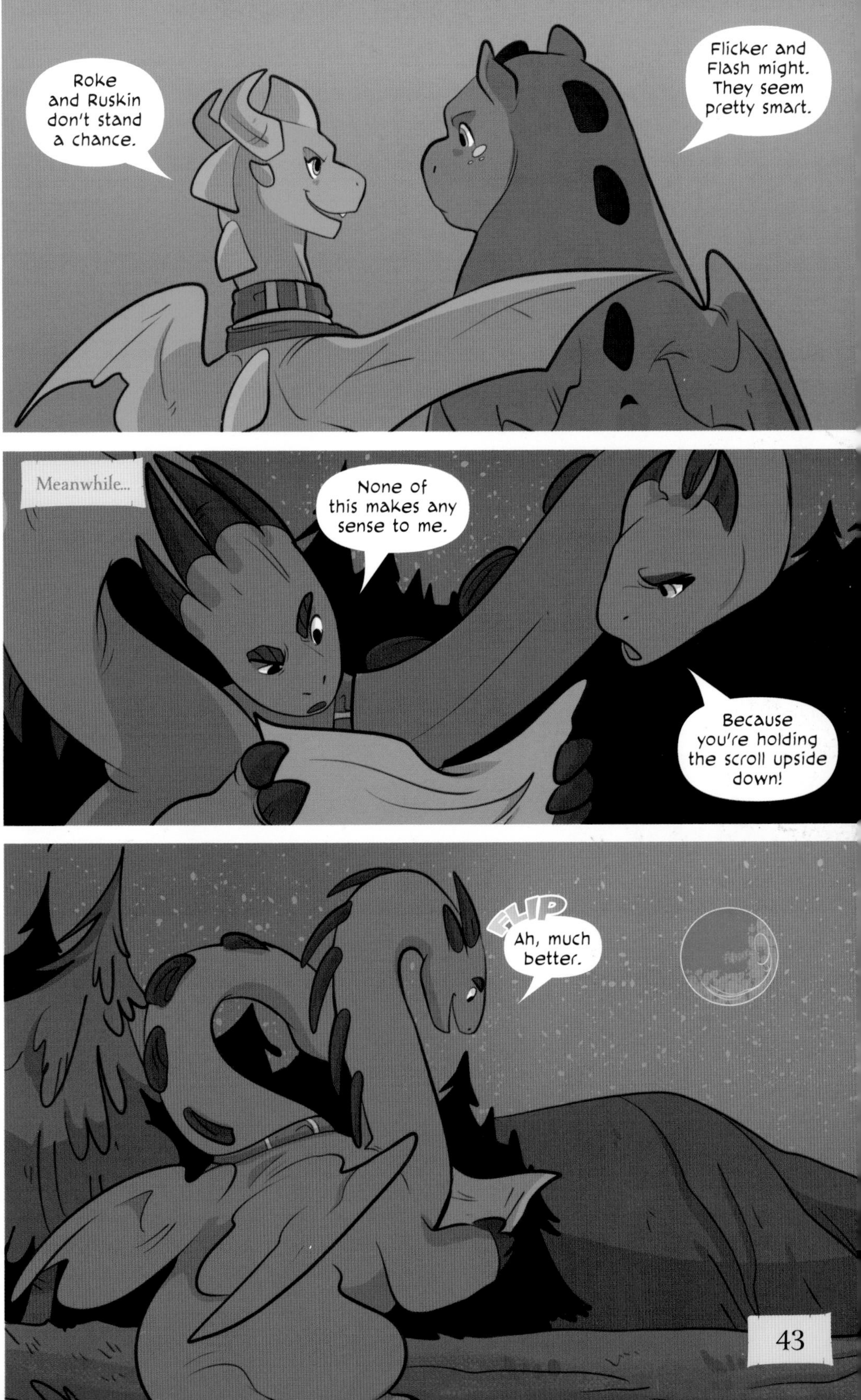

Roke and Ruskin don't stand a chance.
Flicker and Flash might. They seem pretty smart.
Meanwhile...
None of this makes any sense to me.
Because you're holding the scroll upside down!
FLIP
Ah, much better.

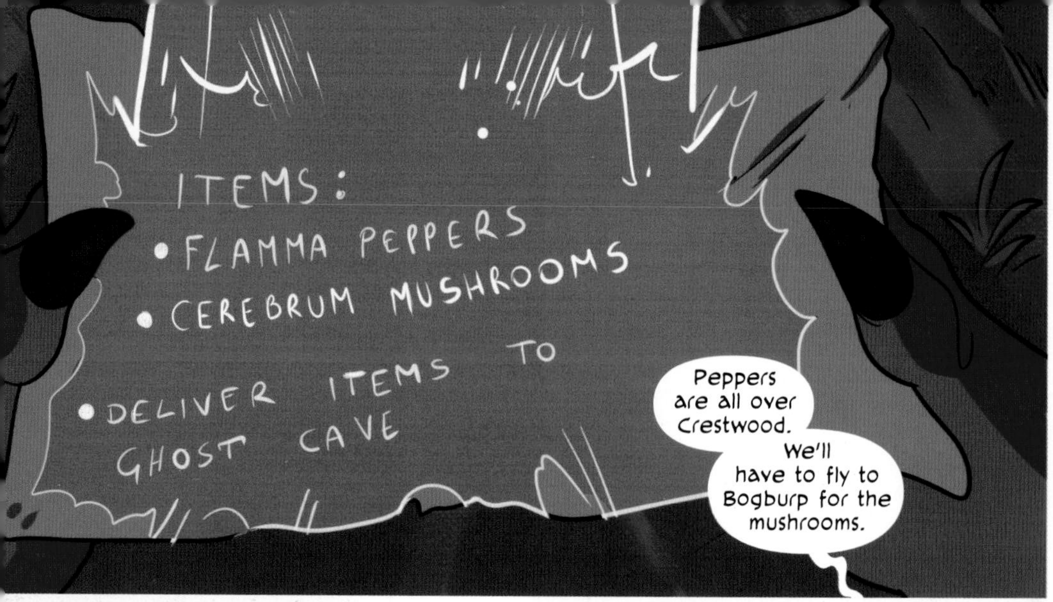
ITEMS:
• FLAMMA PEPPERS
• CEREBRUM MUSHROOMS
• DELIVER ITEMS TO GHOST CAVE
Peppers are all over Crestwood.
We'll have to fly to Bogburp for the mushrooms.

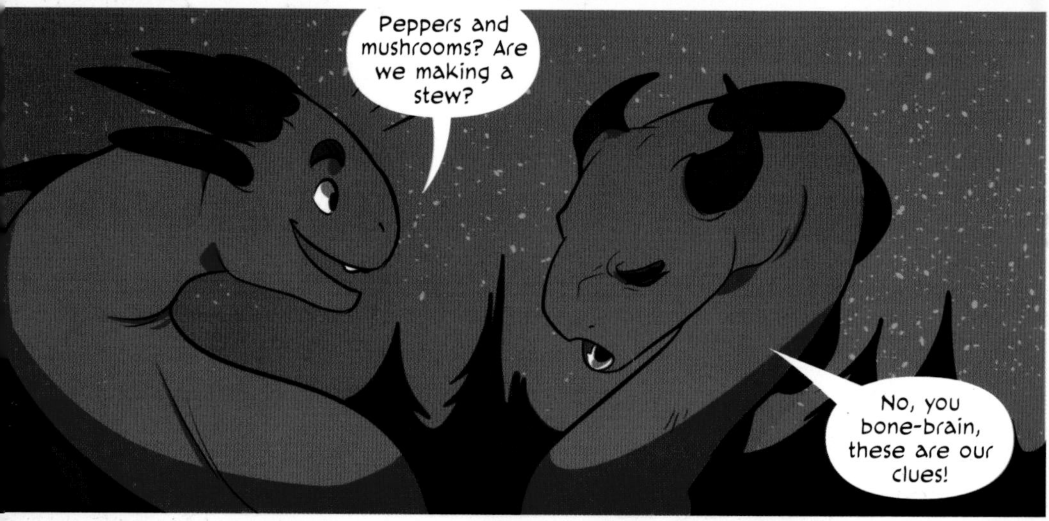
Peppers and mushrooms? Are we making a stew?
No, you bone-brain, these are our clues!

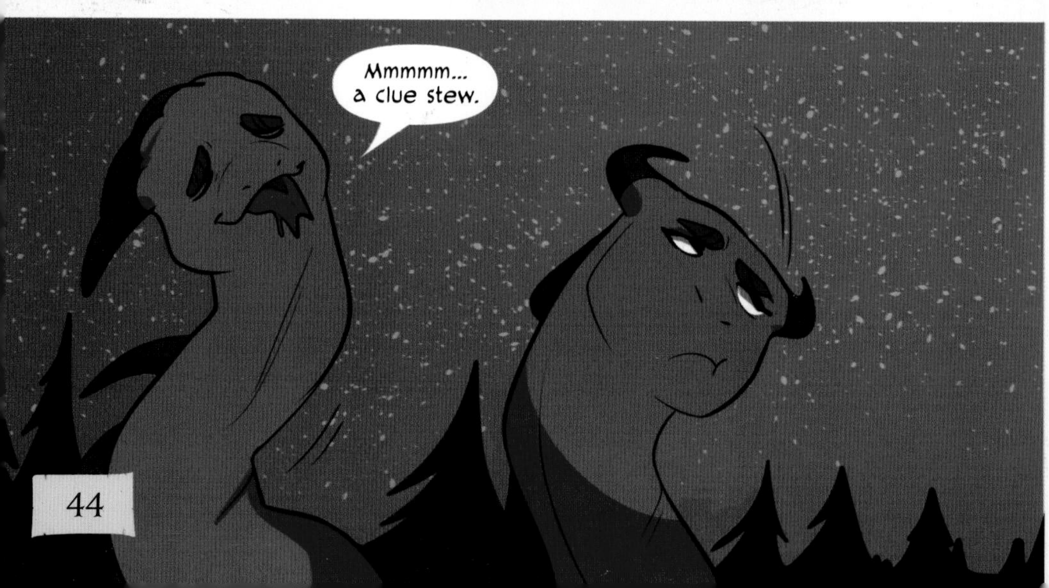
Mmmmm... a clue stew.

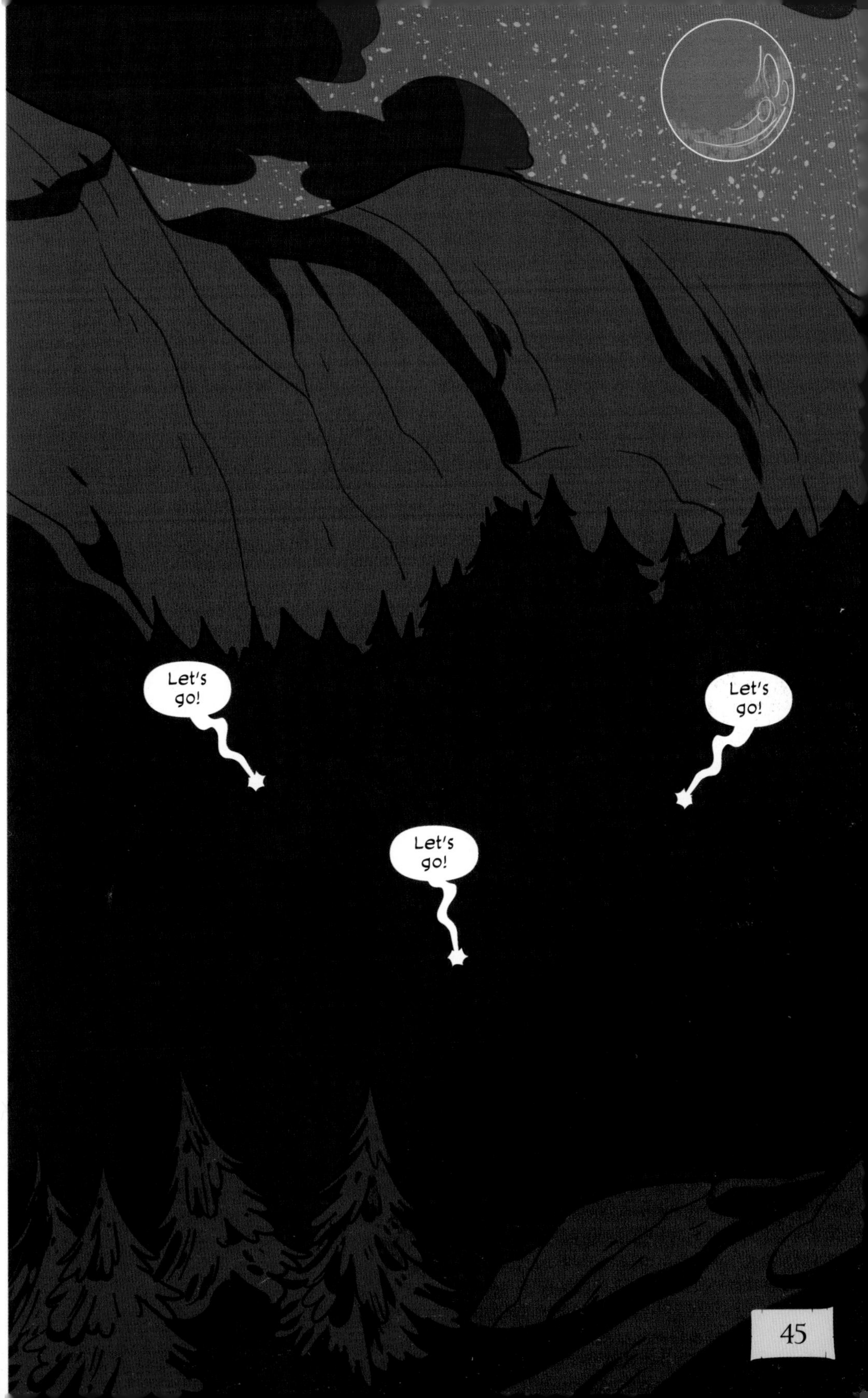
Let's go!
Let's go!
Let's go!

Chapter 4

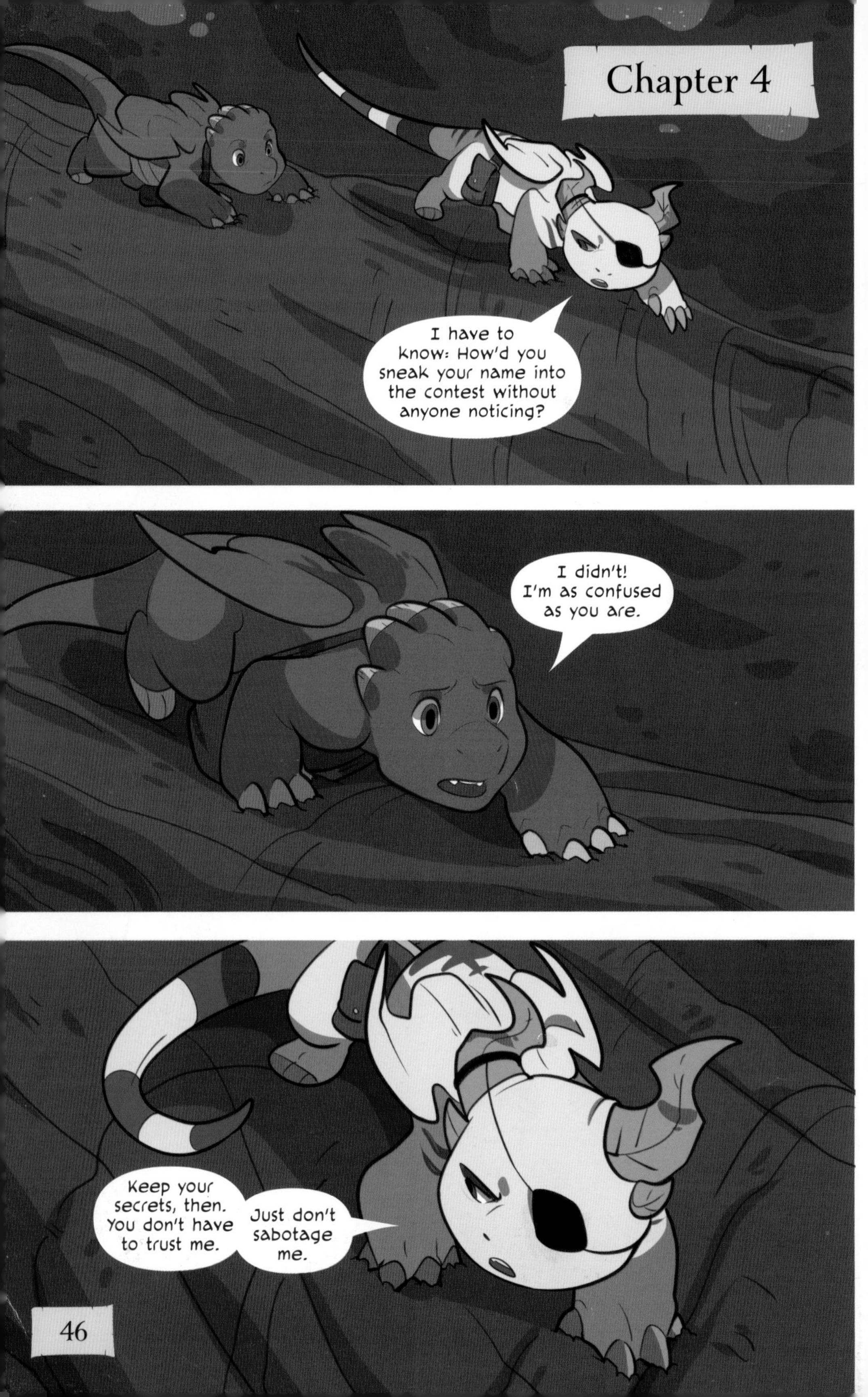
I have to know: How'd you sneak your name into the contest without anyone noticing?
I didn't! I'm as confused as you are.
Keep your secrets, then. You don't have to trust me.
Just don't sabotage me.

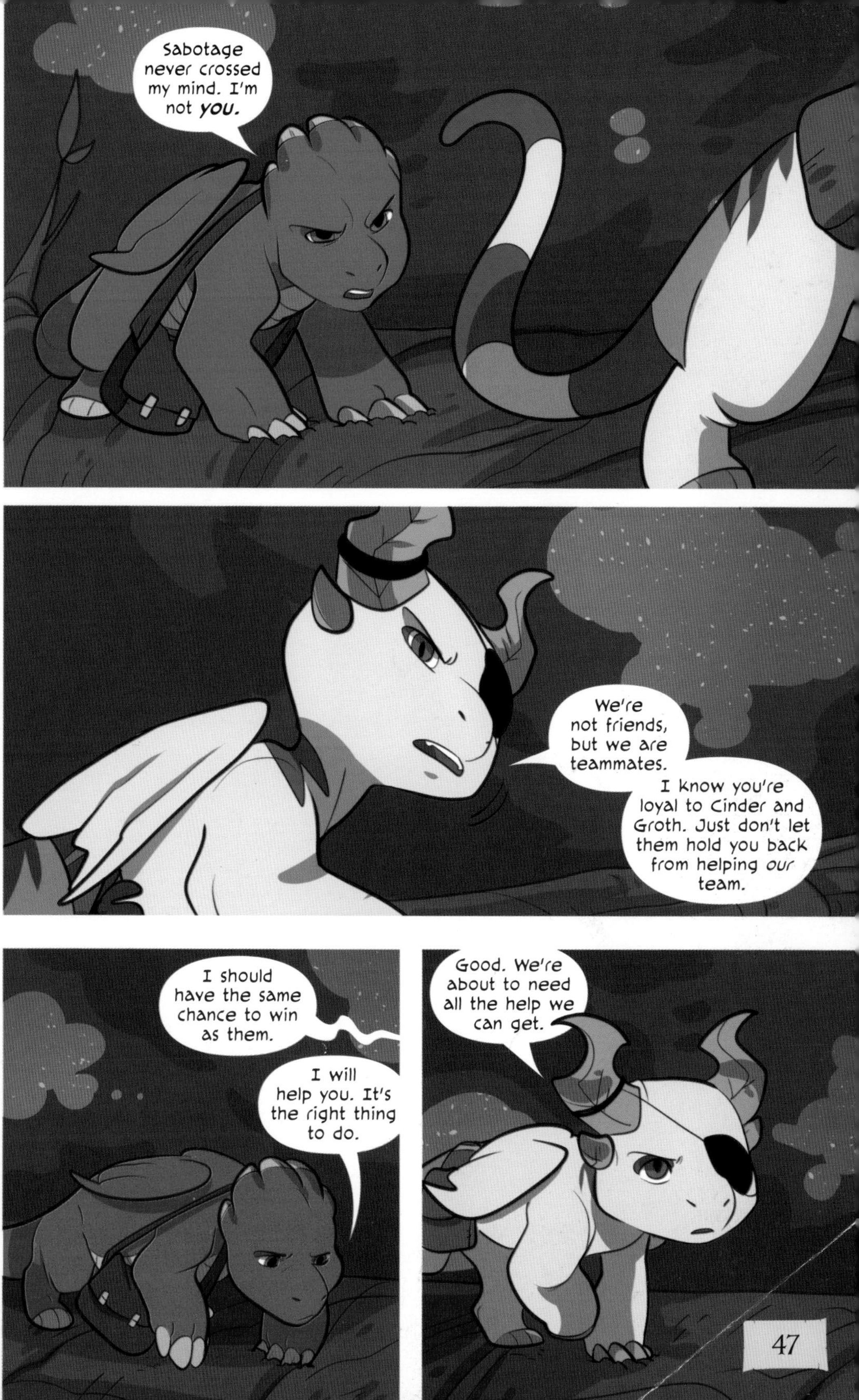
Sabotage never crossed my mind. I'm not *YOU.*
We're not friends, but we are teammates.
I know you're loyal to Cinder and Groth. Just don't let them hold you back from helping *our* team.
I should have the same chance to win as them.
I will help you. It's the right thing to do.
Good. We're about to need all the help we can get.

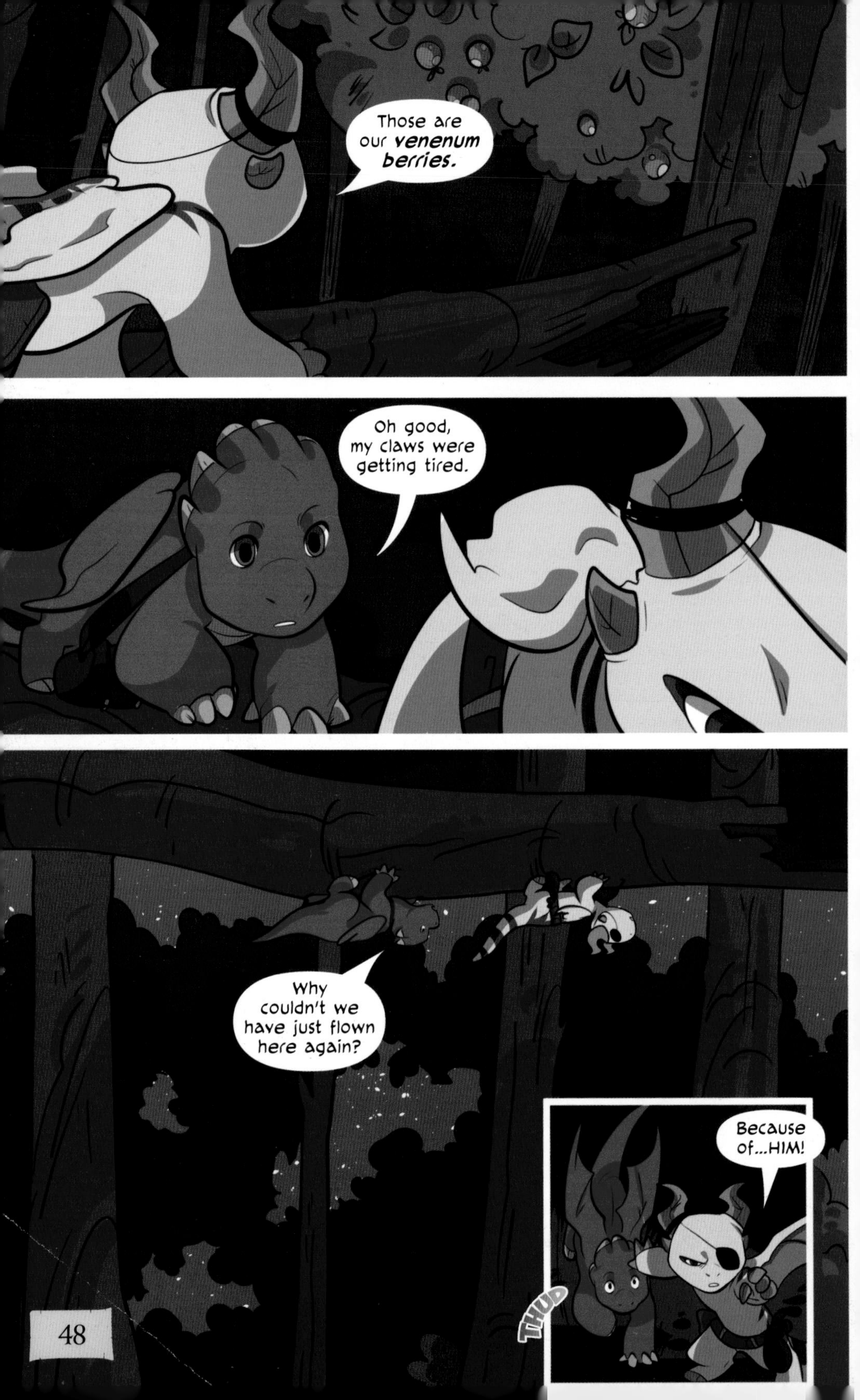
Those are our *venenum berries.*
Oh good, my claws were getting tired.
Why couldn't we have just flown here again?
Because of...HIM!
THUD

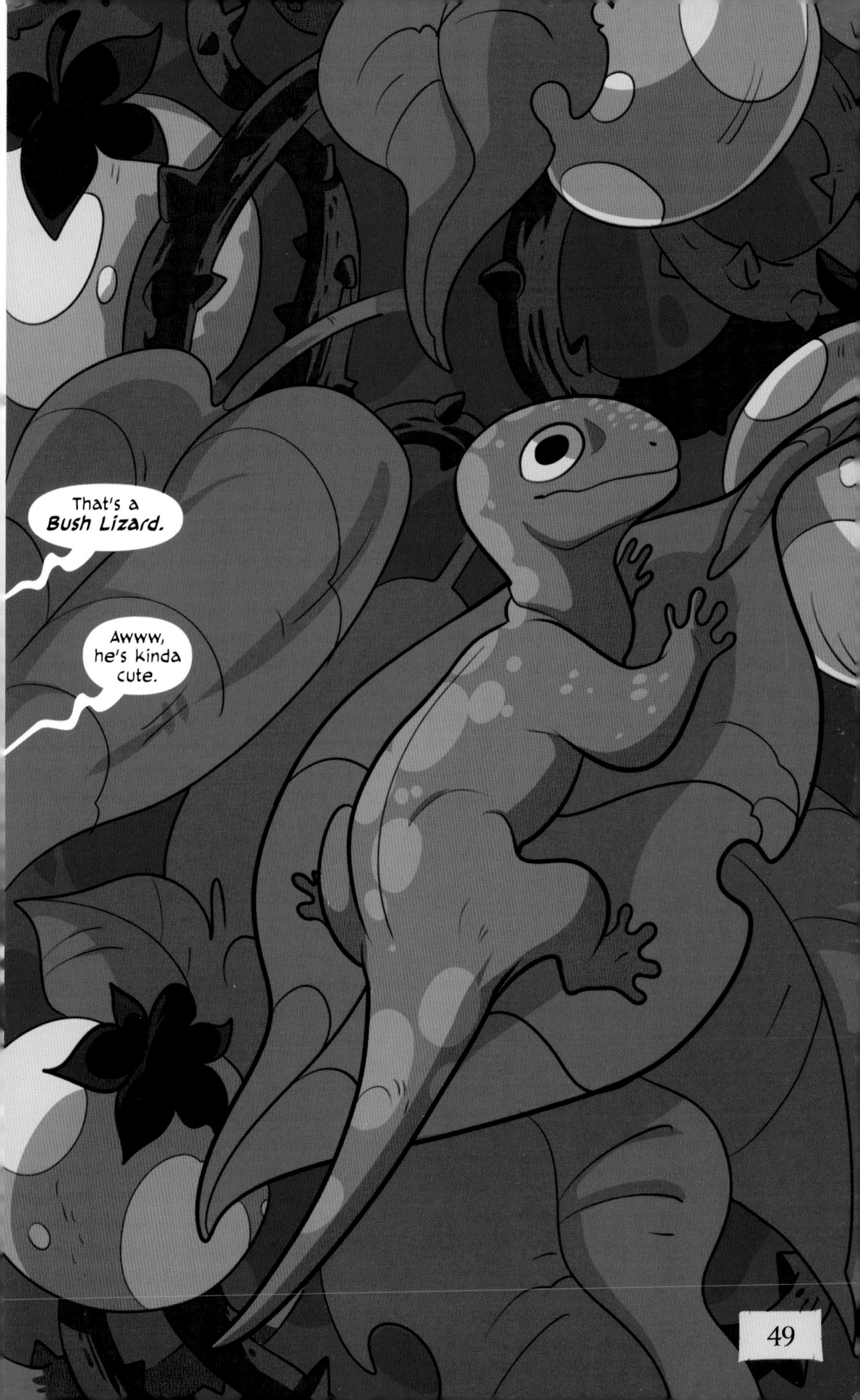
That's a *Bush Lizard.*
Awww, he's kinda cute.

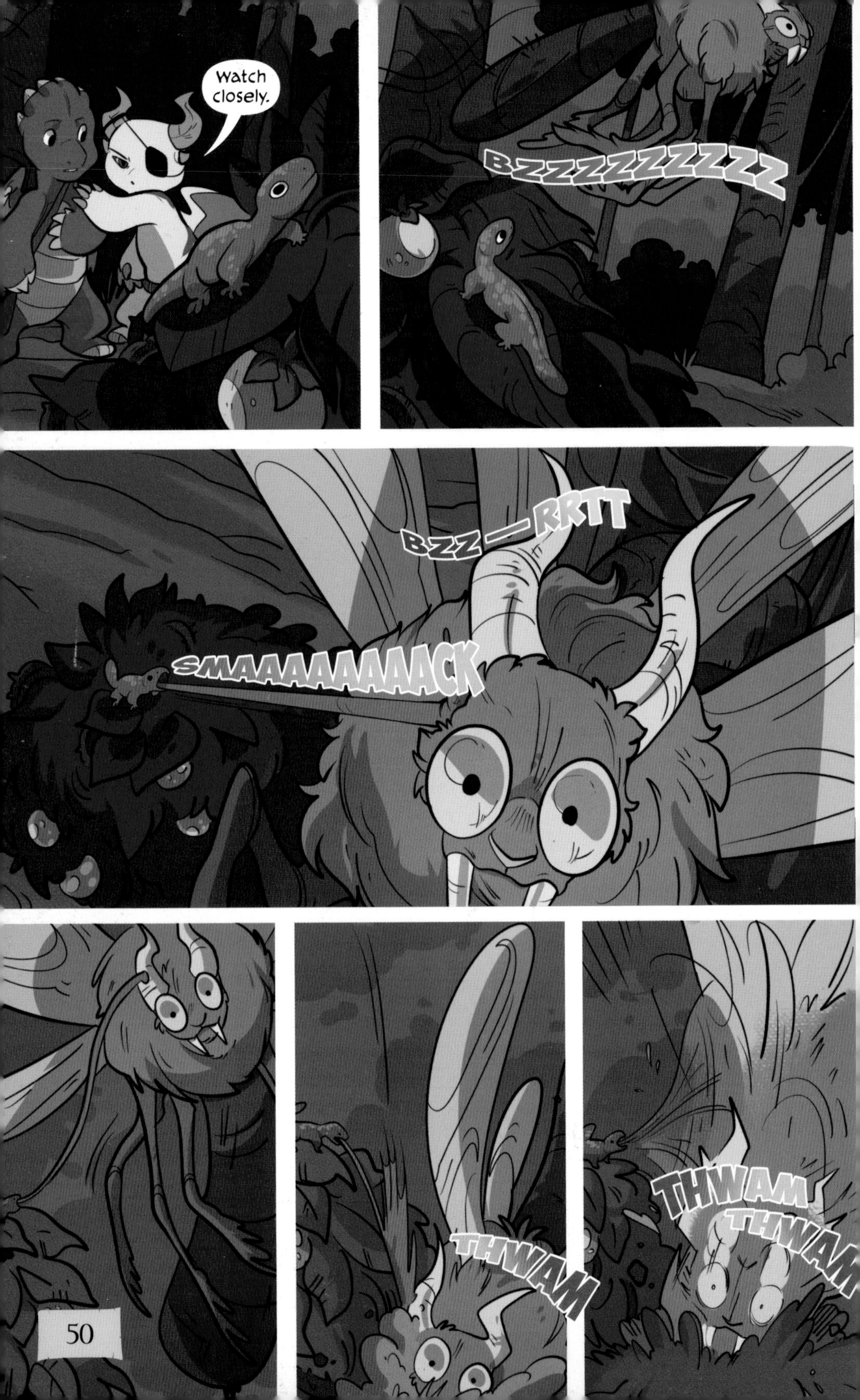

Watch closely.
BZZZZZZZZZZ
BZZ—RRTT
SMAAAAAAAACK
THWAM
THWAM
THWAM

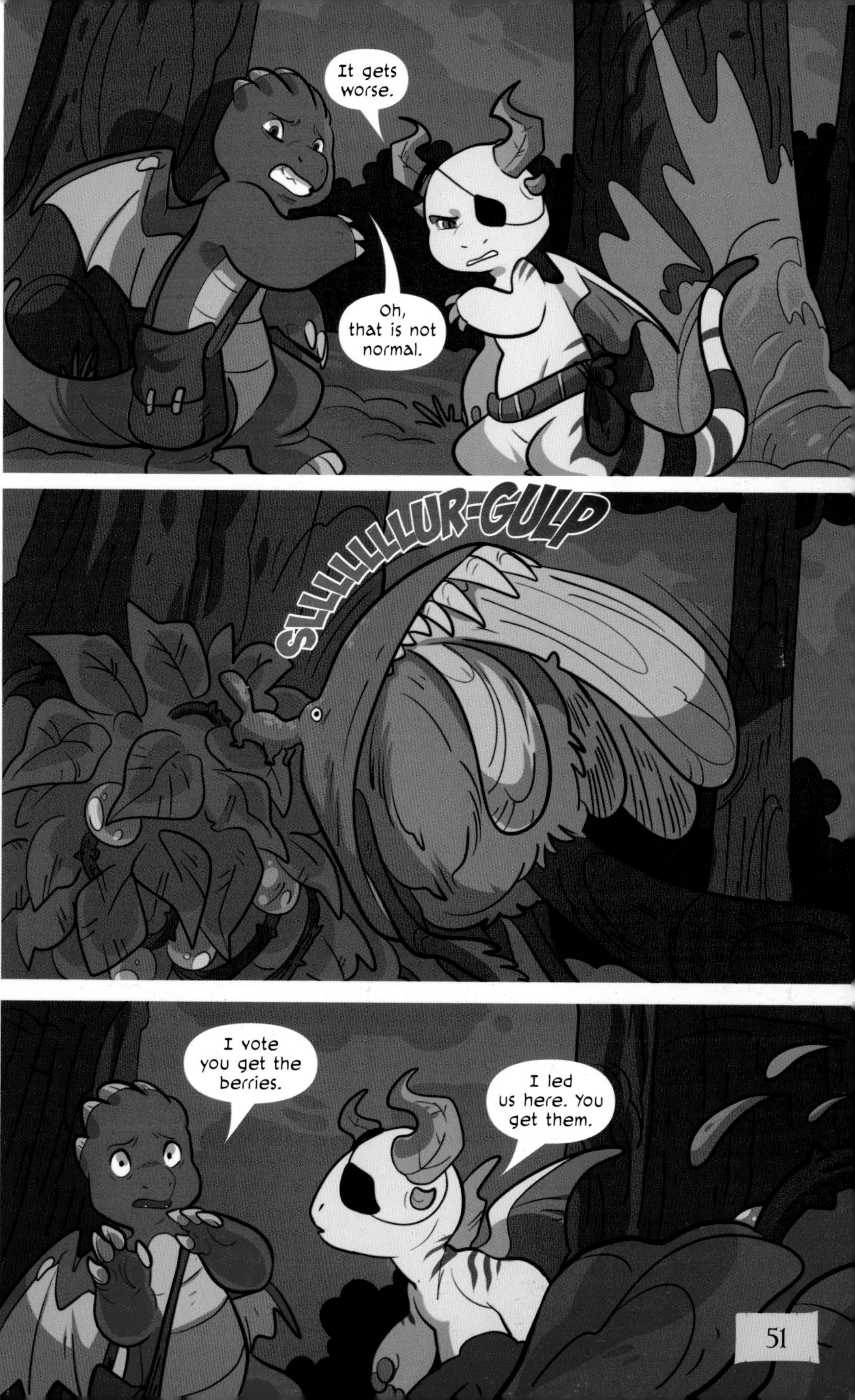
It gets worse.
Oh, that is not normal.
SLLLLLLLUR-GULP
I vote you get the berries.
I led us here. You get them.

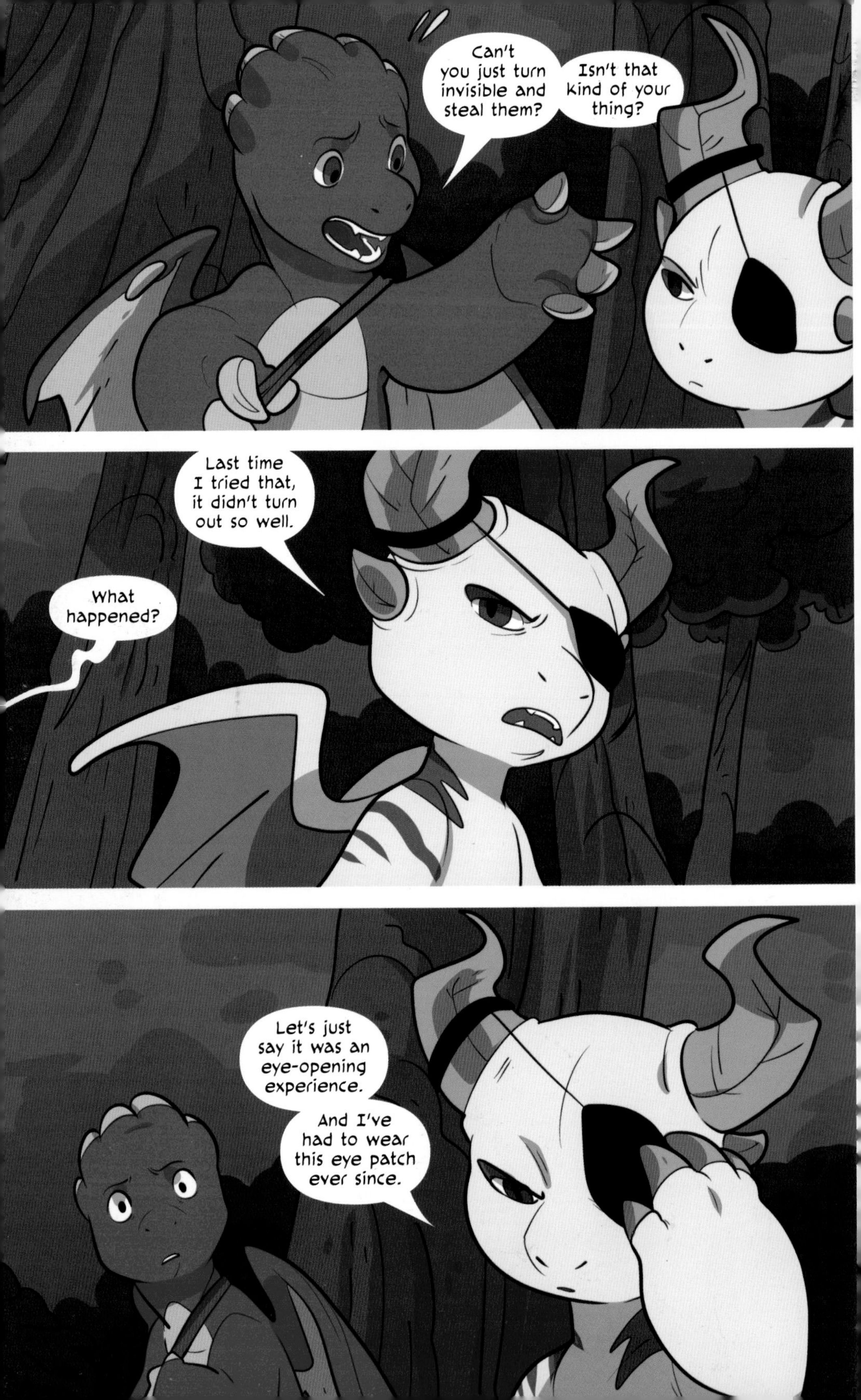
Can't you just turn invisible and steal them?
Isn't that kind of your thing?
Last time I tried that, it didn't turn out so well.
What happened?
Let's just say it was an eye-opening experience.
And I've had to wear this eye patch ever since.

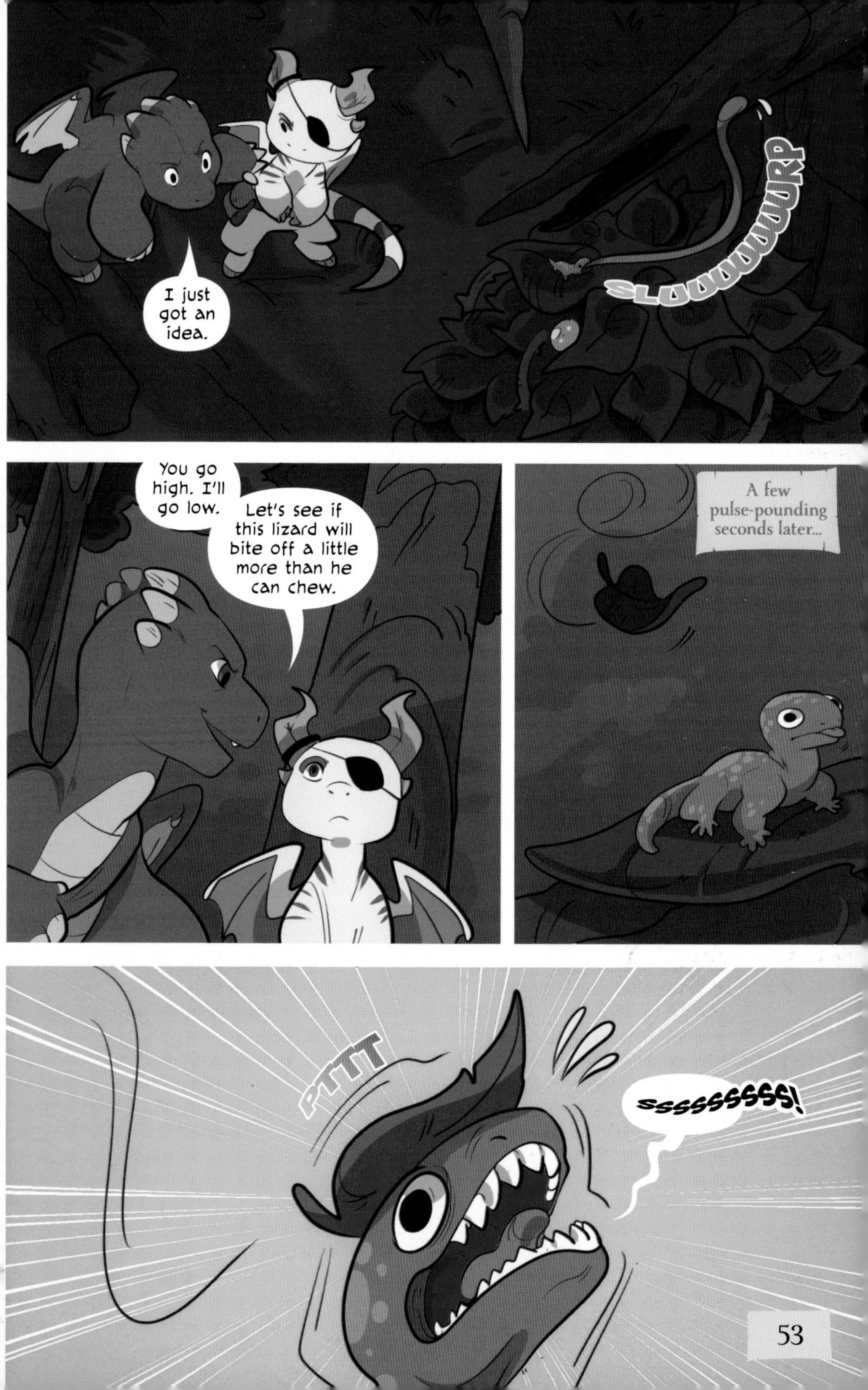
SLUUUUUURP
I just got an idea.
You go high. I'll go low.
Let's see if this lizard will bite off a little more than he can chew.
A few pulse-pounding seconds later...
PTTT
SSSSSSSSS!

Remember me...?
ROARRRRR!
Now, Roke!
FWOOOOOM
WWWUPISHHHHHH

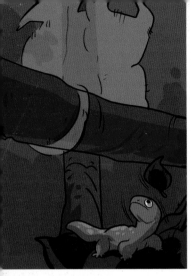

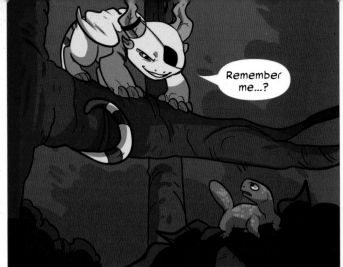

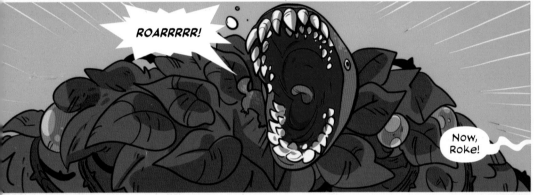

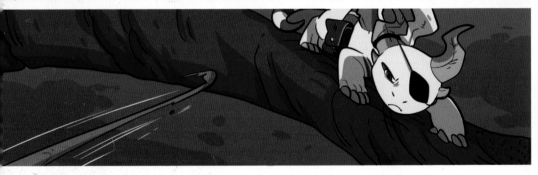

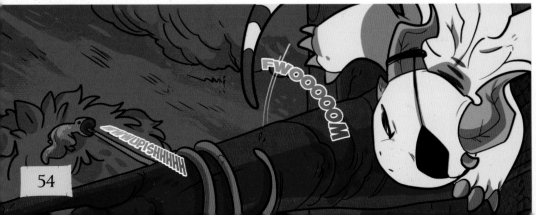

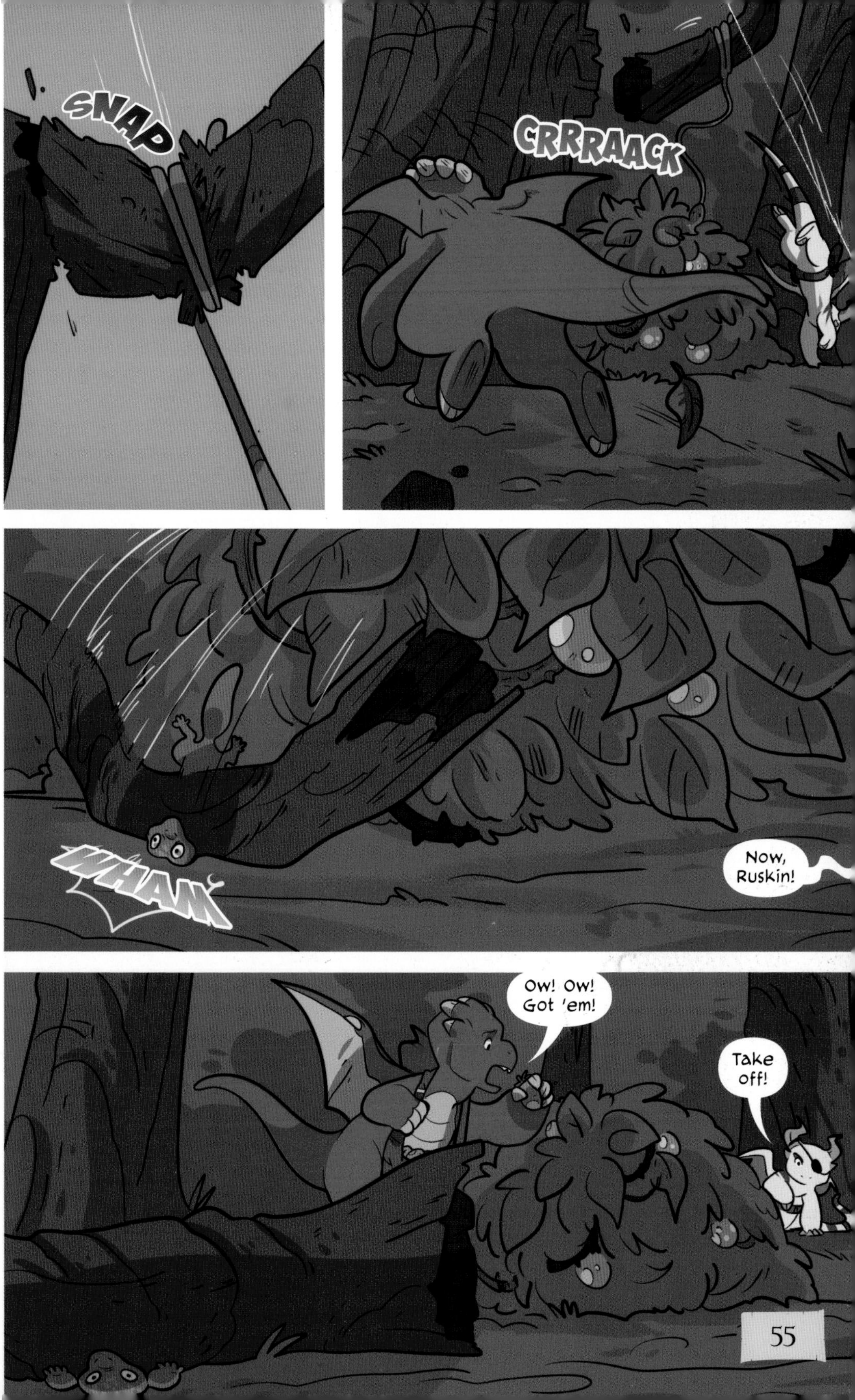
SNAP
CRRRAACK
WHAM
Now, Ruskin!
Ow! Ow! Got 'em!
Take off!

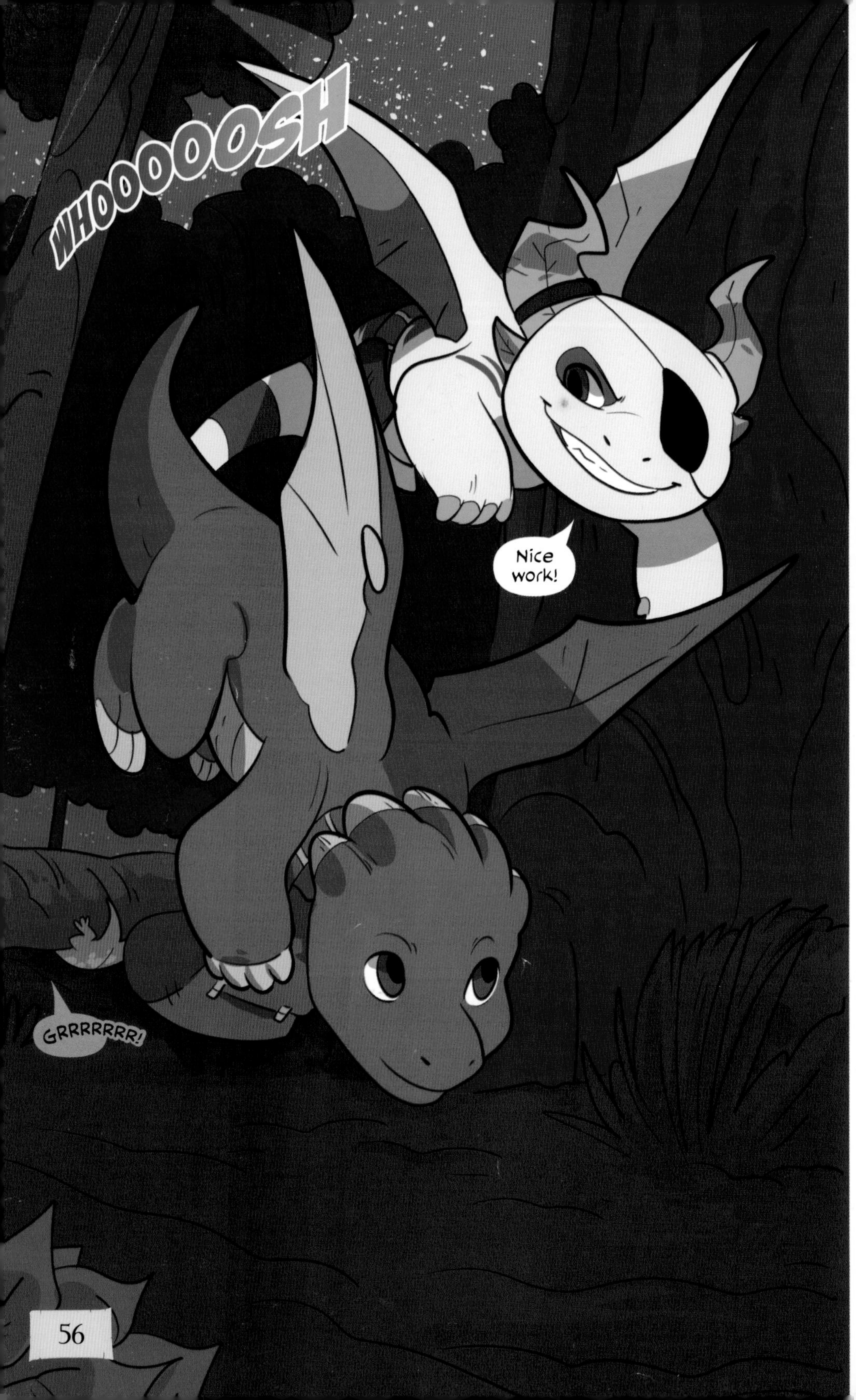
WHOOOOOOSH
Nice work!
GRRRRRRR!

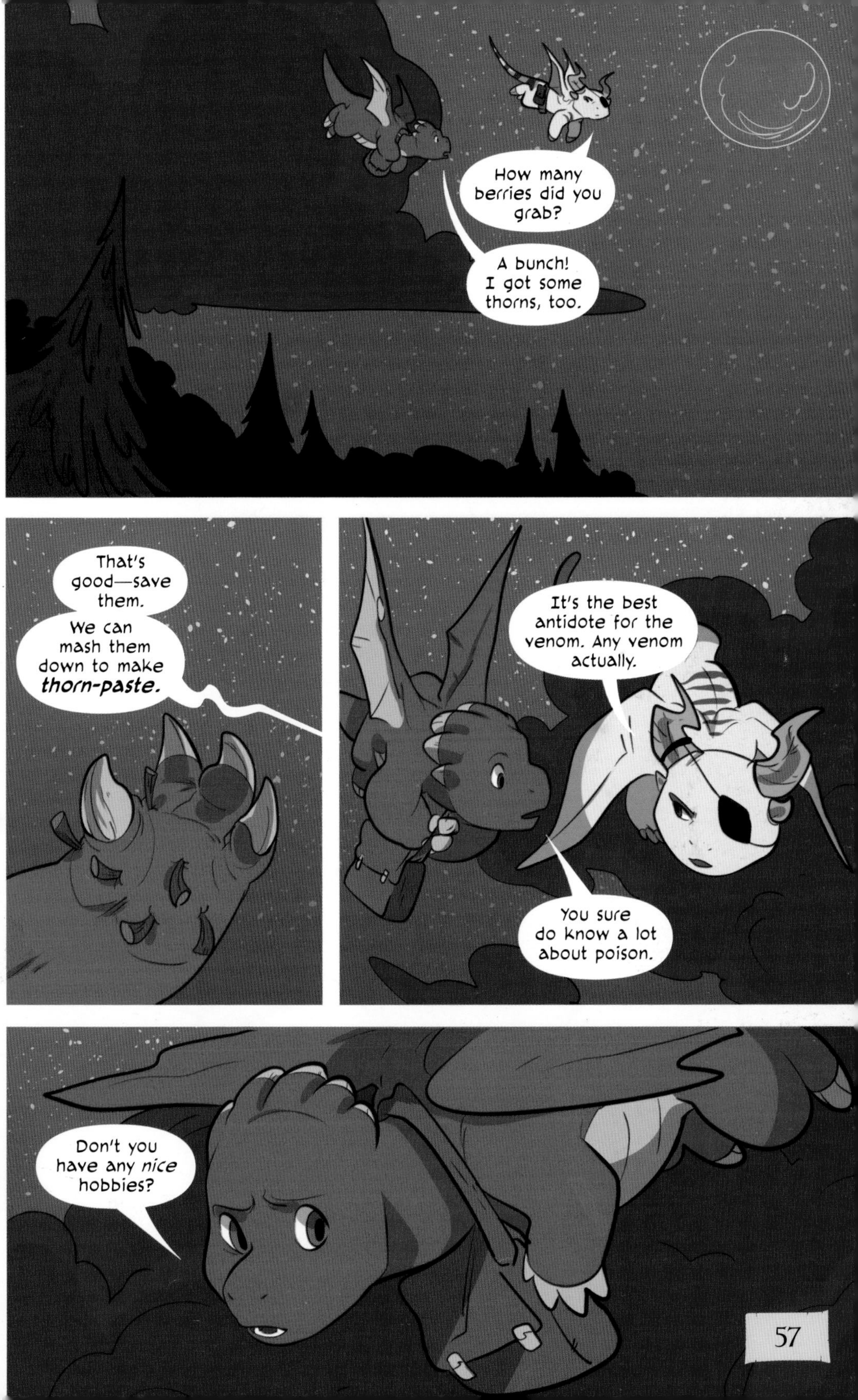
How many berries did you grab?
A bunch! I got some thorns, too.
That's good—save them.
We can mash them down to make *thorn-paste.*
It's the best antidote for the venom. Any venom actually.
You sure do know a lot about poison.
Don't you have any *nice* hobbies?

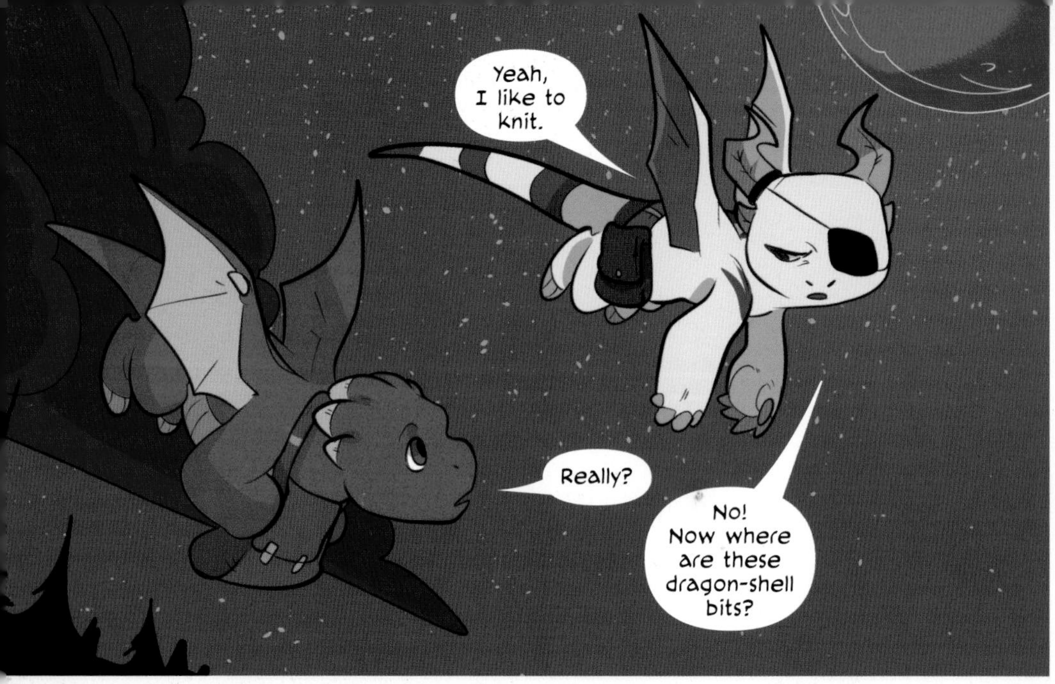
Yeah, I like to knit.
Really?
No! Now where are these dragon-shell bits?

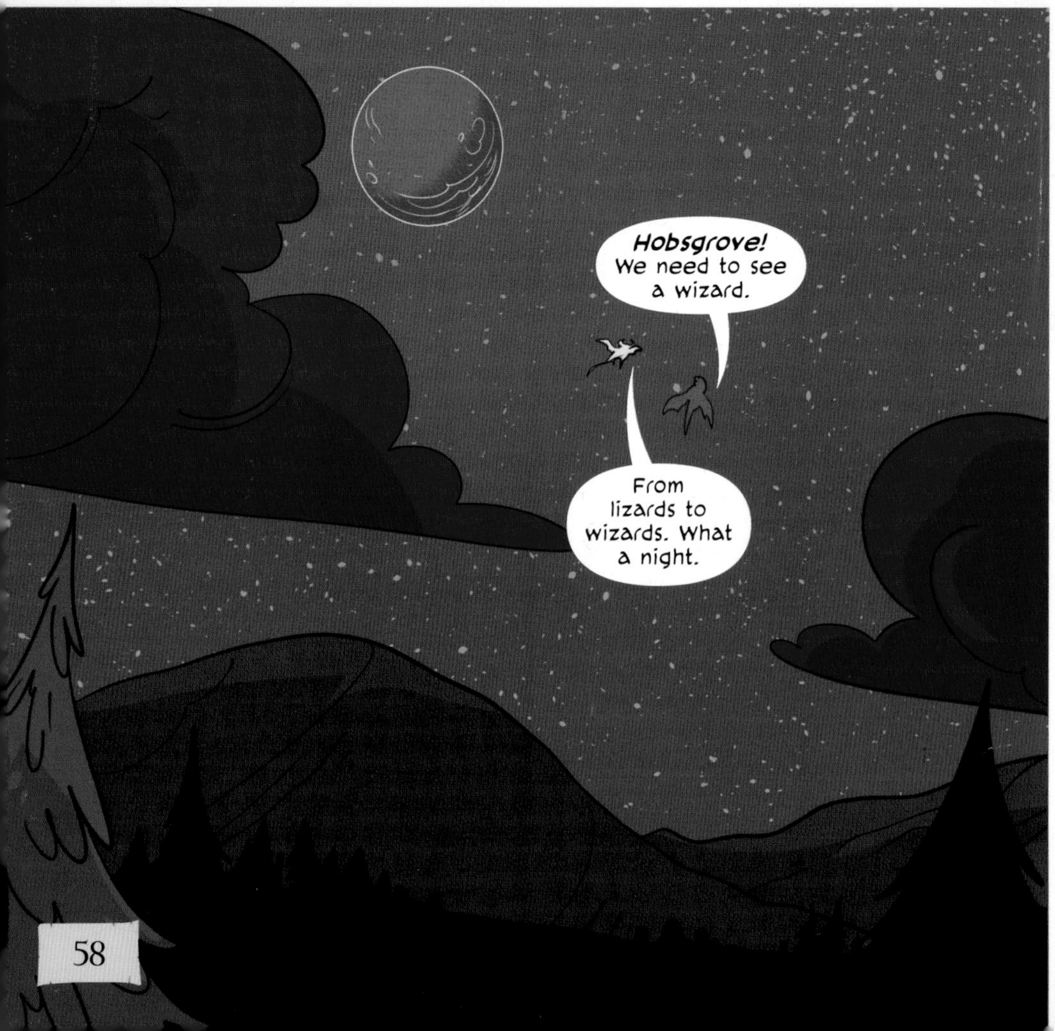
Hobsgrove! We need to see a wizard.
From lizards to wizards. What a night.

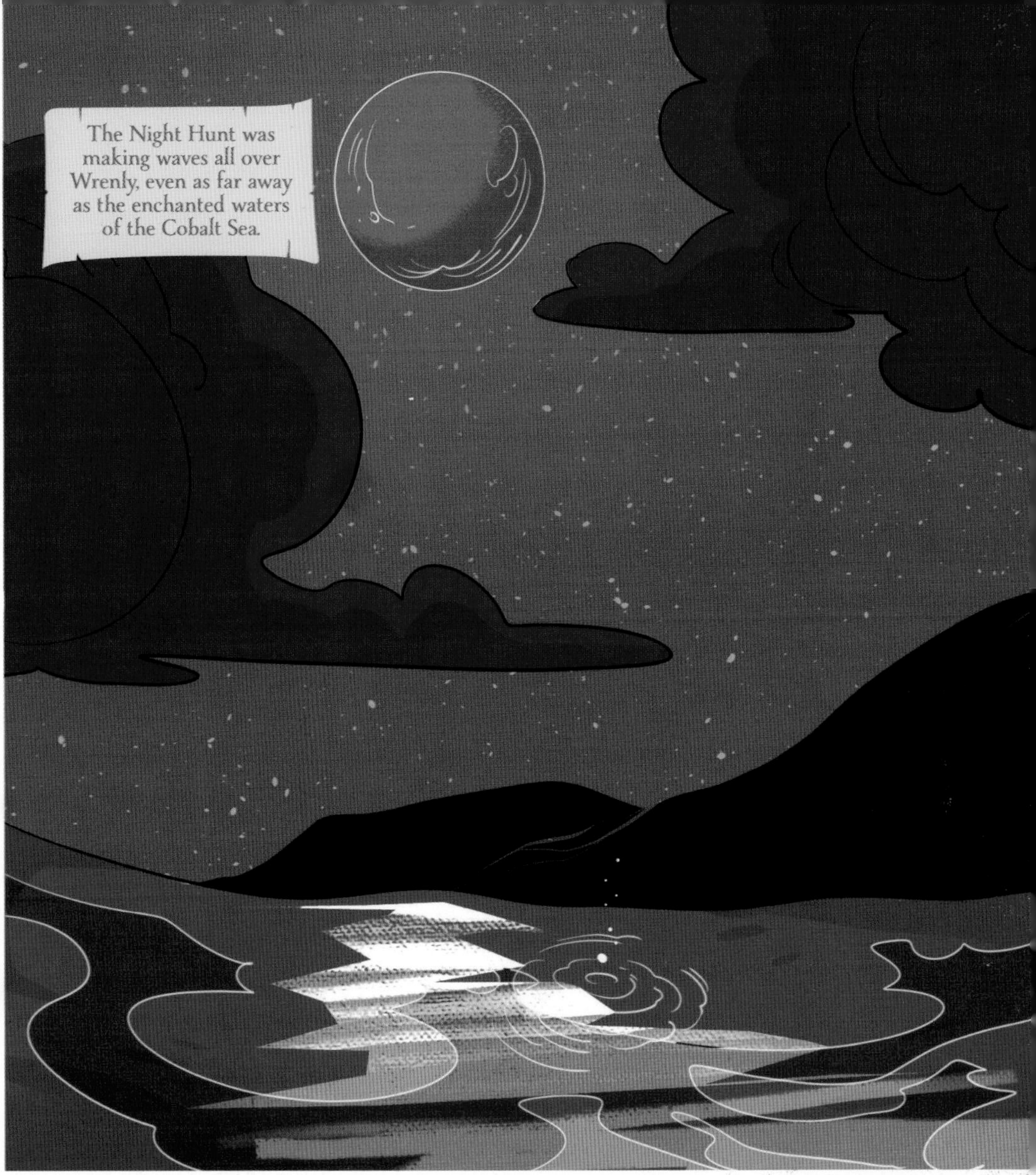
The Night Hunt was making waves all over Wrenly, even as far away as the enchanted waters of the Cobalt Sea.

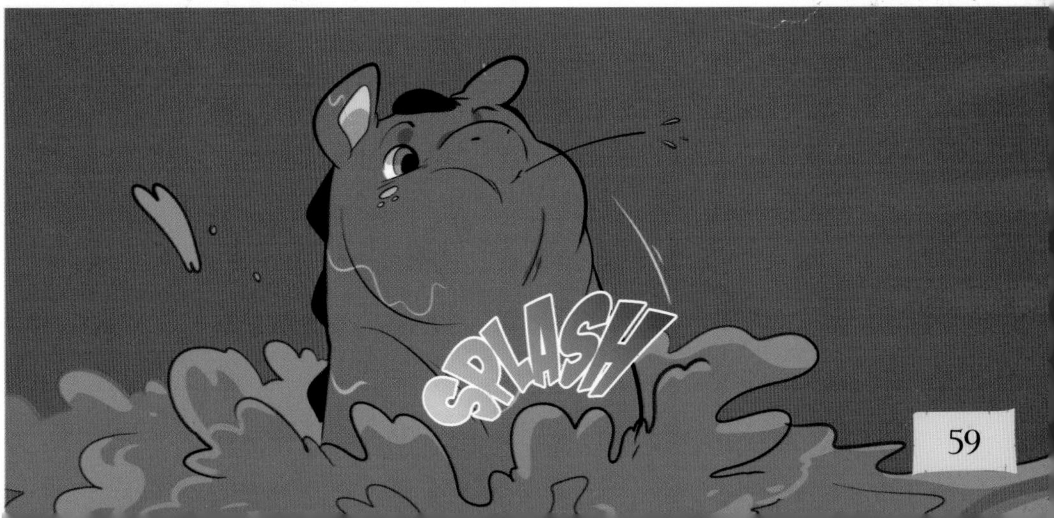
SPLASH

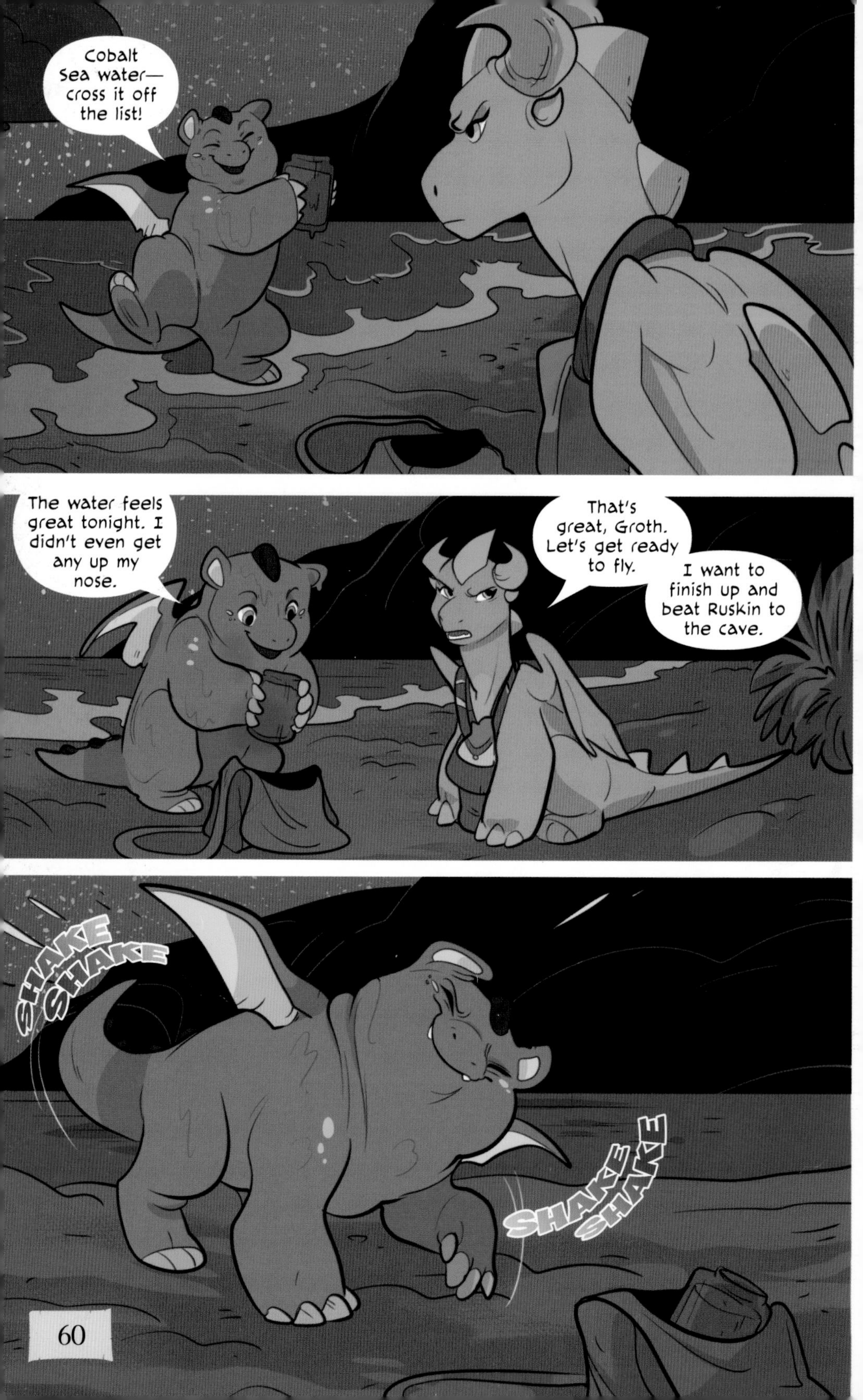
Cobalt Sea water—cross it off the list!
The water feels great tonight. I didn't even get any up my nose.
That's great, Groth. Let's get ready to fly.
I want to finish up and beat Ruskin to the cave.
SHAKE SHAKE
SHAKE SHAKE

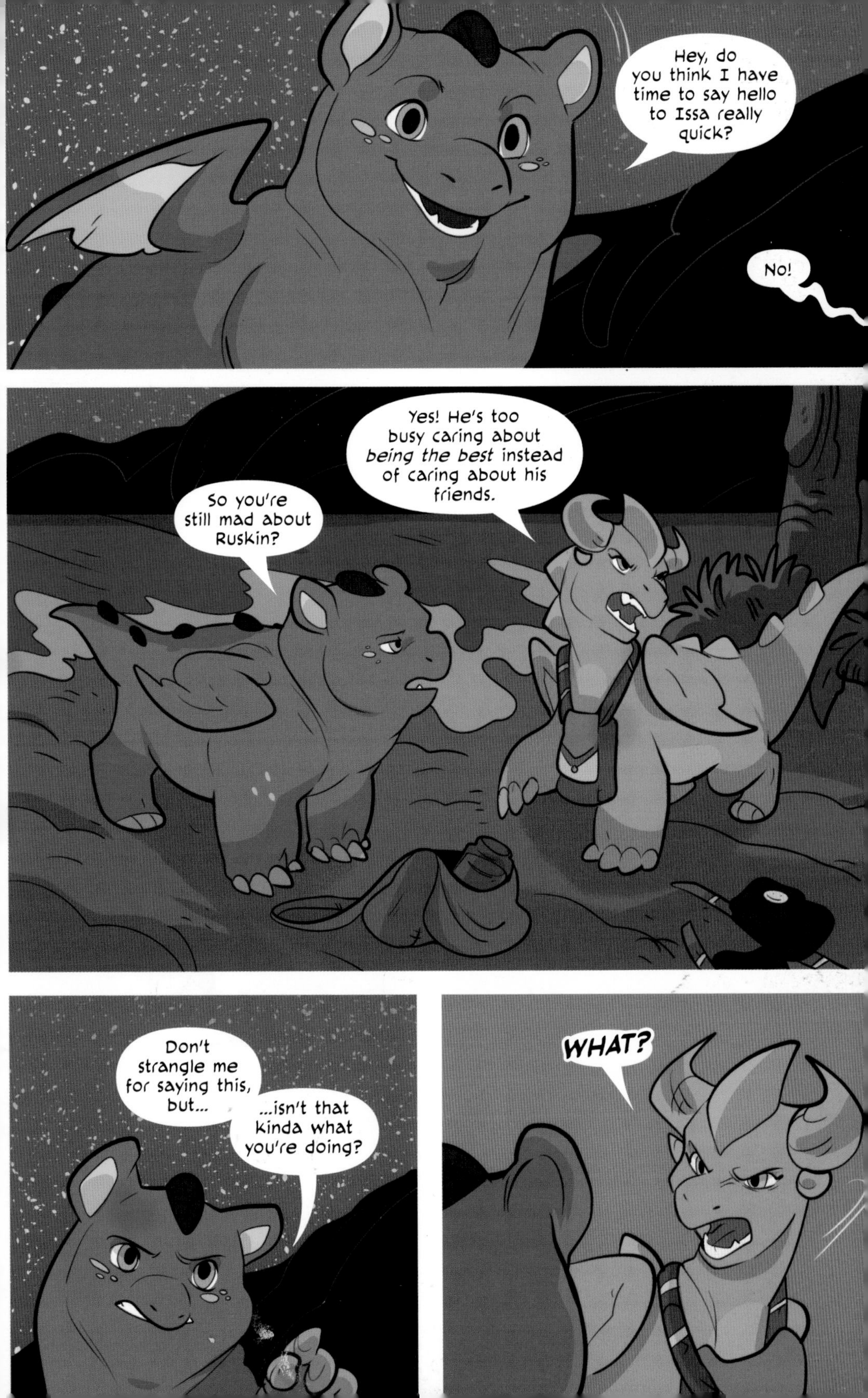
Hey, do you think I have time to say hello to Issa really quick?
No!
So you're still mad about Ruskin?
Yes! He's too busy caring about *being the best* instead of caring about his friends.
Don't strangle me for saying this, but...
...isn't that kinda what you're doing?
WHAT?

Chapter 5

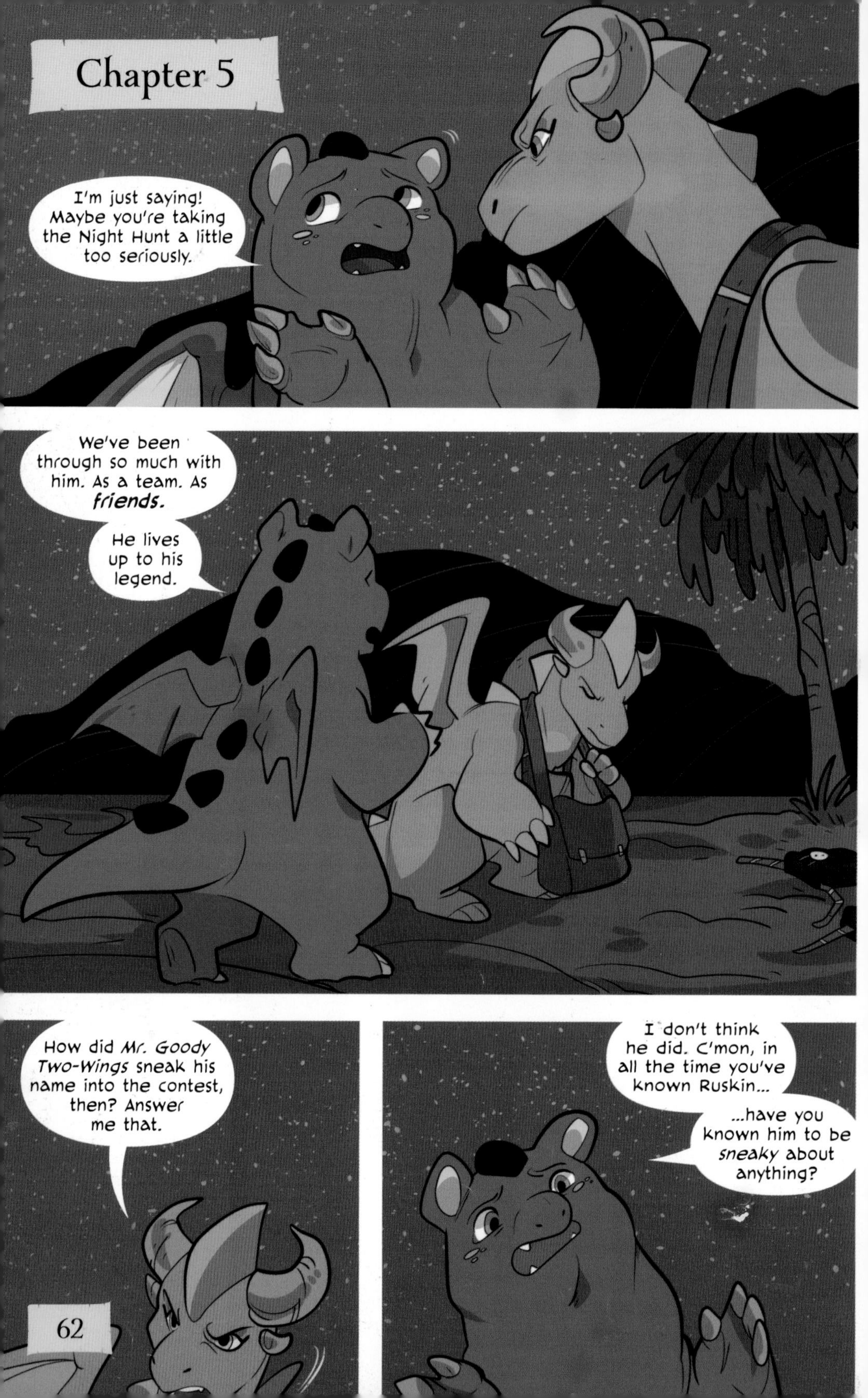
I'm just saying! Maybe you're taking the Night Hunt a little too seriously.
We've been through so much with him. As a team. As ***friends.***
He lives up to his legend.
How did *Mr. Goody Two-Wings* sneak his name into the contest, then? Answer me that.
I don't think he did. C'mon, in all the time you've known Ruskin...
...have you known him to be *sneaky* about anything?

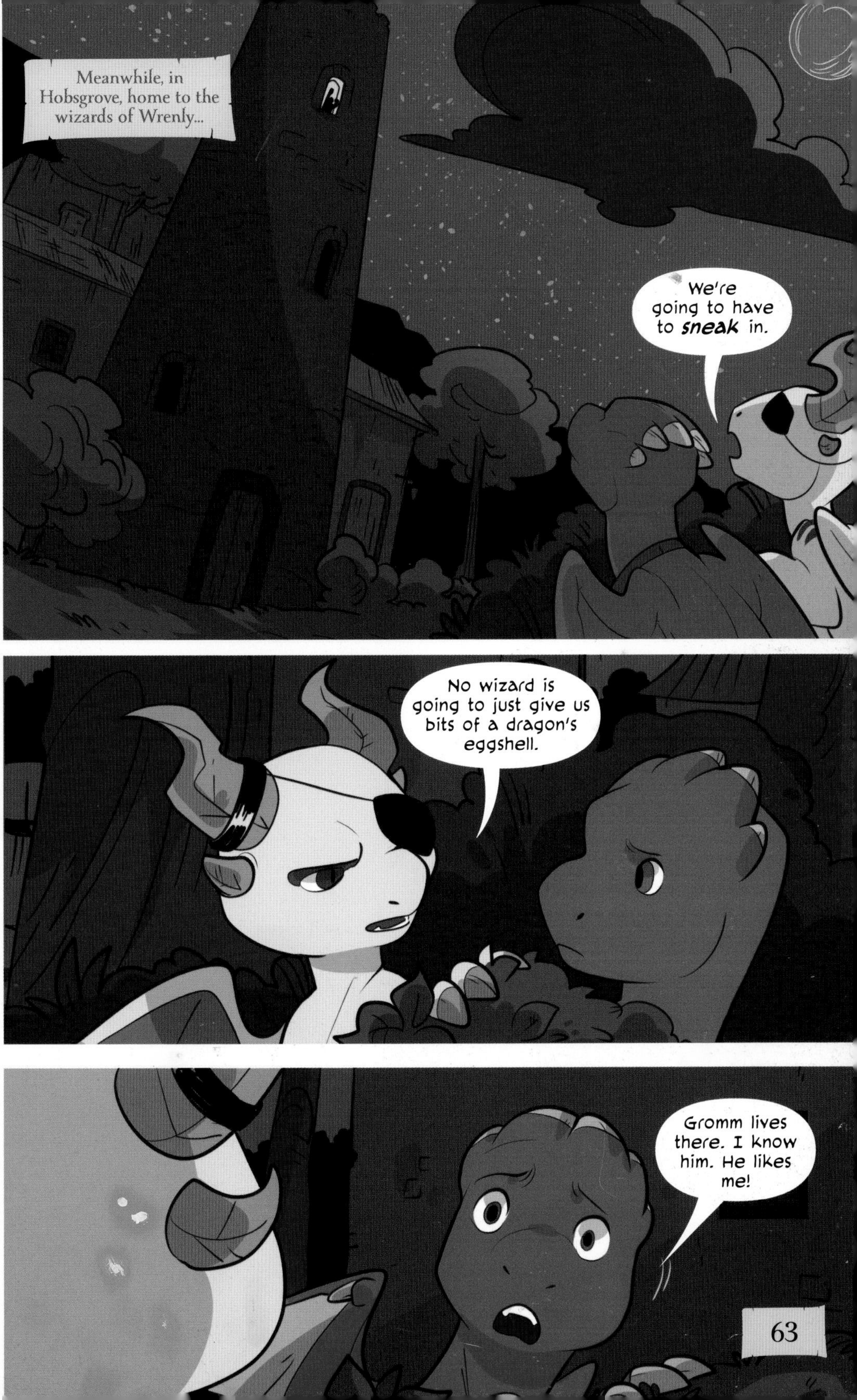
Meanwhile, in Hobsgrove, home to the wizards of Wrenly...
We're going to have to *sneak* in.
No wizard is going to just give us bits of a dragon's eggshell.
Gromm lives there. I know him. He likes me!

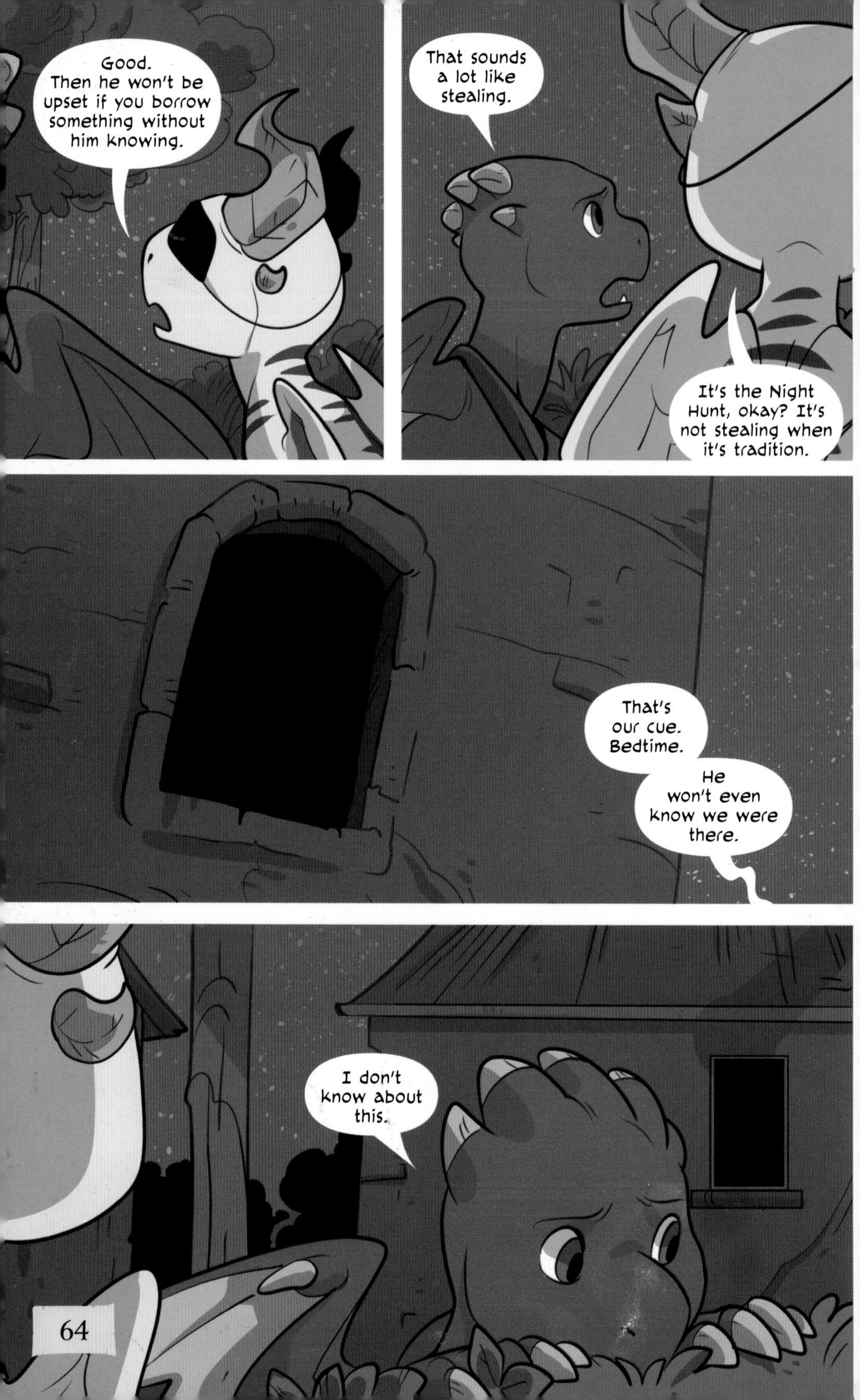
Good. Then he won't be upset if you borrow something without him knowing.
That sounds a lot like stealing.
It's the Night Hunt, okay? It's not stealing when it's tradition.
That's our cue. Bedtime.
He won't even know we were there.
I don't know about this.

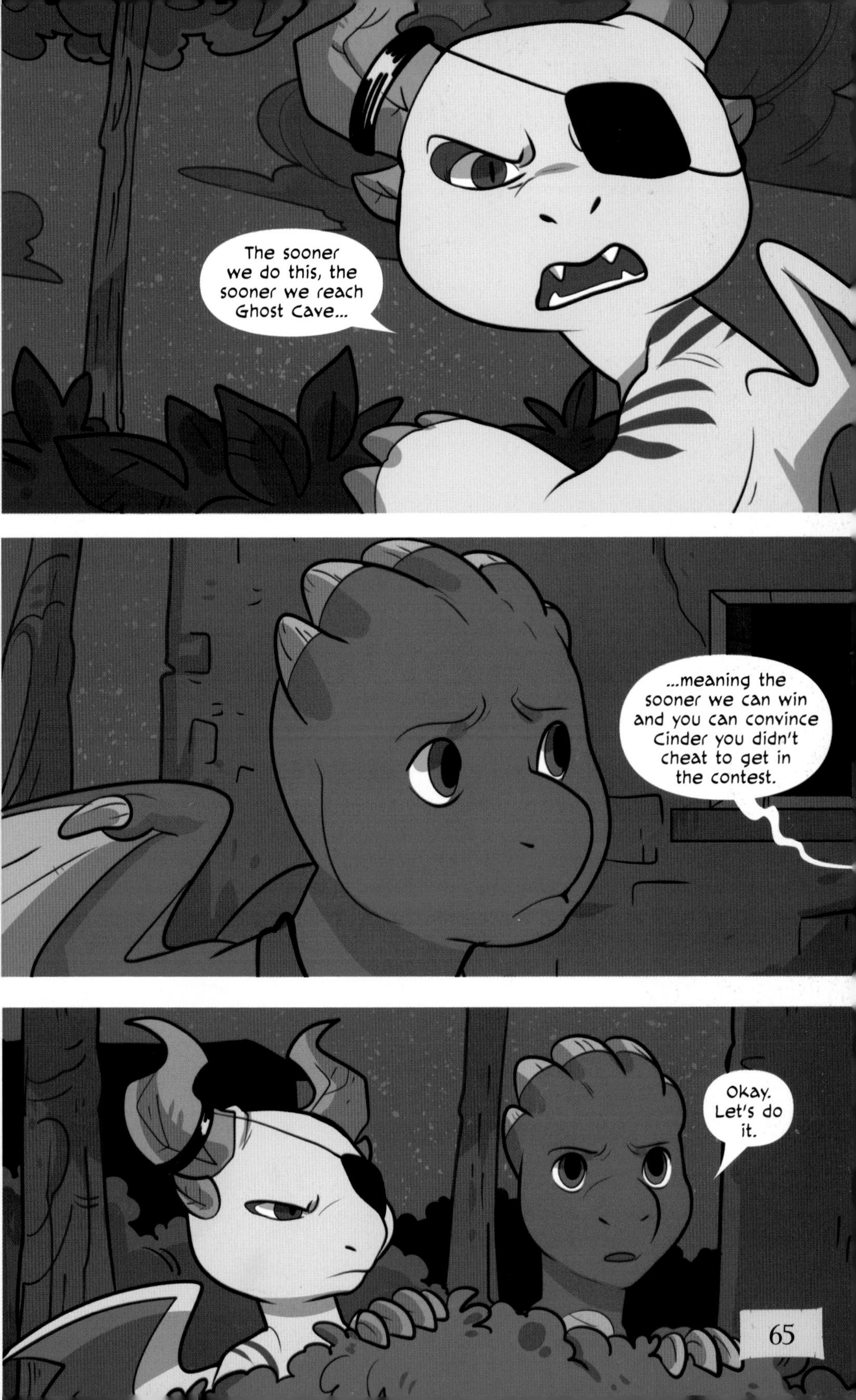
The sooner we do this, the sooner we reach Ghost Cave...
...meaning the sooner we can win and you can convince Cinder you didn't cheat to get in the contest.
Okay. Let's do it.

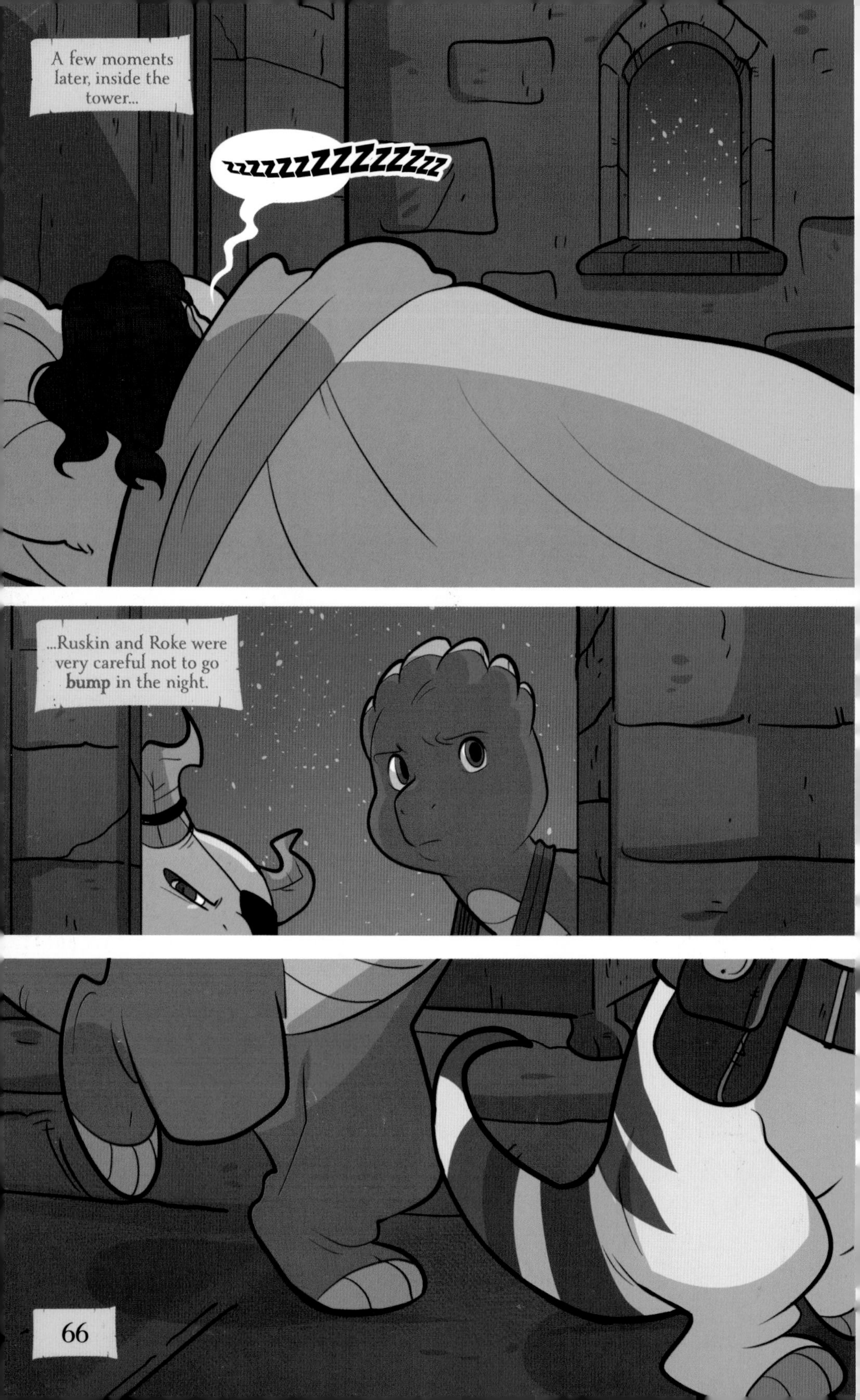
A few moments later, inside the tower...
zzzzzzZZZZZZzz
...Ruskin and Roke were very careful not to go **bump** in the night.

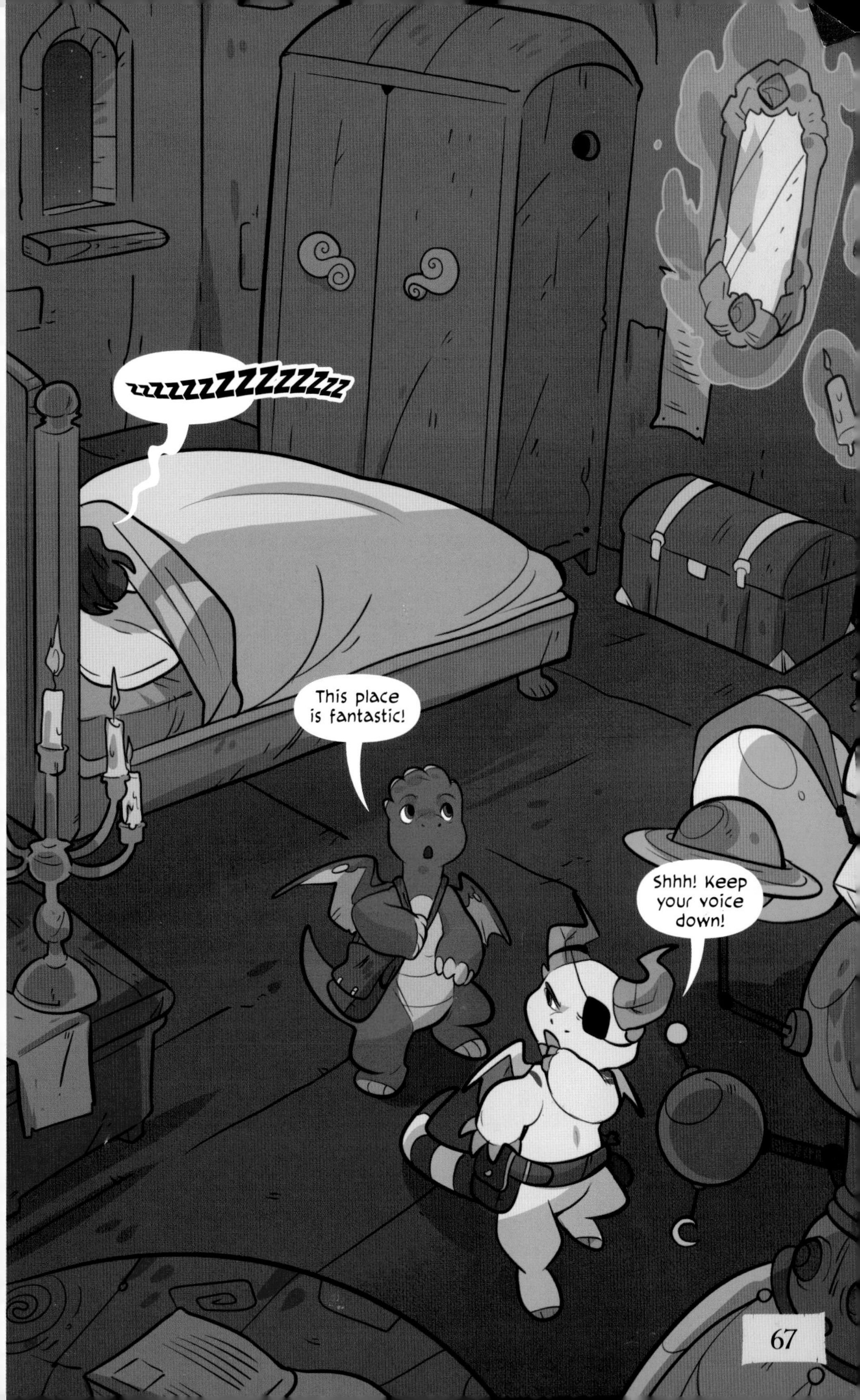
zzzzzzZZZZzzzzz
This place is fantastic!
Shhh! Keep your voice down!

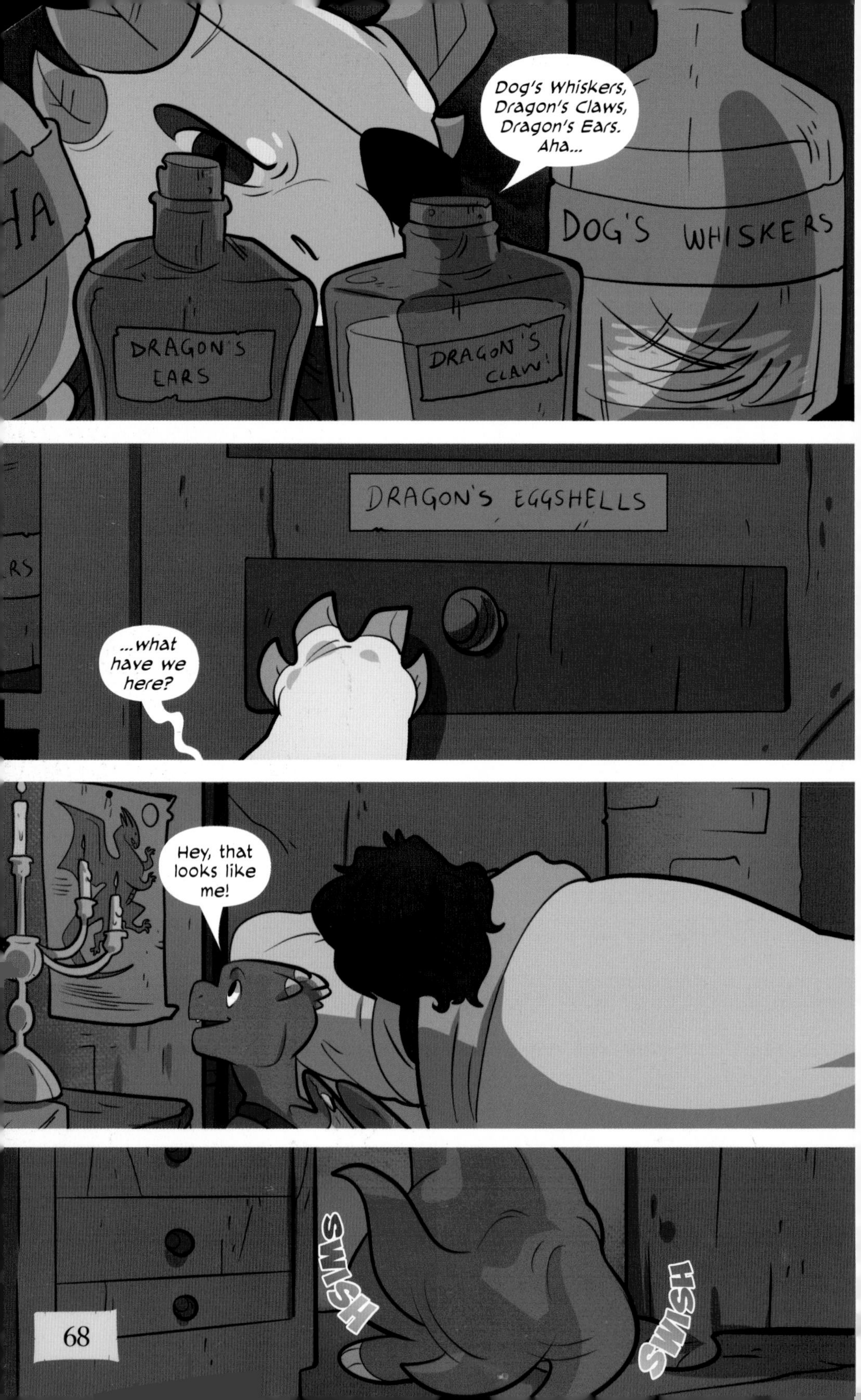
Dog's Whiskers,
Dragon's Claws,
Dragon's Ears.
Aha...
DOG'S WHISKERS
DRAGON'S EARS
DRAGON'S CLAW!
DRAGON'S EGGSHELLS
...what have we here?
Hey, that looks like me!
SWISH
SWISH

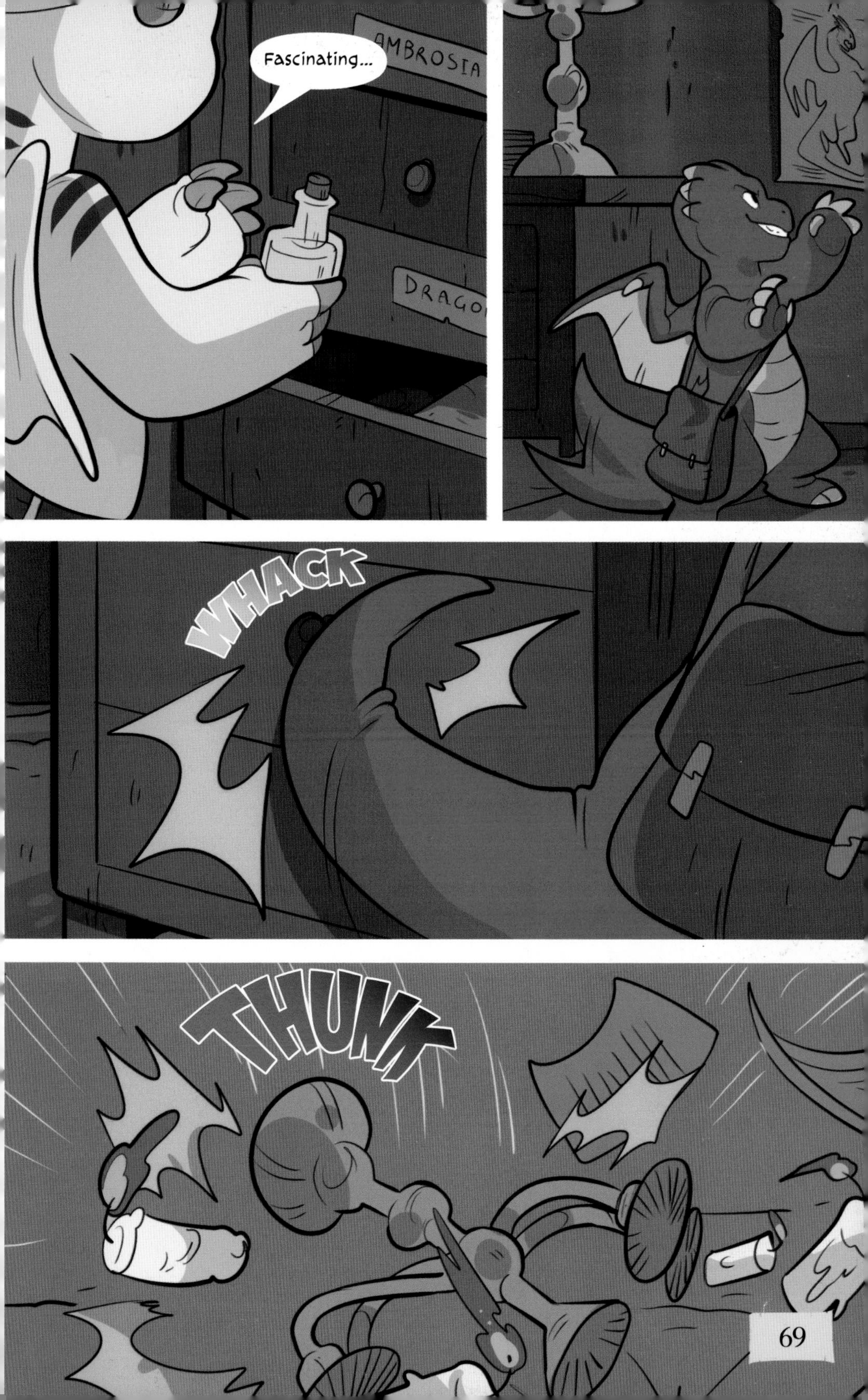
Fascinating...
AMBROSIA
DRAGO
WHACK
THUNK

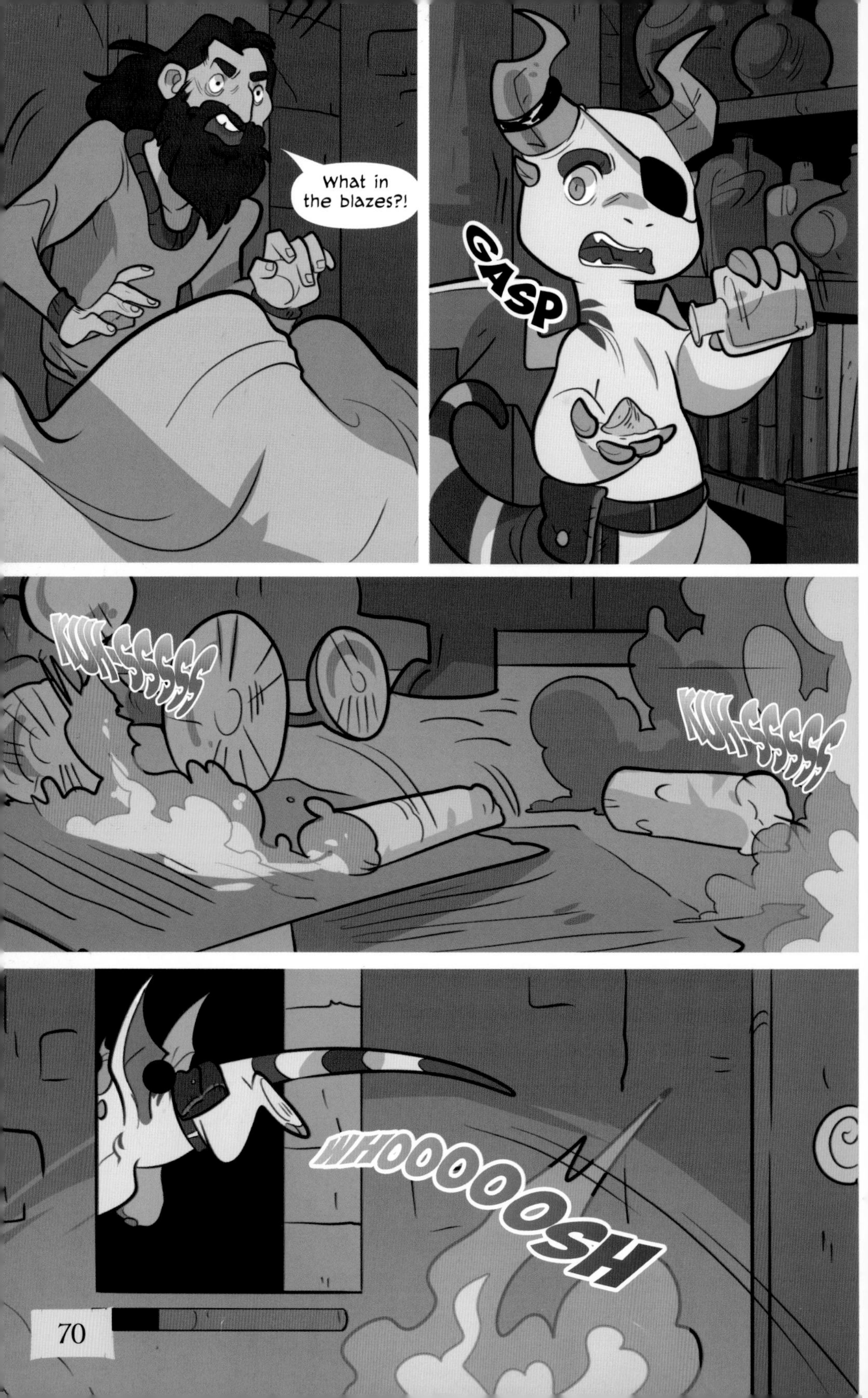
What in the blazes?!
GASP
KUH-SSSSS
KUH-SSSSS
WHOOOOOOSH

Hey, wait!

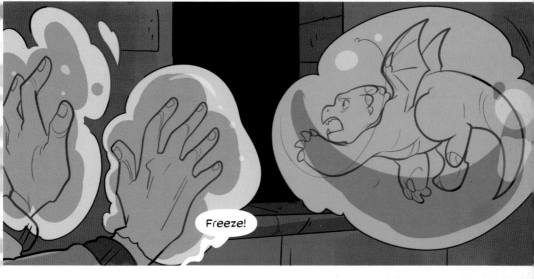

Freeze!

I meant... EVERYTHING FREEEEZE!

71

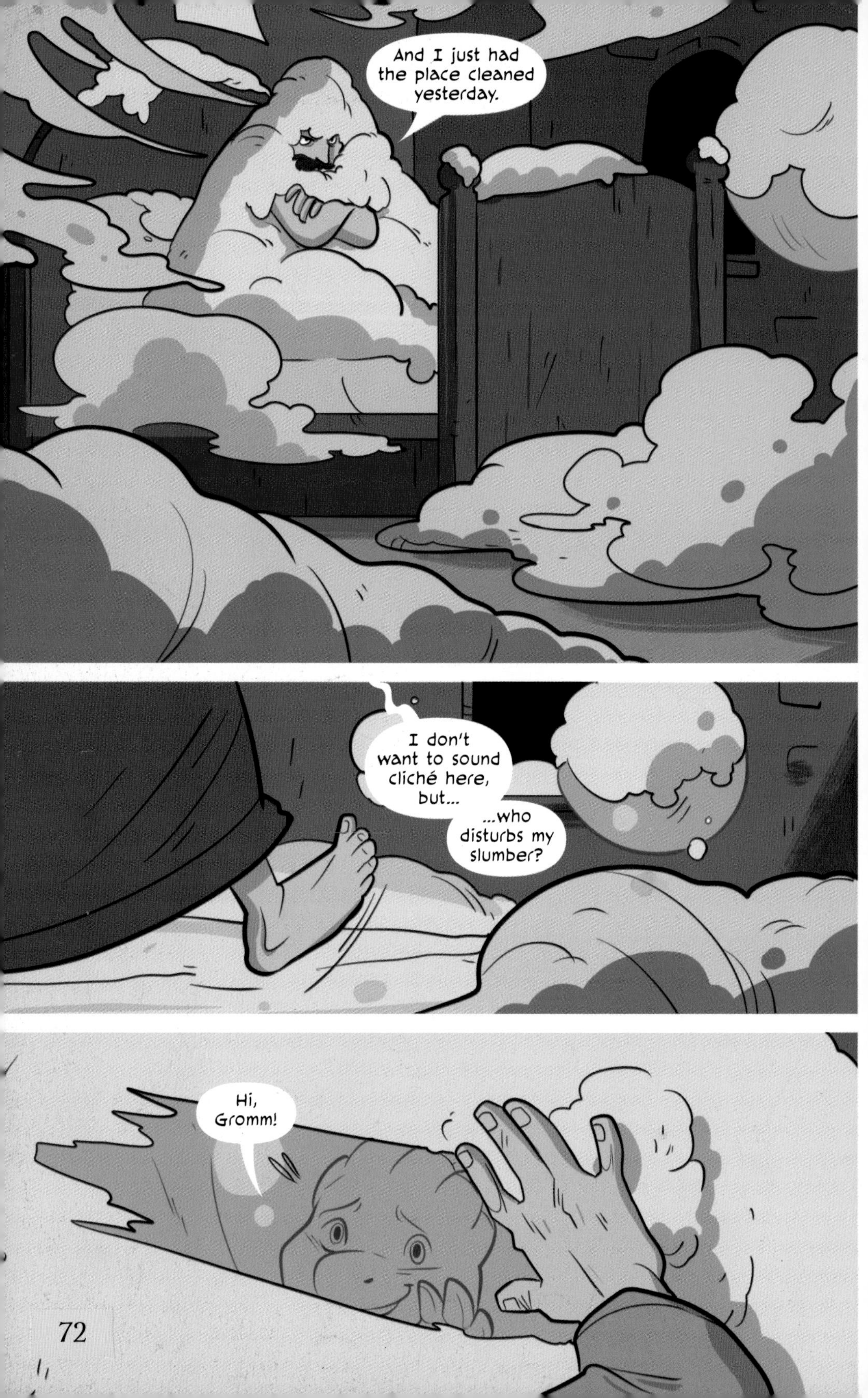
And I just had the place cleaned yesterday.
I don't want to sound cliché here, but...
...who disturbs my slumber?
Hi, Gromm!

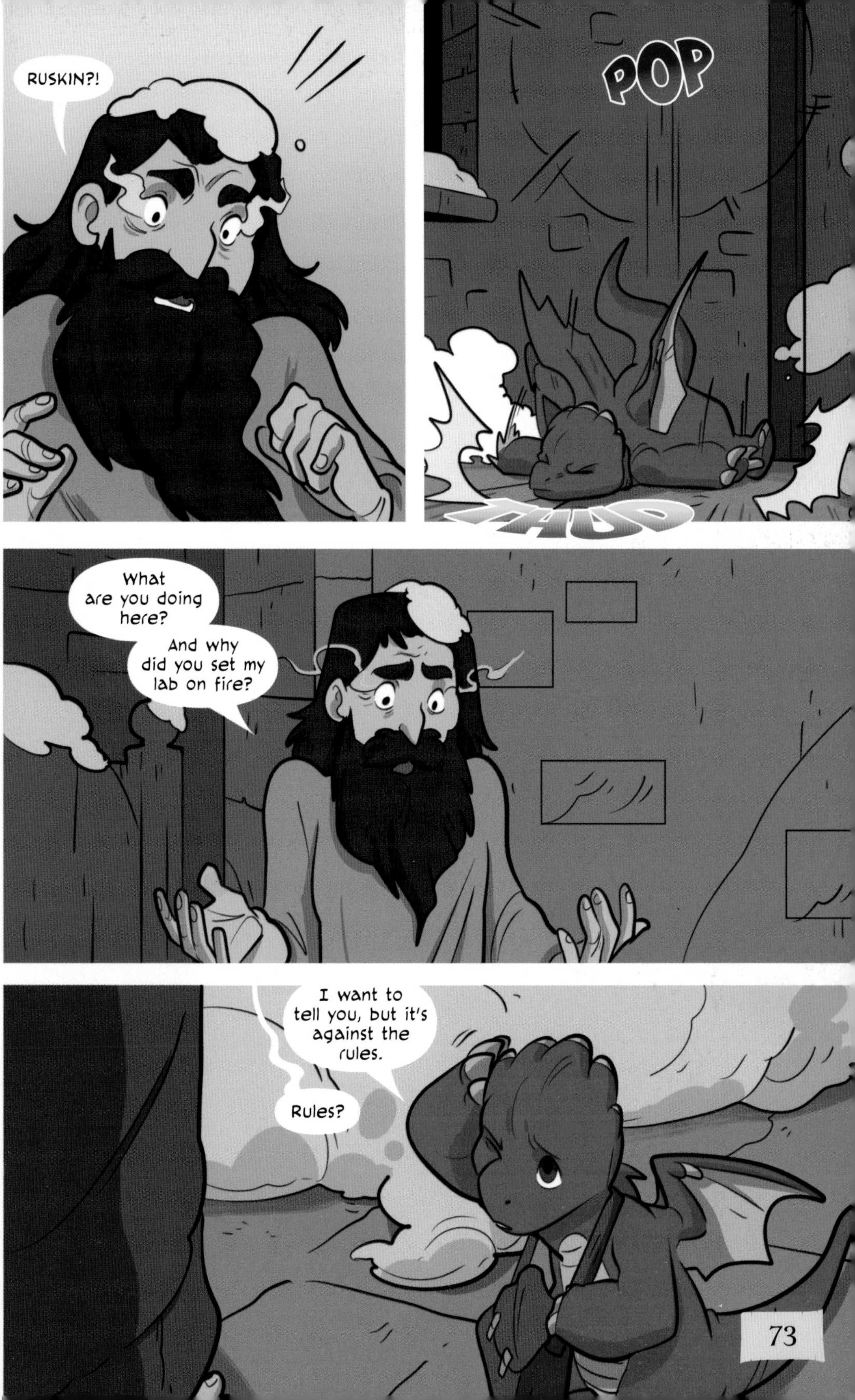
RUSKIN?!
POP
THUD
What are you doing here?
And why did you set my lab on fire?
I want to tell you, but it's against the rules.
Rules?

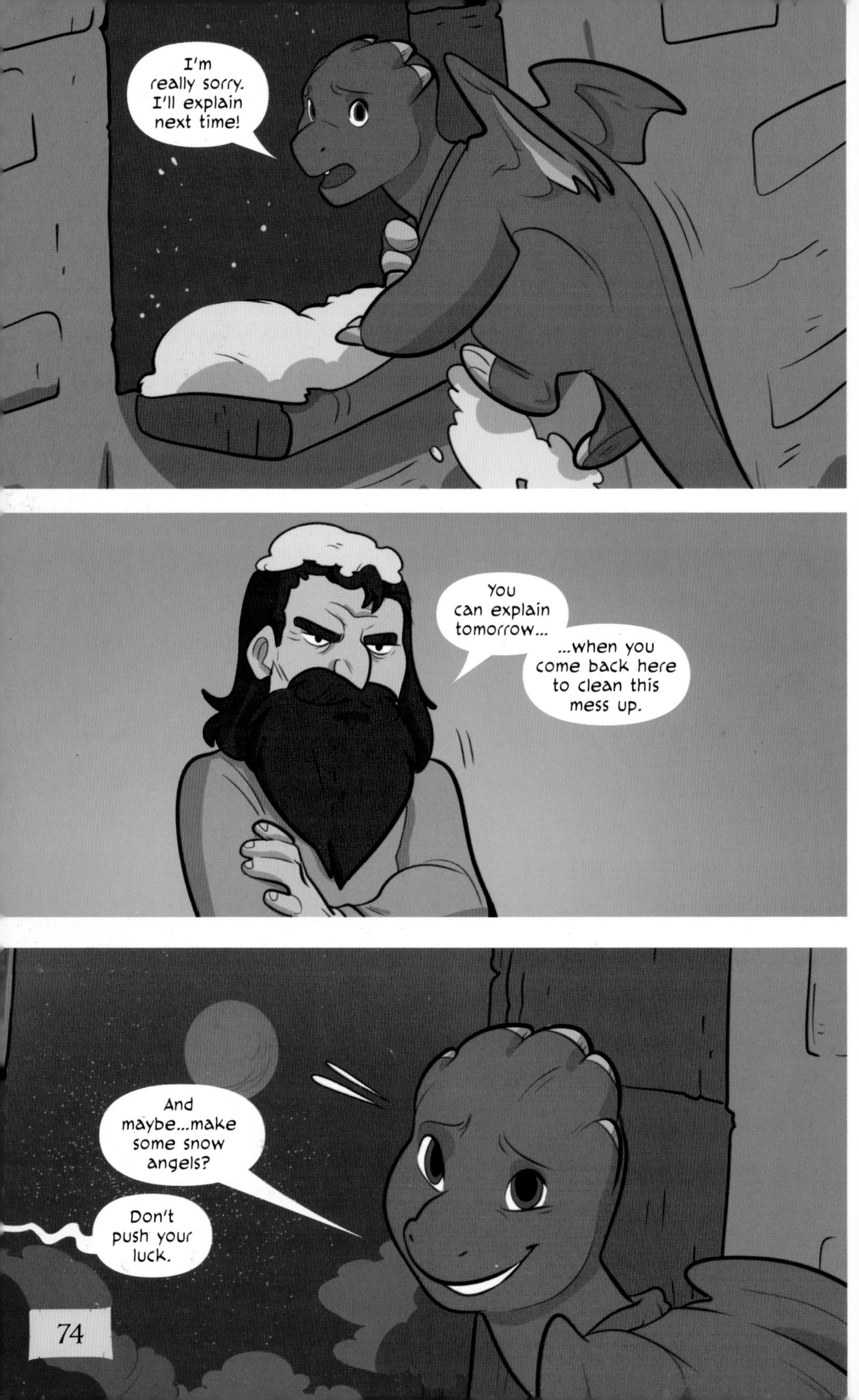
I'm really sorry. I'll explain next time!
You can explain tomorrow...
...when you come back here to clean this mess up.
And maybe...make some snow angels?
Don't push your luck.

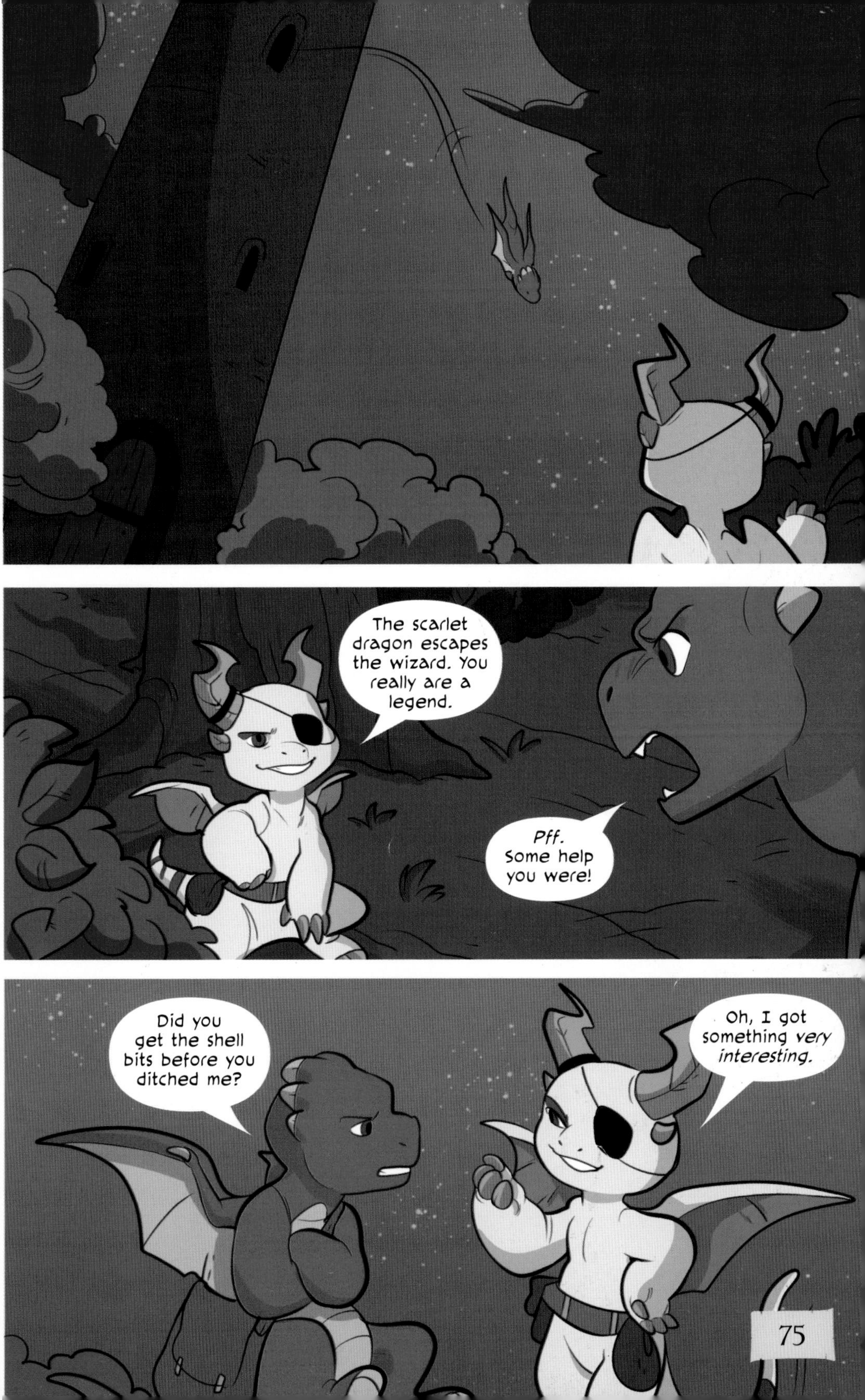

The scarlet dragon escapes the wizard. You really are a legend.
Pff. Some help you were!
Did you get the shell bits before you ditched me?
Oh, I got something *very interesting.*

Chapter 6

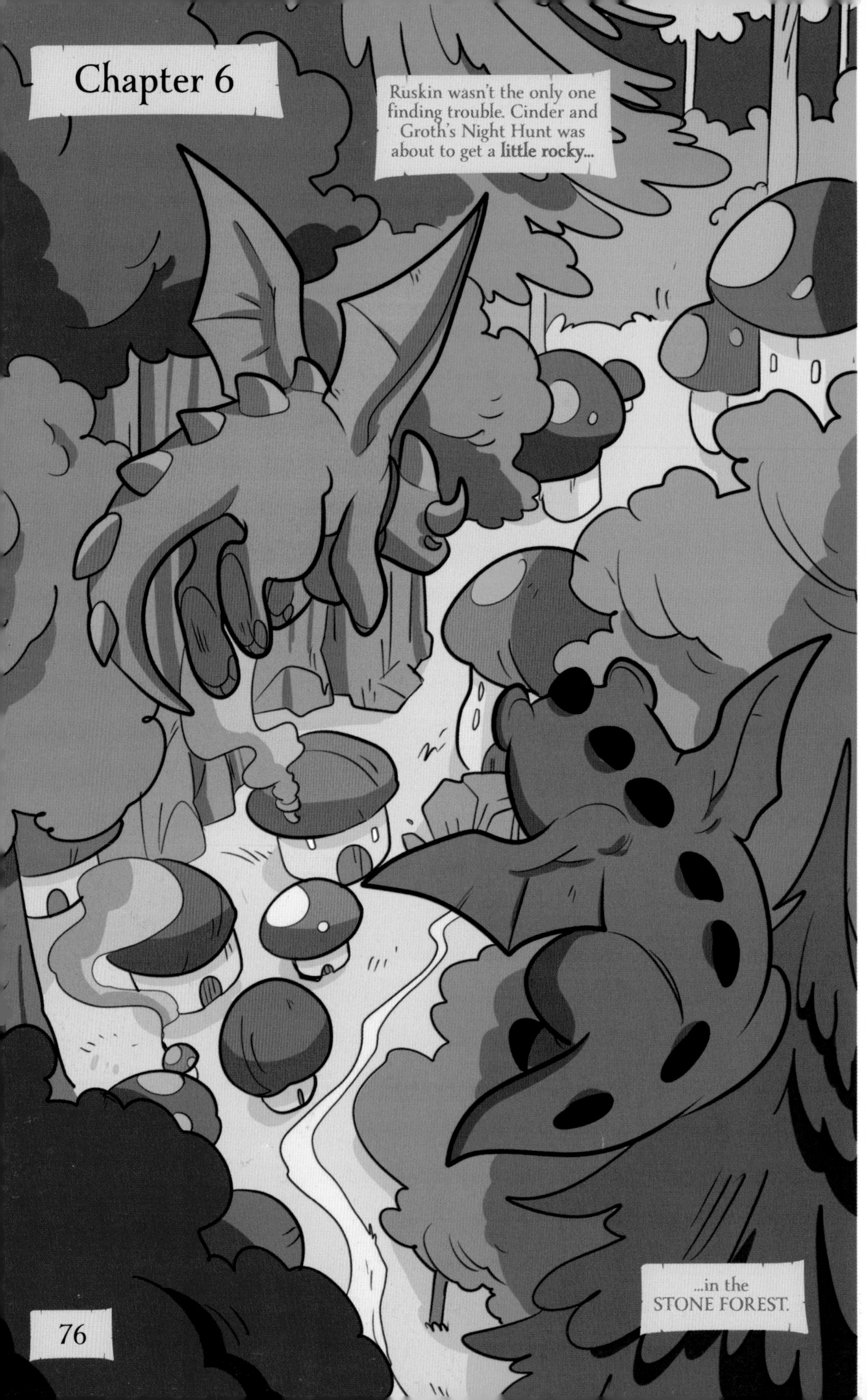
Ruskin wasn't the only one finding trouble. Cinder and Groth's Night Hunt was about to get a **little rocky**...
...in the STONE FOREST.

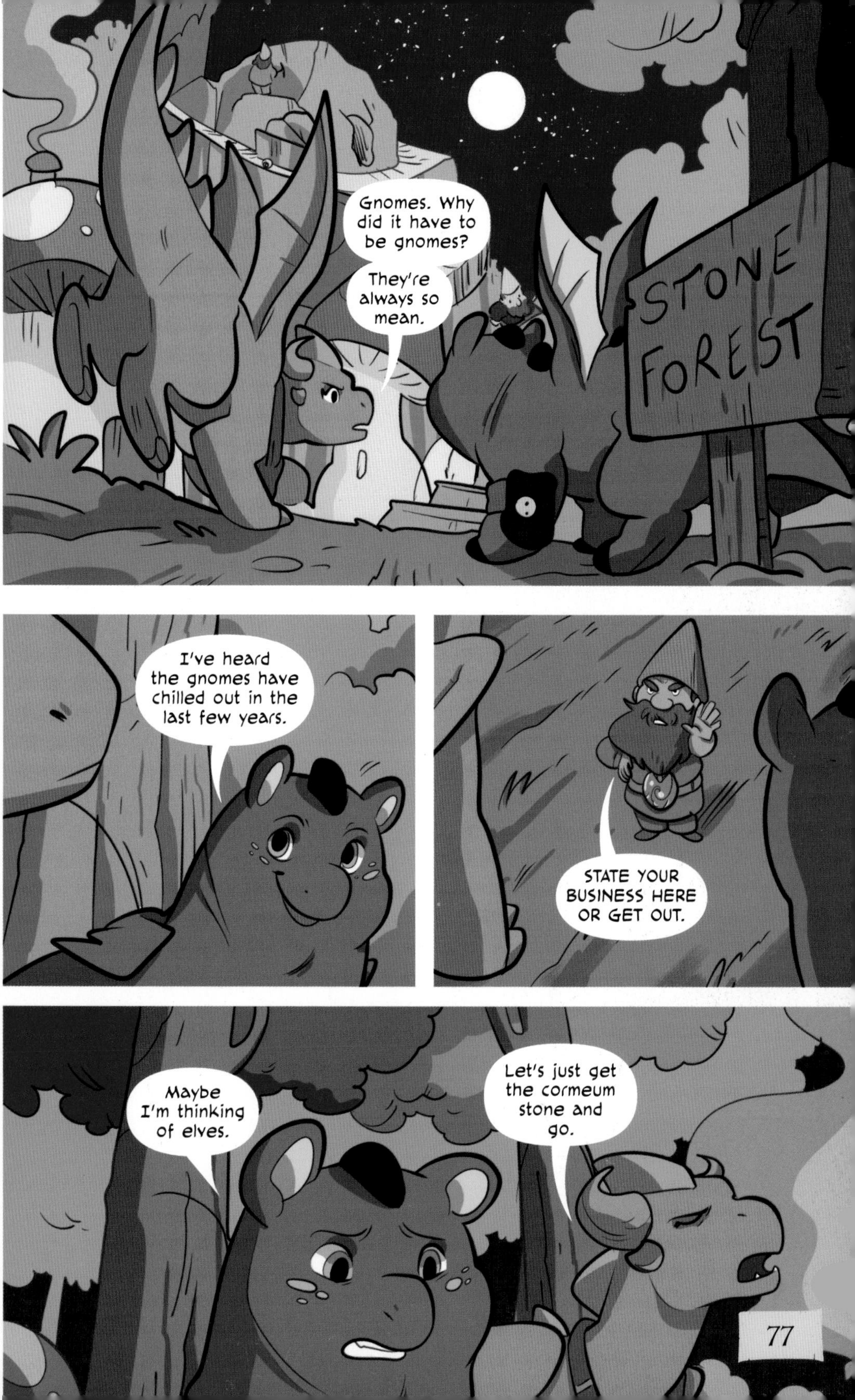
Gnomes. Why did it have to be gnomes?
They're always so mean.
STONE FOREST
I've heard the gnomes have chilled out in the last few years.
STATE YOUR BUSINESS HERE OR GET OUT.
Maybe I'm thinking of elves.
Let's just get the cormeum stone and go.

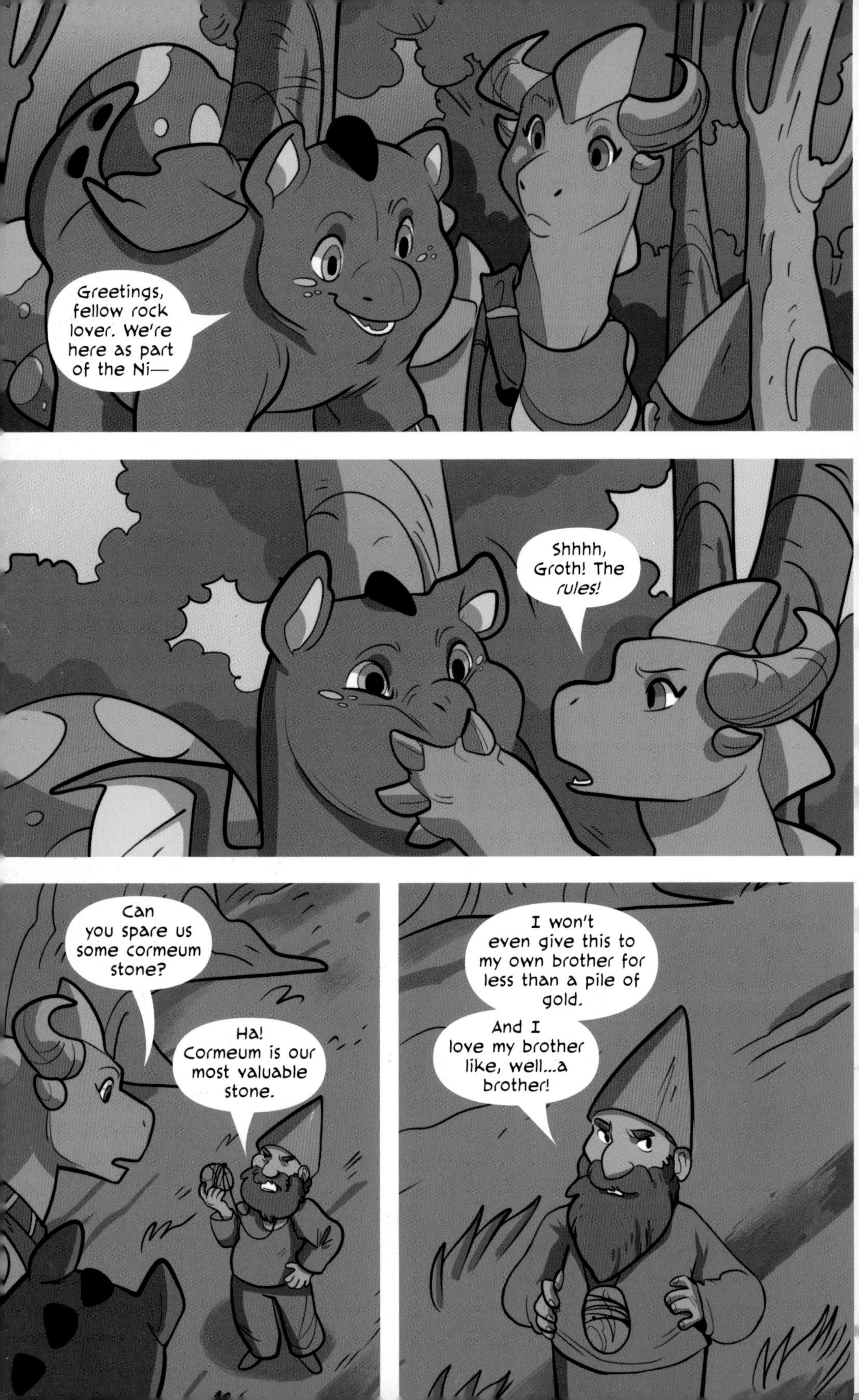
Greetings, fellow rock lover. We're here as part of the Ni—
Shhhh, Groth! The *rules!*
Can you spare us some cormeum stone?
Ha! Cormeum is our most valuable stone.
I won't even give this to my own brother for less than a pile of gold.
And I love my brother like, well...a brother!

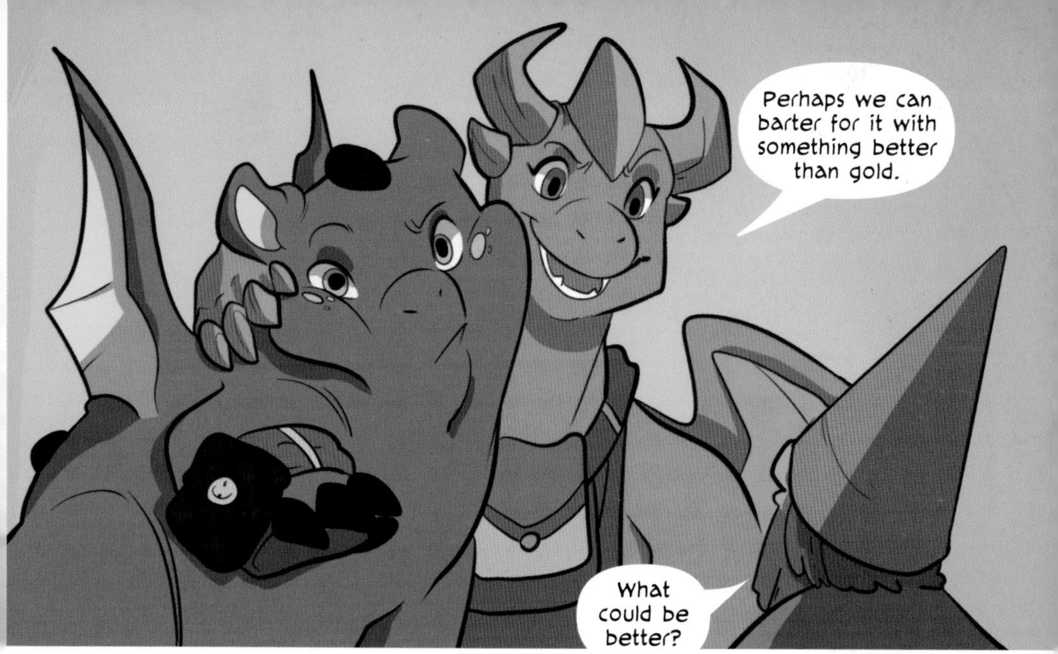
Perhaps we can barter for it with something better than gold.
What could be better?
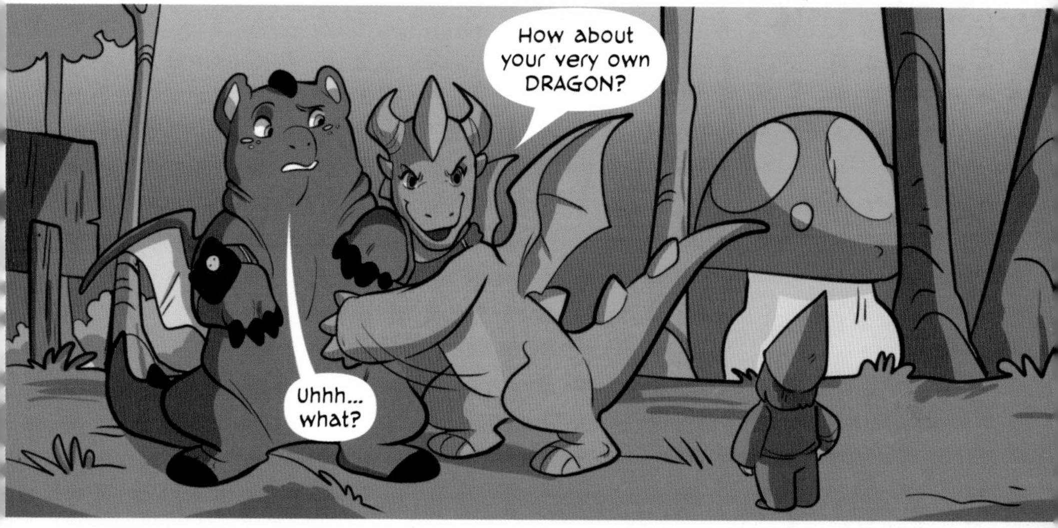
How about your very own DRAGON?
Uhhh... what?
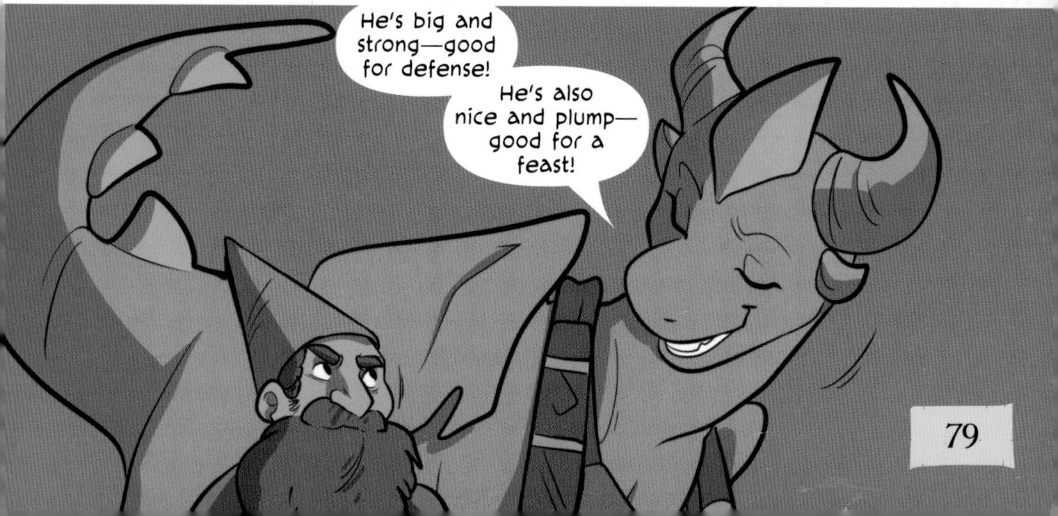
He's big and strong—good for defense!
He's also nice and plump—good for a feast!

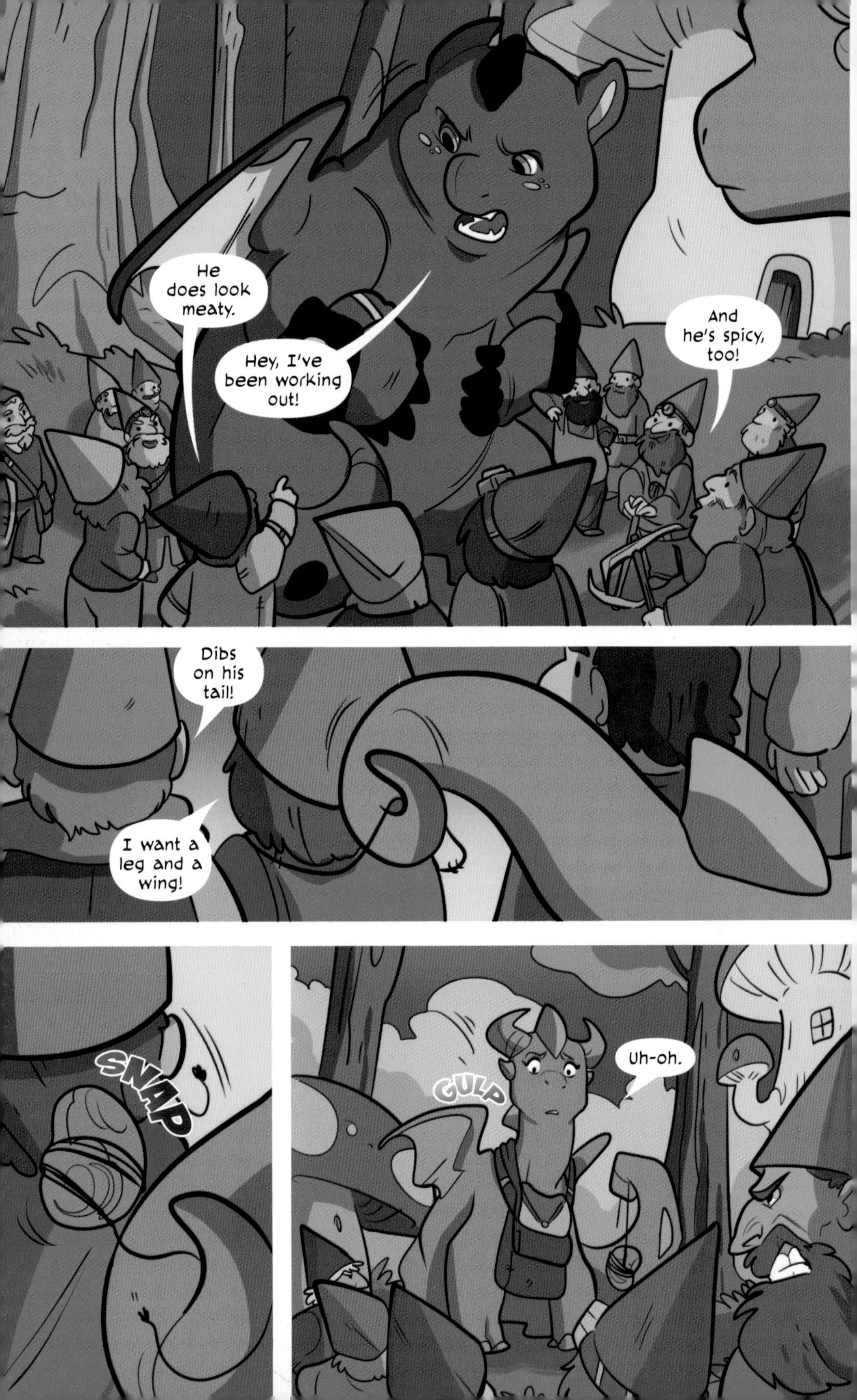
He does look meaty.
Hey, I've been working out!
And he's spicy, too!
Dibs on his tail!
I want a leg and a wing!
SNAP
GULP
Uh-oh.

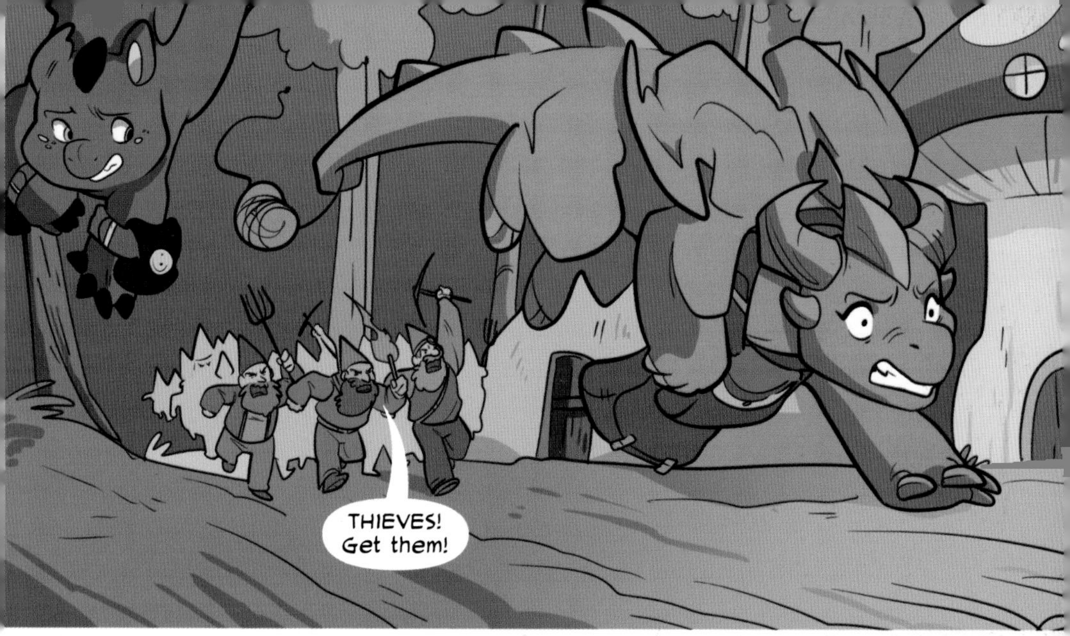
THIEVES! Get them!

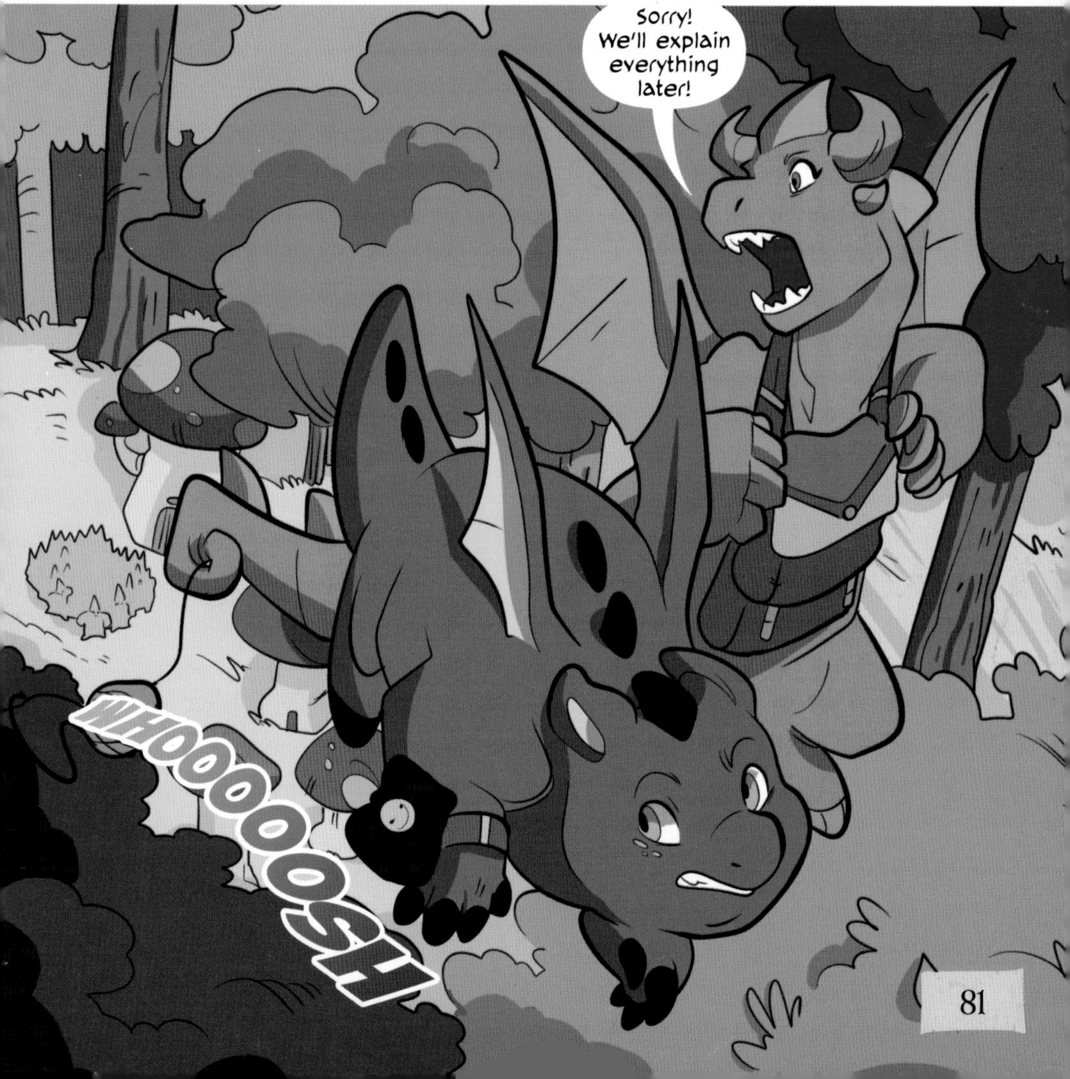
Sorry! We'll explain everything later!
WHOOOOOSH

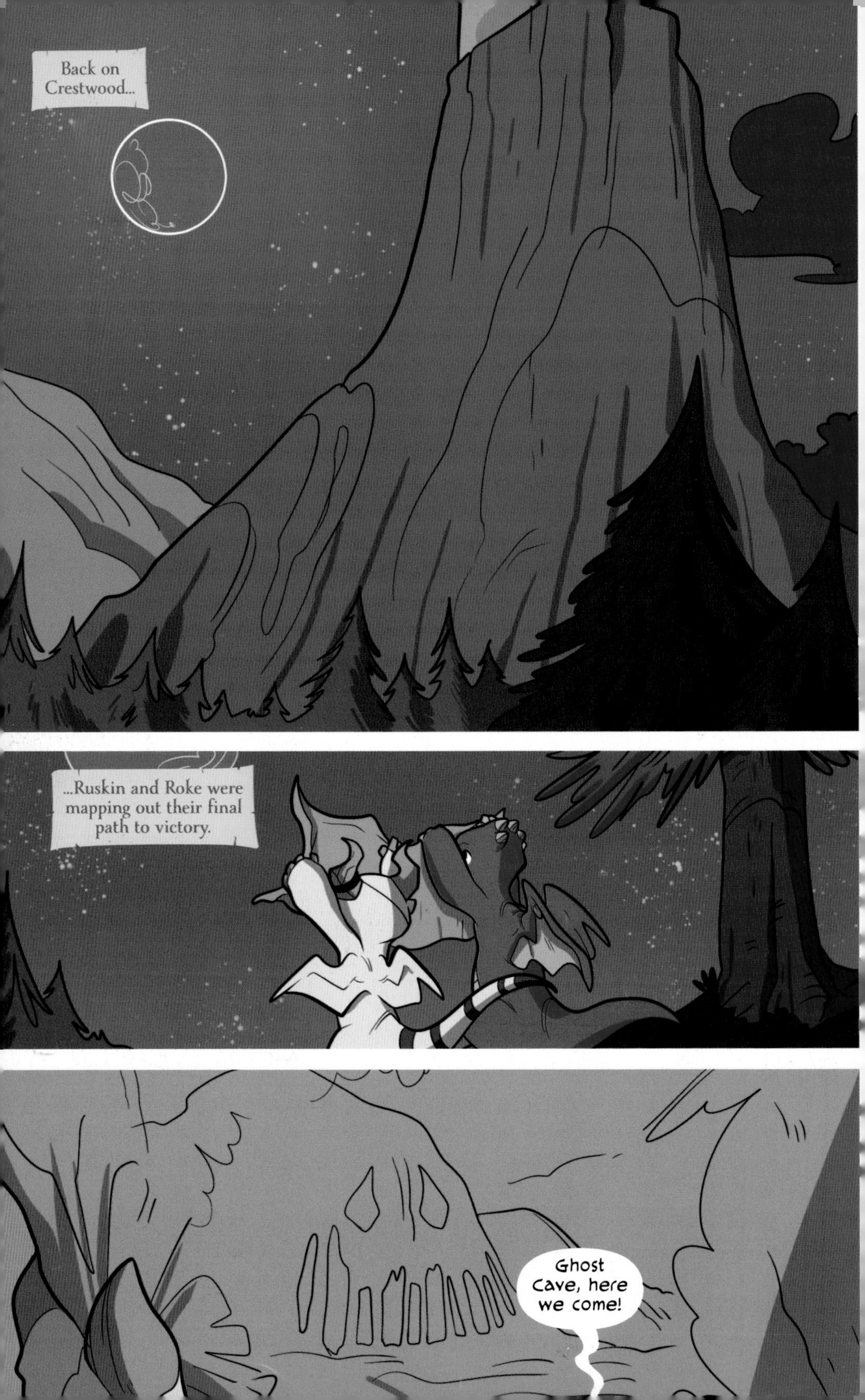
Back on Crestwood...
...Ruskin and Roke were mapping out their final path to victory.
Ghost Cave, here we come!

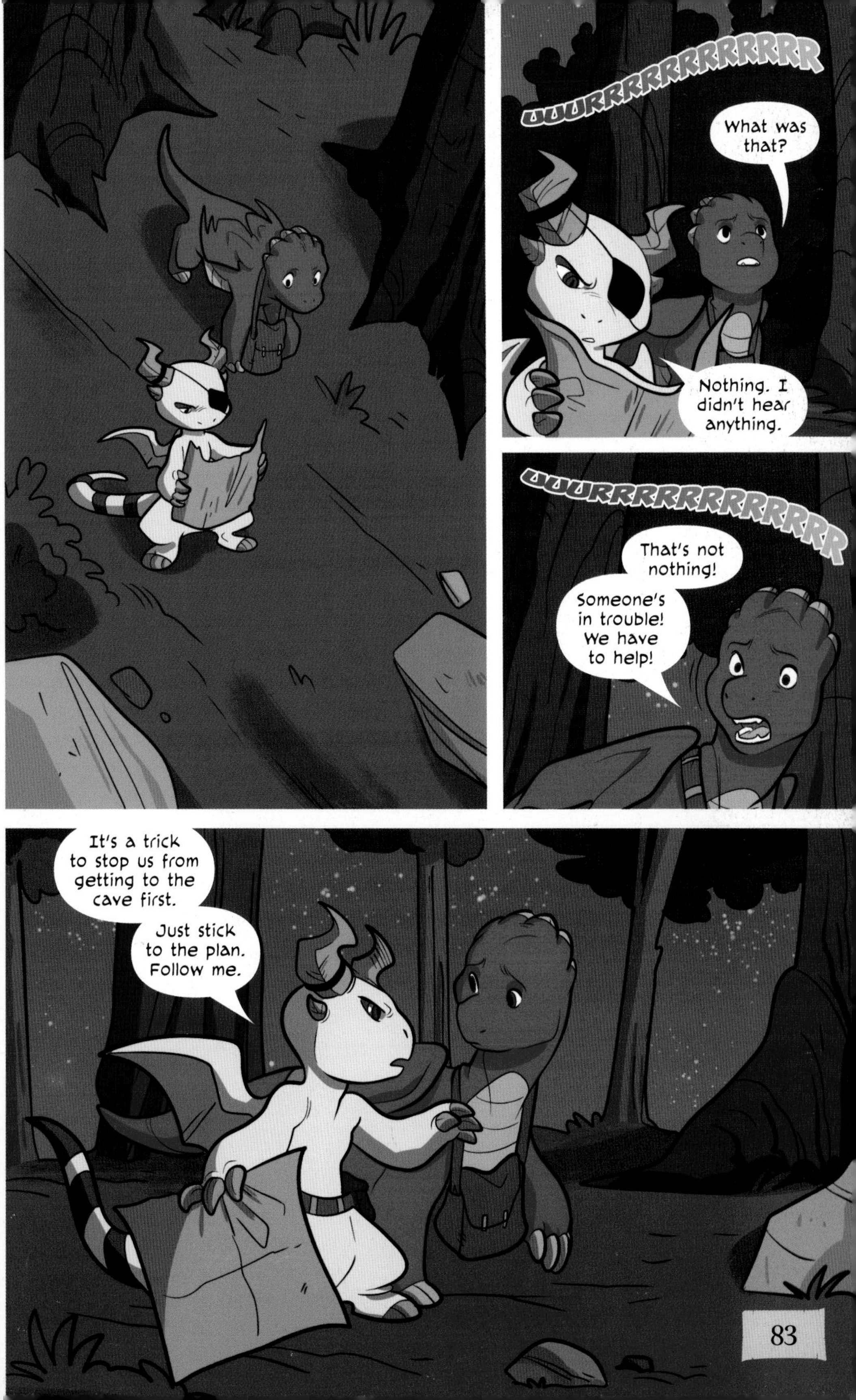
UUURRRRRRRRRRRR
What was that?
Nothing. I didn't hear anything.
UUURRRRRRRRRRRRR
That's not nothing!
Someone's in trouble! We have to help!
It's a trick to stop us from getting to the cave first.
Just stick to the plan. Follow me.

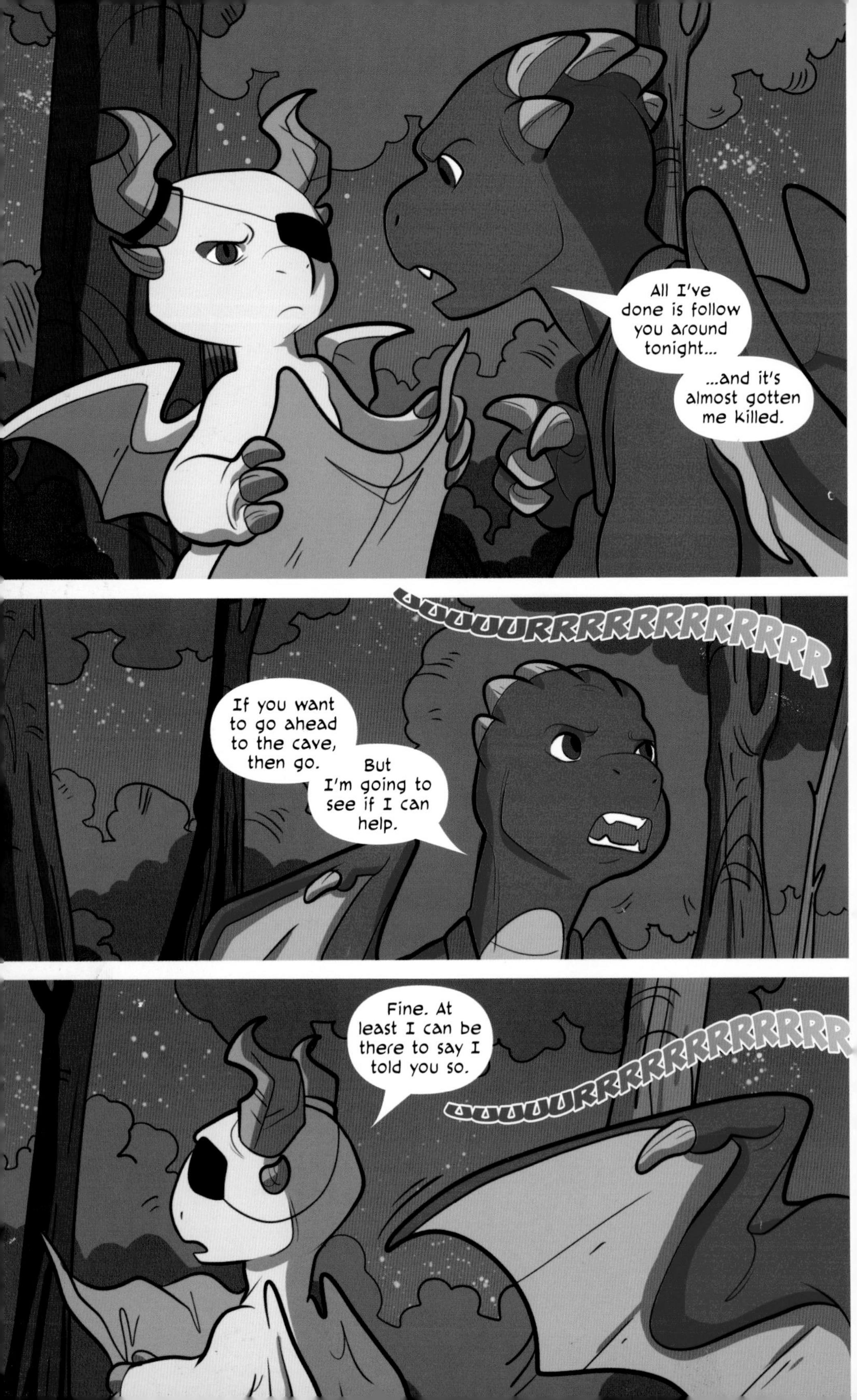
All I've done is follow you around tonight...
...and it's almost gotten me killed.
UUUUURRRRRRRRRRRR
If you want to go ahead to the cave, then go.
But I'm going to see if I can help.
Fine. At least I can be there to say I told you so.
UUUUURRRRRRRRRRRR

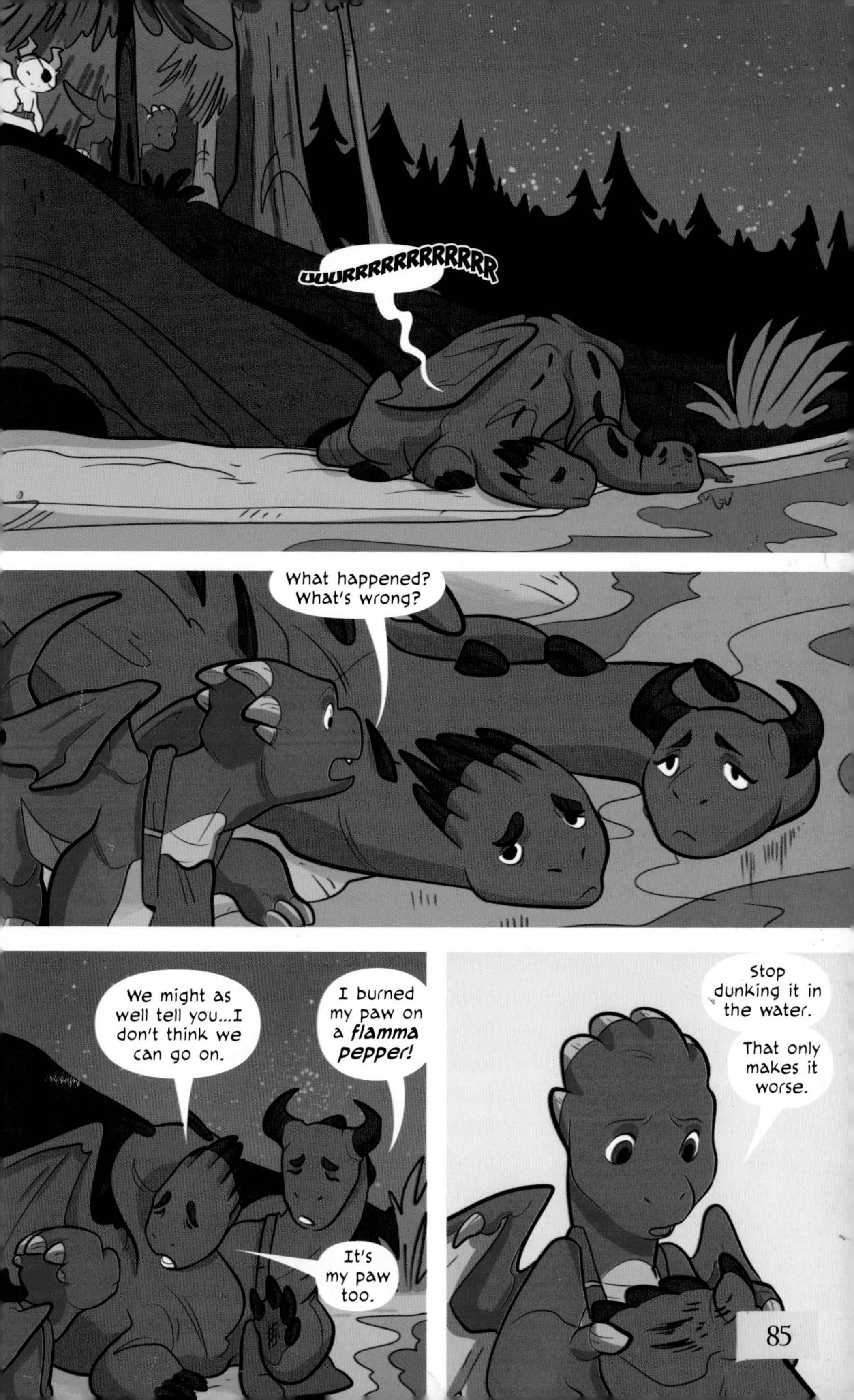
UUURRRRRRRRRRRR
What happened? What's wrong?
We might as well tell you...I don't think we can go on.
I burned my paw on a *flamma pepper!*
It's my paw too.
Stop dunking it in the water.
That only makes it worse.

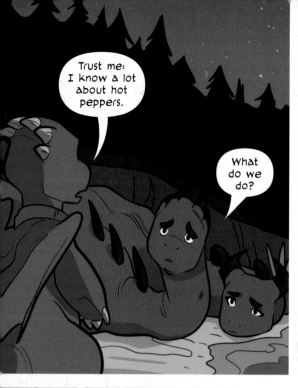

Trust me: I know a lot about hot peppers.

What do we do?

SNAIL SLIME!

Whenever I burn my tongue, Prince Lucas gives me some snail slime to cool it.

I saw some snail trails on our way over here.

You can scoop some up in a leaf.

URRRRRRRR...

You go. I'll stay and watch over them.

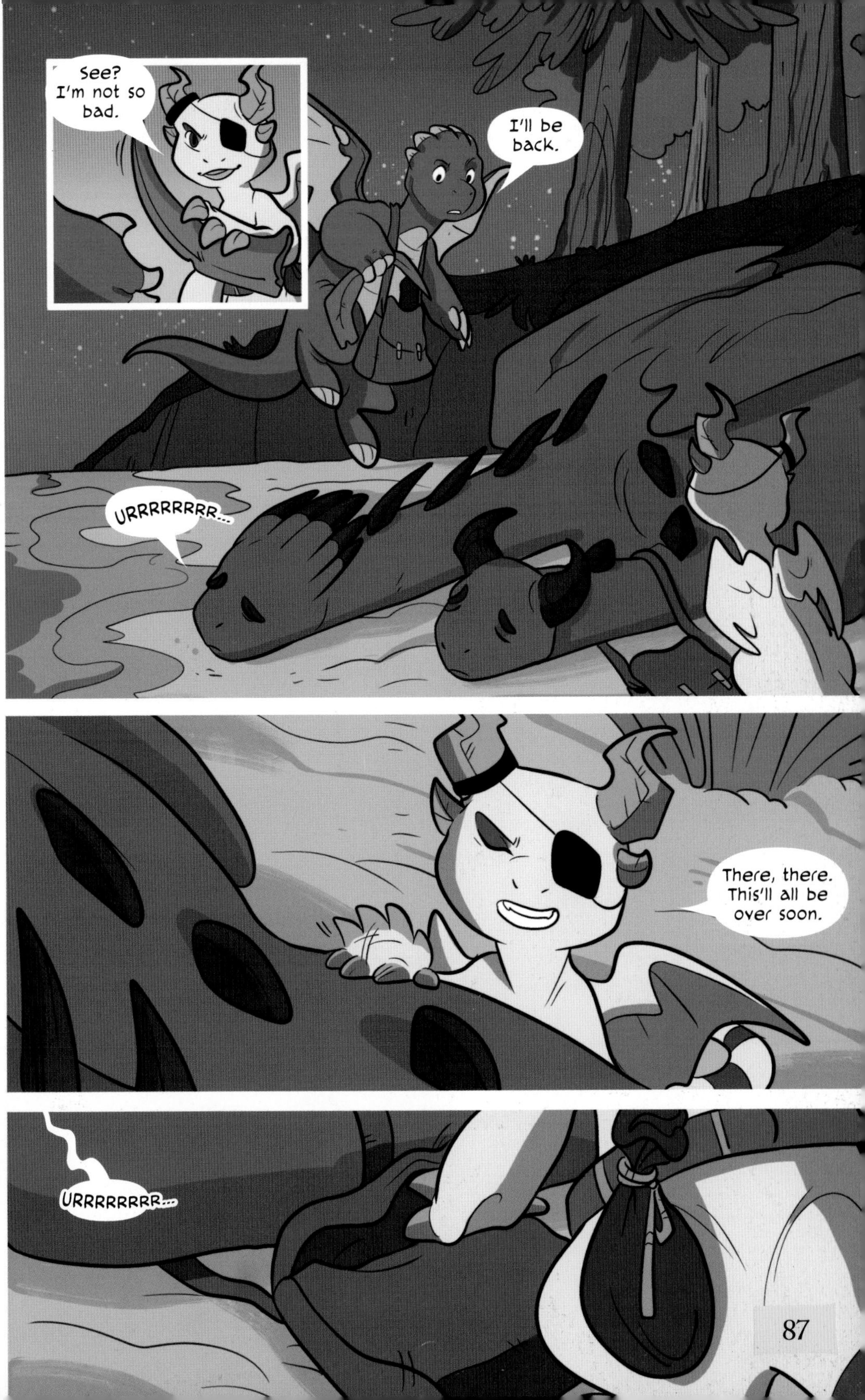
See? I'm not so bad.
I'll be back.
URRRRRRRR...
There, there. This'll all be over soon.
URRRRRRRR...

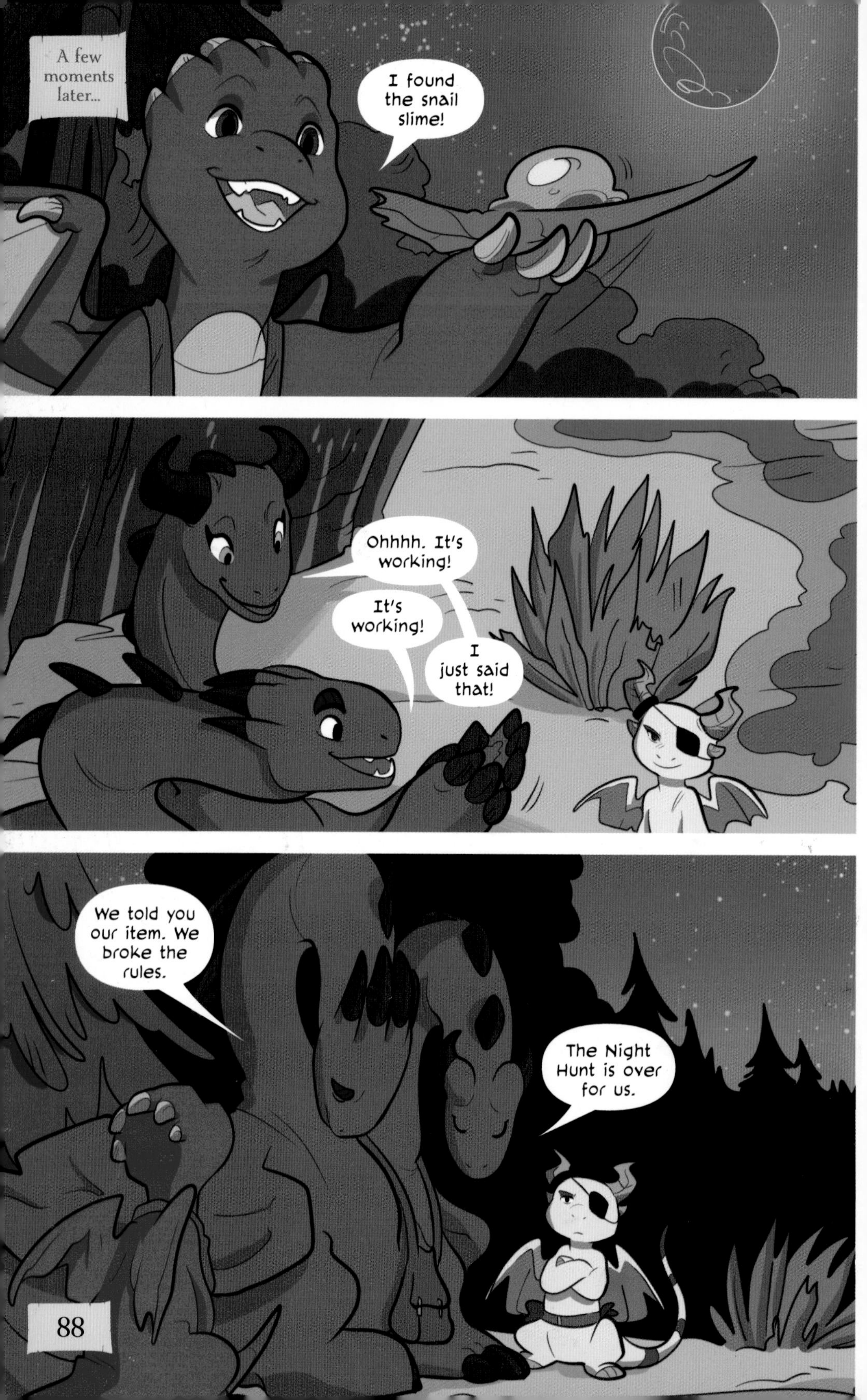
A few moments later...
I found the snail slime!
Ohhhh. It's working!
It's working!
I just said that!
We told you our item. We broke the rules.
The Night Hunt is over for us.

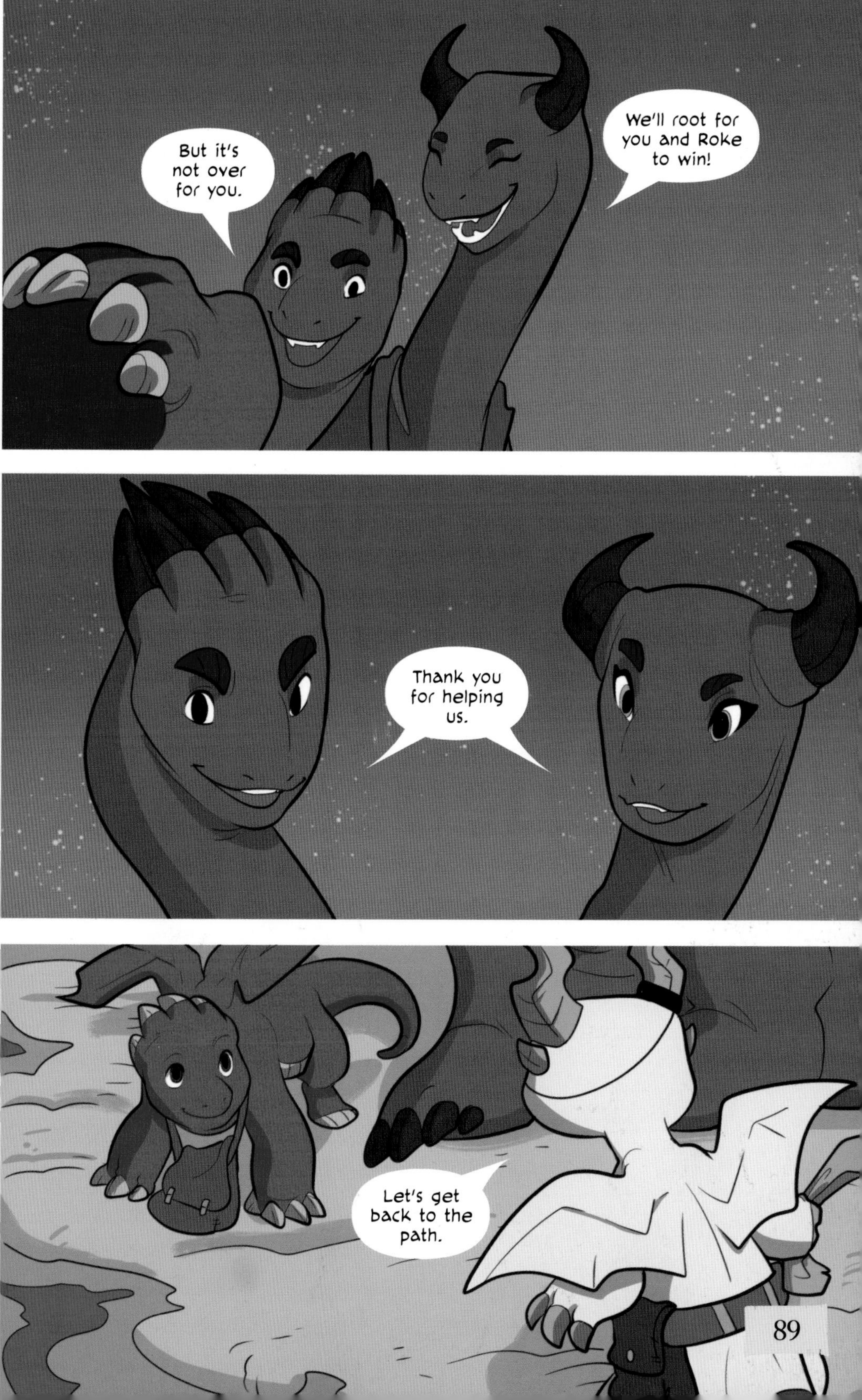
But it's not over for you.
We'll root for you and Roke to win!
Thank you for helping us.
Let's get back to the path.

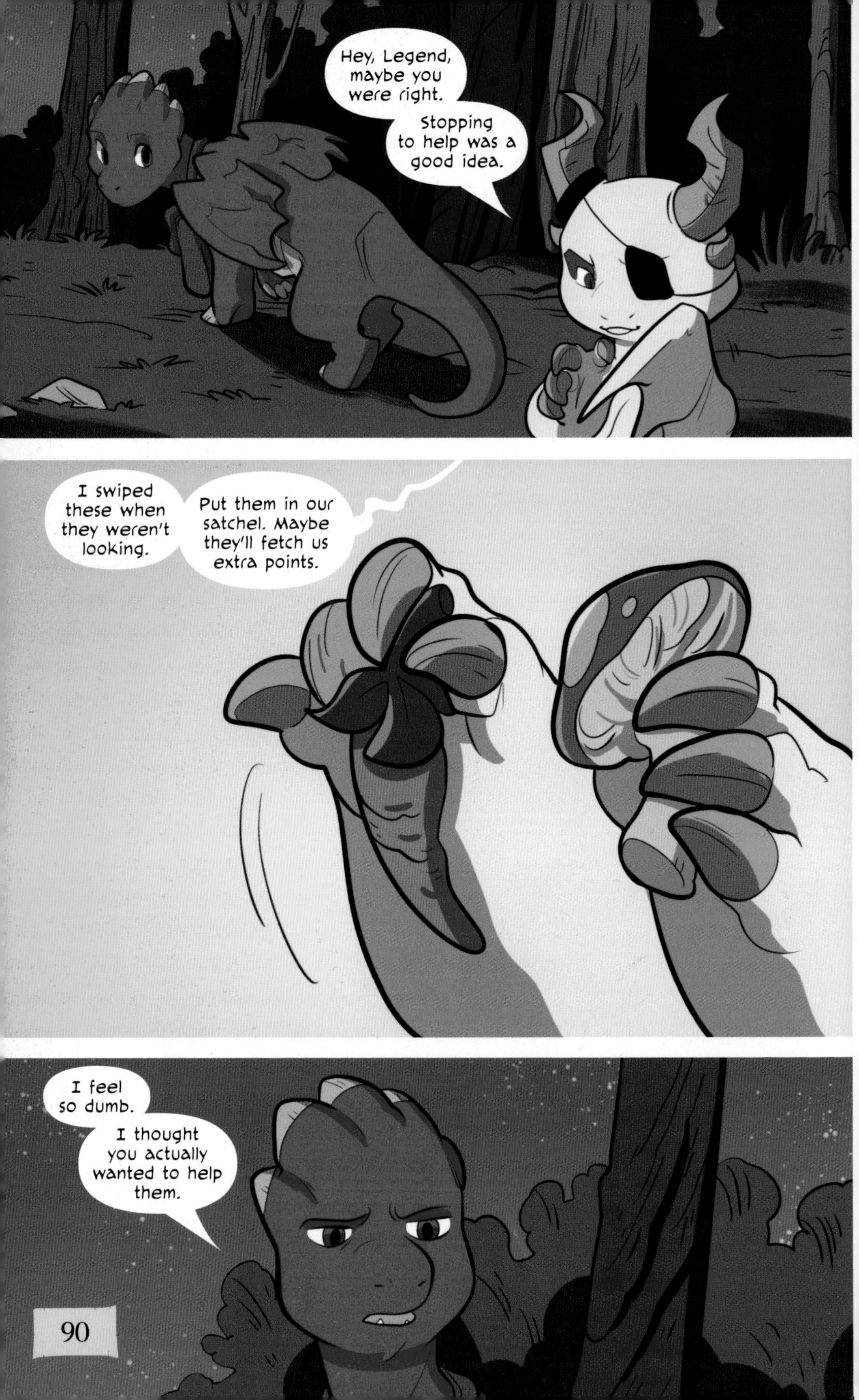
Hey, Legend, maybe you were right.
Stopping to help was a good idea.
I swiped these when they weren't looking.
Put them in our satchel. Maybe they'll fetch us extra points.
I feel so dumb.
I thought you actually wanted to help them.

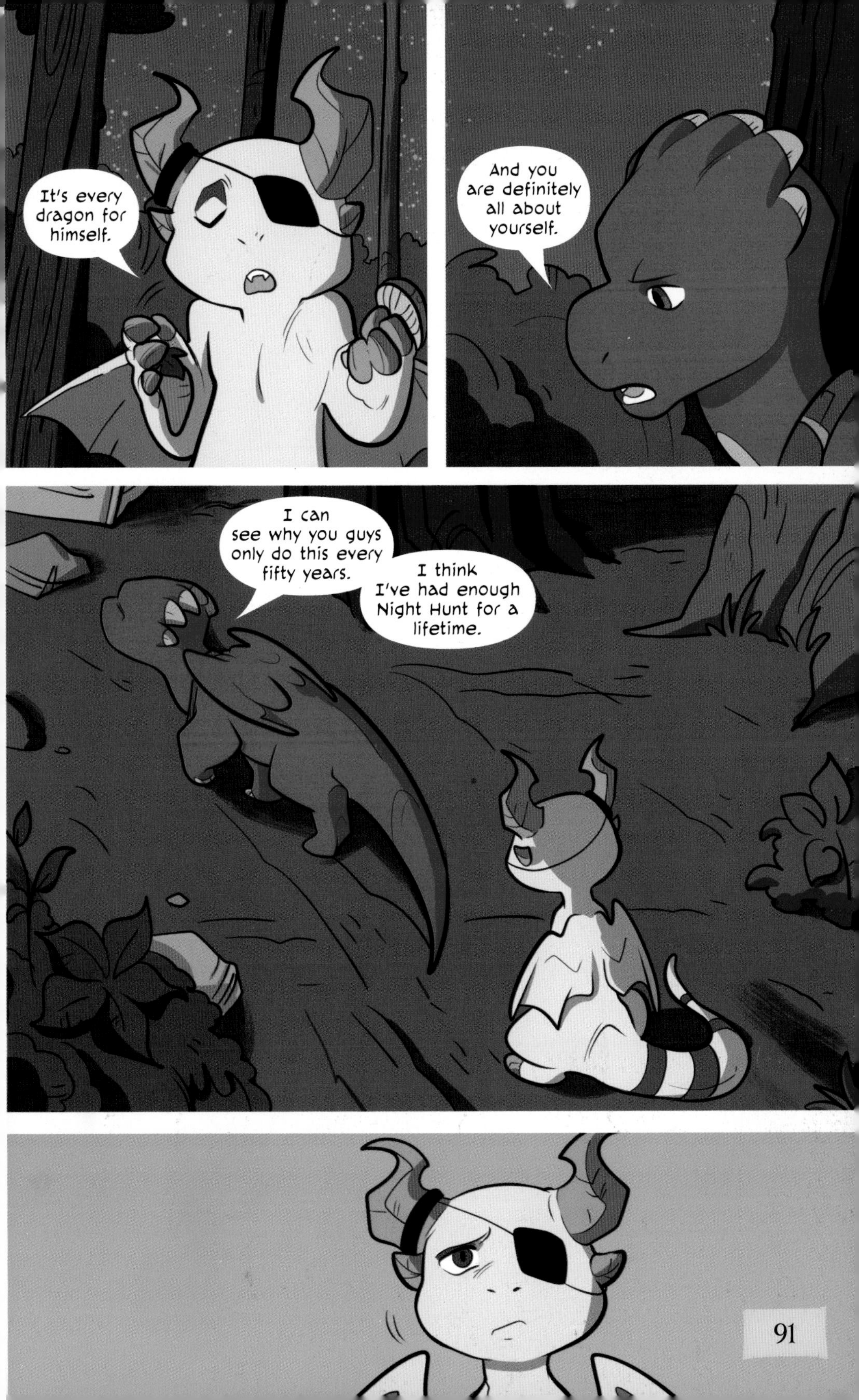
It's every dragon for himself.
And you are definitely all about yourself.
I can see why you guys only do this every fifty years.
I think I've had enough Night Hunt for a lifetime.

Chapter 7

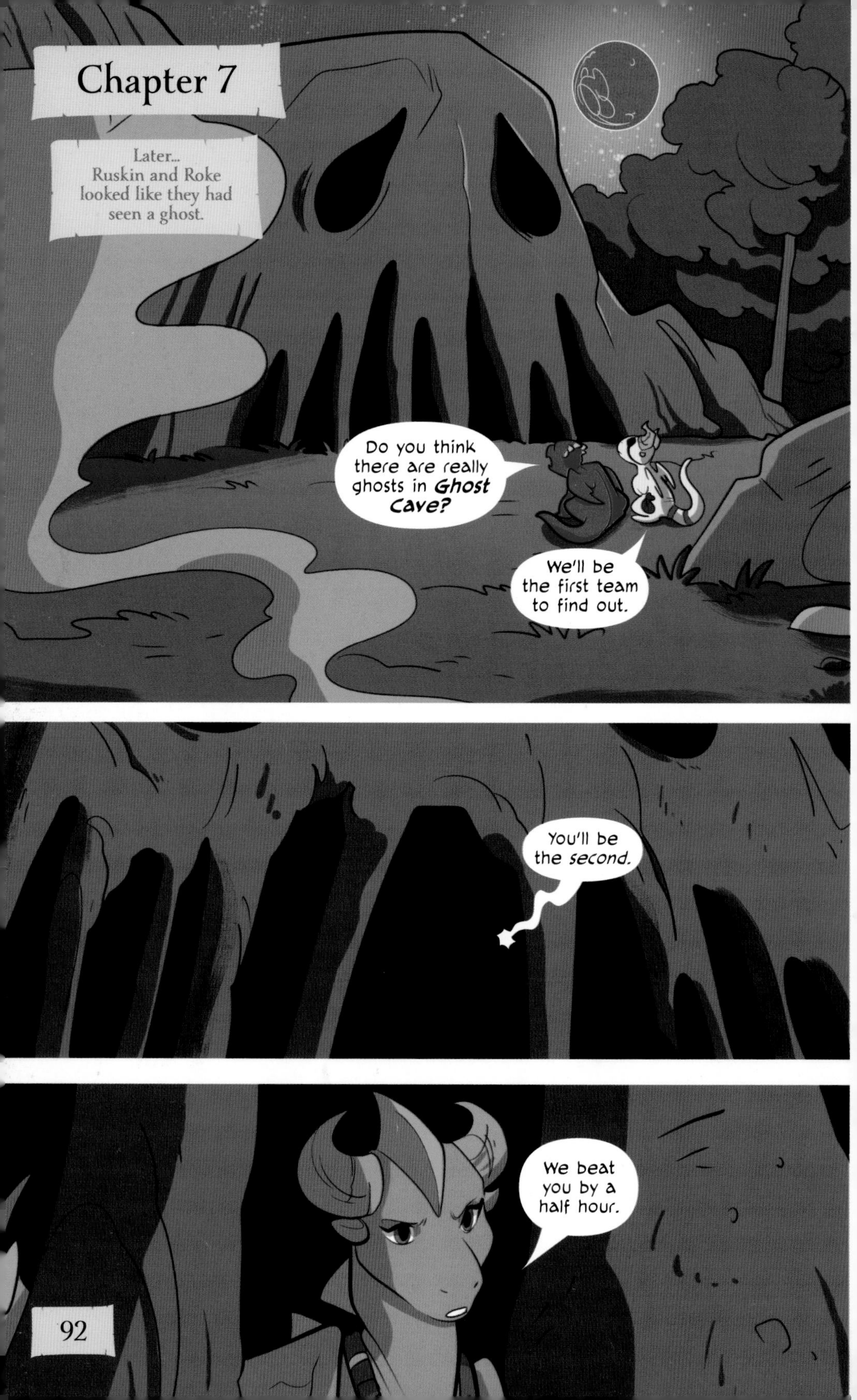
Later...
Ruskin and Roke looked like they had seen a ghost.
Do you think there are really ghosts in Ghost Cave?
We'll be the first team to find out.
You'll be the second.
We beat you by a half hour.

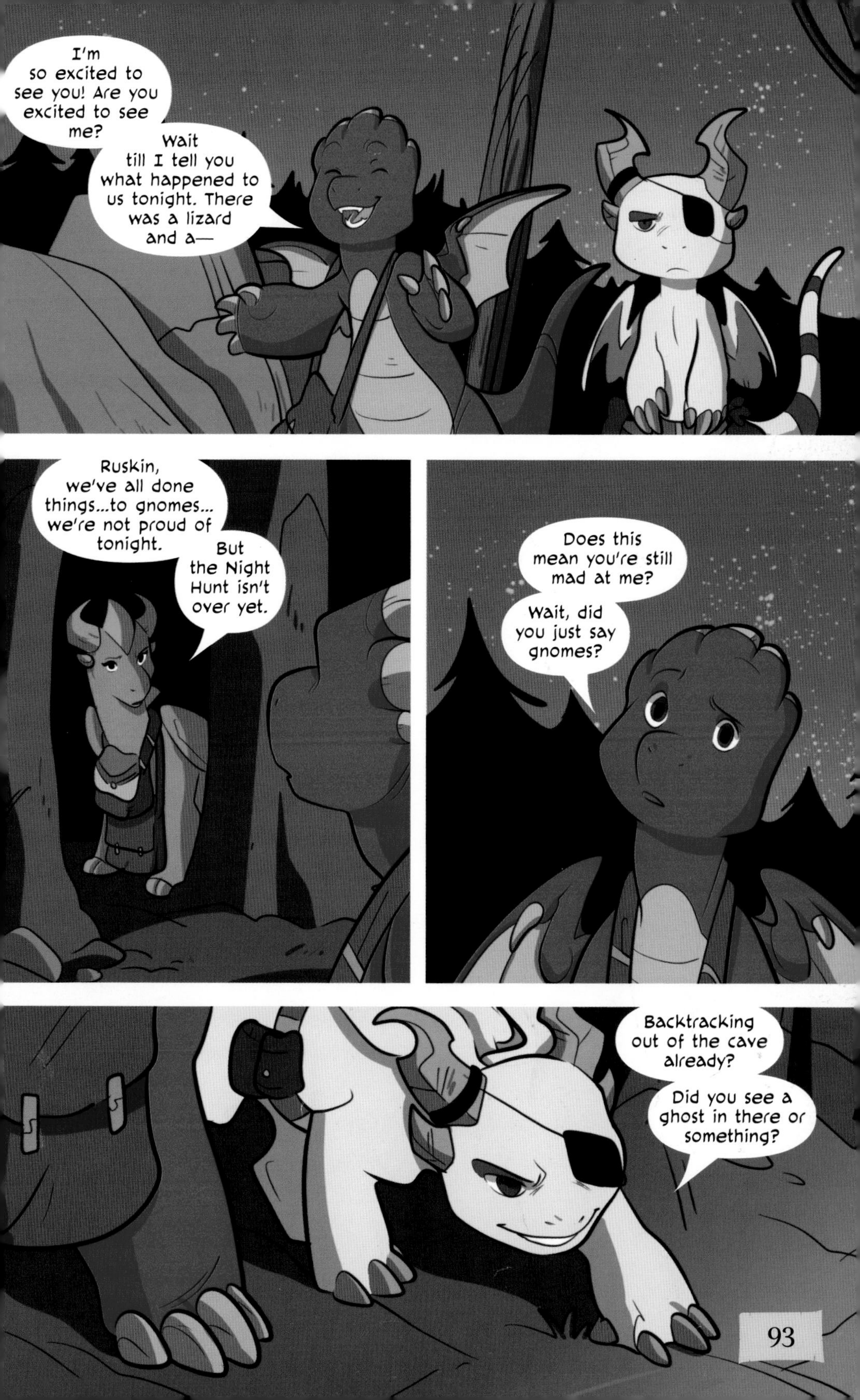
I'm so excited to see you! Are you excited to see me?
Wait till I tell you what happened to us tonight. There was a lizard and a—
Ruskin, we've all done things...to gnomes... we're not proud of tonight.
But the Night Hunt isn't over yet.
Does this mean you're still mad at me?
Wait, did you just say gnomes?
Backtracking out of the cave already?
Did you see a ghost in there or something?

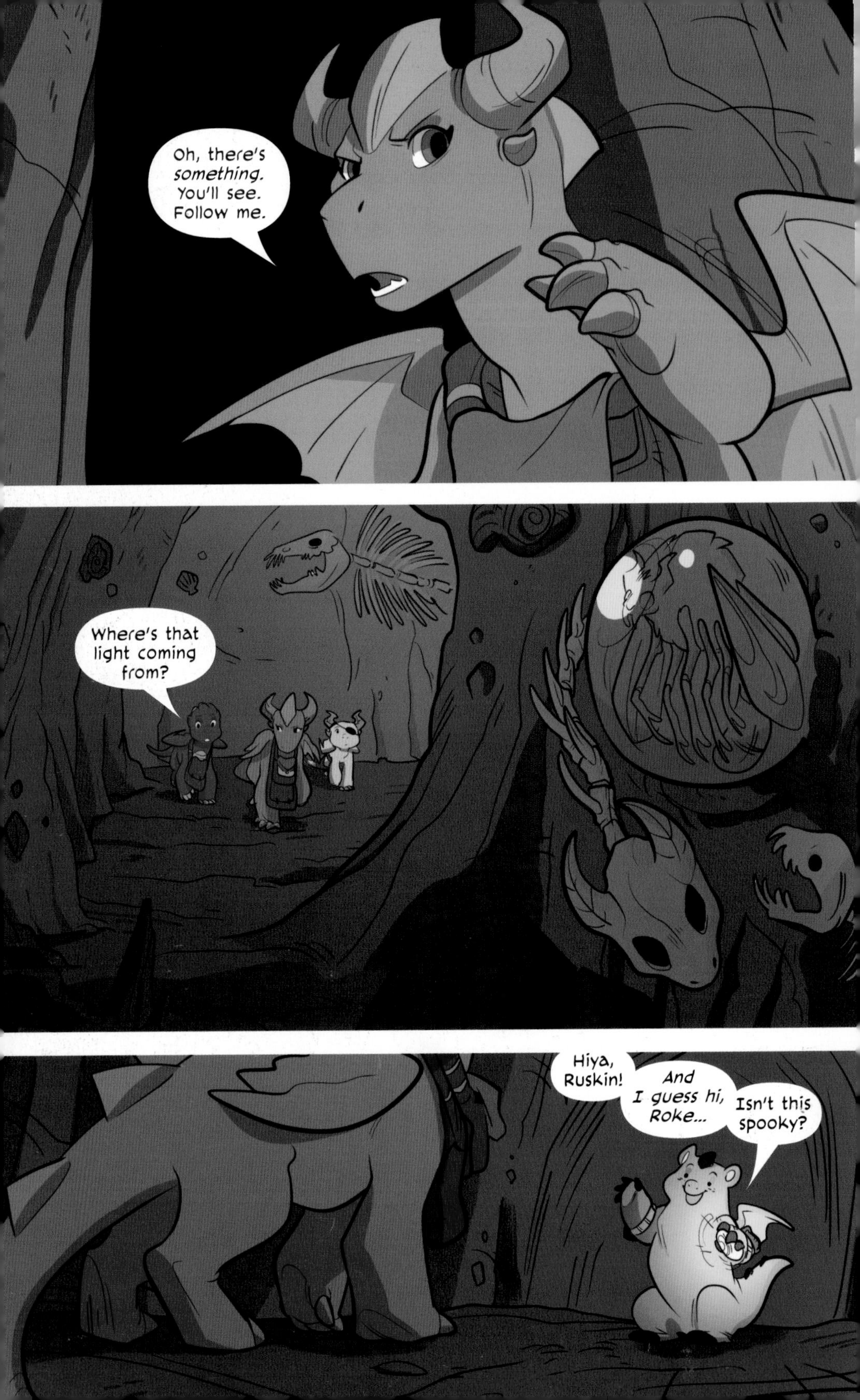
Oh, there's *something.* You'll see. Follow me.
Where's that light coming from?
Hiya, Ruskin!
And I guess hi, Roke...
Isn't this spooky?

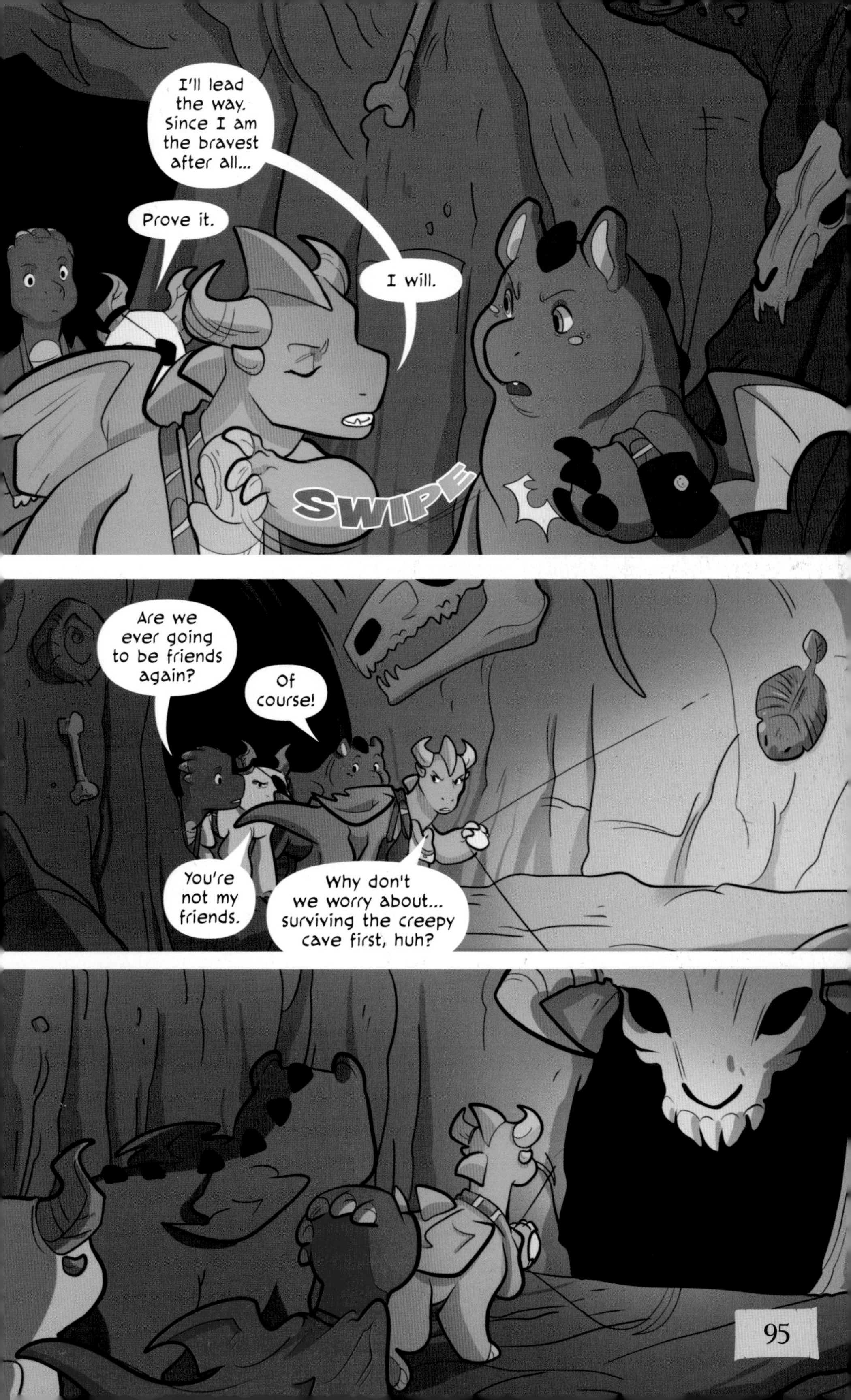
I'll lead the way. Since I am the bravest after all...
Prove it.
I will.
SWIPE
Are we ever going to be friends again?
Of course!
You're not my friends.
Why don't we worry about... surviving the creepy cave first, huh?

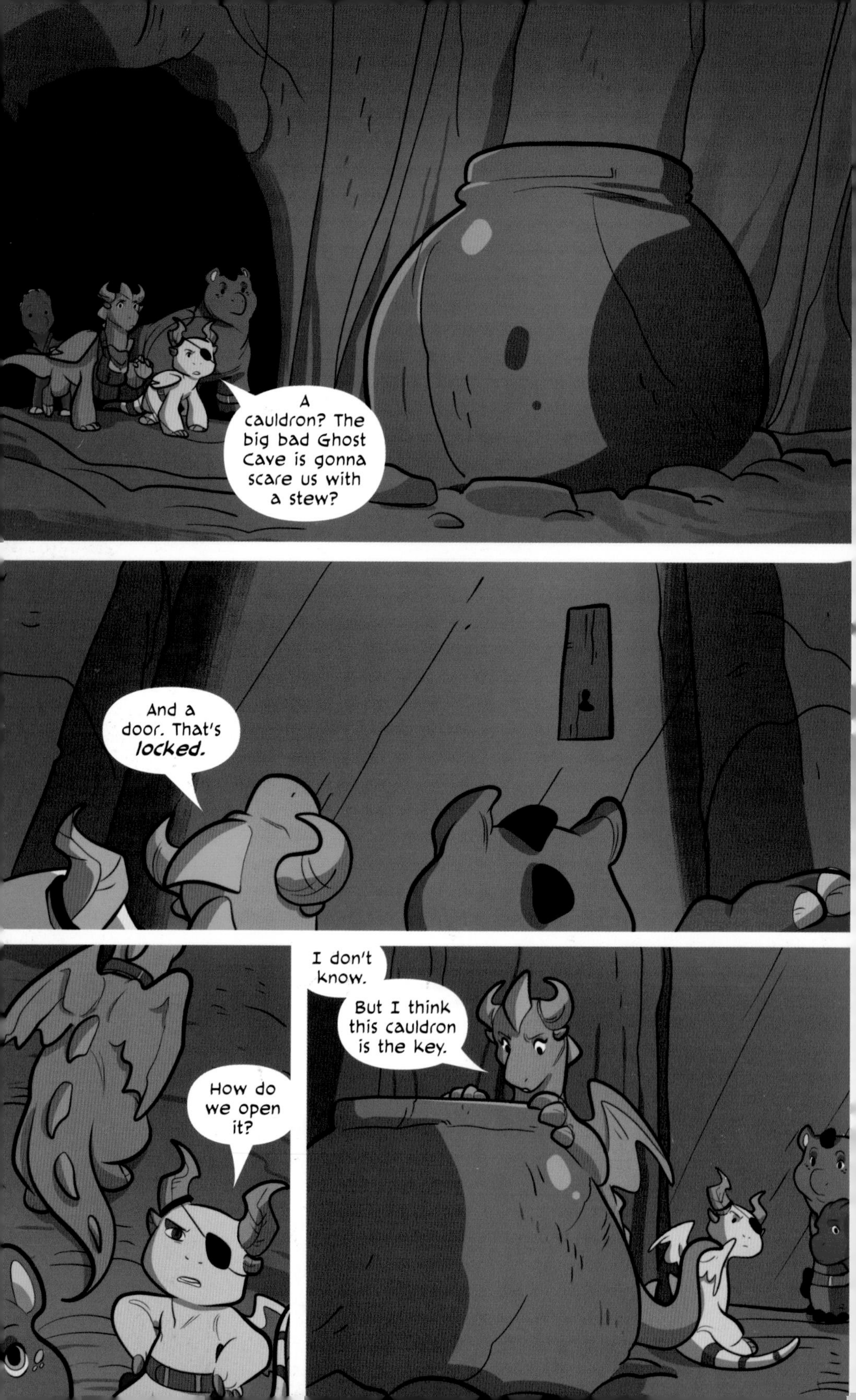
A cauldron? The big bad Ghost Cave is gonna scare us with a stew?
And a door. That's *locked.*
How do we open it?
I don't know.
But I think this cauldron is the key.

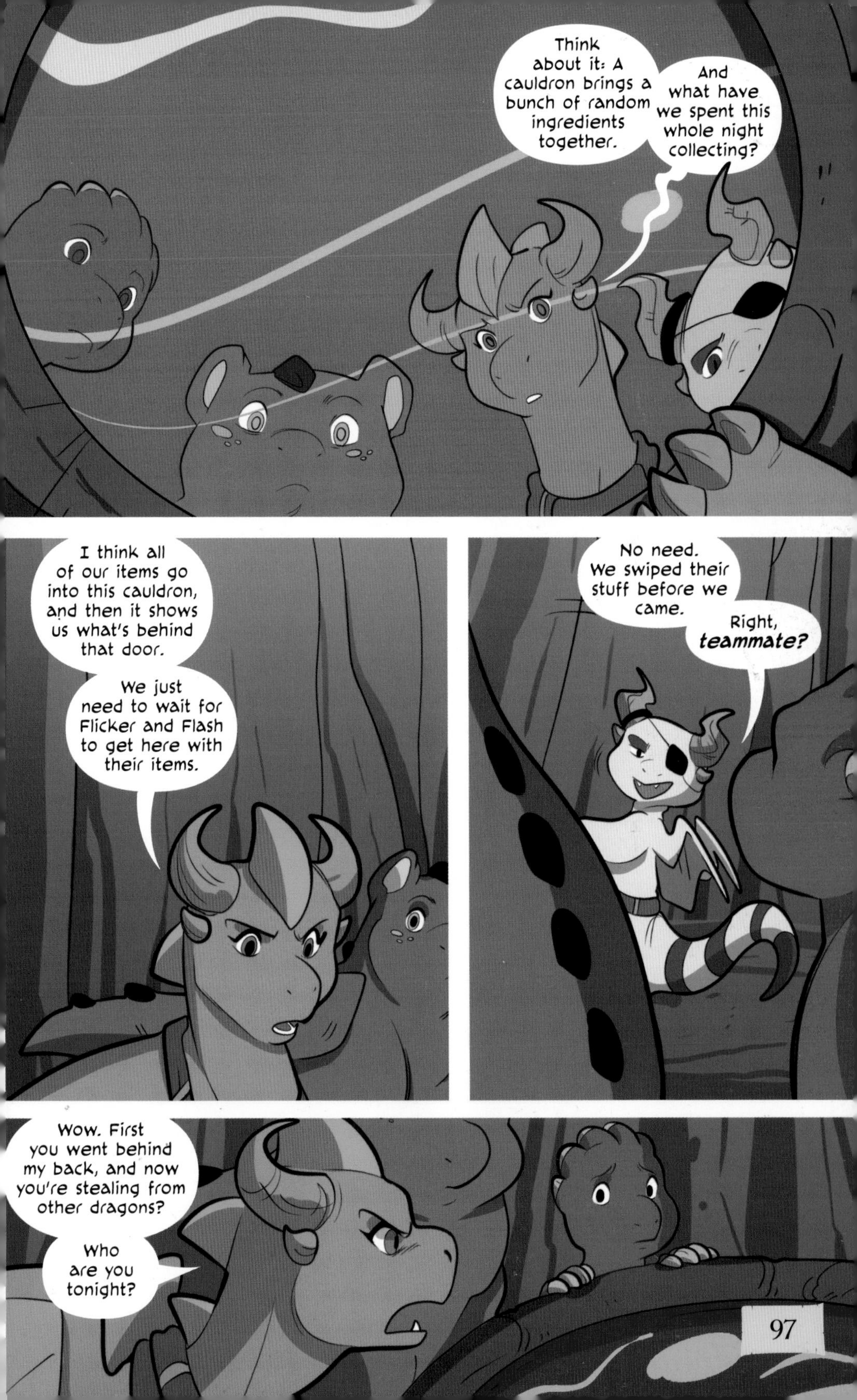
Think about it: A cauldron brings a bunch of random ingredients together.
And what have we spent this whole night collecting?
I think all of our items go into this cauldron, and then it shows us what's behind that door.
We just need to wait for Flicker and Flash to get here with their items.
No need. We swiped their stuff before we came.
Right, ***teammate?***
Wow. First you went behind my back, and now you're stealing from other dragons?
Who are you tonight?

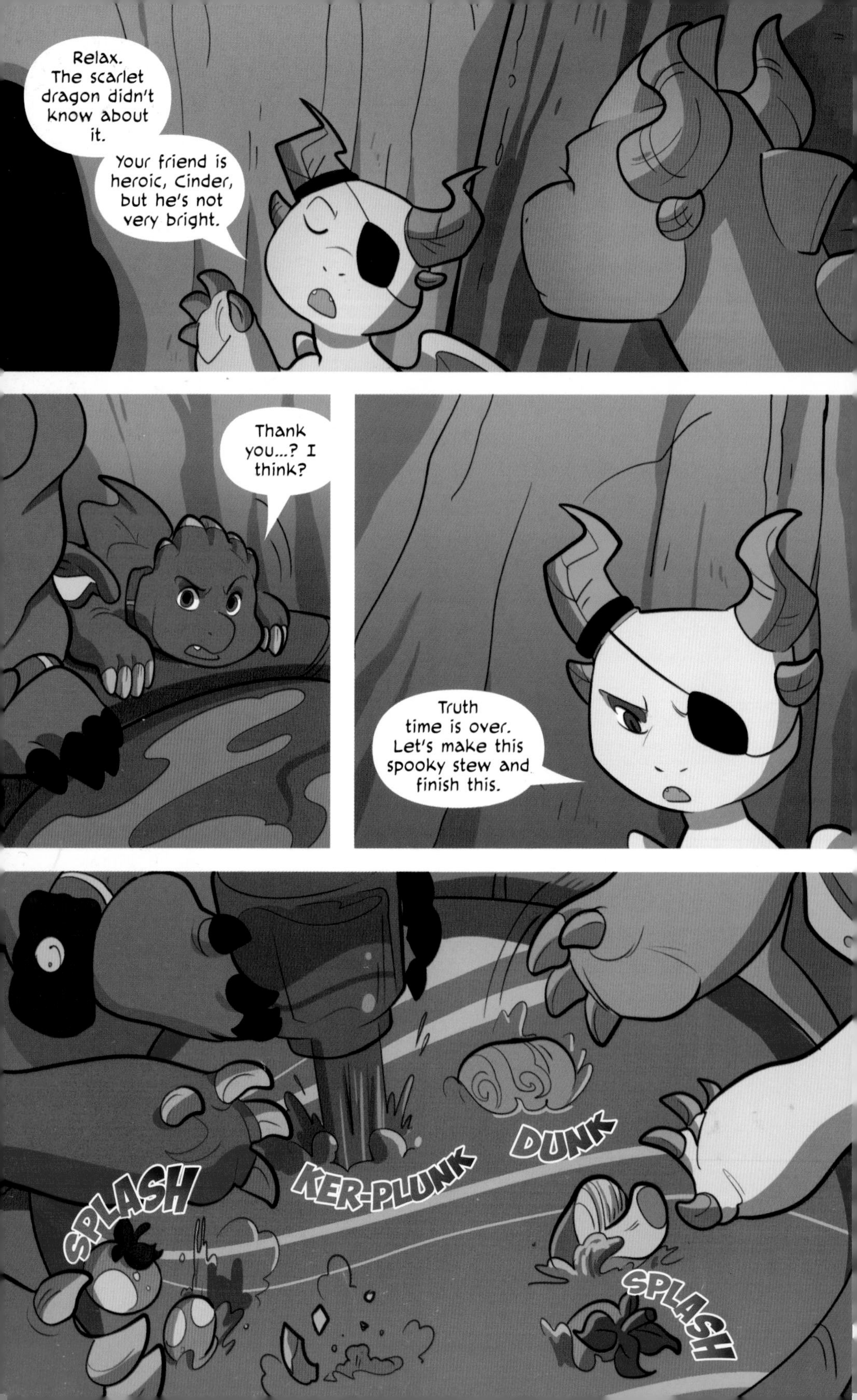
Relax. The scarlet dragon didn't know about it.
Your friend is heroic, Cinder, but he's not very bright.
Thank you...? I think?
Truth time is over. Let's make this spooky stew and finish this.
SPLASH
KER-PLUNK
DUNK
SPLASH

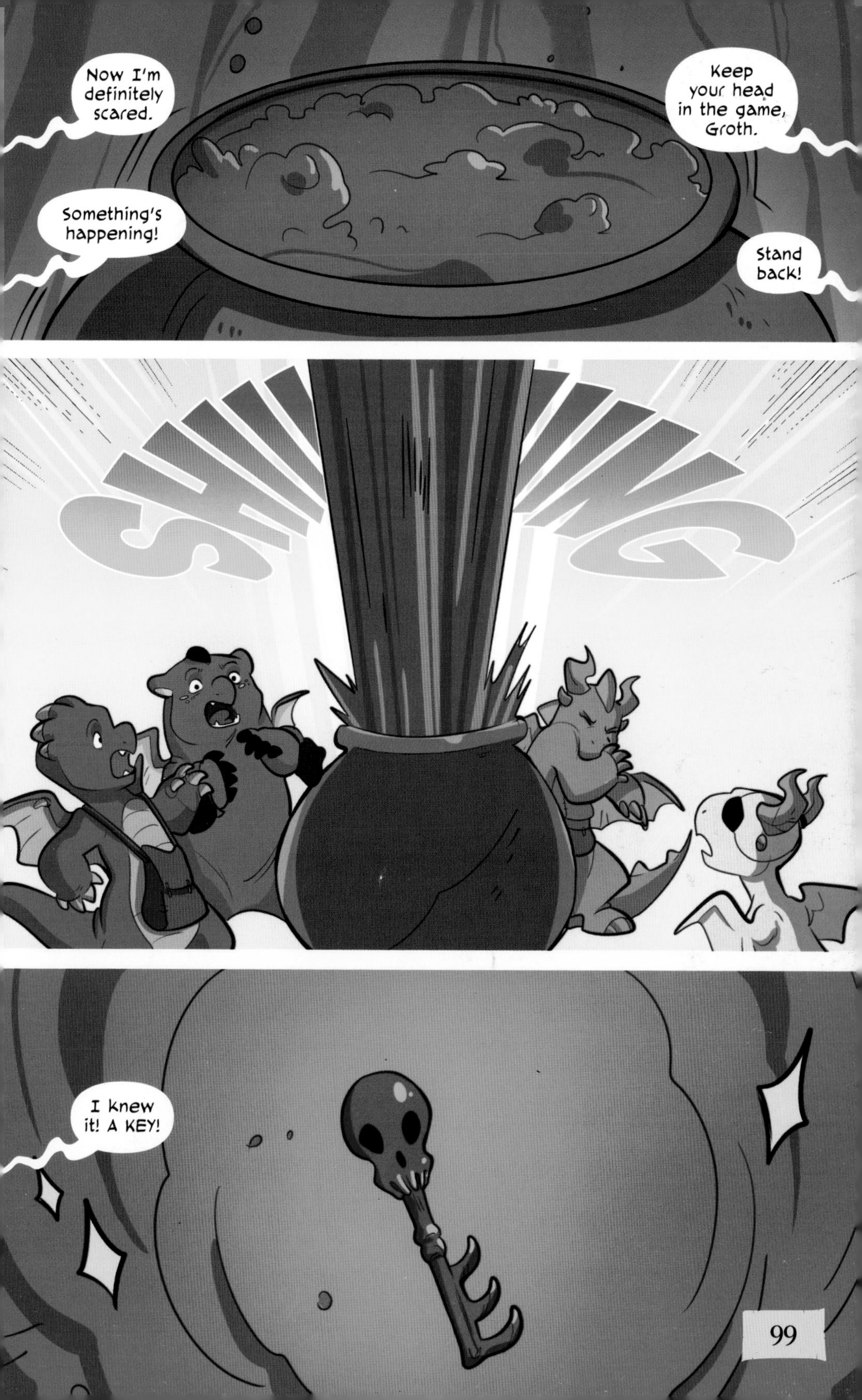
Now I'm definitely scared.
Keep your head in the game, Groth.
Something's happening!
Stand back!
SHHIIING
I knew it! A KEY!

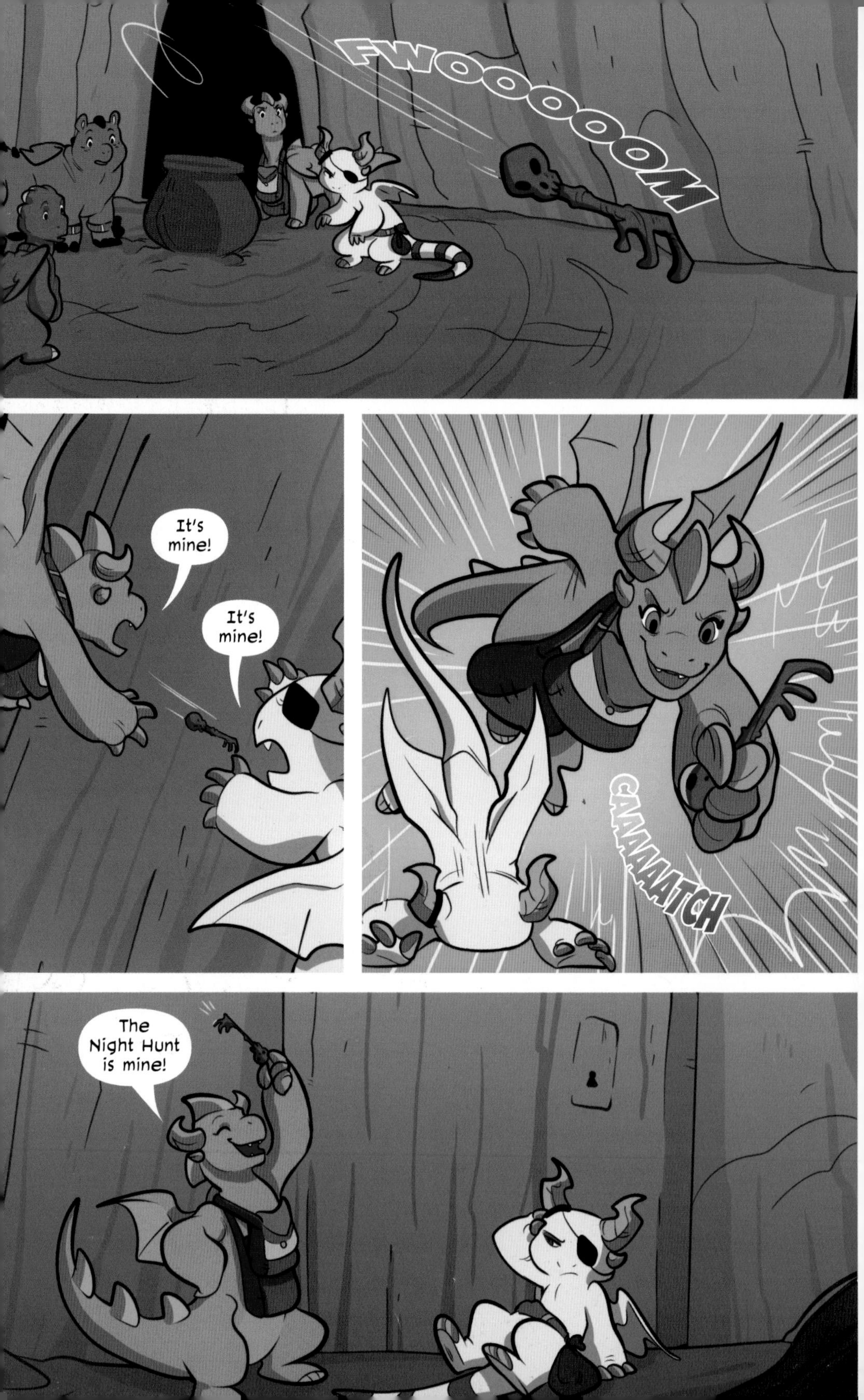
FWOOOOOOM
It's mine!
It's mine!
CAAAAAAATCH
The Night Hunt is mine!

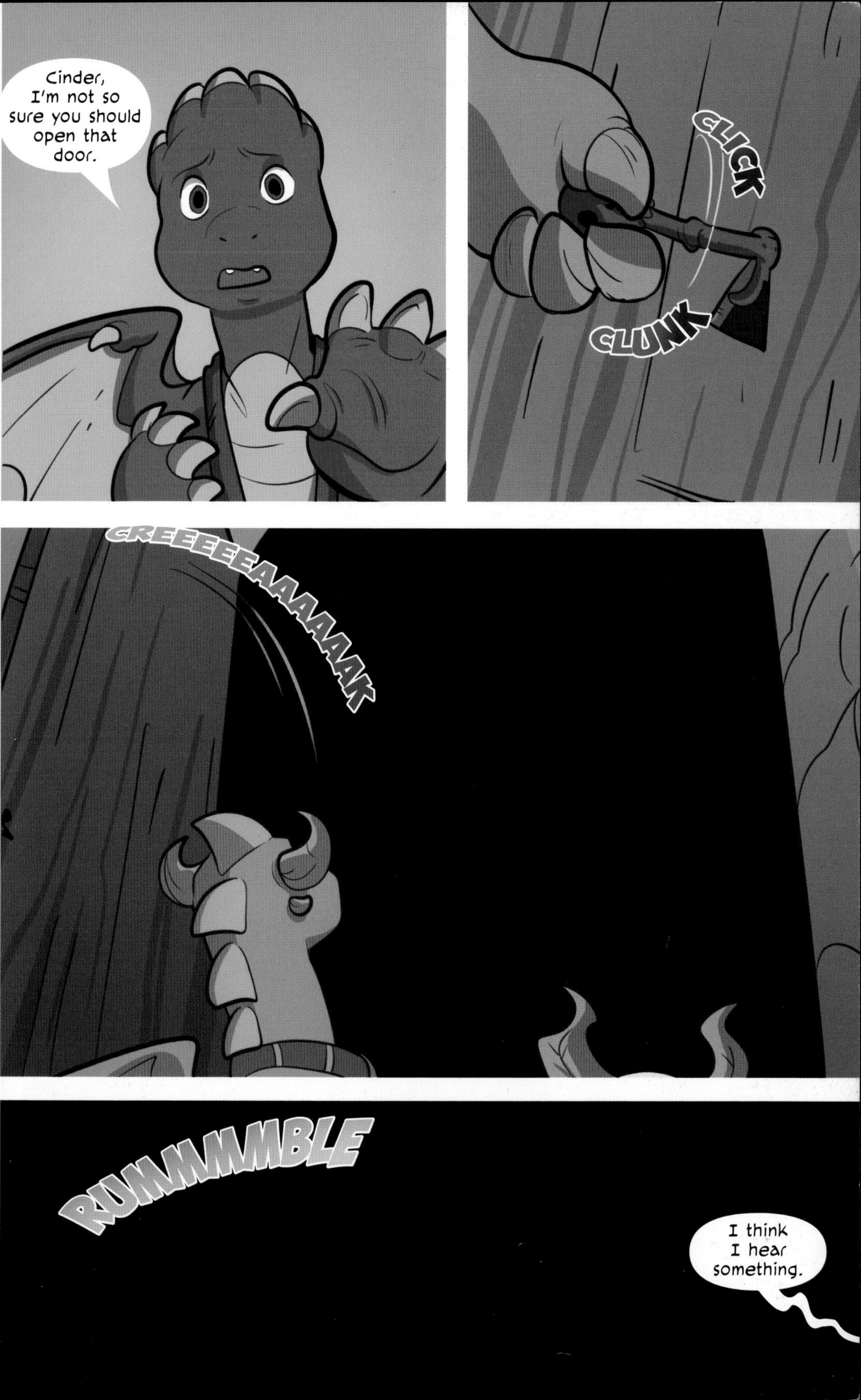
Cinder, I'm not so sure you should open that door.
CLICK
CLUNK
CREEEEEEAAAAAAAK
RUMMMMBLE
I think I hear something.

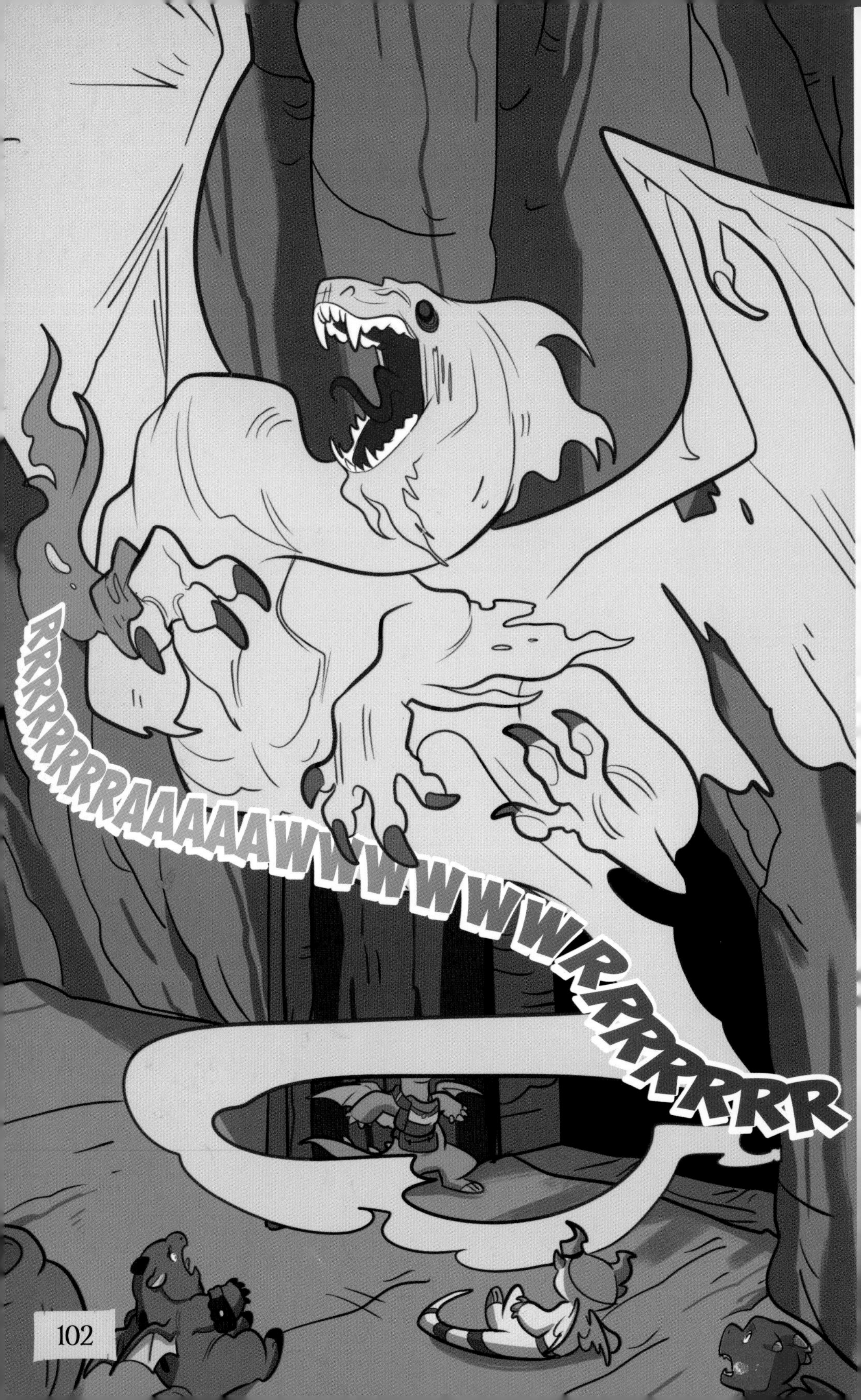
RRRRRRRRRAAAAAAWWWWWWRRRRRRR

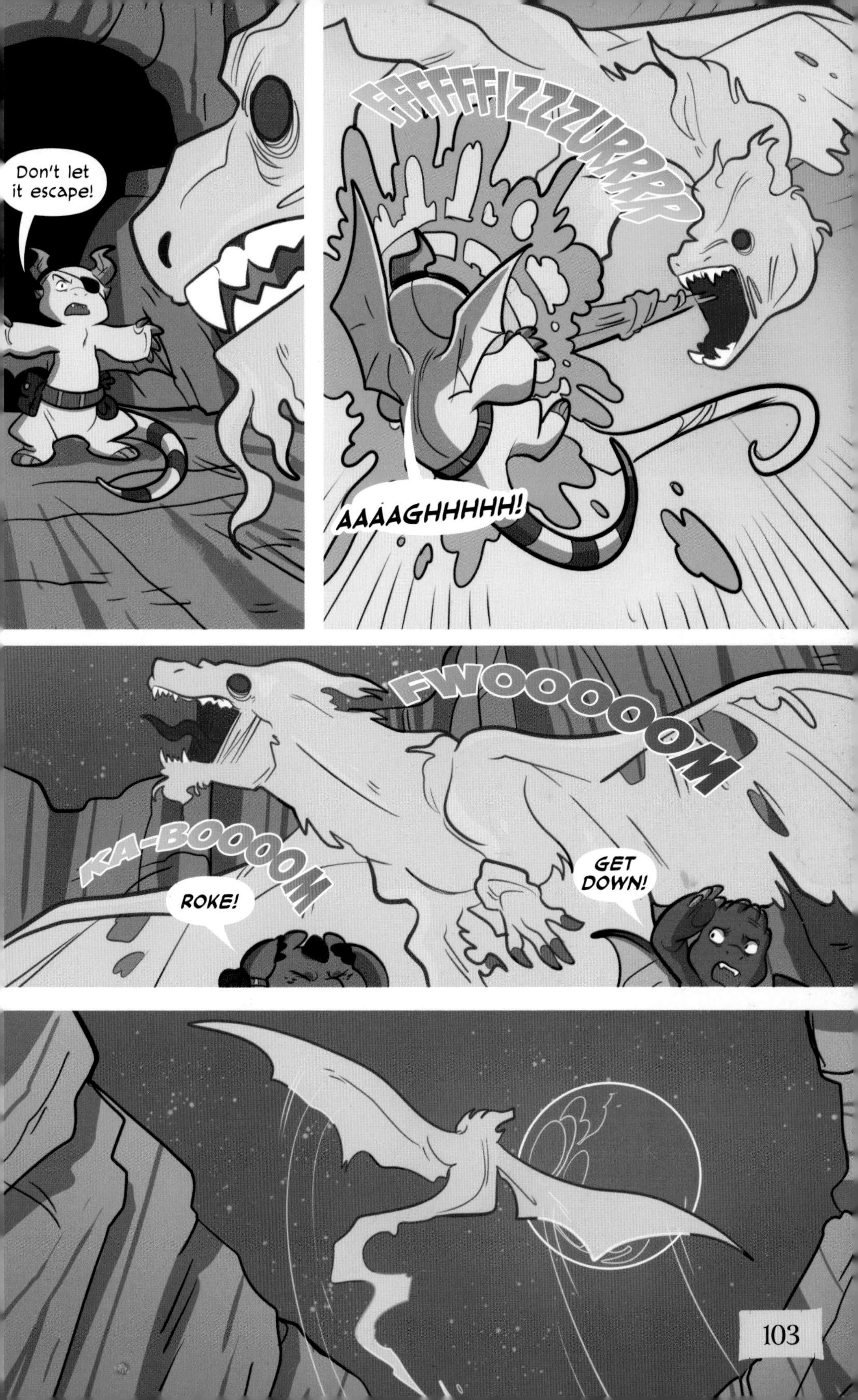

Don't let it escape!
FFFFFFIZZZURRRP
AAAAGHHHHH!
FWOOOOOOM
KA-BOOOOOM
ROKE!
GET DOWN!

Chapter 8

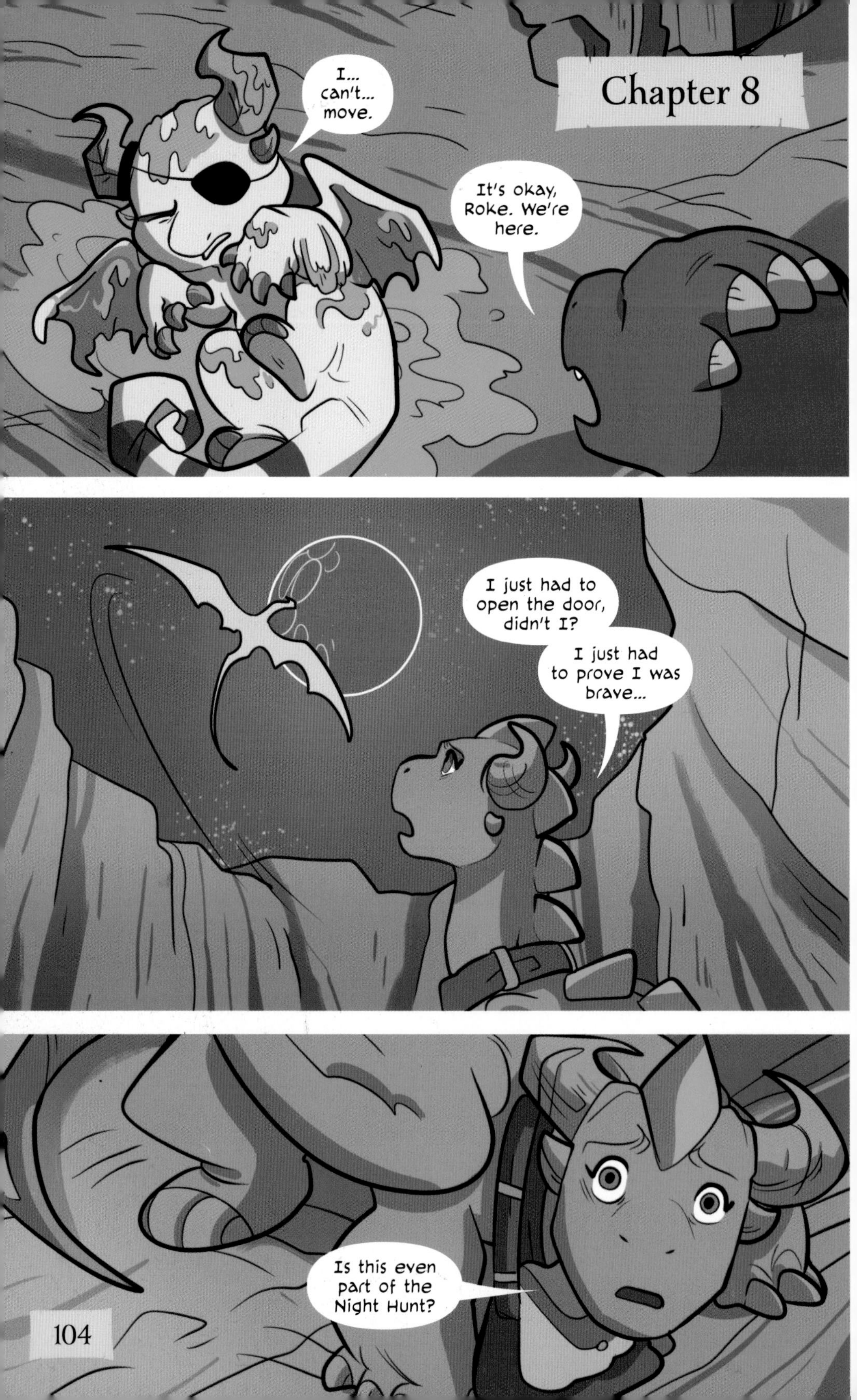

I... can't... move.
It's okay, Roke. We're here.
I just had to open the door, didn't I?
I just had to prove I was brave...
Is this even part of the Night Hunt?

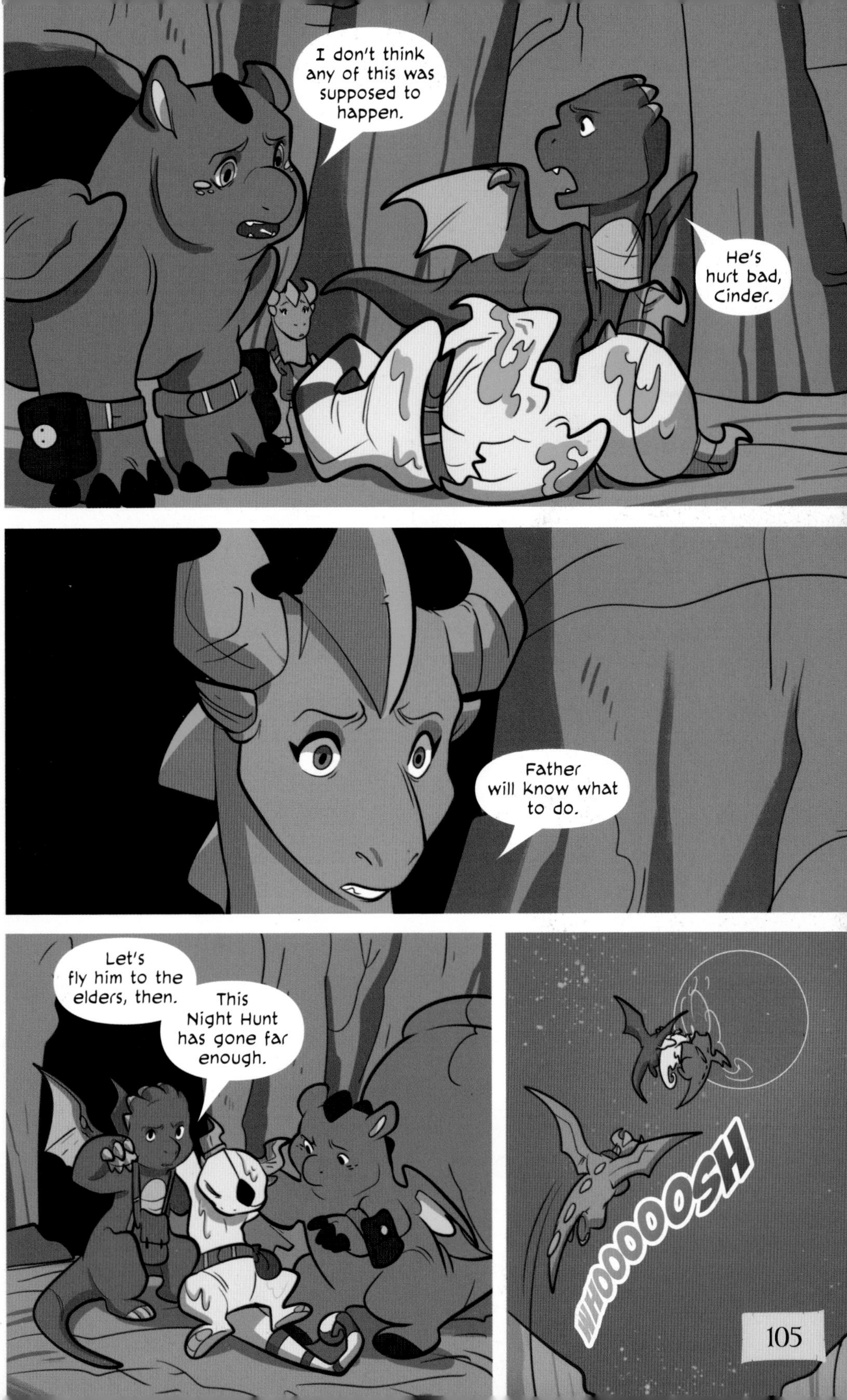
I don't think any of this was supposed to happen.
He's hurt bad, Cinder.
Father will know what to do.
Let's fly him to the elders, then.
This Night Hunt has gone far enough.
WHOOOOOOSH

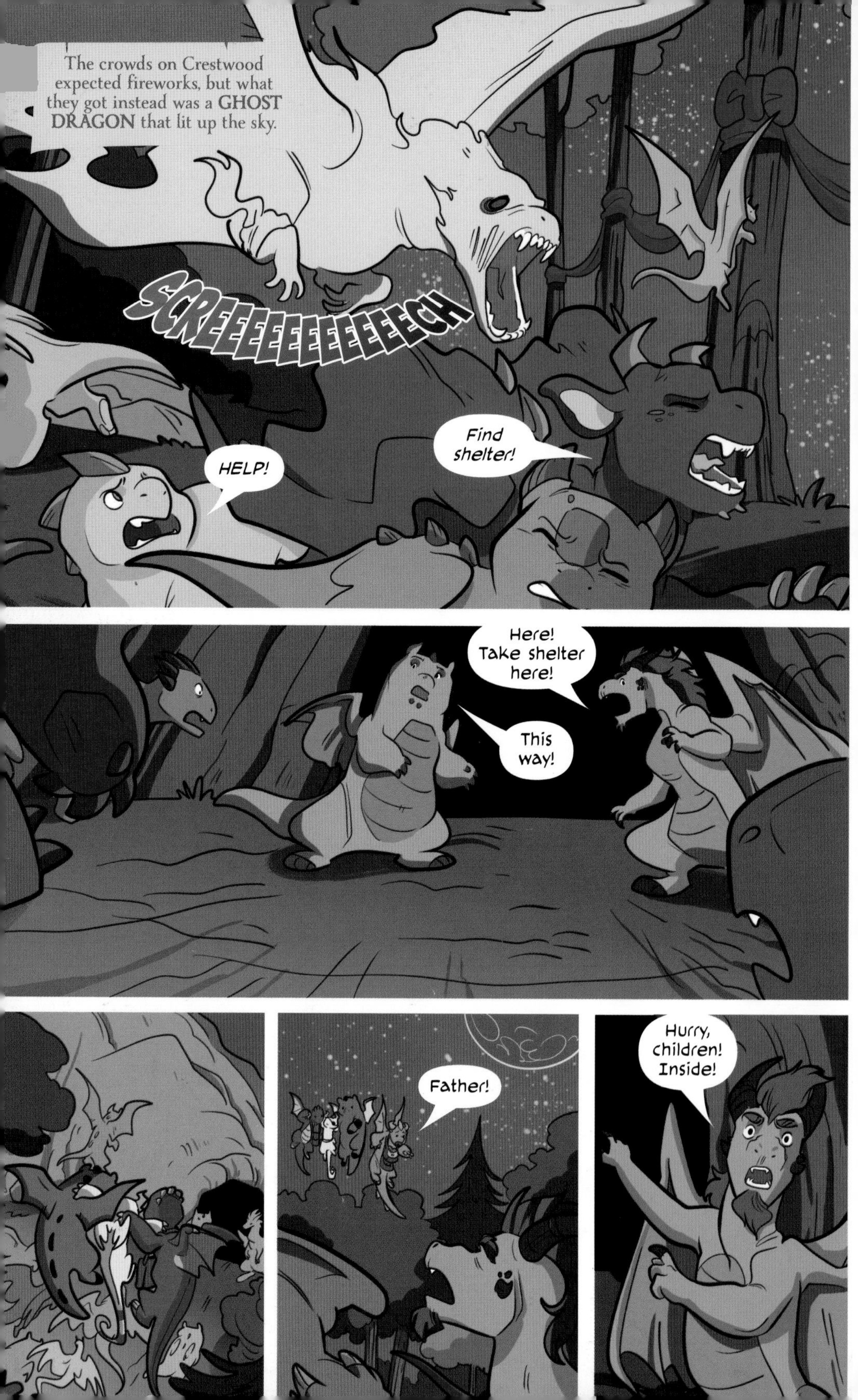
The crowds on Crestwood expected fireworks, but what they got instead was a GHOST DRAGON that lit up the sky.
SCREEEEEEEEEEEECH
Find shelter!
HELP!
Here! Take shelter here!
This way!
Father!
Hurry, children! Inside!

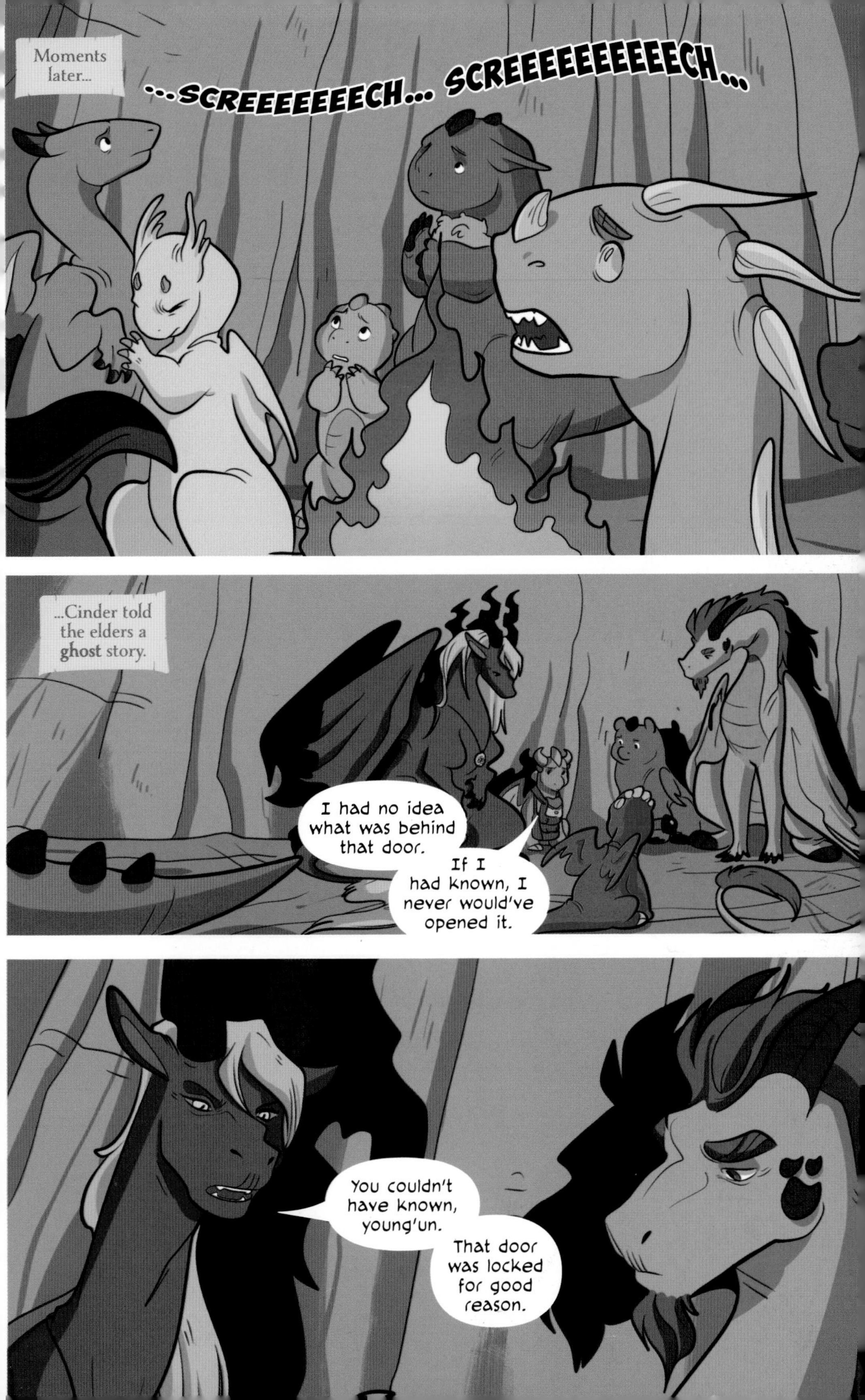
Moments later...
...SCREEEEEEEECH... SCREEEEEEEEEEECH...
...Cinder told the elders a ghost story.
I had no idea what was behind that door.
If I had known, I never would've opened it.
You couldn't have known, young'un.
That door was locked for good reason.

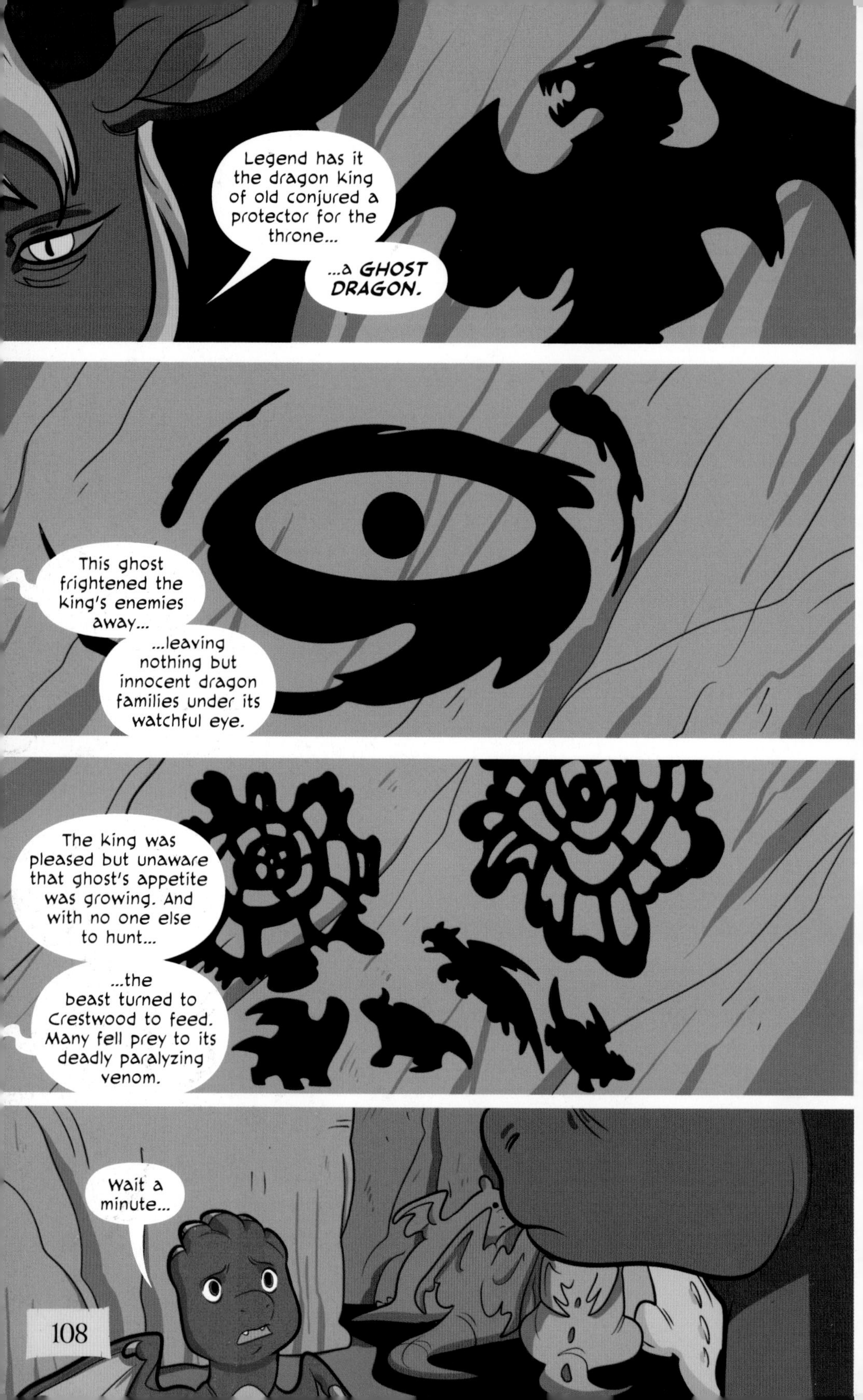
Legend has it the dragon king of old conjured a protector for the throne...
...a GHOST DRAGON.
This ghost frightened the king's enemies away...
...leaving nothing but innocent dragon families under its watchful eye.
The king was pleased but unaware that ghost's appetite was growing. And with no one else to hunt...
...the beast turned to Crestwood to feed. Many fell prey to its deadly paralyzing venom.
Wait a minute...

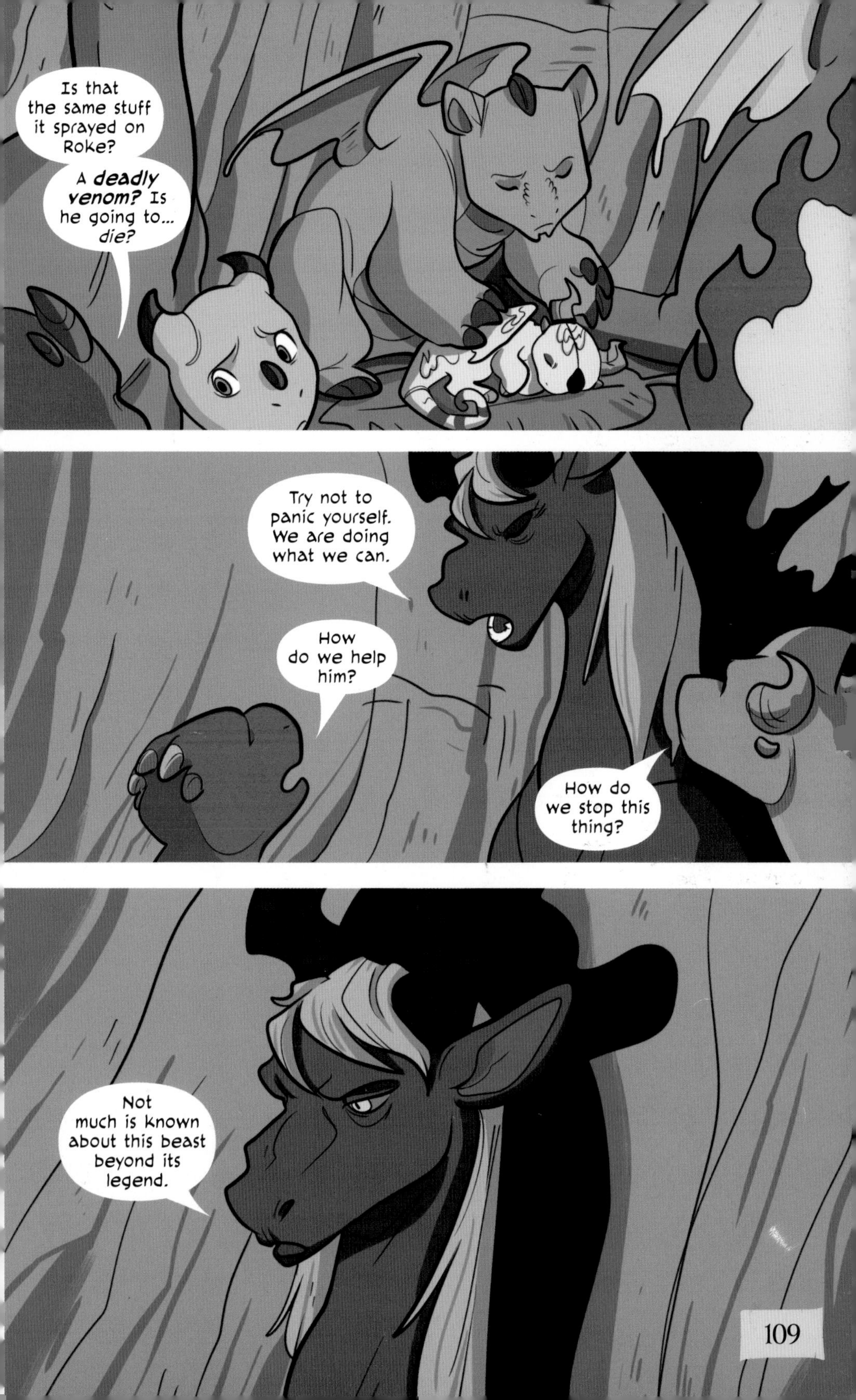
Is that the same stuff it sprayed on Roke?
A **deadly venom?** Is he going to... *die?*
Try not to panic yourself. We are doing what we can.
How do we help him?
How do we stop this thing?
Not much is known about this beast beyond its legend.

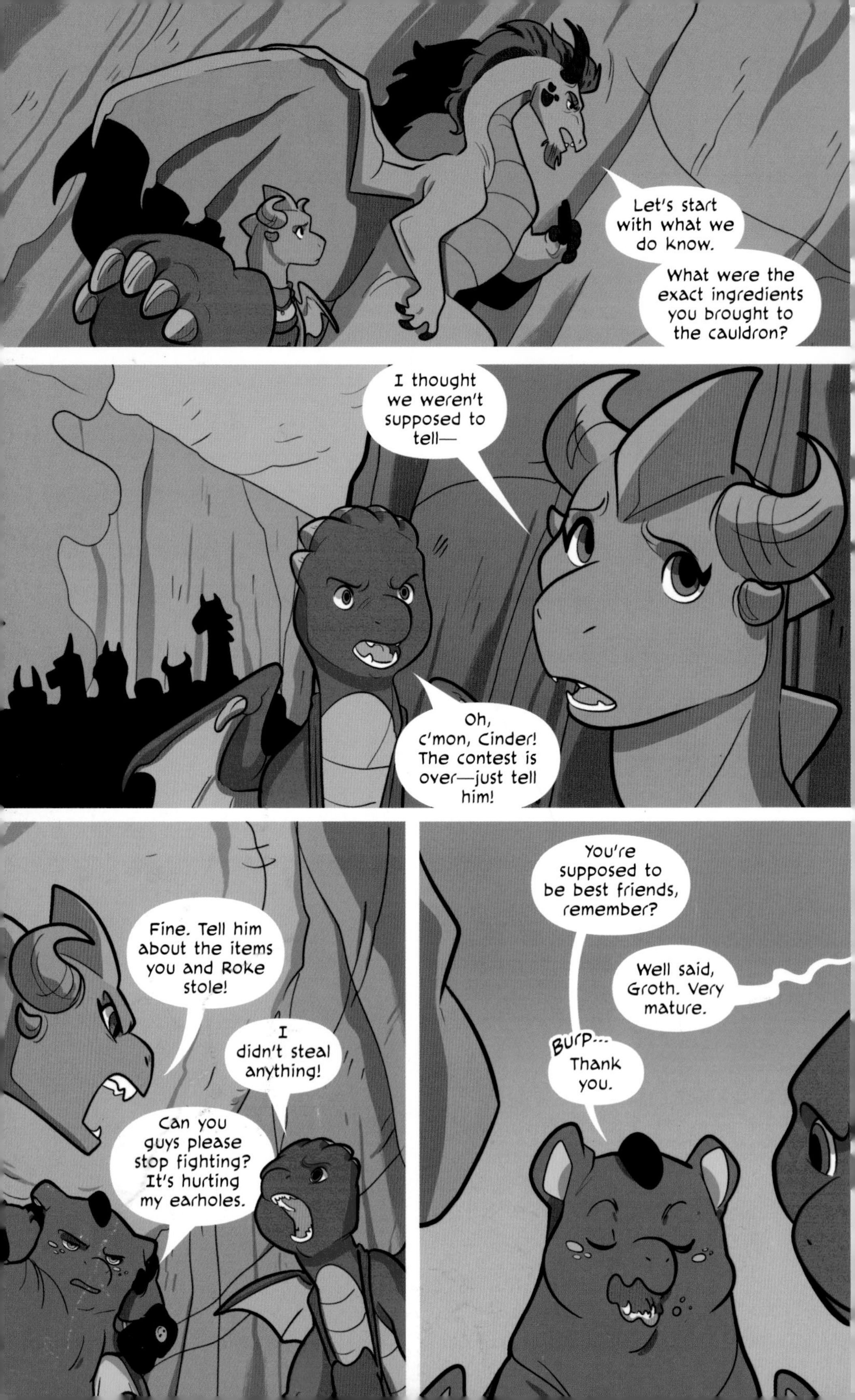
Let's start with what we do know.
What were the exact ingredients you brought to the cauldron?
I thought we weren't supposed to tell—
Oh, c'mon, Cinder! The contest is over—just tell him!
Fine. Tell him about the items you and Roke stole!
I didn't steal anything!
Can you guys please stop fighting? It's hurting my earholes.
You're supposed to be best friends, remember?
Well said, Groth. Very mature.
BURP...
Thank you.

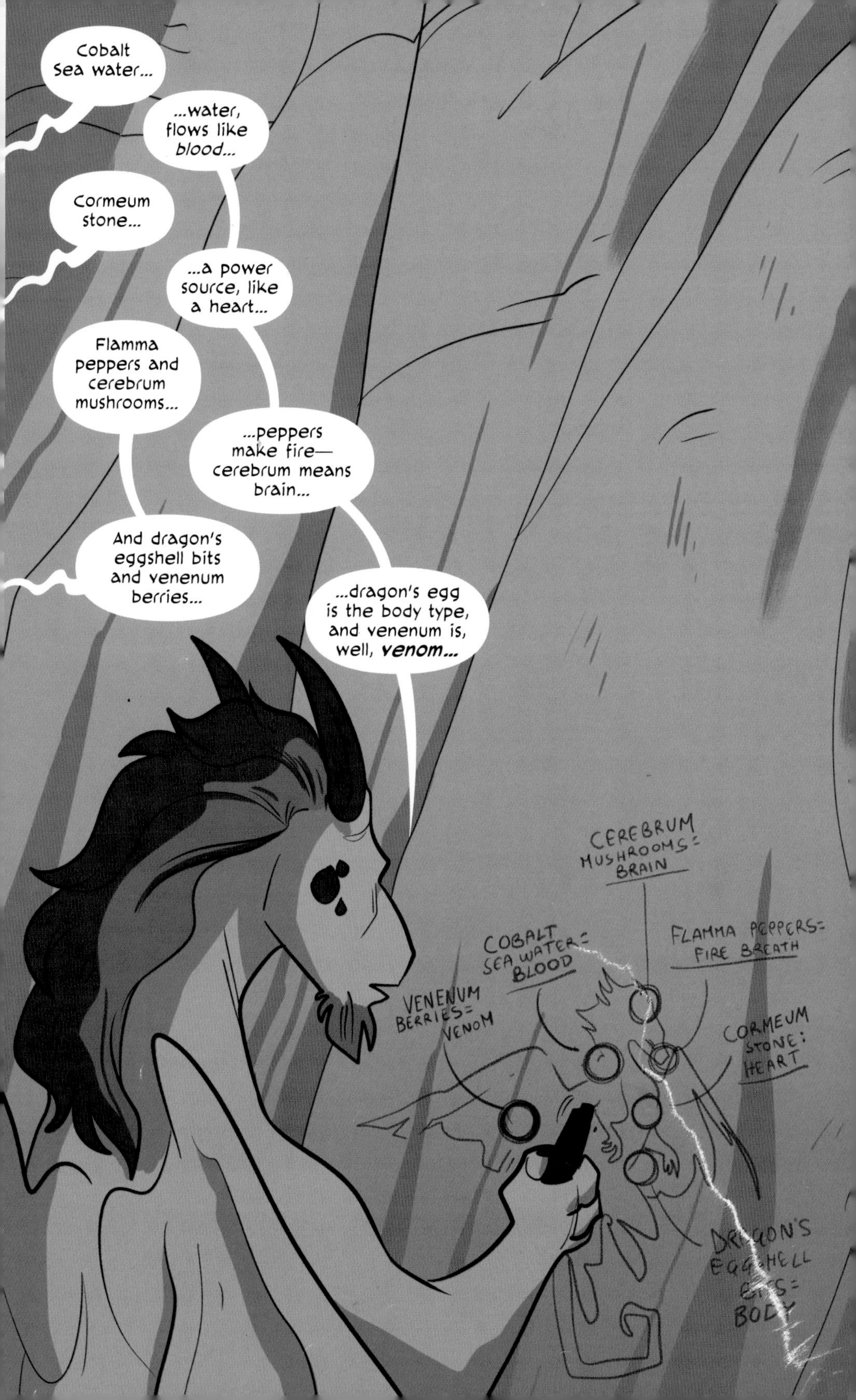
Cobalt Sea water...
...water, flows like *blood*...
Cormeum stone...
...a power source, like a heart...
Flamma peppers and cerebrum mushrooms...
...peppers make fire—cerebrum means brain...
And dragon's eggshell bits and venenum berries...
...dragon's egg is the body type, and venenum is, well, ***venom...***
CEREBRUM MUSHROOMS= BRAIN
COBALT SEA WATER= BLOOD
FLAMMA PEPPERS= FIRE BREATH
VENENUM BERRIES= VENOM
CORMEUM STONE: HEART

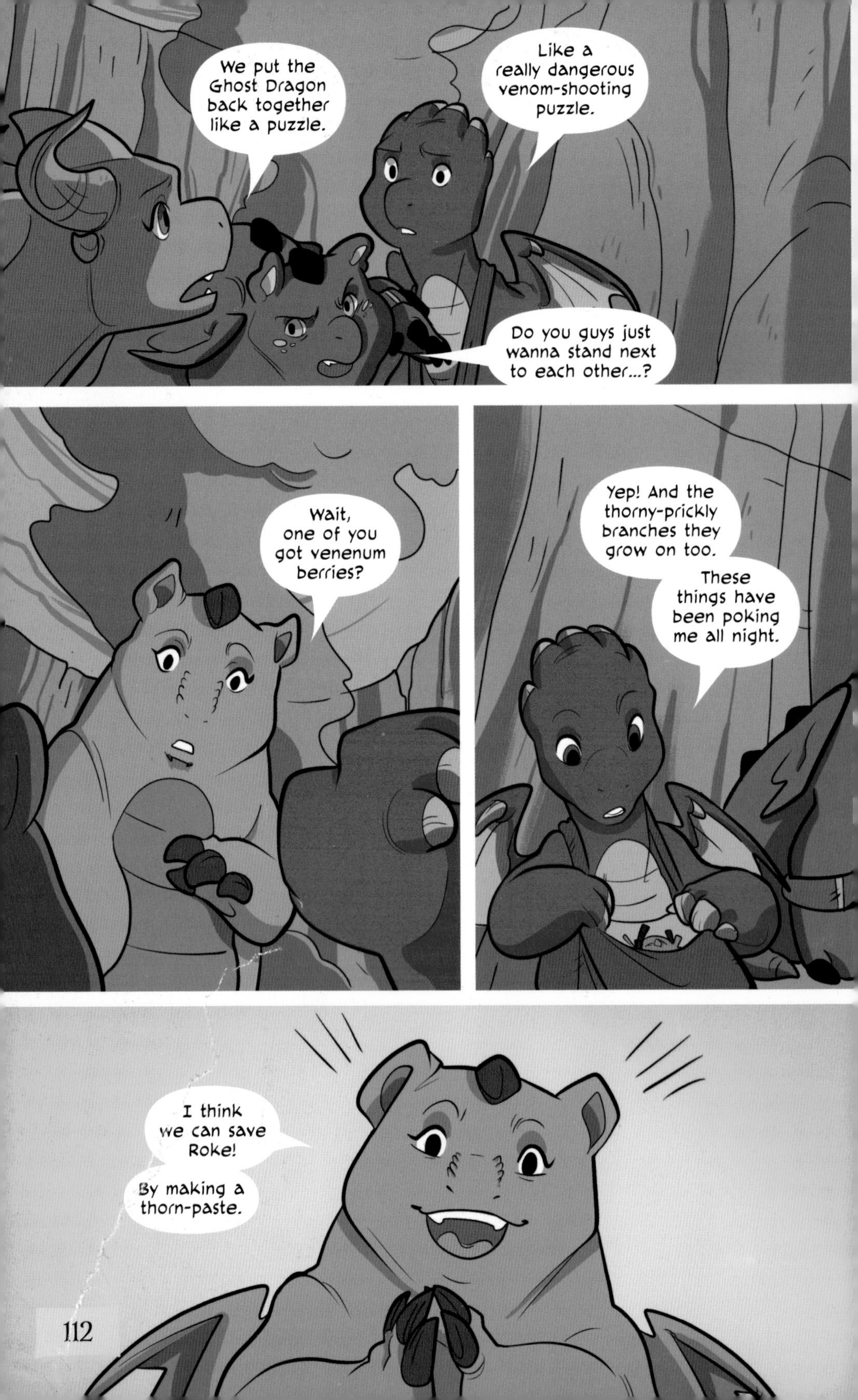
We put the Ghost Dragon back together like a puzzle.
Like a really dangerous venom-shooting puzzle.
Do you guys just wanna stand next to each other...?
Wait, one of you got venenum berries?
Yep! And the thorny-prickly branches they grow on too.
These things have been poking me all night.
I think we can save Roke!
By making a thorn-paste.

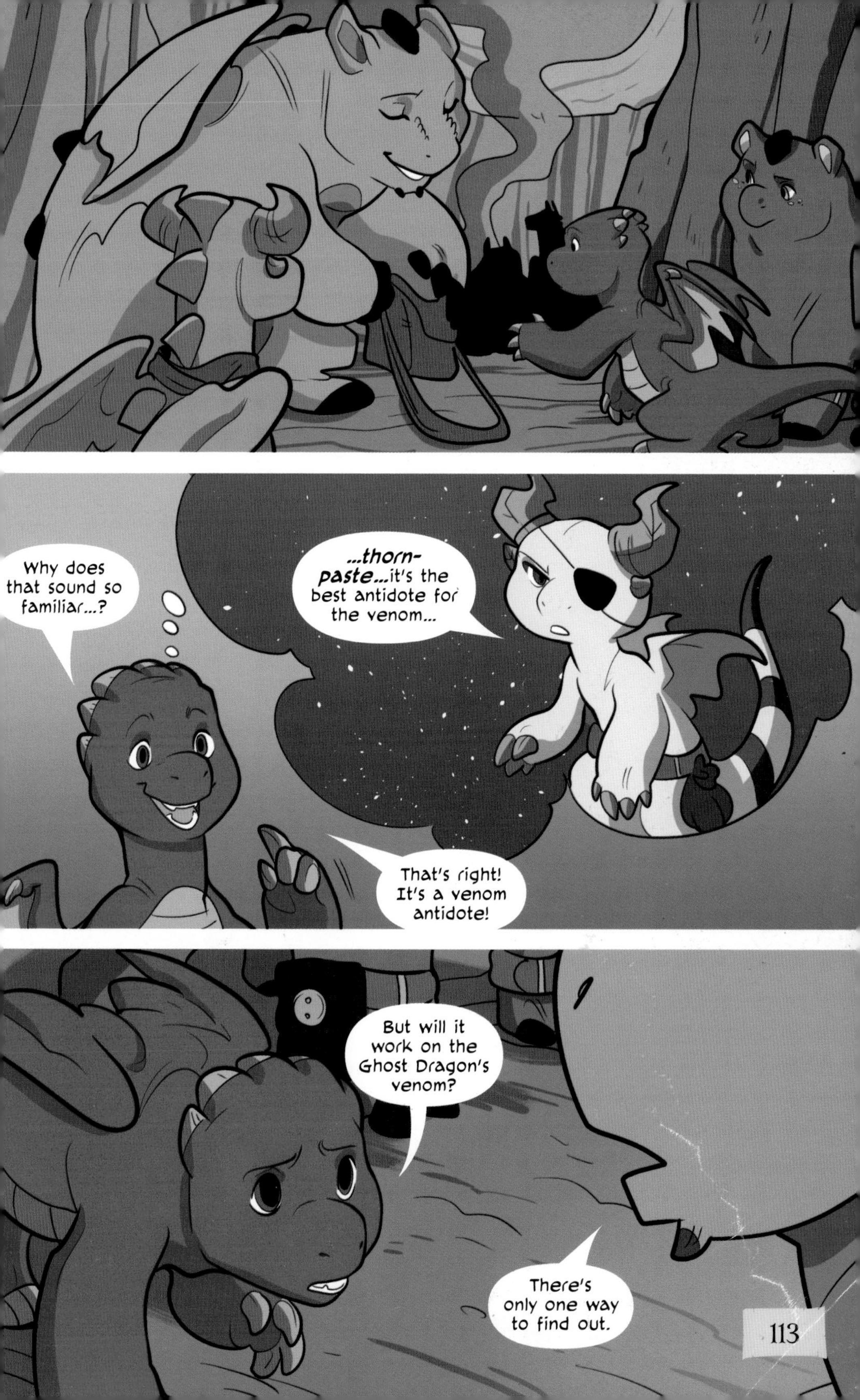
Why does that sound so familiar...?
...thorn-paste...it's the best antidote for the venom...
That's right! It's a venom antidote!
But will it work on the Ghost Dragon's venom?
There's only one way to find out.

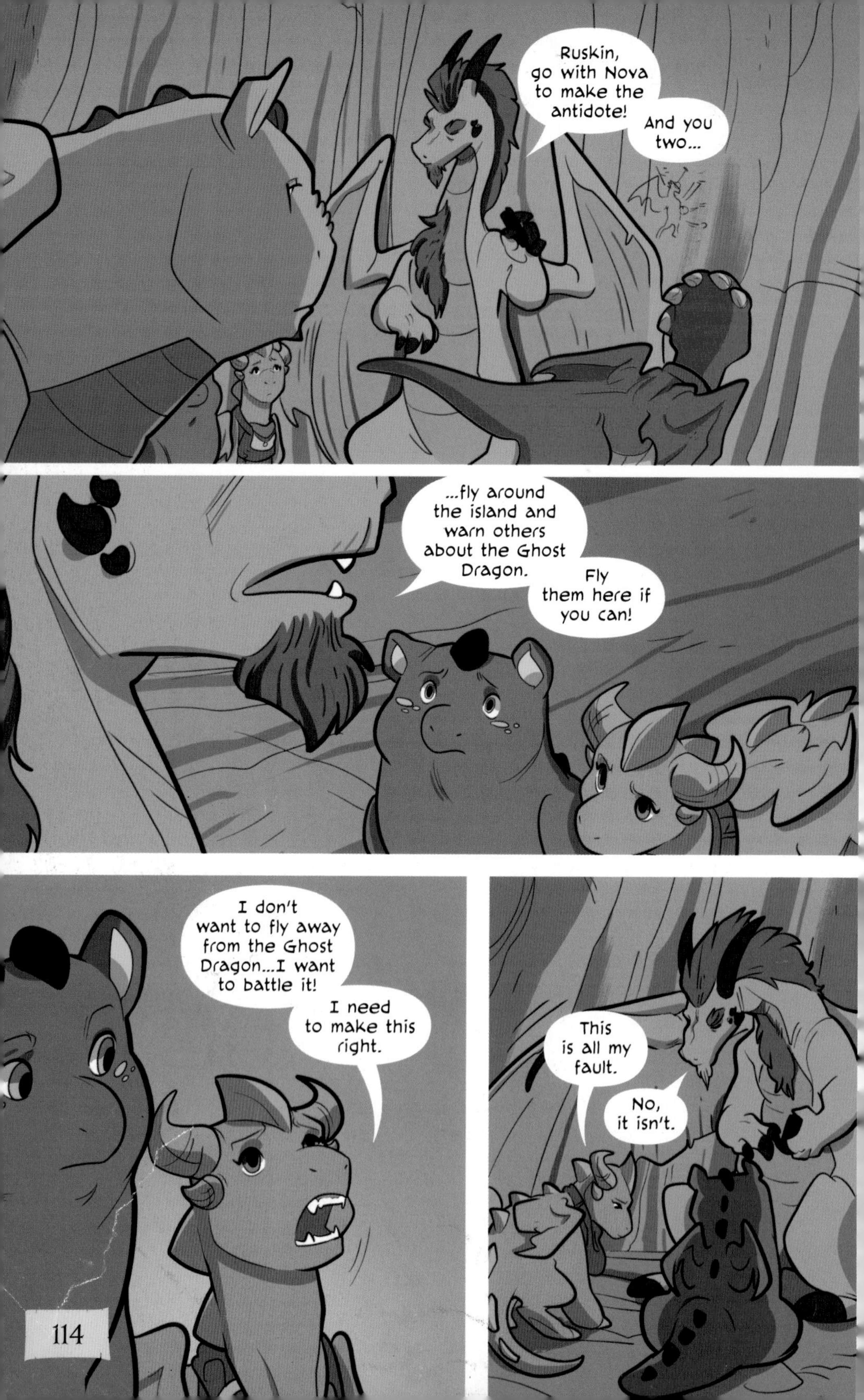
Ruskin, go with Nova to make the antidote!
And you two...
...fly around the island and warn others about the Ghost Dragon.
Fly them here if you can!
I don't want to fly away from the Ghost Dragon...I want to battle it!
I need to make this right.
This is all my fault.
No, it isn't.

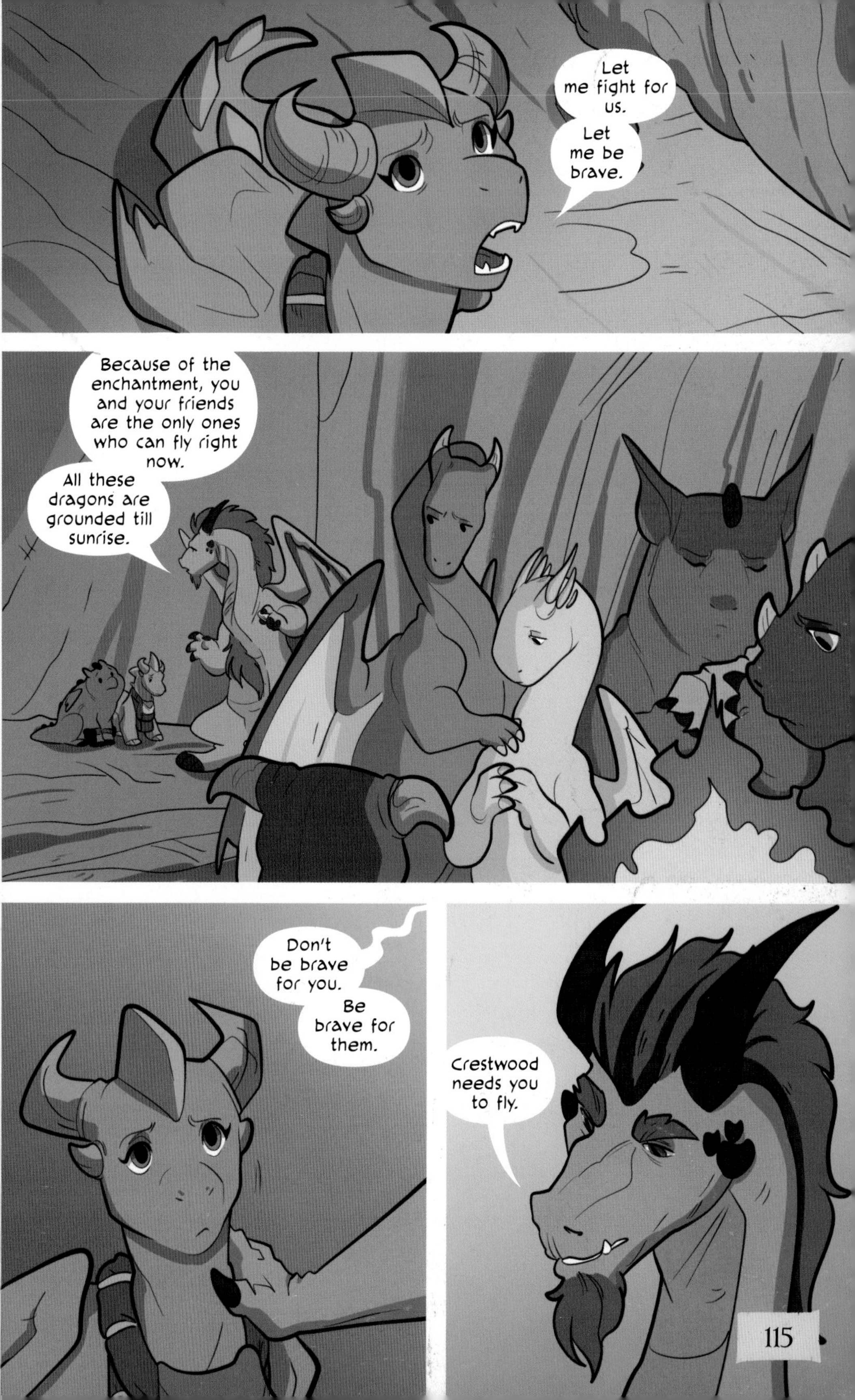

Let me fight for us.
Let me be brave.
Because of the enchantment, you and your friends are the only ones who can fly right now.
All these dragons are grounded till sunrise.
Don't be brave for you.
Be brave for them.
Crestwood needs you to fly.

Chapter 9

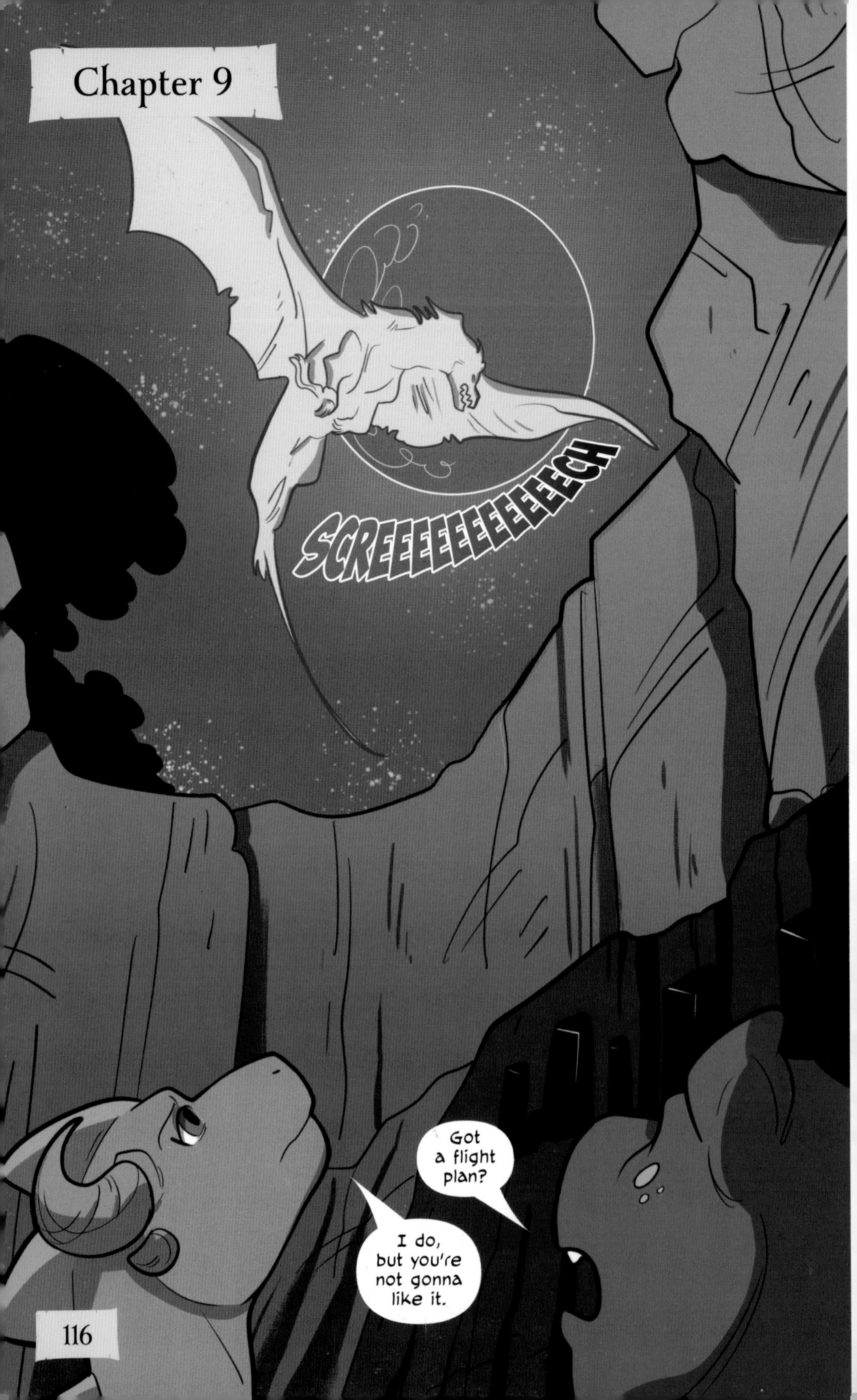
SCREEEEEEEEEEEECH
Got a flight plan?
I do, but you're not gonna like it.

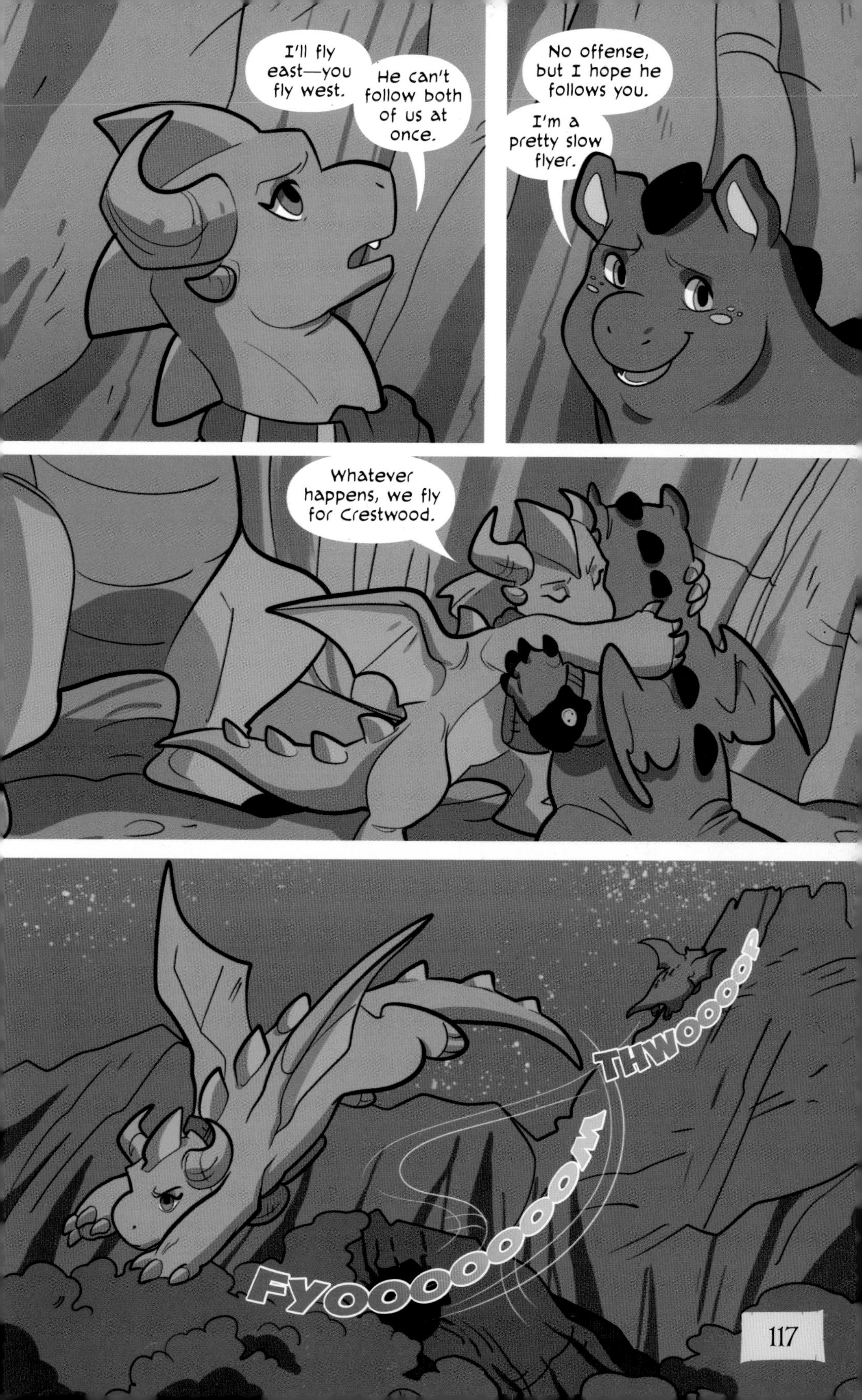

I'll fly east—you fly west.
He can't follow both of us at once.
No offense, but I hope he follows you.
I'm a pretty slow flyer.
Whatever happens, we fly for Crestwood.
THWOOOOOP
FYOOOOOOOOOM

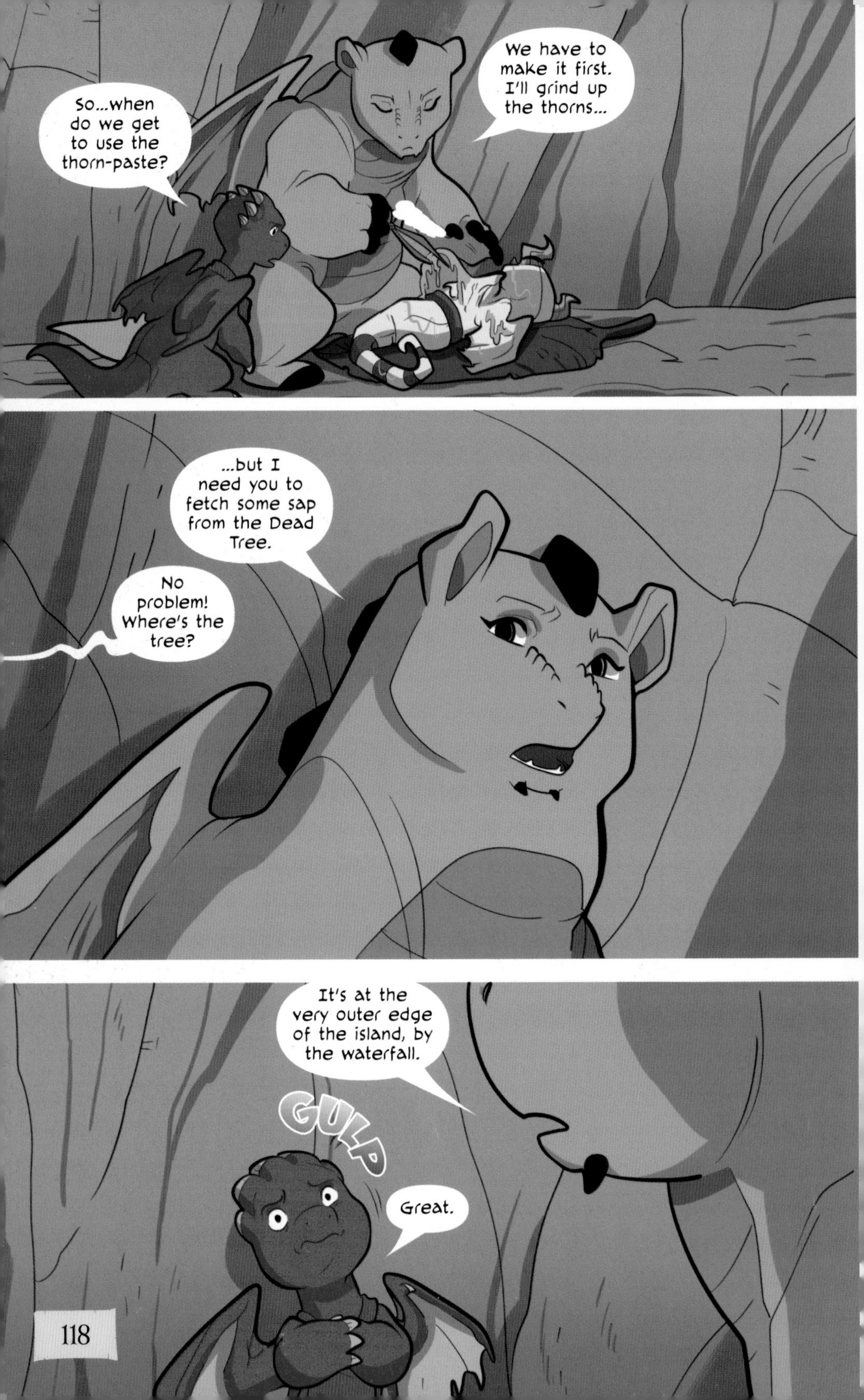
So...when do we get to use the thorn-paste?
We have to make it first. I'll grind up the thorns...
...but I need you to fetch some sap from the Dead Tree.
No problem! Where's the tree?
It's at the very outer edge of the island, by the waterfall.
GULP
Great.

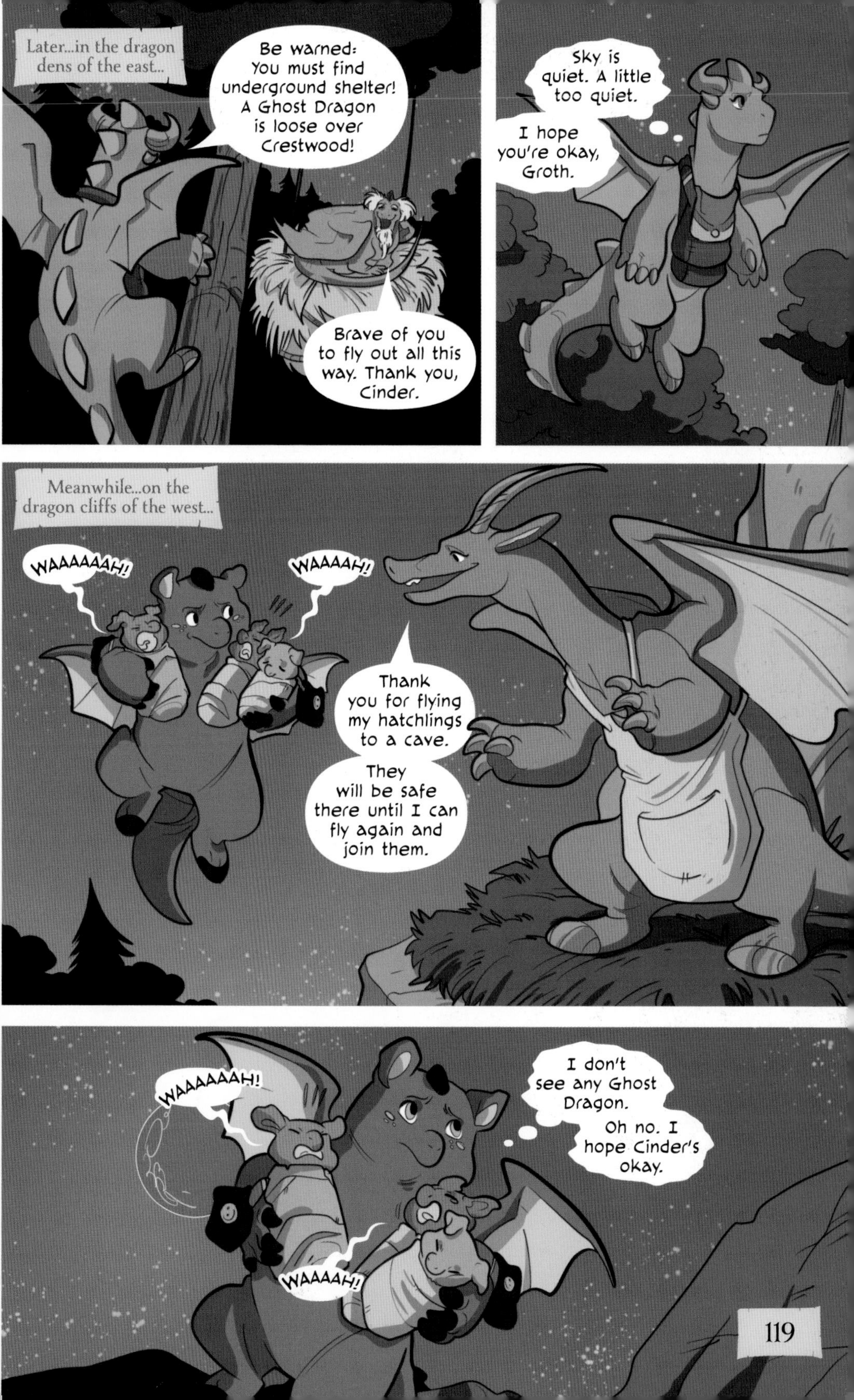
Later...in the dragon dens of the east...
Be warned: You must find underground shelter! A Ghost Dragon is loose over Crestwood!
Brave of you to fly out all this way. Thank you, Cinder.
Sky is quiet. A little too quiet.
I hope you're okay, Groth.
Meanwhile...on the dragon cliffs of the west...
WAAAAAAH!
WAAAAH!
Thank you for flying my hatchlings to a cave.
They will be safe there until I can fly again and join them.
WAAAAAAH!
I don't see any Ghost Dragon.
Oh no. I hope Cinder's okay.
WAAAAH!

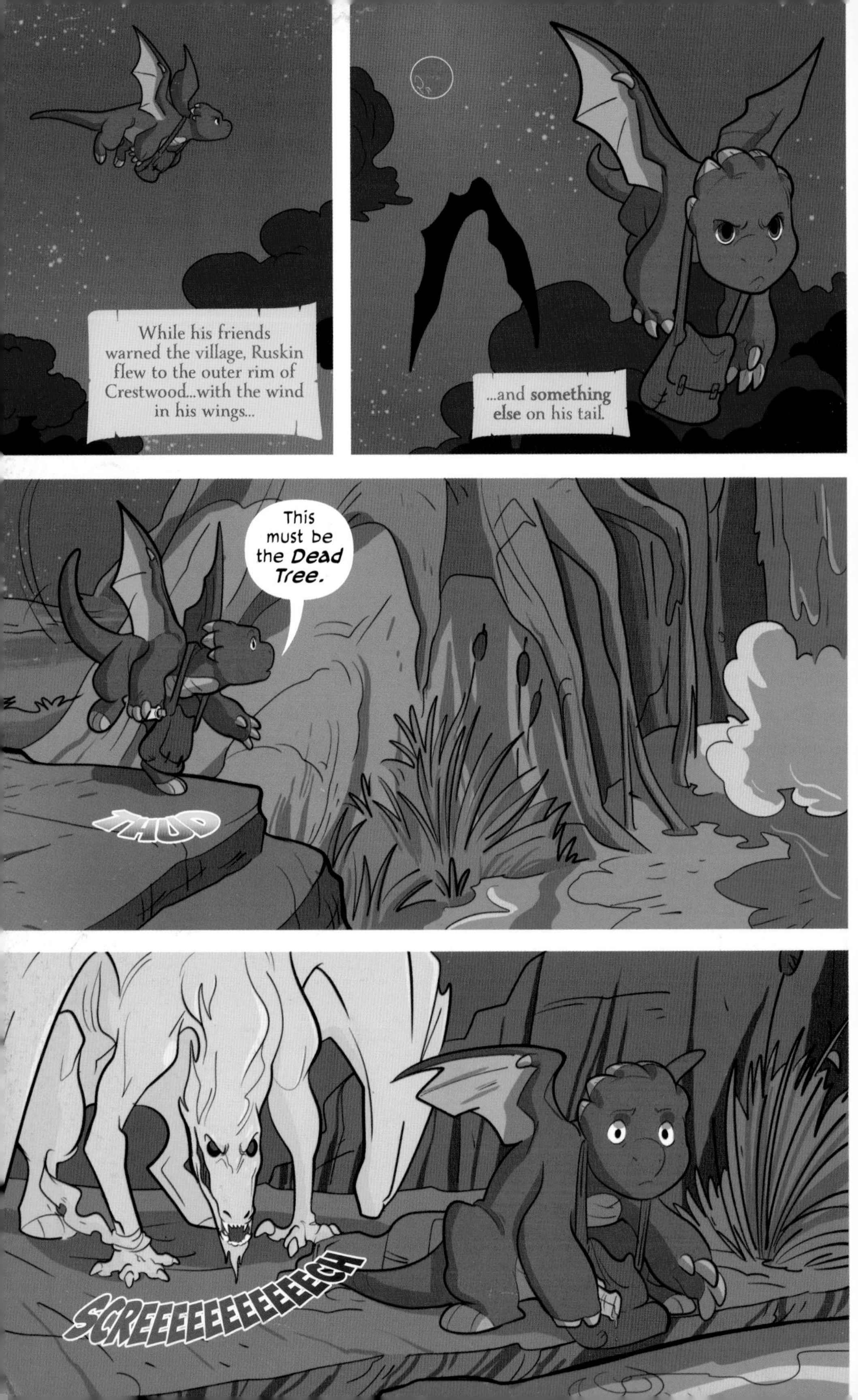
While his friends warned the village, Ruskin flew to the outer rim of Crestwood...with the wind in his wings...
...and something else on his tail.
This must be the Dead Tree.
THUD
SCREEEEEEEEEEECH

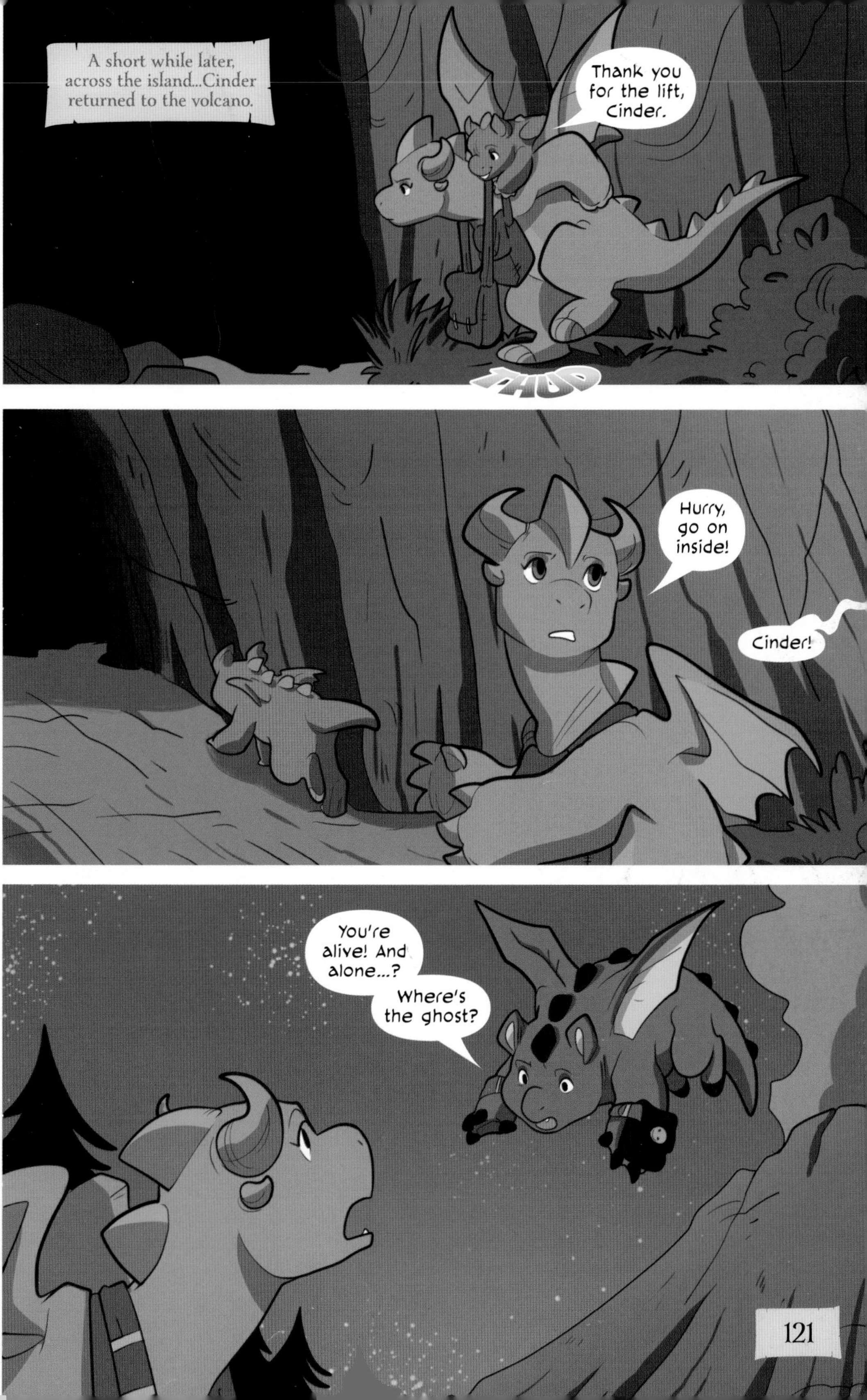
A short while later, across the island...Cinder returned to the volcano.
Thank you for the lift, Cinder.
THUD
Hurry, go on inside!
Cinder!
You're alive! And alone...?
Where's the ghost?

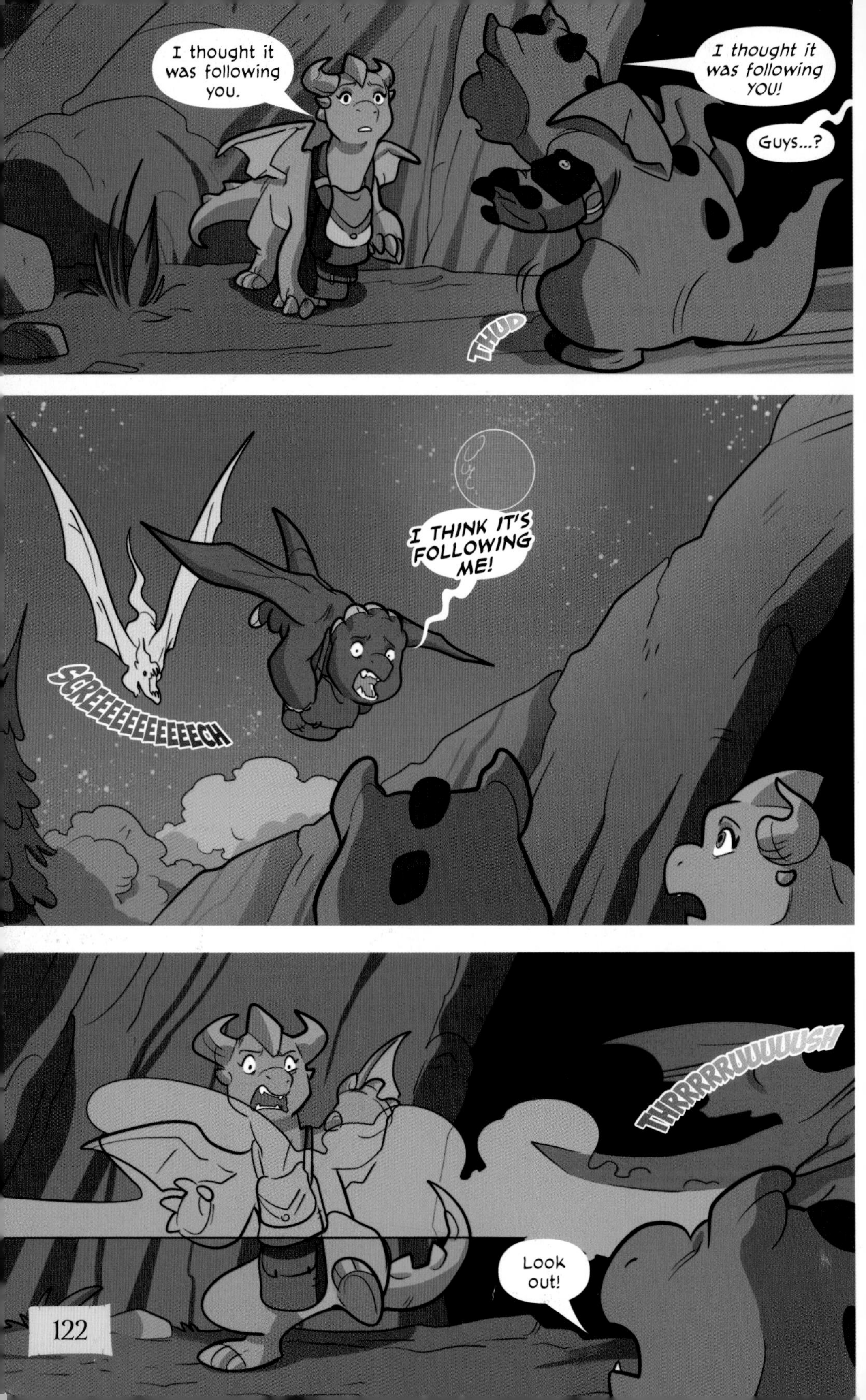
I thought it was following you.
I thought it was following YOU!
Guys...?
THUD
SCREEEEEEEEEEECH
I THINK IT'S FOLLOWING ME!
THRRRRUUUUUSH
Look out!

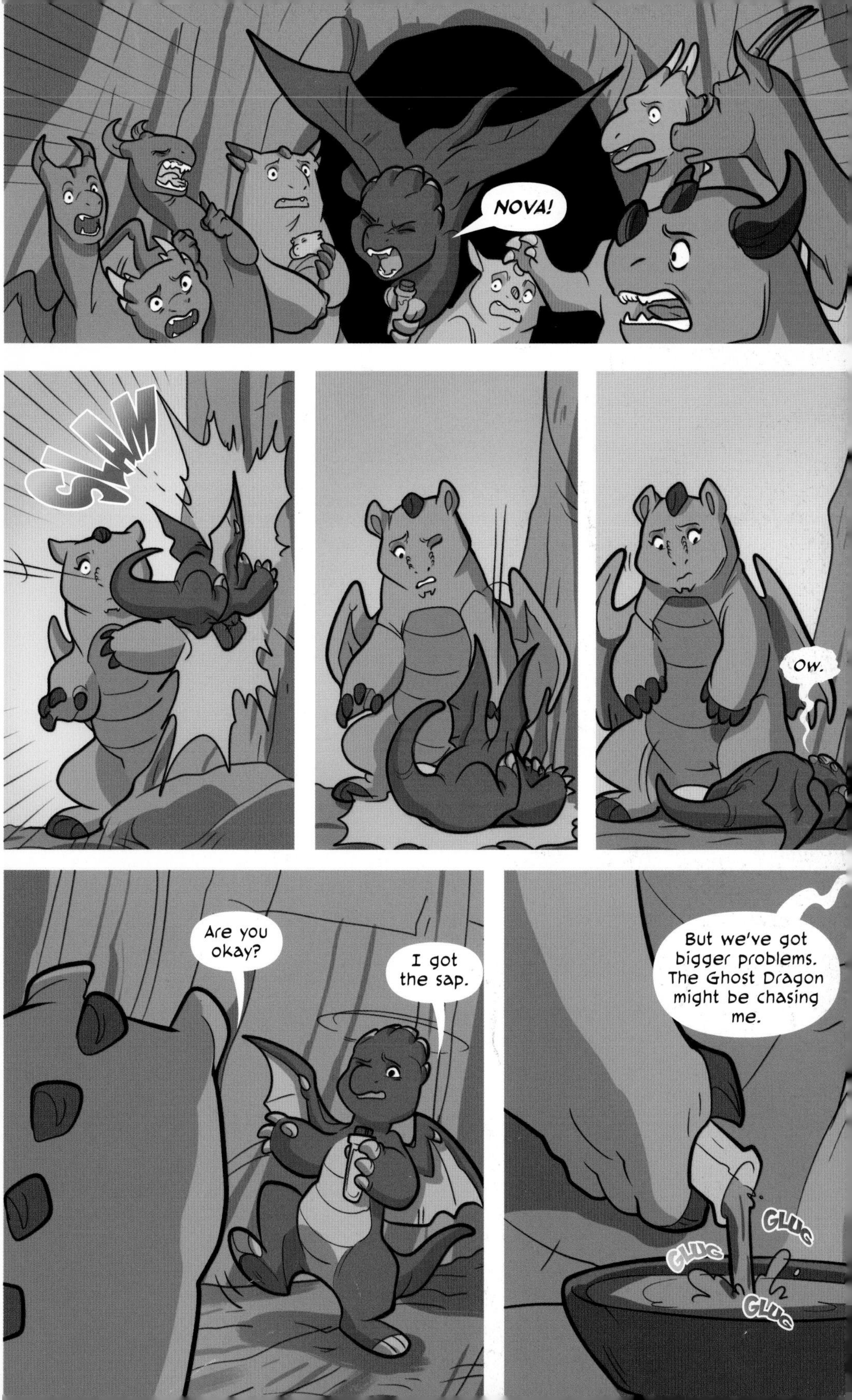
NOVA!
SLAM
Ow.
Are you okay?
I got the sap.
But we've got bigger problems. The Ghost Dragon might be chasing me.
GLUG
GLUG
GLUG

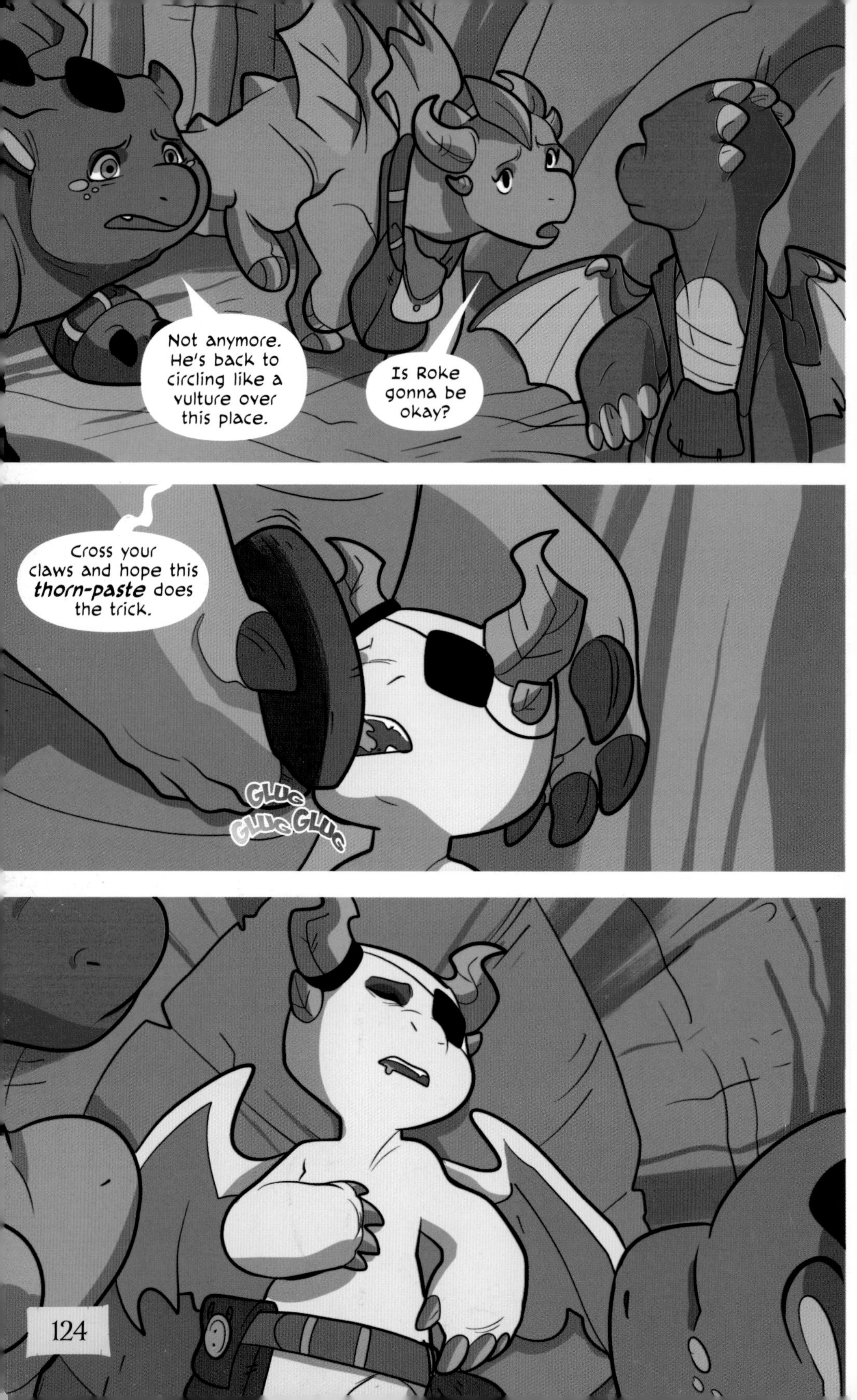
Not anymore. He's back to circling like a vulture over this place.
Is Roke gonna be okay?
Cross your claws and hope this *thorn-paste* does the trick.
GLUG GLUG GLUG

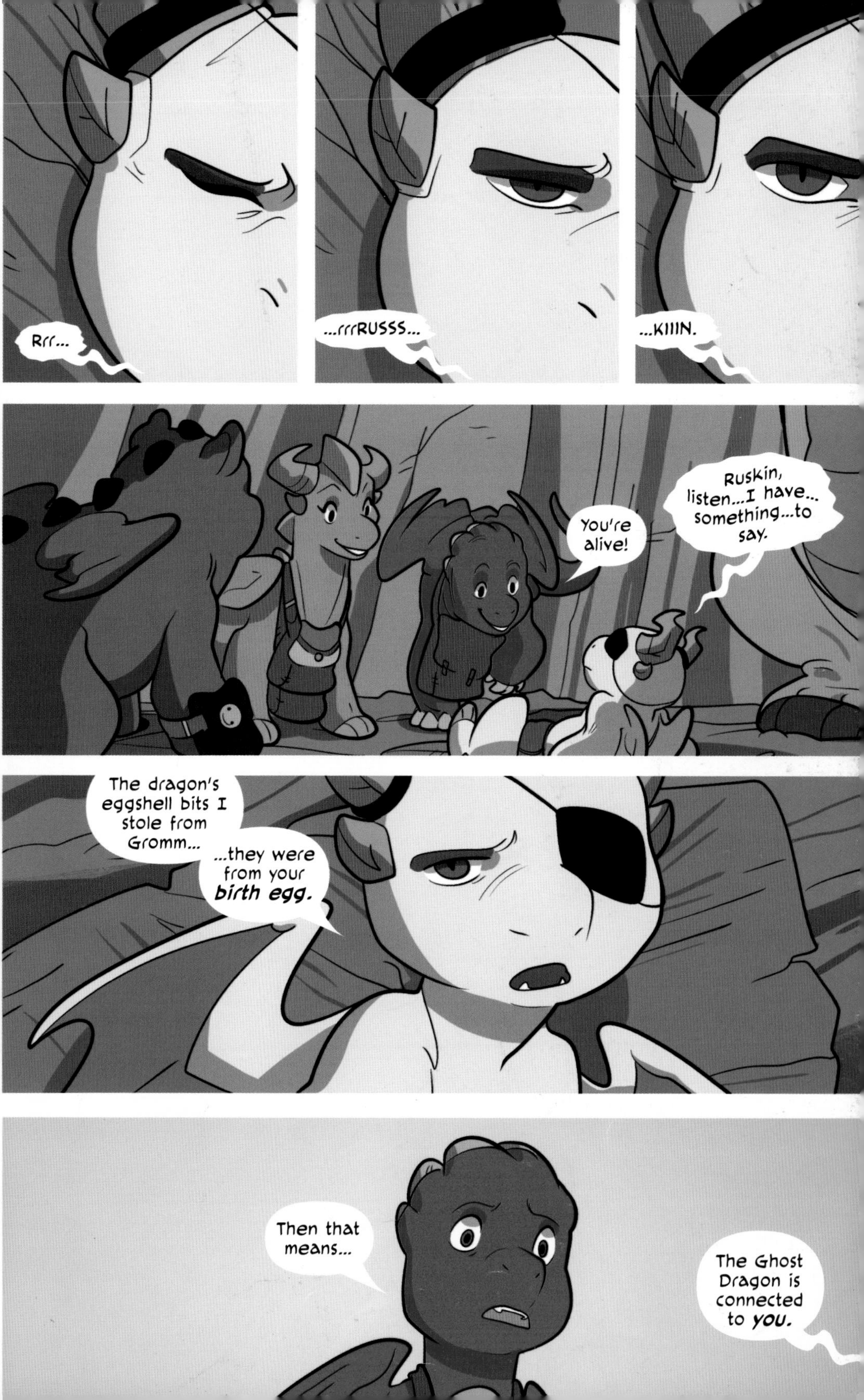
Rrr...
...rrrRUSSS...
...KIIIN.
You're alive!
Ruskin, listen...I have... something...to say.
The dragon's eggshell bits I stole from Gromm...
...they were from your *birth egg.*
Then that means...
The Ghost Dragon is connected to *you.*

Chapter 10

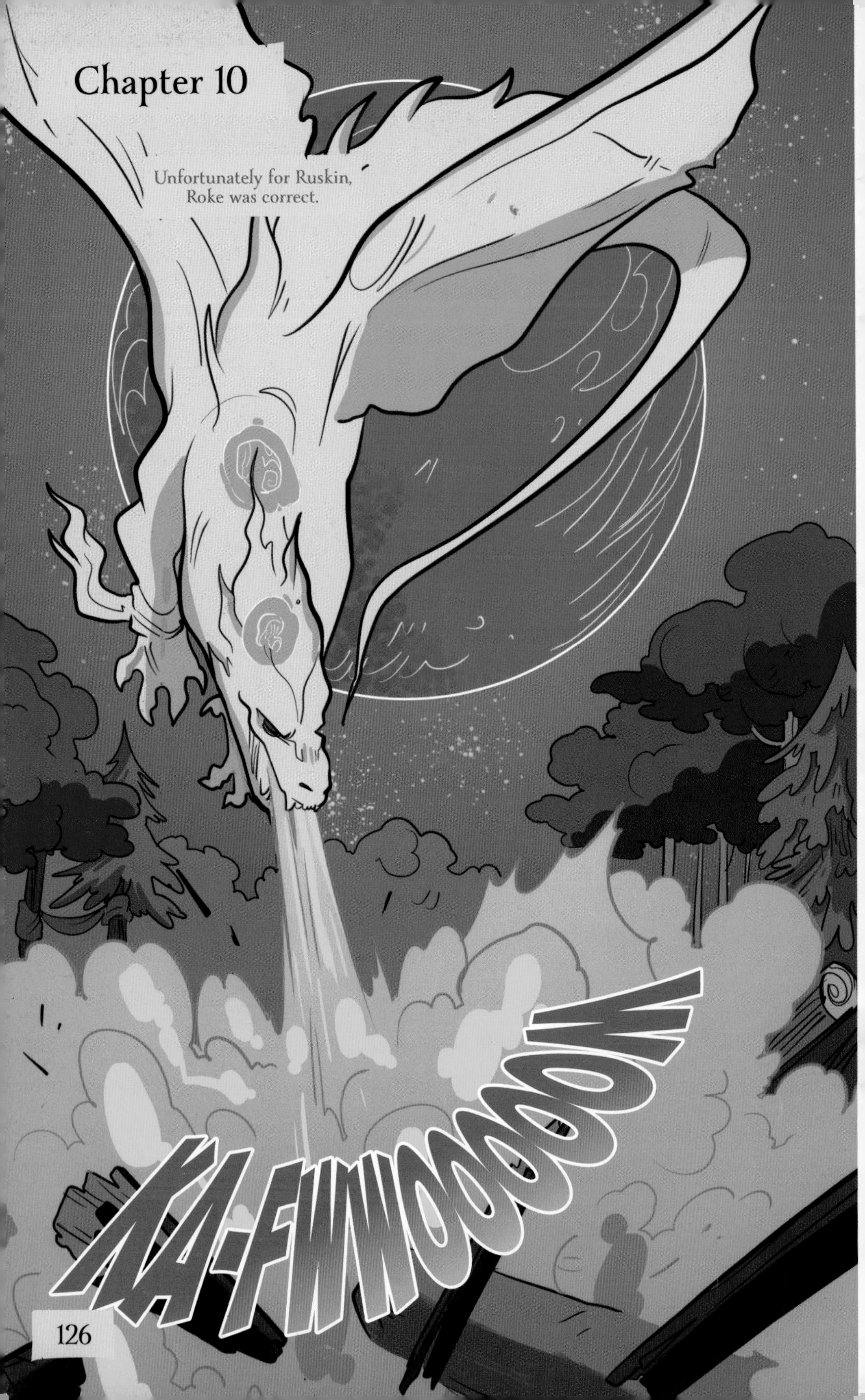
Unfortunately for Ruskin,
Roke was correct.
KA-FWWOOOOOM

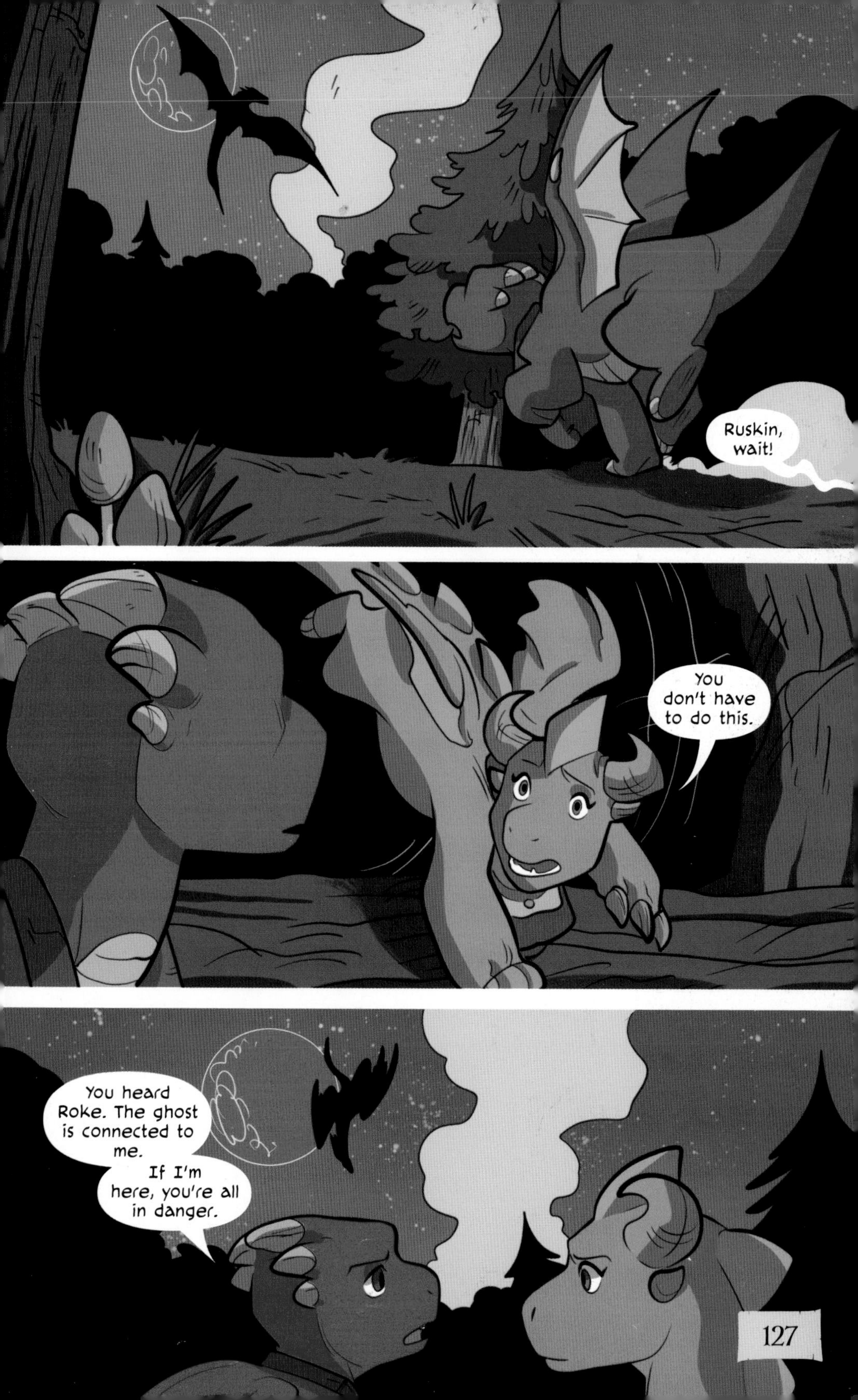
Ruskin, wait!
You don't have to do this.
You heard Roke. The ghost is connected to me.
If I'm here, you're all in danger.

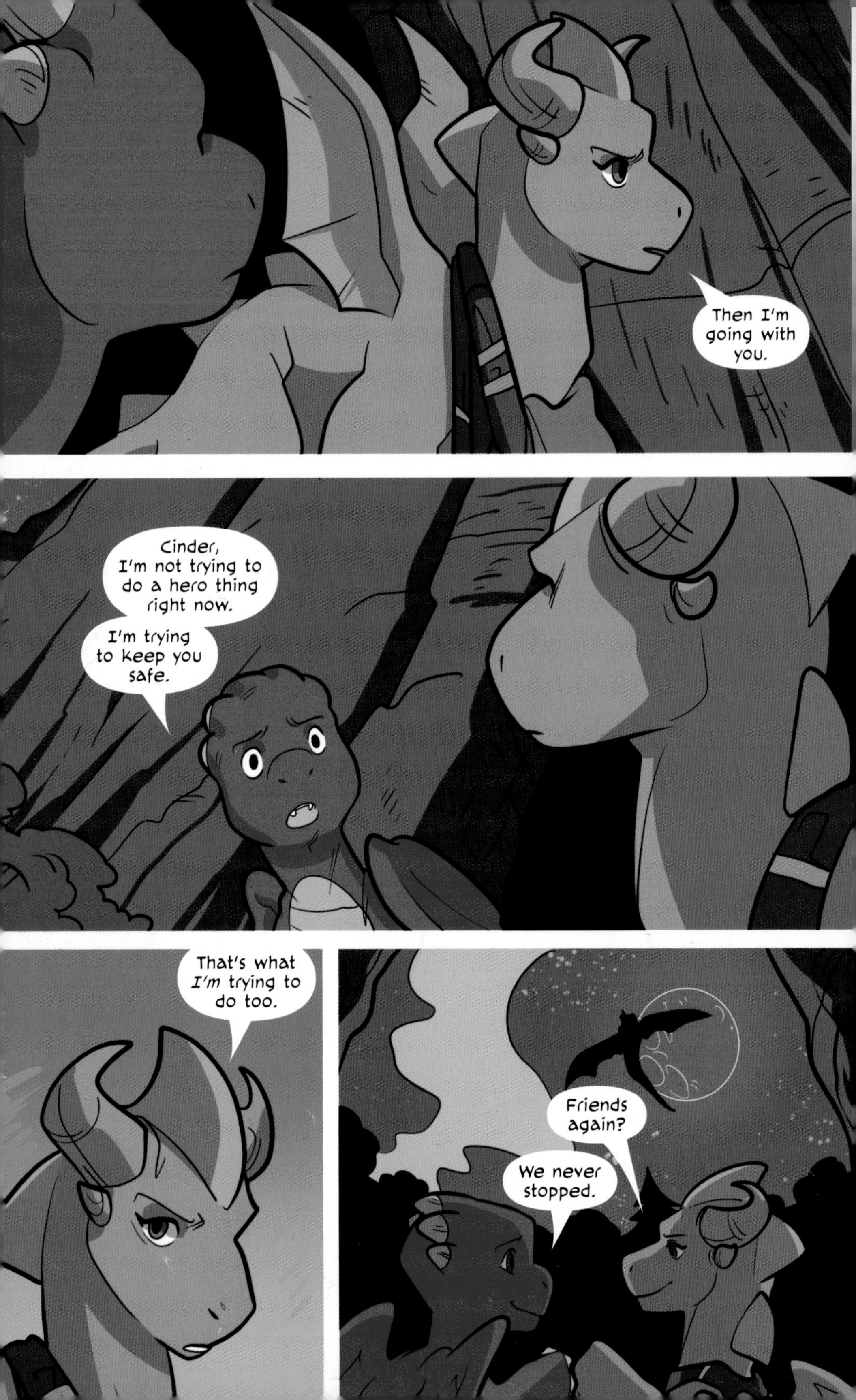
Then I'm going with you.
Cinder, I'm not trying to do a hero thing right now.
I'm trying to keep you safe.
That's what *I'm* trying to do too.
Friends again?
We never stopped.

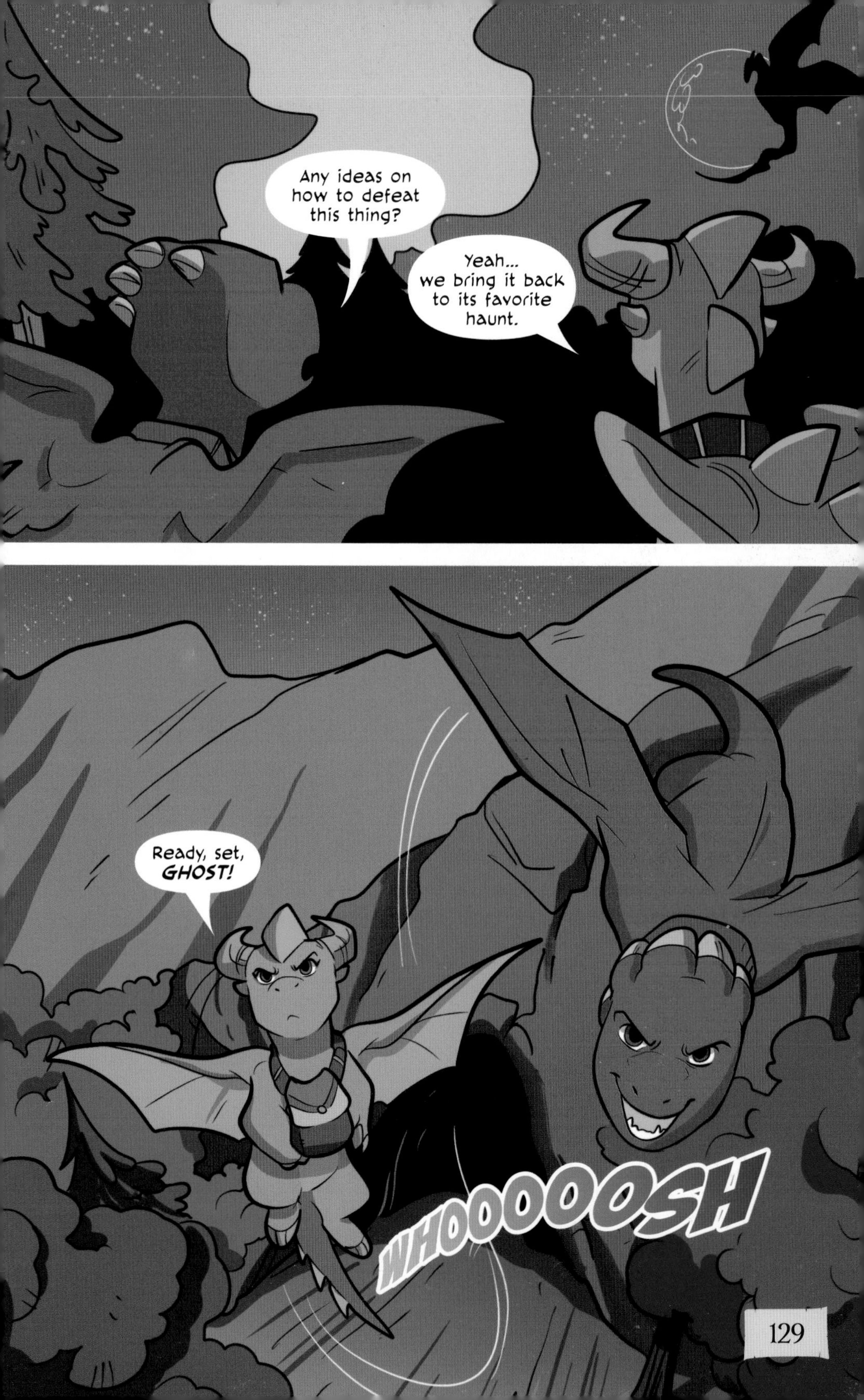

Any ideas on how to defeat this thing?
Yeah... we bring it back to its favorite haunt.
Ready, set, GHOST!
WHOOOOOOSH

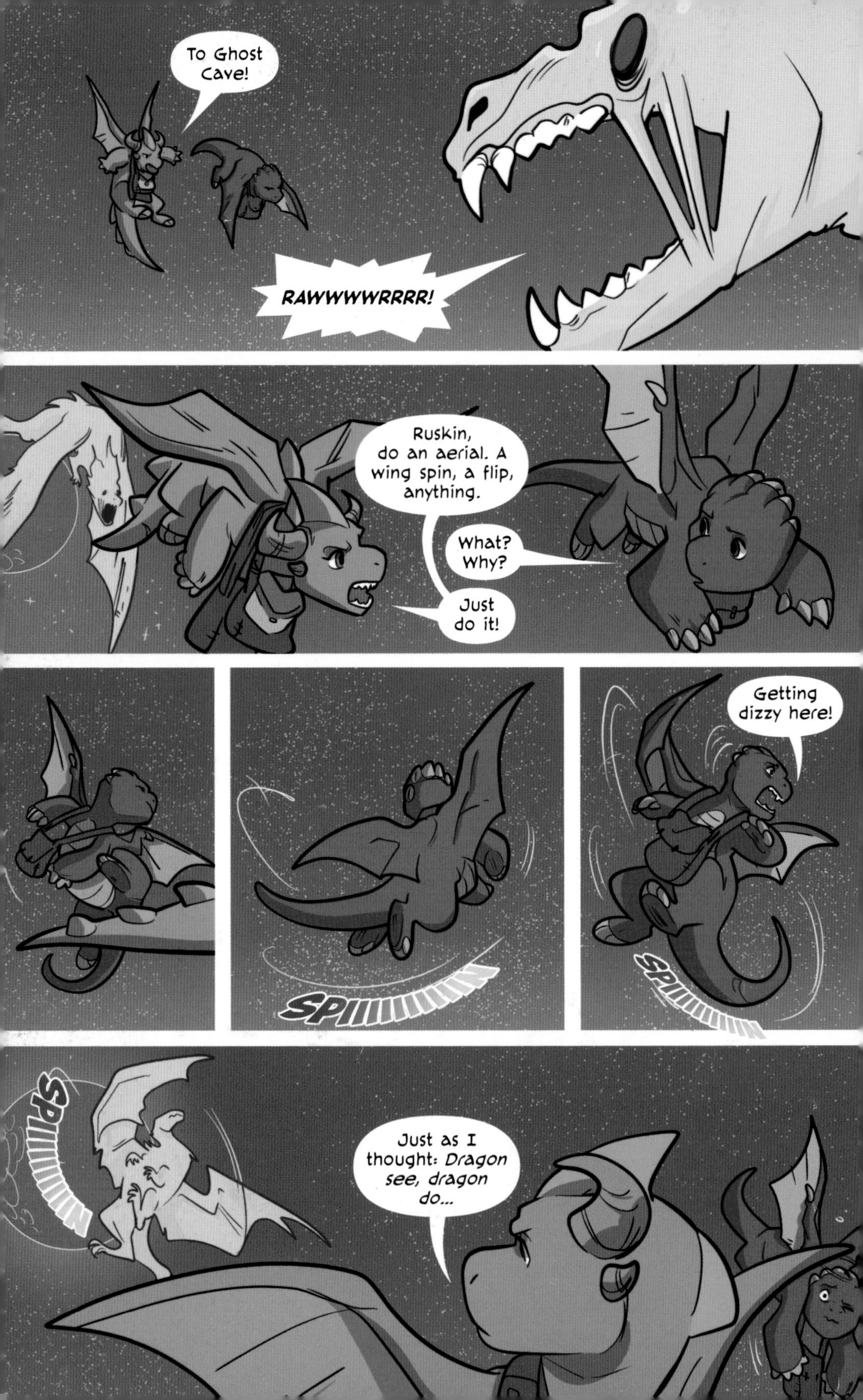
To Ghost Cave!
RAWWWWRRRR!
Ruskin, do an aerial. A wing spin, a flip, anything.
What? Why?
Just do it!
SPIIIIIIIIIIIN
SPIIIIIIIIIIIN
Getting dizzy here!
SPIIIIIIIIIIIN
Just as I thought: *Dragon see, dragon do...*

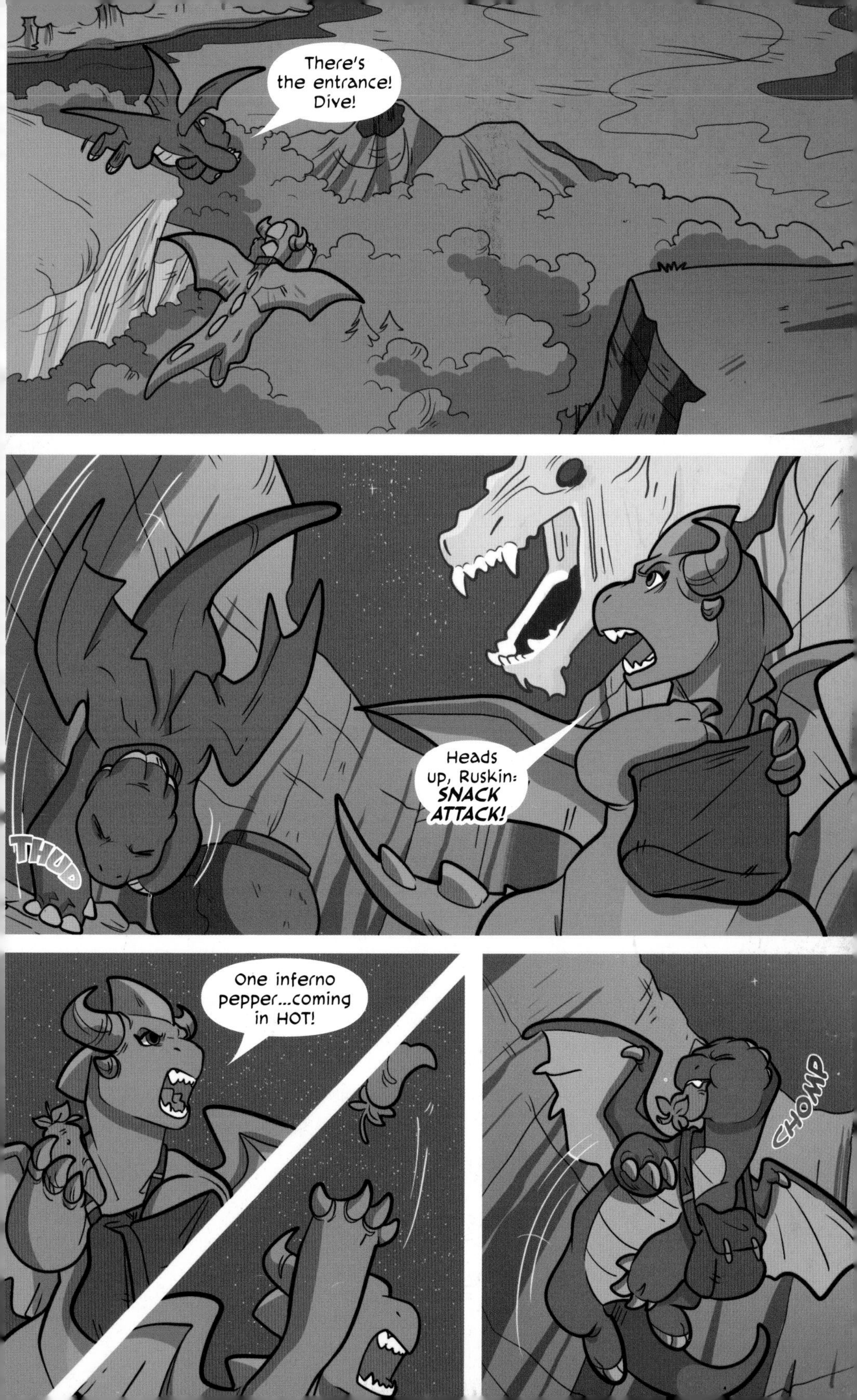
There's the entrance! Dive!
Heads up, Ruskin: SNACK ATTACK!
THUD
One inferno pepper...coming in HOT!
CHOMP

How did you know I wanted a snack?

FfffffffffffTT!

If you want one, so does he.

WHOOOOOSH

Dragon see, dragon do...

...dragon DONE!

CLUNK

SHUT

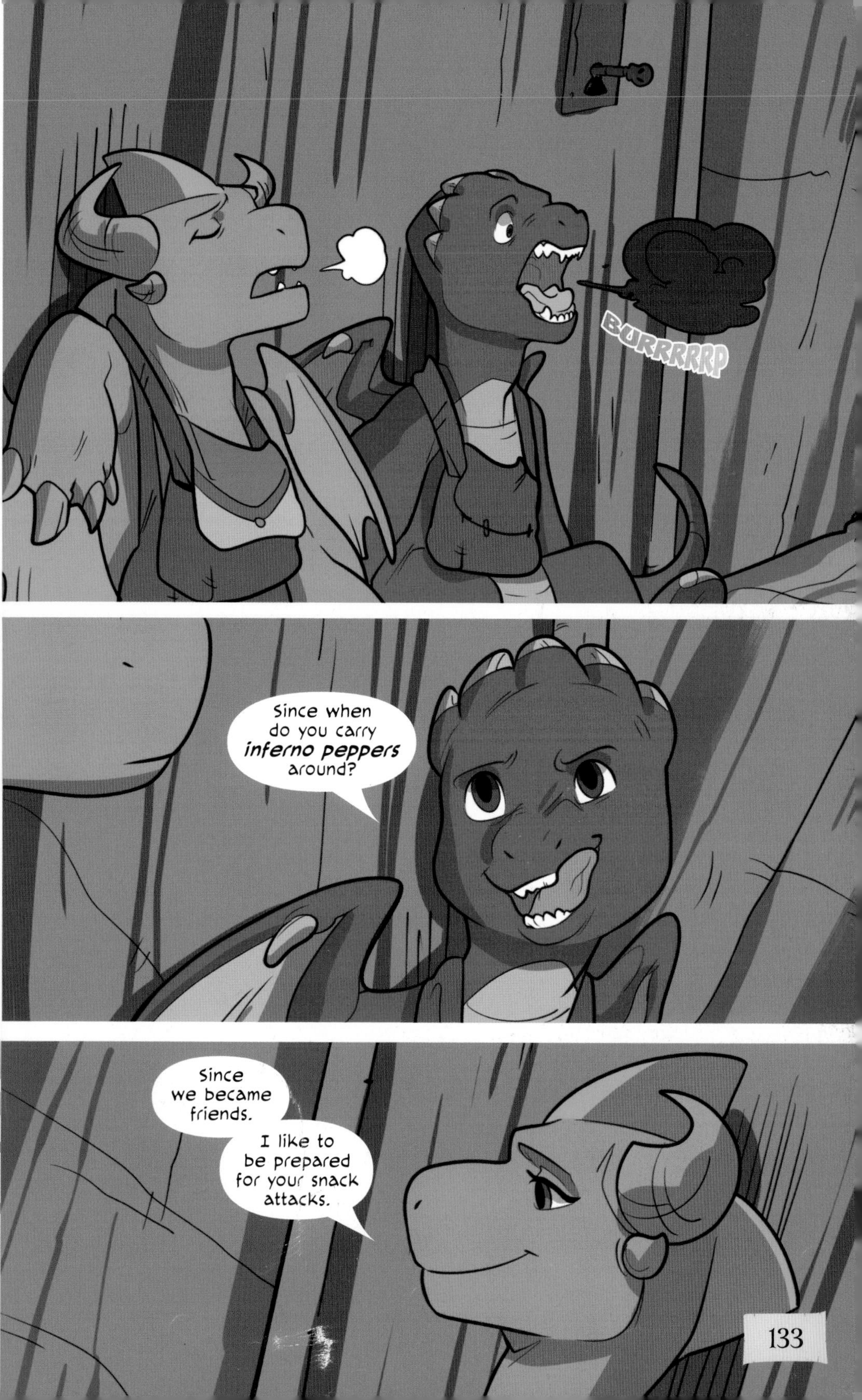
BURRRRRP
Since when do you carry *inferno peppers* around?
Since we became friends.
I like to be prepared for your snack attacks.

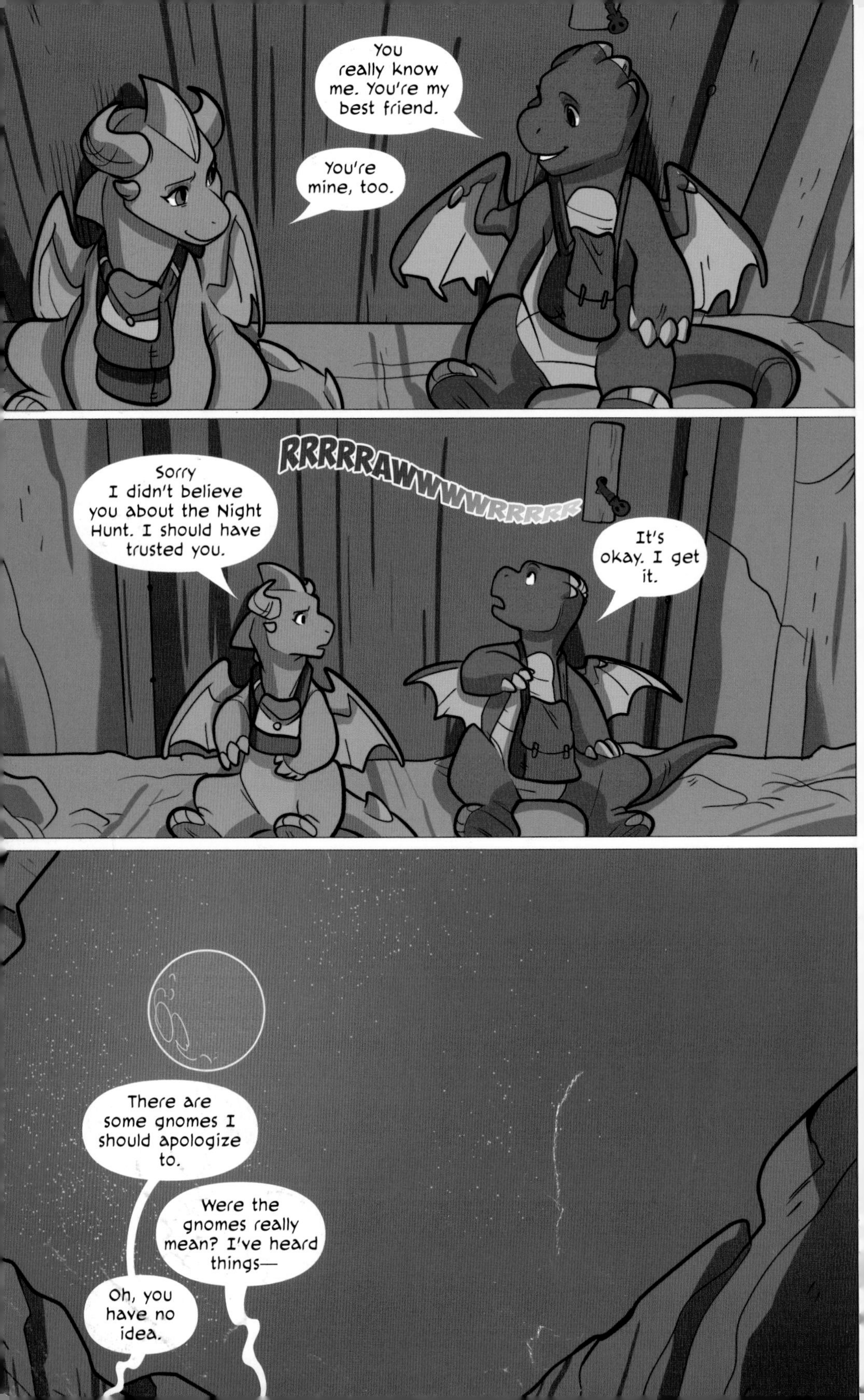
You really know me. You're my best friend.
You're mine, too.
RRRRRAWWWWRRRRR
Sorry I didn't believe you about the Night Hunt. I should have trusted you.
It's okay. I get it.
There are some gnomes I should apologize to.
Were the gnomes really mean? I've heard things—
Oh, you have no idea.

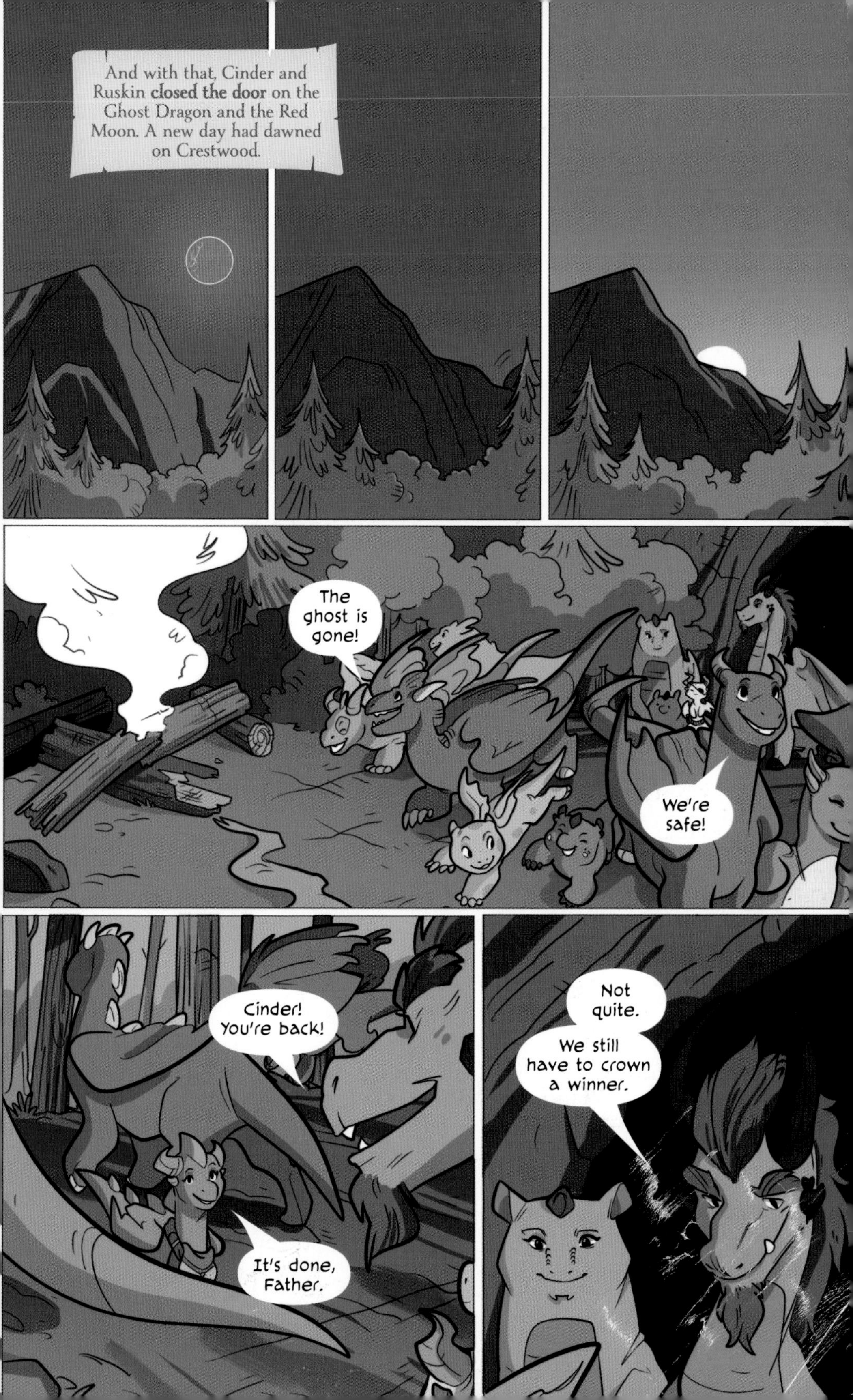
And with that, Cinder and Ruskin **closed the door** on the Ghost Dragon and the Red Moon. A new day had dawned on Crestwood.
The ghost is gone!
We're safe!
Cinder! You're back!
It's done, Father.
Not quite.
We still have to crown a winner.

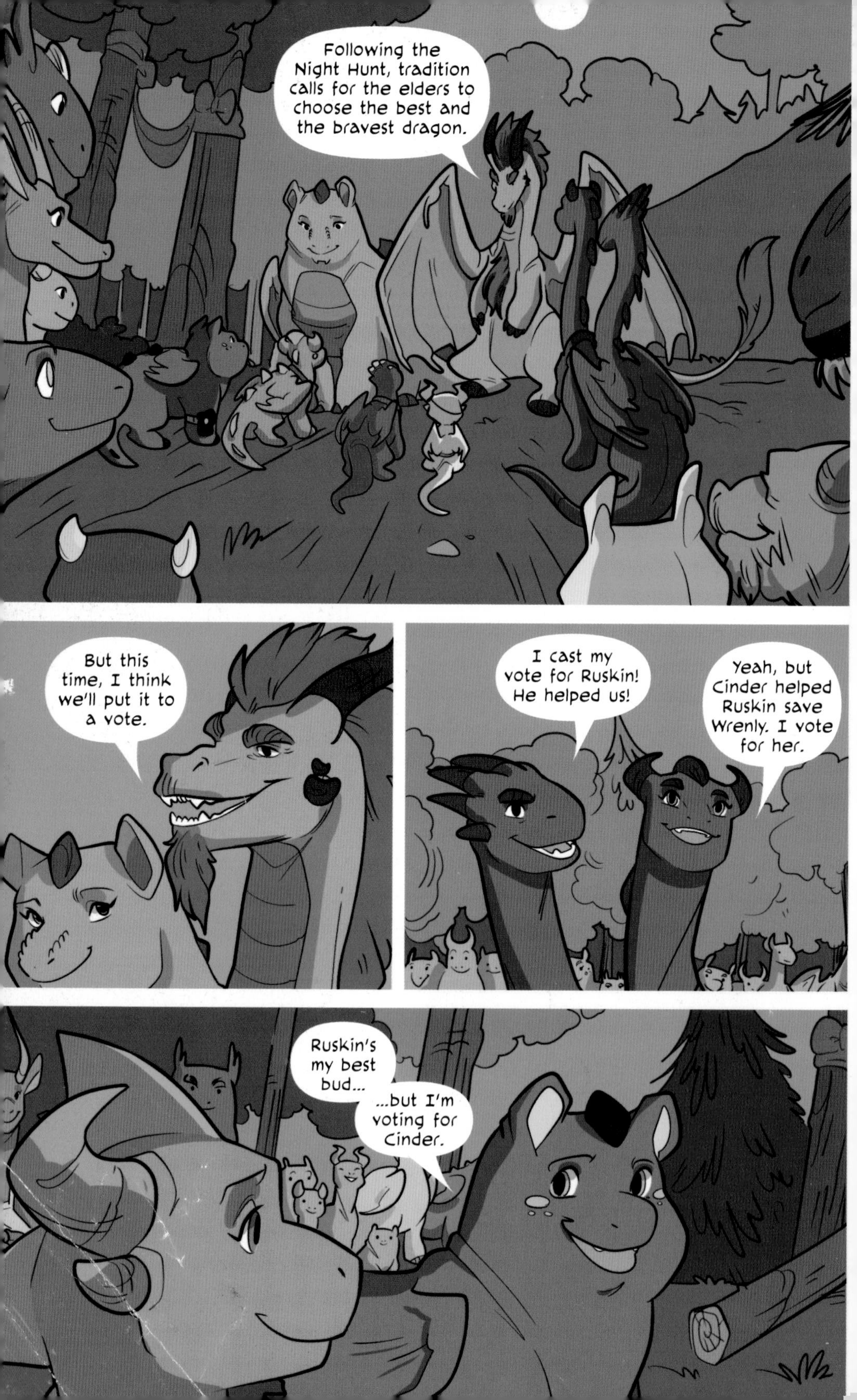
Following the Night Hunt, tradition calls for the elders to choose the best and the bravest dragon.
But this time, I think we'll put it to a vote.
I cast my vote for Ruskin! He helped us!
Yeah, but Cinder helped Ruskin save Wrenly. I vote for her.
Ruskin's my best bud...
...but I'm voting for Cinder.

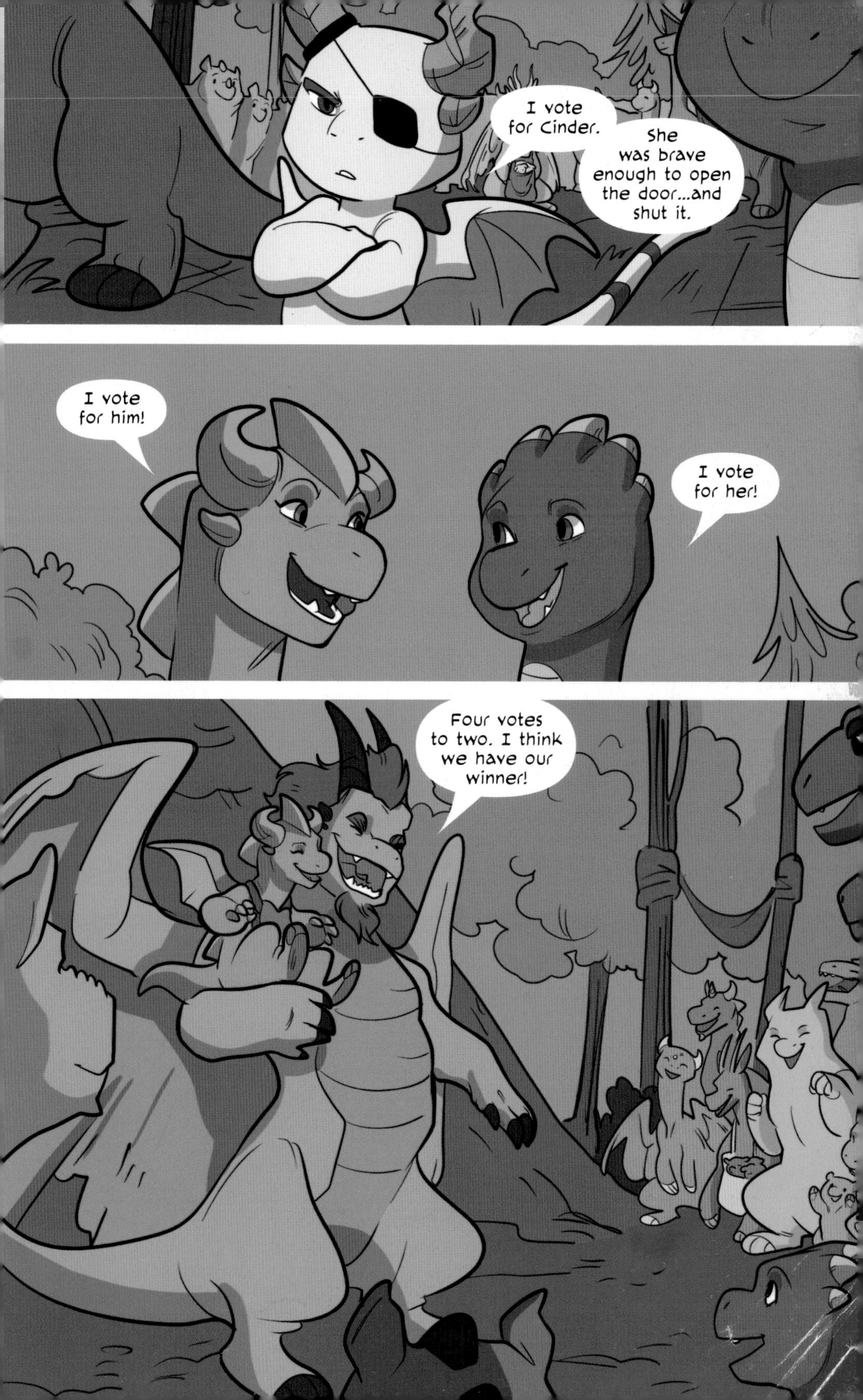
I vote for Cinder.
She was brave enough to open the door...and shut it.
I vote for him!
I vote for her!
Four votes to two. I think we have our winner!

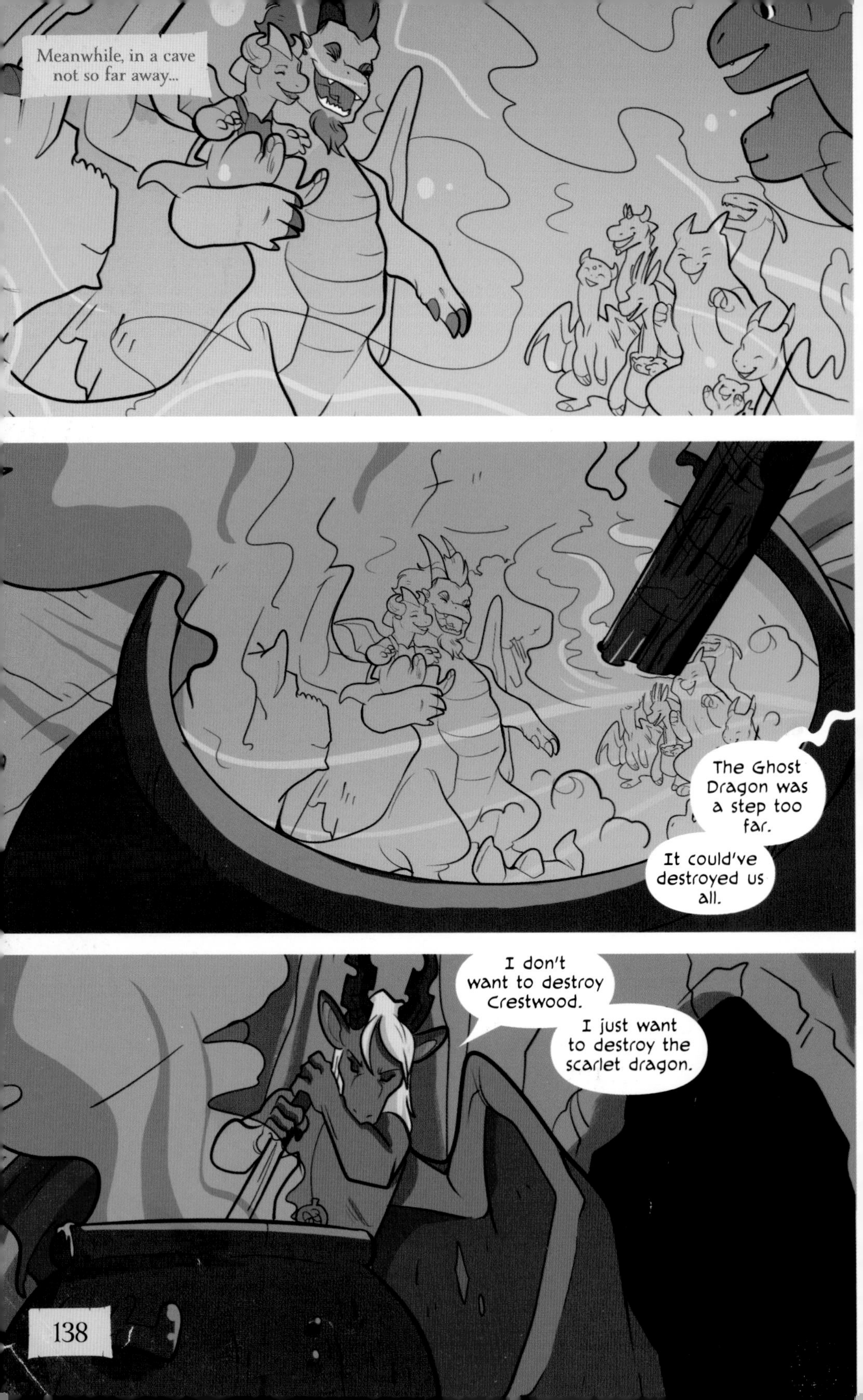
Meanwhile, in a cave not so far away...
The Ghost Dragon was a step too far.
It could've destroyed us all.
I don't want to destroy Crestwood.
I just want to destroy the scarlet dragon.

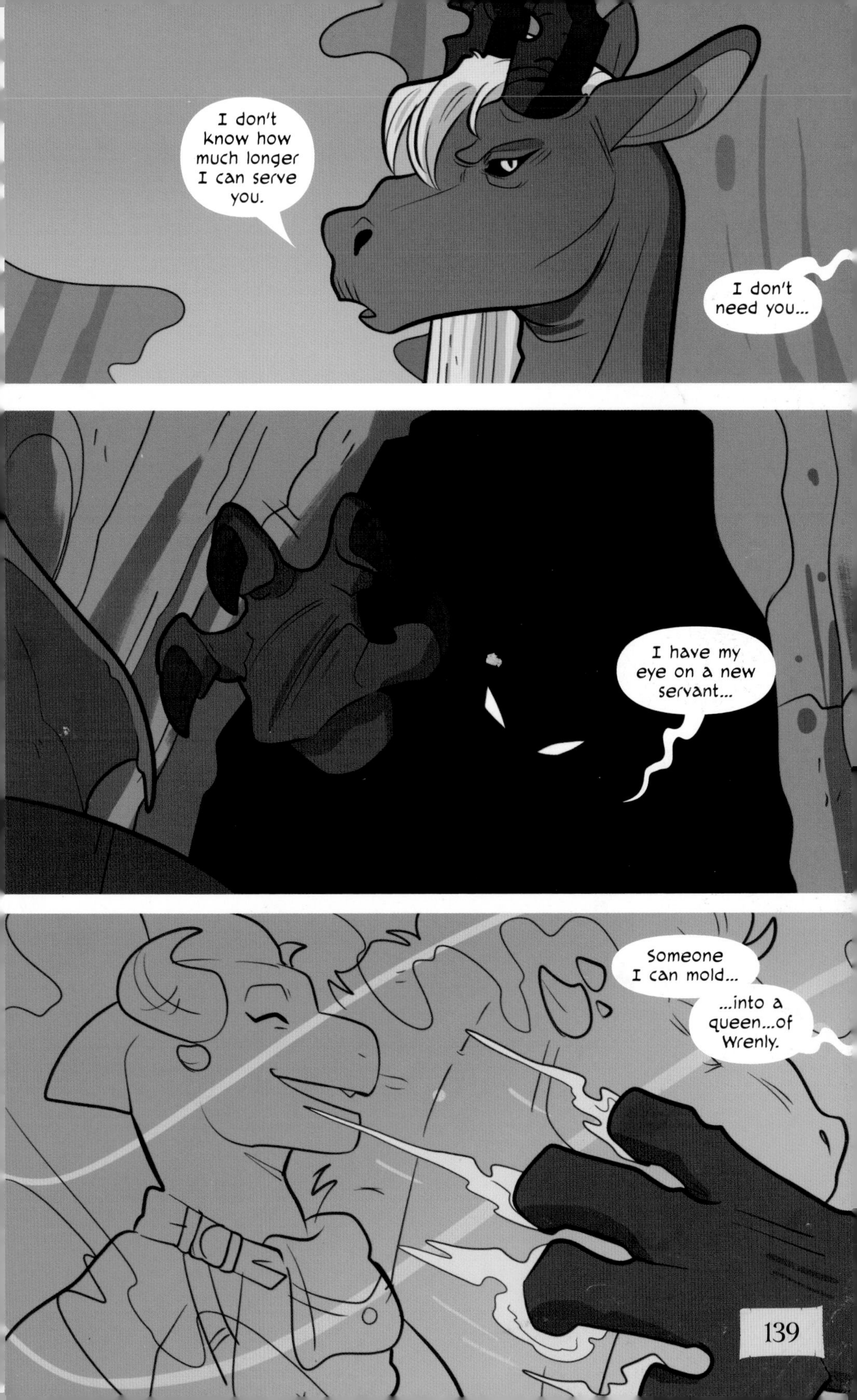
I don't know how much longer I can serve you.
I don't need you...
I have my eye on a new servant...
Someone I can mold...
...into a queen...of Wrenly.

What's in store for Ruskin and his friends next? Find out in . . .

Graphic Novel
Dragon Kingdom
of Wrenly
Ghost Island

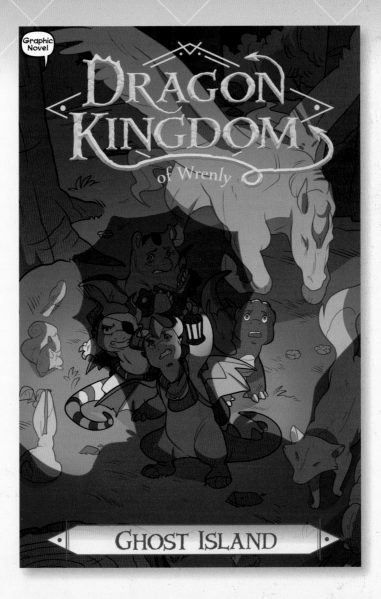

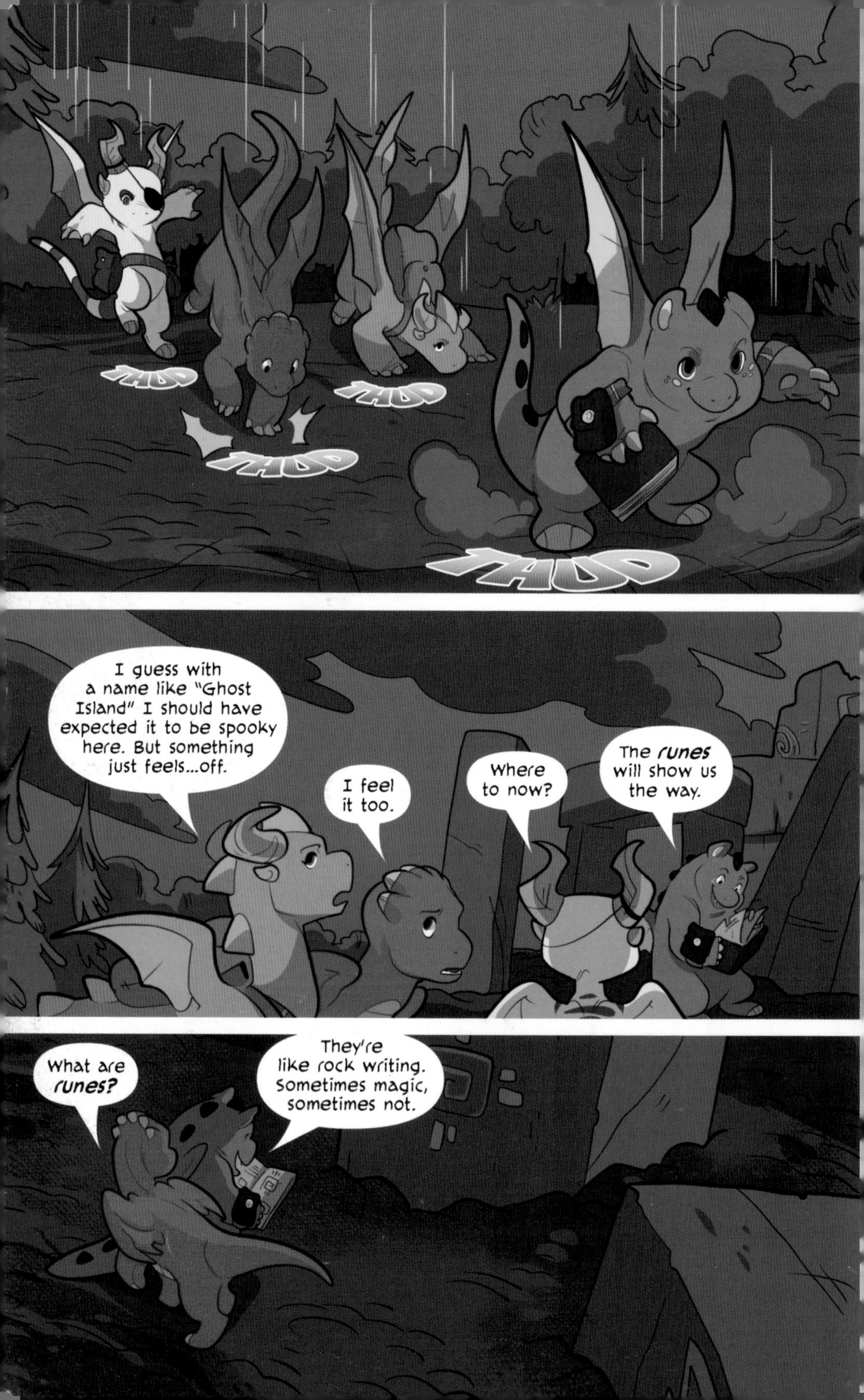
THUD
THUD
THUD
THUD
I guess with a name like "Ghost Island" I should have expected it to be spooky here. But something just feels...off.
I feel it too.
Where to now?
The *runes* will show us the way.
What are *runes?*
They're like rock writing. Sometimes magic, sometimes not.

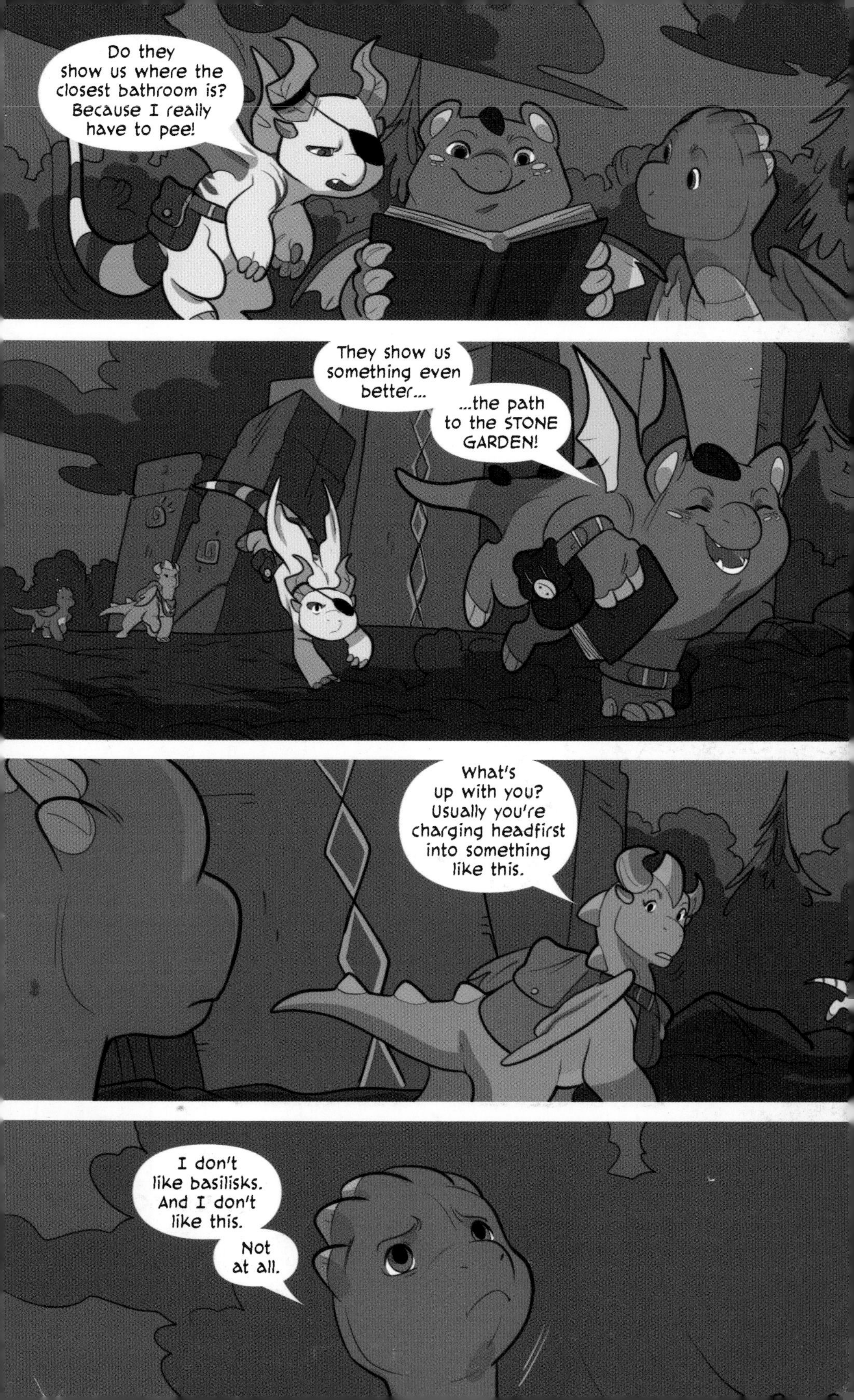
Do they show us where the closest bathroom is? Because I really have to pee!
They show us something even better...
...the path to the STONE GARDEN!
What's up with you? Usually you're charging headfirst into something like this.
I don't like basilisks. And I don't like this.
Not at all.